Praise for *The Thief of Blackfriars Lane*

Talented Michelle Griep delivers an act⸺⸺⸺, romantic adventure set on the dangerous streets of Victorian London.
–Julie Klassen, author of *A Castaway in Cornwall*

The Thief of Blackfriars Lane spins danger, mystery, and romance into a story sure to captivate fans of Griep's fast-paced style. Thrilling storytelling from first page to last.
–Elizabeth Ludwig, *USA Today* bestselling author and speaker

Just when I think she can't top the last book, Griep does it again! *The Thief of Blackfriars Lane* is spellbinding from page one until the end. Kit and Jackson will steal your breath and your heart.
–Ane Mulligan, Amazon bestselling author of *Chapel Spring Revival*

Come with me to Blackfriars Lane, run the underground rails and sewers, and if you're the police, just try to keep up! Gosh, this book was a fun, feisty, and female-empowering story. I thoroughly enjoyed the spots of humor, the mystery, and the action. A little bit of Enola Holmes and a lotta fun!
–Jaime Jo Wright, author of Christy Award–winning *The House on Foster Hill*

Romance, crime drama, mystery, adventure, and suspense! Only this author can weave all those into one fabulous book! Add in quirky, fun characters, a heartfelt love story, and twists and turns even I didn't see coming, and you have another bestselling page-turner from this incredible author.
–MaryLu Tyndall,
author of award-winning Legacy of the King's Pirates series

Griep is such a talent and she shines in *The Thief of Blackfriars Lane*. Well-told, romantic, and clever, this is one you don't want to miss. It will delight you!
–Rachel Hauck, *New York Times* bestselling author

Sparkling with intrigue, danger, adventure, and romance, this is one of Griep's finest stories yet! Each page drips with nail-biting suspense and pulls the reader deeper into Kit and Jackson's world. A spellbinding tale from a master storyteller!
–Tara Johnson,
author of *Engraved on the Heart* and *Where Dandelions Bloom*

The Thief of Blackfriars Lane will take you through Victorian London, from the black-as-night sewer tunnels to glittering parties at the Lord Mayor's mansion. With Kit and Jackson as your guides, you'll be breathless to keep up with their clever intrigues. This duo sparkles on the page as they right wrongs, fight for the light, and pursue God-given purpose in every life.

–Jocelyn Green,
Christy Award–winning author of *Shadows of the White City*

A Charles Dickens-like Victorian tale full of intrigue, adventure, and romance. Delightful!

–Morgan L. Busse, author of the award-winning Ravenwood Saga

If there is an *it* quality to writing Victorian fiction, Michelle Griep has it! Action? Check! Setting? Check! Snappy dialogue? Check, check! Meticulous research meets impeccable story crafting in this fast-paced, many-layered novel. I give it an A-plus!

–Erica Vetsch, author of the Serendipity & Secrets Regency series

I've never before rooted for a thief, but Griep has magical storytelling power that will convince you to join whatever escapade she's thought up. The unexpected plot and unlikely but dynamic leads pop with the color and life of a Dickens novel, but with a style that is uniquely—and delightfully—Griep's own.

–Joanna Davidson Politano, author of *The Love Note* and
other Victorian-era mysteries

Take one earnest, well-meaning but slightly bumbling hero matching wits with a nefarious female villain—or is she our heroine in disguise?—and you have the perfect recipe for a delicious romp across (and underneath) Victorian London. I loved Jackson and Kit! Too fun to miss!

–Shannon McNear, 2014 RITA® finalist
and author of *The Rebel Bride* and *The Blue Cloak*

What an absolutely delightful mystery! A fast-paced adventure through the underbelly of Victorian London led by a smart heroine you can't help but fall in love with. Exceptional research. Characters that sizzle off the page!

–Abigail Wilson, author of *Masquerade at Middlecrest Abbey*

THE THIEF OF
BLACKFRIARS
LANE

MICHELLE GRIEP

BARBOUR
PUBLISHING

Print ISBN 978-1-64352-715-4

eBook Editions:
Adobe Digital Edition (.epub) 978-1-63609-062-7
Kindle and MobiPocket Edition (.prc) 978-1-63609-063-4

Cover Design: Kirk DouPonce, DogEared Design

Published in association with the Books & Such Literary Management, 52 Mission Circle, Suite 122, PMB 170, Santa Rosa, CA 95409-5370, www.booksandsuch.com.

Published by Barbour Publishing, Inc., 1810 Barbour Drive, Uhrichsville, Ohio 44683, www.barbourbooks.com

Our mission is to inspire the world with the life-changing message of the Bible.

Member of the
Evangelical Christian
Publishers Association

Printed in the United States of America.

To Cheryl Higgins and Maria Nelson, two lovely ladies whose gardening legacy leaves the world a better place. And as always, to the One who began time in a garden and will someday bring those who love Him to a better place.

Chapter One

April 1885
London

For want of a properly working pocket watch, Jackson Forge failed to save the world today—or at least the City of London. Now he'd be lucky to save himself.

With no time to run a comb through his hair, Jackson flew out the door of the Hutton Street boardinghouse and entered the fray of early morning pedestrians. Of all the days to be tardy to work, this was the absolute worst. Half the City filled the streets, and the other half was likely already gathered outside St. Paul's—which stood between him and the station. State funerals always attracted attention. And criminals. A perfect opportunity to start his career off with a rousing bang. He upped his pace. Crowds or not, he'd be hanged if he arrived late for his first briefing as a newly hired constable.

But his step hitched as he turned onto Blackfriars Lane. Loaded drays, street hawkers, skirts, suits, and even a chicken or two clogged the pavement from gutter to gutter, all slowly moving towards the cathedral. The noise boxed his ears. The stink wrinkled his nose. Yet he grinned. This—*this!*—was why he'd come to London. Humanity in all its complex glory.

He plowed forward—and promptly collided with an old man in a green-checkered sack coat. The grizzly-faced fellow teetered on one foot, his beat-up bowler skewing sideways as he grabbed on to Jackson for support.

"I beg your pardon." Jackson lent a strong arm, righting the old fellow. "I was—"

"Tut-tut, young man! I'll tell you what you were doing." He jammed a finger in Jackson's chest. "You were bib-bobbing about, not caring a fig-nackety for who might be in your way. That's the trouble with people these days. Rushing! Always rushing."

He was right. All of Blackfriars was awhirl at the moment—but that didn't give Jackson license to go crashing into law-abiding citizens. He dipped his head. "I stand guilty as charged, sir. But I assure you I have good reason."

"Save your excuses for God, sonny, not me." The man's fingers curled around the lapel of his coat. "Now, if you don't mind, I should like to be on my way."

"Yes, of course." Jackson let him pass, then drew a deep breath and once again set off at a good clip. This time he paid particular attention to what was in front of him, until a feminine voice and a tug on his sleeve turned him around.

"I believe you dropped this, sir."

A worn leather pouch balanced on the woman's upturned palm, drawstrings frayed at the ends. In reflex, he patted his pocket. Empty. Blast! The thing must've fallen out when he bumped into the old man.

The woman blinked up at him, eyes twilight blue with peculiar silver flecks. Raven hair and a tatty brown bonnet framed her heart-shaped face—a rather comely face despite a few cinder smudges. She wore a ragged gown, smelling of dust and coal smoke, and clutched the fingers of a boy who leaned into her skirts. Despite her ignoble appearance, the woman captivated like none other. Where did she and her son lay their heads at night? Were they safe? Maybe not, judging by the small triangular scar near her eye.

"Sir?"

The question snapped him back to attention. He retrieved the coin pouch and offered her a shilling from it. "For your honesty, madam. You could have simply walked on and been long gone before I noticed my purse missing, and I thank you for being forthright."

She staved him off with a wave of her hand. "No need, sir. My boy and I do not take charity."

What was this? Turning down money? He blinked, his tongue lying dormant. Clearly the woman and her son were in want.

"Here." Jackson deposited the coin in the boy's hand. "Get your mother and yourself a meat pie, hmm?"

Wide-eyed, the lad nodded, then buried his dirty face in the woman's gown.

Rising, Jackson pulled out a sovereign. A goodly amount, one that would require weeks of hard work to replace, but this poor woman and her son were in far more need than he. Taking her hand, he pressed the money into it and curled her fingers over the coin. "For you and your boy. I will not take no for an answer."

"Oh sir, I. . . You have no idea. . ." Her eyes shimmered, and she clutched the coin to her breast. "I cannot thank you enough. This means the world to little Frankie and me."

"May God bless you, madam."

The low bong of church bells filled the air, and instinctively he glanced towards the sound. Dash it! Eight o'clock. He turned back to the woman to say goodbye, but she was gone. Just as well. He didn't have time for such niceties at the moment.

Jamming his coin pouch back into his pocket, Jackson set off at a run. He'd never be able to protect those on the street if the sergeant fired him on his first day as a constable.

He arrived at the station on Old Jewry winded and drenched in sweat, but he'd made it in only eight minutes instead of ten. A small miracle, considering. He raced up to the clerk's desk and snapped a crisp salute before the front door slapped shut. "Constable Third Class Jackson Forge reporting for duty, sir."

A wan man in a blue uniform lifted his face, though the way his neck cracked, the movement required much effort. Everything about him looked tired, from the flatness of his hat to the flaccid skin hanging off his neck. "Stand down, Forge. I'm only a clerk." He shook his head. "New recruits. . .far too young and fresh faced if you ask me."

"I'll have you know I'm three and twenty, sir."

"Oh are you now?" He clicked his tongue as he paged through a sheaf of papers with painstaking lethargy. "Practically ready to be put to pasture then, eh?"

Jackson hid a smile. The man's raillery reminded him of his outspoken father.

The clerk—Beanstaple, according to his name badge—shoved a document across the desk. "Sign that one."

Jackson reached for a pen and scrawled his signature in record time.

The clerk tucked away the paper then glanced sidelong at a closed door across the corridor. "You'd better make haste suiting up, Constable Forge. Briefing's already started and Sergeant Graybone don't take kindly to latecomers."

Beanstaple listed sideways, and for one horrid moment, Jackson worried the fellow might be suffering an apoplexy—but then he withdrew a folded uniform and a helmet from a bottom shelf. "Here you be."

"Thank you." He snatched the bundle before the man could eke it across the desk and took off at a good clip. Every second spent here in the lobby was one less getting briefed.

Three strides later, he paused. "Oh, uh, where should I. . . ?" He nodded at the garments.

"Sarge will eat this one for breakfast," Beanstaple mumbled as he edged his thumb up and over his shoulder. "Last room on the right."

Jackson dashed to the indicated chamber and peeled off his garments, tucking them into the only remaining empty cubby. Then he shoved his arms and legs into the blue woolen dream he'd clung to since boyhood. Snatching up his officer's helmet, he snugged it under his arm and did a quick once-over in the small mirror on the wall. A white *172* was embroidered on the collar. *His* number. His validation. The official authorization to right the wrong that had happened so many years ago.

Oh James.

After a quick smooth of his moustache, he raced back down the corridor, dipped his head at Beanstaple in gratitude, then opened the door to the briefing room and slid into a vacant seat near the rear. Rows of blue-shouldered men filled the stools to the side and in front of him. Only one gazed his way—the bear of a man at the front of the room with sergeant stripes on his sleeve. He stood impossibly rigid, a military stance. How many campaigns had this man seen before trading uniforms?

Silence fell like a sledgehammer. The sergeant shifted his gaze to the clock on the wall, then skewered Jackson with a squinty-eyed stare. "Name?"

Jackson shot to his feet and instantly cut a sharp salute. "Constable Third Class Jackson Forge, sir."

"Forge." The sergeant heaved out the name. "Are you able to tell time, Constable?"

Throat tight, Jackson prayed his voice wouldn't mewl like a girl's. "Yes, sir."

"Don't lie to me, Forge!"

The words reverberated in his chest, loud and clear enough to be heard in battle, but despite the volume, Jackson would be deuced if he could understand the man's meaning. He schooled his face, holding in check brows that desperately wanted to rise. "Sir?"

"Clearly, Constable, if you were able to read the hands of a clock, you'd have been here at eight, and not a minute later. But congratulations." The sergeant clapped hands the size of kidney pies, the sharp rap of it bouncing off the walls and pelting him like grapeshot. Jackson stiffened to keep from wincing.

"You've just earned your first demerit." Graybone's clapping stopped, the absence of the noise jarring. "Two more and you're out. Understood?"

"Yes, sir!" Once again Jackson saluted, then lowered onto the stool, aware of the perspiration trickling between his shoulder blades.

The officer next to him slid a sympathetic glance his way.

"As I was saying. . ." The sergeant shot one more choleric look at Jackson, then clasped his hands behind his back while he paced the length of the front row. "Lord Twickenham's recent disappearance makes two high-profile men unaccounted for this past week. The commissioner is calling on us, gentlemen, to not only find them, but to put a stop to this nefarious trend. I will not have our precinct tarnished, especially today when all eyes are upon us. If I so much as hear of one pickpocketing incident during the Lord Mayor's funeral procession, you'll all be written up. Is that clear?"

"Yes, sir!" the officers' voices thundered.

"Good." The sergeant strode to a podium near the front door. "Here are your assignments. Harper, Jones."

Two men made their way to the front, and as they did so, the fellow next to Jackson leaned sideways, speaking for him alone. "I'd wager you'll never be late again."

He tugged at his collar. The man had no idea how right he was. "Lesson learned." He offered his hand. "Jackson Forge."

"So I heard." Amusement gleamed in the man's brown eyes as he returned the handshake. "Charles Baggett. I think you just set a record for fastest-earned demerit."

Jackson couldn't help but grin. "I tend to be an overachiever."

"You may want to rethink what you'd like to achieve." Baggett chuckled. "Where you from, Forge?"

"Haywards Heath."

Baggett's brow scrunched. "Is that north?"

Jackson shook his head. "South. Nearer to Brighton than London."

"Baggett and Williams!" the sergeant boomed.

Baggett rose at once and cuffed him on the shoulder. "Well, Forge from Haywards Heath, good luck on your first day."

Jackson watched the man go. Charles Baggett seemed a logical candidate for an ally, since no other man had acknowledged him.

Two by two, the room emptied until only Jackson remained. Sergeant Graybone slammed shut his ledger, tucked it on the shelf beneath the podium, then strolled towards the door.

"Sir?" Jackson rose. Surely the man hadn't forgotten him already. "My assignment?"

"Hmm?" The sergeant's lips pursed, his thick black moustache a dark slash against his white skin. "Oh, right. Forge. Listen, I can't spare a First Class for you to shadow today. You'll have to guard the station."

The order was a yanked rug, knocking him off balance. Ever since that fateful day when he and his brother had learned firsthand the ruthlessness of London's streets, he'd dreamed of this moment to make things right. Prevent others from falling victim to villains and cutthroats. Yet the only thing he'd be safeguarding against was a possible paper cut to Beanstaple's fingers?

"But surely you can use me on the streets, sir. You said you'll not tolerate so much as a pickpocket today." He puffed out his chest. "I can do that, Sergeant. I can protect against thievery of all sorts."

"Can you, now? Well, well, I could use a man like that."

The knotted muscles in his shoulders untwined. Given the chance, he'd make Graybone proud.

The sergeant pulled a small paper from his pocket and handed it over. An odd size for a task sheet, an even odder place to keep it, but who was Jackson to question?

He unfolded the paper. A receipt of some sort—for a Skye Terrier puppy. He angled his face at the sergeant. "Sir?"

"I'm expecting that pup to arrive in a few hours." Sergeant Graybone aimed a podgy finger at the invoice. "A gift for my niece. If you're as good at protecting as you say you are, then keep that dog safe until I arrive back at the station. Dismissed."

The sergeant stalked to the door, leaving a slack-jawed Jackson alone with nothing but a scrap of paper in his hand and a rock of disappointment in his gut.

Chapter Two

God's mercies were new every day. Hopefully Sergeant Graybone's would be as well. With a final snug-down on his helmet and a quick flick of a straggling dog hair on his sleeve, Jackson strolled from the boardinghouse onto streets much less chaotic than yesterday. Amazing how a mere twenty-four hours could effect such a change.

Or maybe the extra tuppence he'd slipped the house matron to rap on his door before dawn was already paying off. He turned onto Blackfriars Lane. At this rate, he'd be at the station a half hour before the briefing began, despite even taking time to pen a letter home to Father. Not that he had much to write. Yet.

Ahead, a raised voice snagged his attention. He cocked his head.

"—bib-bobbing about, not caring a fig-nackety for who might be in your way. That's the trouble with people these days. Rushing! Always rushing."

Not only was the voice familiar, but the words as well. And the flash of a green-checkered sack coat. Coincidence the same fellow had once again been jostled? Or could it be something a bit more devious? Jackson's eyes narrowed.

He dodged a kipper cart and ducked into a passageway between two buildings that lent a great vantage, from which he could see yet not be seen. A boon—and a curse. Too eerily like the crevice he'd hidden in thirteen years ago, when his world upended.

The old fellow finished his upbraiding then strolled down the pavement towards Jackson. The other man continued the opposite direction. Hmm. Other than the repeated words, nothing else seemed amiss. Perhaps he'd been hasty in his assessment.

Then a woman in a brown skirt with a boy scampering beside her rendezvoused with the old man. Jackson leaned out a bit farther, every sense on alert. He knew that tatty bonnet and threadbare shawl. Recognized the smudgy cheeks on the freckle-faced lad. Confound it! Jackson had given the woman enough coin to not only clean up but find lodgings in a better part of town. Why was she still here?

From his sleeve, the old man pulled out a coin purse and transferred it to the woman—then she and the boy dashed after the fellow who had clearly been pickpocketed. When she caught up to him, she tugged on his sleeve, turning him about.

Jackson's jaw dropped. He could still feel the press of her fingers on his own arm. What a little swindler!

He set off at a dead run, and as she handed the man his wallet, Jackson caught her by the shoulder. "Your thieving days are done, madam."

The boy scampered away, and two sets of wide eyes turned to Jackson. Defiance flashed in the woman's gaze.

"Surely you are mistaken, Constable." The man hefted his leather pouch to eye level. "This woman was merely returning my property."

"This woman is a thief." Jackson tightened his grip on her collar. "Using you as a mark, setting you up for—"

Her elbow caught him sharp in the gut. He gasped. She sprang. Fabric ripped.

And the woman shot down a narrow neck of a corridor.

Shoving the handful of torn material into his pocket, Jackson charged after her. At the end of the building, she veered left, pushing over a broken cask as she went. Jackson sidestepped it. Did she truly believe her antics would hold him at bay?

"Stop in the name of the Crown!" he roared.

Her laughter bounced off the brick walls, prodding him to pump his legs all the harder. She wouldn't be laughing for long. He was gaining on her.

Once again the woman turned, right this time. Onto a busy street. Her slim figure easily sliced between suits and skirts, skittering like a field mouse through a plot of corn. Jackson plowed after her, not nearly as graceful, and though he called out, "Stop that thief!" he took the brunt of blowback from disgruntled pedestrians.

"Nick off, bobby!"

"Watch where yer going, man!"

"Cod's heads! What an ox."

Hang it all! *She* was the criminal, not him. He lengthened his stride. "Out of my way, in the name of the Crown!"

Ahead, by the greengrocers, another figure swerved in from around the corner, joining her side. The boy. She nodded as she fled past him, and he dropped to a crouch. Surely the lad wasn't foolish enough to think he could take down a man of Jackson's size simply by springing at him.

But then the boy dashed into the street—and once again a choice must be made. Continue chasing the woman or pursue the lad? Judging by his own heaving breaths, Jackson bounded after the woman. She had to be winded, weary, and getting very wobbly of step.

From the corner of Jackson's eye, he noted the boy ran only a few steps before he crouched yet again. Strange, but—

Pain cut into Jackson's shin. The world tipped. Headlong, he whumped to the ground, shards of gravel cutting into the heels of his hands as he broke his fall. His chin scraped hard against the cobbles.

The boy laughed and scrambled away, his nearly invisible wire now tangled around Jackson's boots.

Blast!

He shook off the snare and shot to his feet, then sprinted ahead, undaunted. It would take more than a booby trap to stop him from snagging that thief. He *would* have her, and eventually the boy and the old man as well.

The lane ended in a T. The woman glanced over her shoulder at him, then dodged eastward. He tore after her. But as he rounded the corner, entering the same lane she'd taken only moments before, a scream rent the air.

"Stop! I beg you." Pain bled through the woman's words.

Confused, he slowed. She stood but twenty paces from him, clutching her stomach, somewhat doubled over. Was she hurt? Colour leached from her face, and her skirts trembled. Of all the inopportune times for the woman to take sick! Hauling a dead-weight body back to the station would be a lot harder than escorting her on her feet.

He held up his hand, as he might to a spooked mare, and softened his tone while he approached. "Allow me to help you to the station where you can receive medical help." He advanced a few more careful steps. "There will be a lesser charge if you cooperate."

"I—I don't feel so very well." Her shoulders sank.

As he studied her face for any sign of swooning, a low rumbling vibrated beneath his feet. Traveling fast. Coming closer. Hopefully the noise and jittering of the underground railway wouldn't worsen whatever ailment the woman suddenly suffered.

"We have a doctor on call at the station," he encouraged. Ten more paces and he'd have her. "I will help you and—"

She bolted. Fleet of foot. Light of step. Transforming from weak and ailing female to street rat bent on scrabbling off to her warren. Of all the ploys to slow him down! He rocketed ahead.

And was hit by a blast of steaming, sooty vapor belching up from an iron grate in the middle of the lane—a blow hole she had neatly hidden with the hem of her gown.

Jackson stumbled like a blind man, rubbing the grit from his eyes, goaded by the pain and even more by the woman's taunting voice.

"Ha-ha! Don't worry none fer me, love. Get yerself to the doctor, eh?"

Rage hotter than the blistering puff of smoke burned through his veins. Squint-blinking, Jackson charged after her, tears leaking out the sides of his stinging eyes. The lane narrowed ahead, a perfect place to tackle her. She'd lost her chance for gentle handling.

She beat him to the opening and slipped through the gap. He barreled on, vision still watery—then stopped when the lane emptied into a market square that stretched wide and long. Dozens of brown skirts ambled about, women with baskets in hand, bending over crates of swedes and apples or haggling at stalls. Jackson rubbed his eyes, and though his vision cleared, the action did nothing to distinguish one feisty swindler in a tatty bonnet from the vast sea of shoppers who looked exactly the same. It would take him forever to find her in this crowd.

And by now, time was surely not his friend. Sergeant Graybone would show no mercy were he late again.

Defeat tasted as acrid as the blast of steam, though he tried to swallow it down as he trudged to the station. What kind of constable couldn't apprehend a woman? Maybe it would be better to just turn in his uniform now before anyone realized how ill-suited he really was for this job, no matter how much he wanted it. The sergeant already suspected his incompetence anyway.

Jackson scrubbed a hand over his face. His fingers came away black, and he winced. He probably looked no better than a chimney sweep on a bad day. Wouldn't the sergeant love that?

He fished about for a handkerchief, but instead he pulled out the scrap of fabric he'd torn from the woman's collar. There, tangled in the piece, was a broken chain with a curious token attached. He narrowed his eyes, studying the worn bit of brass. It was a button, shiny on one side, tarnished on the other. Two letters and a date were engraved on the back: H.G. 1854. And on the front, a few embossed words. *"Nulli Secundus."* Second to none. The slogan of the Coldstream Guards, if he remembered correctly.

He shoved the handful back into his pocket and eased out his own cloth, wiping the remnants of soot, sweat, and a smear of blood from his chin while his mind whirred.

Why would a woman wear such a thing near her heart? Did it belong to a lover? A brother? A father? Not that it mattered. What did matter was now he had a link to the little thief. Finding the button's owner would bring him one step closer to locating the woman and her accomplices. And when he brought in all three, he'd be vindicated.

Now that would be something to write home about.

Chapter Three

Something was wrong. Off a wee bit. Not surprising in a world that didn't care a fig, but still the queer feeling chafed like a wet petticoat. With her free hand, Kit snugged her collar higher up her neck, the basket on her other arm swinging wildly in the morning breeze. Was it nothing but the unusual chill in the air that shivered across her shoulders? Or maybe the niggling dread of what she knew she'd soon face?

Nah. She discarded those ideas as deftly as she sidestepped a pile of manure. Whatever it was that twinged her stomach was undefinable and completely baffling. Like the time she'd stood in front of a gilt-framed portrait of Miss Lila's great-grandfather and known the painting was slanted just a smidgen, but even when she'd turned her head and squinted, she'd not been able to figure out which side needed a nudge to make it right.

Tossing back her loosely bound hair, she left behind the wide yawn of Upper Thames Street and turned into the narrow throat of Angel Lane. Hah! As if an angel would dare taint the hem of his snowy robe in this neighborhood. Unless the rag-and-bone man she passed, reeking of onions and sweat, happened to be a heavenly being in disguise. Could be. Kit fought the urge to glance back at him. She knew better than most that people were often not what they appeared to be.

Several paces later, she rapped her knuckles against a flimsy door that was more of an idea of wood and nails than a functioning defense.

A few childish voices argued inside. Another sang an off-colour ditty at the top of his lungs. Had anyone even heard her knocking?

She had lifted her hand to strike again when the door swung open to a flop-haired, freckle-faced Frankie, hefting a scowl and a pocketknife.

Kit smiled. Had she been a real threat, the scrapper would've gone down fighting to protect his family. And as quickly as it came, her smile faded. No boy should have to do a man's work.

"Miss Kit!" The boy lowered his knife and his glower, then stepped aside for her to pass. Since their last great escape from the constable nigh on two weeks ago now, he'd been furloughed from further street escapades, too busy caring for his mother.

Kit blinked, adjusting her eyes to the darkness inside the room, the grimy window as abysmally dysfunctional as the door. She turned to Frankie, practically shouting to be heard over his siblings' noise. "How is your mum today?"

His angular shoulders lifted in a shrug. "Same."

The worry in his brown eyes said more than his lips. Kit forced a chipper smile. "Well, let me see if I can brighten her up then, eh? And how about you separate those screech-cat nippers over there?" She tipped her head towards the five- and six-year-old waging a violent tug-of-war with a wooden spoon. "Here, this should help." She handed Frankie her basket. The crusty bread inside ought to calm the spoon battle and quiet the lusty three-year-old marching about in front of the cold hearth with an old pot on his head, singing of wine and women.

Bypassing the circus, Kit ventured to the back of the room, where sickness lived and breathed in dark shadows. Just as there were no angels on Angel Lane, neither did God visit this squalid corner of the earth, leaving Kit to do His work.

Kneeling quietly lest she wake the babe asleep in a nearby cradle—though how the child slept through the raucous caterwauling was anybody's guess—Kit pressed a hand to the brow of the ashen-faced woman on the bed. "Mornin', Martha."

The woman's eyes fluttered open, recognition slow in coming, but when it did, a small smile quivered on her lips. "Kit. You came."

Though it broke her heart to hear the breath rattling in Martha's lungs, Kit snorted as if they bantered about nothing more than the price of potatoes. "Of course I did. It is Thursday."

"Already?" Her voice was a butterfly's wing, airy, light, far too fragile.

And the sound of it kindled a white-hot rage in Kit's belly. It wasn't fair! It wasn't right or good or just in any sense of the word. Death was no respecter, it seemed, of a woman who must fend for herself and her children all on her own. Who would care for the little ones when Martha was gone? A freckle-faced boy with a chipped front tooth who ought to be in school rather than convincing unsuspecting pedestrians to part with a coin? Kit's hands clenched into fists, the responsibility draping over her shoulders like a leaden blanket. Just one more family to add to her growing list of those who needed her help.

But such was not for Martha to fret over. Kit quirked a brow, a saucy look she'd perfected on the streets. "I do not wonder that the day eludes you, my dear. I imagine time flies when you are a lady of leisure."

Reaching into her pocket, Kit pulled out a shilling and several sixpence and pressed them into Martha's cold fingers. "Here. Parcel these out. You know Frankie would spend them all at once on sugar sticks and candied nuts if given the chance."

"No." Martha held up the coins. "Ye already provide him work enough, and thankful I am fer it."

"You know as well as I do that is not enough." Kit leaned back on her haunches, away from the money. "I only wish I could do more."

Martha's hand dropped back to the bed, but thankfully, she kept hold of the offering. "Without ye, I dunno what we'd do, what with my man tossed in Newgate and me feeling so poorly."

"Well, then you must get better, hmm?"

A squall in the cradle began, the baby girl's cries winding tighter and tighter. Kit rose and retrieved the small bundle, holding the babe to her shoulder and bouncing a bit. "Hush, my sweet."

Kit nuzzled the girl's fuzzy head, a host of emotions normally kept at bay rising up as the little one rubbed her fist against her chin. She was a fighter, this one. A wildcat slugger every bit as capable as her brother—and as Kit had been, or to put it more aptly, as she'd had to be. Discarded at the Foundling Hospital when only weeks old. Hired out before she could even start school. And then the streets, knowing that she was well and truly alone in this world.

She hugged the babe tighter and whispered against the soft down near the babe's ear. "Do not worry, my love. Such will not happen to you."

Bending, she nestled the child to her mother's breast. "There, now. All is well."

Martha instinctively wrapped her arm around the babe. "God bless ye, miss."

"May God bless you as well." The words, while heartfelt, didn't quite match the doubt in her soul. Of course God could bless the woman, but would He? Or was He leaving it up to Kit to provide comfort and care for Martha?

Footsteps neared and soon Frankie held out a leftover crust of the bread. "Take a bite to eat, Mum?"

Martha smiled at him. "Aye, maybe in a bit, Son." Her eyes fluttered closed.

Frankie peered up at Kit, a rare show of emotion clouding his gaze. Fear. The sight of it punched Kit in the stomach.

She cuffed him on the arm, overly playful, a weak attempt to lighten his grim mood. "You need to get out of the house, my boy. How about today at noon sharp?"

And just like that, the fear vanished, replaced with a hopeless sort of determination. He nodded.

"Right, then." She gathered her basket, the other children sated and quiet. At least she was leaving the home better than she'd found it, for now at any rate.

Kit pulled the door shut behind her, and for a moment she lifted her face to a sky as sullen and unsettled as she felt. There was nothing she could do to make Martha hold on to life—and that irked.

"Kitty!"

She snapped her gaze to a faded blue skirt racing gimp-stepped down Angel Lane. The older woman grabbed on to Kit's arm then bent double, chest heaving for air. Grey hair frizzled out of the sides of her straw bonnet, a few patches frayed into holes. Little wheezes sang on her inhales.

Alarmed, Kit braced her up. "Natty? What's wrong?"

"He's gone," she cried. "I dunno where." She gasped. "Or why." She rasped. "Or how."

"Hold on now, Natty. Slow it down. In and out. In. And. Out." She coaxed her old friend through several breathing patterns, and finally the veins at Natty's temples flattened, her puffs slowing into steady breaths. Kit smoothed the woman's collar. "There. Much better. So tell me, exactly who is gone?"

Natty's face folded, tears sprouting in the creases at the corners of her eyes. "My Joe. He din't come home last night nor this morn, and I tell ye somethin's wrong. I know it in here." She flapped the flat of her hand against her chest. "Ye got to do somethin', Kitty. Ye know it ain't like him. I'm afeared somethin' terrible's happened."

Natty's panic seeped past Kit's sleeve and slid into her heart. Joe was the only semblance of a father she'd ever known. The one who'd saved her off the streets when he found her coughing away her life at the tender age of twelve and taken her in as one of his own. She'd had no one to depend upon during those lean years except for Natty and Joe—though they were stretched wire thin with their own seven mouths to feed. But now it was Joe who needed saving.

And she would.

"Don't worry. I'll find him and bring him home, Natty." She pulled away and tossed back her hair. "Whoever thought to cross our Joe just crossed me as well."

Chapter Four

Of the many duties Jackson had expected to perform, been trained for, *yearned* for, the guarding of a fabric warehouse was not one.

Yet here he was.

Day after infernal day for more than a fortnight, he whiled away monotonous hours walking the beat around Hamstock's Storage—a great wooden box of a building belonging to the sergeant's brother-in-law. The assignment was a favor to Graybone's relative and a slap in the face to Jackson. All for one smear of soot on his cheek that he'd missed. Not a single second smacked of danger or intrigue in this quiet crook of the City. Who in their right mind would snooker off with a bolt of linen?

He yanked his helmet lower in the face of a chill north wind banking around the building. He ought to be working with the other officers, combing back alleys for clues, for yet another man had gone missing—a barrister this time. But all the senior constables were paired up with other recruits. None to spare for him, even though Baggett had offered to let Jackson tag along with him and Officer Smith. No, the sergeant was determined to punish his earlier infractions by stationing him here, where the liveliest action was the few customers who patronized the nearby pawnshop or waited for an omnibus at the corner. If that were not bad enough, when the clock struck eleven bells, Jackson was expected to clip the lead on Hamstock's rat terrier for a turn around the block. And more often than not the dog wore a bonnet.

A bonnet!

Jackson tugged the leash. What a ridiculous bit of fur. Must the little beast stop to sniff every cobble as it ambled along? Graybone and his family's love affair with dogs perplexed him as much as the brass button of the Blackfriars thief.

While waiting for the dog to finish its business, Jackson pulled out the button. Not much to go on. Especially not for him. What experience did he have in such matters?

So he'd gone to Baggett, who affirmed what he already knew. It *wasn't* much to go on. But his friend had said, merely on a whim and a gut feeling, that he might try the Foundling Hospital on the off chance it was a token, which would be identifiable.

That very morning Jackson had paid a visit, voicing such a hope, and the matron matched the button to her records—but only after a sound education that such tokens were no longer in use. Paper receipts were apparently the thing. Which was neither here nor there to him. He just wanted to know if the button was linked with a name. And it was. Quite the victory, until the stalwart matron would not be moved to give any information from said receipt save to the mother who'd dropped off the child.

From there, he'd trudged over to the 1st Infantry Brigade head-quarters at the Wellington Barracks, for he had no doubt whatsoever that the button belonged to a former Coldstream Guard. Again, fruitless. The colonel of the regiment had been too occupied to grant him a meeting. But not to worry. Persistence had ever been his strong point—a trait that thief on Blackfriars Lane would soon discover.

"Oy! That be you, young Mr. Forge? Or should I say *Constable*, now?"

Shoving the button back into his pocket, Jackson looked up to see a hyena of a man, all legs with a short torso, wearing a perpetual smile. Scruffy patches of facial hair smattered his face from cheeks to chin, a failed attempt at muttonchops. Mr. Thicket—Father's friend from the village, and the biggest tongue-wagger in all of Essex, hobbled towards him. The man could outgossip each and every member of the

Women's Aid Committee without breaking a sweat.

With a quick sidestep, Jackson relegated the dog to behind his legs, hopefully hiding the disgraceful thing, or at least the bonnet. "Mr. Thicket, what a surprise."

The man chuckled. "Indeed, what a windfall to cross paths with ye! I daresay yer father will scarce believe me. What are the chances?"

Exactly. What were the chances that a fellow all the way from Haywards Heath would see him here, now? And how would he explain why he wasn't stopping a theft or hauling in a criminal like he'd boasted before leaving home? Jackson forced a smile and pumped the man's hand in greeting. "What brings you to London, sir? Particularly these parts?"

A rare frown shaded Thicket's face. "I'm here on a sorry business. Afraid my lady wife's cousin recently passed, God rest him. And a good rest it should be. His final years weren't no patch o' posies. Ended up selling off most o' the family heirlooms just to keep a roof o'er his head. Died without a penny in his pocket, I'm told."

"I am sorry to hear it."

A sharp bark yipped out its own condolences, or more like an annoyed-to-be-waiting-in-one-spot warning. Whatever the reason, Mr. Thicket craned his neck to peer at the dog. Once again Jackson sidestepped, blocking the thing.

"Well then, Mr. Thicket, please, do not let me keep you."

"Aye, I ought not tarry, so off I am to redeem a particular brooch from that pawnshop." He hitched his thumb at the establishment. "Hopefully it won't be the breaking of my wallet. But tell me, young Forge." A knowing smile curved his lips. "What are you doing in this quiet corner o' town? Yer father told me you were bent on cleaning up the streets o' London, not strolling about with a dog in tow."

Blast! What a merry time Thicket would have at the pub embellishing what he'd seen. Father would be sure to hear, and though he'd never voice his chagrin aloud, he'd have to be disappointed. Jackson's conscience chafed red and raw. Just one more failure in a long line stringing all the way back to that ugly day he'd failed his brother.

But the longer he remained silent, the more Thicket would conjure up his own larger-than-life tale. Tugging at his collar, Jackson glanced at the pawnshop. Would that Thicket might simply go about his business instead of standing here, eyes narrowed, waiting for an explanation.

"A pox on you. A pox, I say!" A raised voice belched out of the pawnshop, followed by a colourful parade of curses. "I'll not take such a theft in silence, ye scabby villain."

All of Jackson's senses snapped to attention. A man dressed head to toe in black dashed out the door, clutching a canvas sack to his chest.

A robbery!

Now here was a story Jackson wouldn't mind Thicket taking home. He shoved the lead into the man's hand. "Take the dog to the back door." He jerked his head at the warehouse. "There is thievery afoot."

He broke into a sprint, silent this time, having learned his lesson on Blackfriars Lane not to announce his pursuit. And it paid off. Catching up to the thief, he sprang and rode the blackguard to the ground before the fellow could know what hit him.

"Help! Police!" The man thrashed beneath him.

"I *am* the police." Jackson made short work of cuffing the man's hands behind his back and hauling him to his feet. "And you are under arrest."

"Are you mad?" the fellow blustered. "What the devil for?"

Jackson reached for the fallen bag and peered inside. Money. Lots of it. Dash it! This was exactly why constables were paired up. He couldn't do everything simultaneously, so what to do first? Return the money? Speak with the shopkeeper about pressing charges? Or use his own initiative to secure the criminal behind bars before such details were ironed out?

Snap decision made, he grabbed the man's arm and yanked him

towards the station. "Caught you red-handed, did I?"

"What on earth are you talking about?" The man writhed.

Jackson tightened his grip. "As if you did not know. Come along now."

"Let me go! You are making a big mistake."

Just as was documented in the officer's handbook, the man unraveled a string of excuses and outright lies all the way to Old Jewry. As recommended, Jackson flattened his lips, unresponsive. Let the lawbreaker tell it to the magistrate.

It was no small feat to yank open the station door while gripping a wriggling criminal and lugging a bag of money, but Jackson relished the task. Finally a worthy duty, something that would make a difference in the world. One less criminal to terrorize innocent citizens.

And a way to get back into the sergeant's good graces.

He pulled the man into the receiving hall, and several sets of eyes turned to them. Beanstaple rose from his seat to peer over the desk. Several paces away, a hunchbacked man in a sateen dress coat lifted a brow, while the other brow sank over a purpled eye with a cut near it. Strange. The almost frail-looking man didn't seem the type to take part in fisticuffs. Next to him, Sergeant Graybone flared his nostrils.

"What is this?" A merlot-coloured stain rose up the sergeant's neck. "Explain yourself at once, Forge."

Jackson released his quarry and threw back his shoulders. "I caught this thief red-handed, sir. Robbing the pawnshop on Coopers Row." In two strides, he shoved the bag of money into the sergeant's hands. "Here is the evidence."

A tic twitched Graybone's right eye. "You muddleheaded greenbow! That is no thief." He slammed the bag onto the clerk's counter. "You have just hauled in Mr. Clarence Boyle. *Banker* Clarence Boyle."

The words circled like vultures, waiting to pick at his flesh. Could it be? But no. A banker could break the law as much as any other man. Jackson widened his stance. "I clearly heard the pawnshop owner accuse this man of robbery. In no uncertain terms, I might add."

If glowers could kill, the one darkening Boyle's face would have Jackson bleeding out on the floor. "He was not talking to me, you oaf. The man was in a tiff with the landlord, who is raising the rents yet again. I was merely making my daily pickup. Which you would know if you had listened to one word I said on the way here."

Jackson shook his head. "I have manned that street for two weeks now, and not once were you present. If what you say is true, then why have I never seen you before?"

"Because I use the back door, you fool, which happened to be blocked today by a dray at the loading dock. Walking about in the public view on the main road is just asking for trouble—which is what I got."

The truth cut as sharp as a broad swipe with a felling axe. Jackson planted his feet to keep from toppling. Behind him, Sergeant Graybone snorted, a bull about to charge.

Jackson turned slowly. Carefully. One wrong move could be fatal. "Sir, I—"

"Loose that man. Now!"

The sergeant's roar reverberated in his chest, and he stifled a flinch. Summoning the last of his dignity, Jackson strode behind Boyle and unlocked the cuffs.

As soon as the banker was free, Sergeant Graybone returned the canvas sack to him. Boyle's red wrists peeked from beneath his sleeves as he reached for it. "My apologies, Mr. Boyle. I assure you this matter will be sorted out at once."

"I hope you will better train your officers to keep their hands off law-abiding citizens." With a sneer at Jackson, the man stormed away, riffling the wanted posters tacked to the wall as he passed. The slam of the door behind him echoed throughout the station.

Jackson's gut clenched in the unnerving silence left behind. Mr.

Beanstaple blinked at him. Pity shone in the gaze of the hunchbacked man standing near the counter. But there was no such mercy in the black eyes of Sergeant Graybone. Only a burning rage.

"In my office, Forge." Each word struck like a deadly blow. "Immediately."

Chapter Five

Some days should be wadded up and thrown in a dustbin before they are finished. This was one of them. And Jackson himself just might be tossed into the bin right along with the day, if the stiff shoulders stretching Sergeant Graybone's uniform into taut lines were any indication.

Sucking in a deep breath, he set off after the sergeant, steeling himself for the firing squad. Though, judging by the pound of Graybone's steps, he was to be drawn and quartered first. Clerk Beanstaple made eye contact with him then looked sharply away, yet not before Jackson caught the pity sparking in his gaze. The same sort of freakish compassion Father had shown when he'd found Jackson huddled in an alcove after his brother had been taken off to hospital.

"Hold up there, Henry." Behind them sounded a bass voice with a heavy accent—a strange mix of French and Dutch.

Graybone halted. Jackson turned. The hunchbacked fellow who'd earlier been chatting with the sergeant strode their way on long, thin legs, bringing the scent of bergamot along with him. Either the man was a particular friend of Graybone or a fool. Even were the sergeant in a merry mood, it was a bold move to call him by his Christian name.

Without turning, the sergeant spoke over his shoulder. "My apologies for cutting short our engagement, Mr. Poxley, but this matter must be dealt with immediately. I bid you good day."

"I understand, my friend, but a word, if you please, before you gut this young pup." He swiped a hand indicating Jackson, the cuff of his shirtsleeves flapping with the movement.

Jackson's gaze bounced between the sergeant's broad back and the twinkle of amusement in Mr. Poxley's green eyes. Beanstaple's chair creaked, and though the clerk appeared to busy himself with a sheaf of papers, his head inclined their way.

Finally, the sergeant pivoted, his face a stoic slate. Whoever this Mr. Poxley was, he must be a powerful fellow indeed to effect such a stay of execution. Curious, Jackson studied him, from the top of his shiny silk hat to the tips of his Italian leather shoes. Quite the dapper fellow. Save for the hump on his back and the bruised eye, he might be a fashion plate model. Curled auburn hair framed his chiseled face, a face that challenged the sergeant with a flicker of a smile.

"All I ask is that you go easy on him, Henry. Lord knows we were both spit and vinegar years ago, were we not? I daresay you wouldn't be where you are today without a measure of mercy."

"Mercy!" The word shot out so forcefully, Graybone's black moustache rippled with the breeze. "Not only did this officer abandon his duty, he accosted a known banker who was merely doing his job. That sort of performance is more than sloppy. It can harm innocent people, or the force, should Boyle decide to press charges against one of our own, namely you, Mr. Forge."

Jackson stiffened. Heaven and earth! How had he inadvertently committed such a magnificent blunder? Maybe the sergeant who had instructed Jackson and the other recruits was right after all. Failure was an undertaker, always waiting in the wings, ready to bear away the bodies of those who made one too many mistakes.

Mr. Poxley clucked his tongue. "Come now. We both know Boyle will not seek legal counsel. He is far too miserly of his pennies to pay for such an excess."

Graybone's eyes narrowed. "I would not be so sure if I were you." He wheeled about and once again marched away. "Step lively, Forge."

So much for Poxley's plea. The man tipped his hat at him and strode towards the front door. Beanstaple turned his face away. And just like that, Jackson stood abandoned, with nothing but the clip of the sergeant's boots echoing like rapid gunfire.

He forced his feet to move, but no sooner had he gone a few paces when a wailing cry burst into the station.

"He's gone. Oh! He's gone." A woman rushed in, skirts aswirl. "Please! He must be found."

Bypassing Mr. Poxley, she dashed over to Jackson, her red-rimmed eyes pleading up into his. "I beg you to find him, Officer."

Sergeant Graybone stalked over to them both, as did Mr. Poxley. "Who must be found, madam?"

"My husband. He ain't come home, and he *always* comes home. I fear he's gone the way of the other missing men." She grabbed Jackson's arm. "Please, you must help."

"Of course, madam. We will do all we can, will we not, Sergeant?"

Sergeant Graybone flattened his lips, then motioned for Beanstaple to hand him a pencil and paper. "Who is your husband? A name, a description, if you please. Where he was last seen and the like."

Her teary gaze drifted from Jackson to the sergeant. "His name is Joseph Card, Joe to those what know him. He's about this man's height, though not so froggish in the legs." She tipped her head at Mr. Poxley. "And he's got a fluff o' hair about his ears. Bald on top. One tooth missing in the front. Wears a red fabric poppy in his hatband. I'm told he were last seen in Blackfriars, where he picked up a gent."

Graybone cocked his head. "Picked up?"

"Aye." Her lower lip trembled as she jutted her chin. "He's a jarvey, my Joe is. Best hack driver in the whole Square Mile."

"I see," the sergeant drawled, as if what he really saw was some manure on his shoe. He set the paper and pencil on the counter. "Well, I have no doubt your husband will turn up, Mrs. Card. Jarveys always do after they have recovered from one pint too many."

Frantic, she swung her head side to side. "No, it's not like that, I tell ye. Joe don't touch a drop. He *ne'er* touches a drop!" Once again her fingers dug into Jackson's arm, panic tightening her voice to a shrill pitch. "Please, you've got to search for my Joe now. Right now."

Her wide-eyed gaze burned into his.

Jackson opened his mouth, but the sergeant's voice bellowed out, "Please return when your husband has been missing more than twenty-four hours and fill out a report here with my clerk. I assure you we shall look into the case in due time. Now"—Graybone cut Jackson a sideways glance—"Mr. Forge, my office, if you please."

What? Was the sergeant still bent on dismissing him even when a clear need for justice wept right here in the front reception hall?

He pulled away from the woman and stepped up to Graybone. "Sir, allow me to redeem myself. Put me on this case. I vow this time I shall not let you down."

The sergeant shook his head. "Absolutely not. Your time here is finished."

Mrs. Card dropped to her knees at the sergeant's feet, grabbing hold of his coat hem. "Please, sir. Have mercy."

A disgusted sigh deflated Graybone's chest as the woman dripped tears onto his shoes. He shuffled from foot to foot, eventually dragging his gaze from the woman to Jackson. "Very well. I will give you two days, Forge. That's forty-eight hours to find this woman's missing husband and save your job in the process. Am I clear?"

Jackson snapped a salute. "Yes, sir. You can count on me, sir."

The sergeant rolled his eyes. "I doubt it," he breathed, just loud enough for Jackson to hear.

Bending, Jackson aided the woman to her feet. "I shall do my utmost to find your husband, Mrs. Card. Leave your contact information here with the clerk. I must be off to the cab company posthaste."

With a tip of his helmet to the woman and to Mr. Poxley—for the sergeant already stalked away from them all—Jackson strode to the front door, throat tingling from the near beheading he'd missed by a last-minute pardon. For now, anyway. If he didn't find the cabby, his head might yet hang on the sergeant's trophy wall.

Forder's Cab Company stood at the corner of Greeley and Graham Streets, a soot-blackened brick building, smelling of horses and wheel grease—which was a far more pleasing scent than what permeated the front office Jackson entered. Was it the man—Burton Forder—who stank of wet dog and boiled eggs? Or did the stench emanate from the ratty cushioned chair in front of the small hearth? Either way, Jackson remained near the open door.

Mr. Forder, ensconced behind a paper-littered desk, lifted baggy eyes his way. "How can I be of service, Officer?"

"One of your drivers, a Mr. Joseph Card, has been reported missing. I should like to know his exact route and examine his cab at once. That is, of course, if the vehicle is here?"

The man shifted in his seat, giving his rump a good long scratch before settling down to answer. "Aye, that it is. First stall to the right just through the big doors. It were found abandoned over near the docks."

"The docks, eh? Which one?"

"Wapping."

Jackson pulled out a notepad and scribbled down the information. "Was that on his regular route?"

"No. Ol' Joe din't have much o' a route, really. Mostly he parked at the Grouse & Gristle over on Bridewell Place. Did a fair enough trade hauling home patrons and the like. Odd he's gone missing. In all his ten years o' service he's never once been late to return his hack. Shame, leaving the pub without a cabby like that after all this time."

Jackson held his pencil aloft. "Can you not simply assign another cab?"

"Pish. Not as easy as you'd think, not where the Grouse & Gristle is concerned." Forder leaned back in his chair. "Their clientele don't take to new faces."

"Yet clearly Joe Card had been able to establish a successful trade therein."

Forder shrugged. "Ol' Joe was one o' them."

"One of who?" Stench or not, Jackson stepped closer, studying Forder's face. "What sort of people are we talking about?"

The man sucked his teeth as if they were chicken bones, stretching the silence for so long that Jackson couldn't help but wonder if he might not answer at all.

"The private sort," he said at length.

Hmm. The man's cryptic words could mean anything from eccentrics to smugglers. Judging by that part of town, the patrons were more than likely of a nefarious shade.

"Tell me, Mr. Forder, being you are familiar with the pub and the people, do you suspect foul play could be afoot in the case of your driver Joe as it relates to the customers of the Grouse & Gristle?"

A great belly laugh burst out of the man. "Hah! That's a good one. No, no. Ol' Joe were safe as a babe in his mother's arms in that place. Like I say, he were one of 'em, and kin don't nip after kin."

"Very well. Did Joe have any known enemies? Anyone at all who might wish him to be gone?"

Forder pushed out his lower lip, clearly giving the question a good think before spit-shining an answer. "Everyone who knew Joe would tell you he were a quiet soul, harmless as a church mouse."

Jackson blew out a long breath. This was getting him nowhere, but before he tucked away his pad and pencil, he skewered Forder with one last look. "Have you anything to add, any detail at all that I should know about, before I examine the cab?"

"Not that I. . ." The manager's voice trailed off and a faraway glaze darkened his eyes.

"Any little thing could be of the utmost importance, sir."

"Well, maybe something," he murmured. "Or maybe not."

"In a case such as this, there is nothing too insignificant to mention."

"Right." Forder snapped his gaze back to Jackson. "Well then, I s'pose ye'll find out soon enough."

Jackson lowered the pencil lead to the paper, ready for anything. "What is that?"

"Joe's cab is empty. *Completely* empty."

Not particularly headlining news. He angled his head in disgust. "Is that really so unusual? You said yourself the vehicle sat near the docks. Hardly a place to expect it would remain untouched."

"O' course. But what I mean is it were clean empty." Forder leaned forward in his seat. "Not a cigar ash. No bits o' gravel on the floor. Not even a stray hair fallen from a patron. Somebody wiped down that vehicle, Officer. Somebody that didn't want to be identified in any way."

Jackson's grip tightened on the pencil. Clearly whoever had abducted Mr. Card was a professional, someone used to covering his tracks. Someone who could be involved in the cases of the other missing men? Might he not only find Joe Card but discover the baronet, barrister, and merchant as well? A flicker of hope burst into flame at the thought of the sergeant clapping him on the back in pride.

Jackson tucked the paper and pencil away then tipped his hat at the man. "Thank you, Mr. Forder. If you think of anything else, leave word for me at the Old Jewry station. Good day."

Bypassing a boy shoveling a pile of horse droppings, he wove his way into the great stable block of stalls. Most were empty, being it was daytime with traffic at a high. But just to his right, as Mr. Forder had said, stood a black hackney with a nearby knock-kneed nag munching a mouthful of provender beside it. Jackson patted the horse's withers. "If only you could tell me what you saw, my friend."

Leaving the horse behind, he first examined the outside of the cab. A bit of dried mud speckled the wheel wells, but other than that and one deep scratch on the door, the carriage practically reflected his face right back at him. The thing hadn't been merely wiped down, but polished.

Next he climbed into the driver's seat, scouring the leather cushion for any sort of leftover blood or scrapes that revealed a scuffle, feeling about in the crevices for anything Joe or his abductor might have left behind.

Nothing.

He jumped to the ground and yanked open the door, giving the inside of it a good going-over. Again, while the paint was worn thin around the handle and the curtains were threadbare, not one thing hinted at any sort of struggle or kidnapping attempt. There weren't even any smudges on the window.

Hefting himself up, he surveyed the carriage box. Years stained the leather seat to nearly black, something that couldn't be erased no matter how much one might scrub them. And clearly someone had. The scent of vinegar and lye soap permeated the cab.

"What happened here, Joe?" Jackson whispered as he dissected every corner. "Why could you not have left me some sort of—"

He squinted at the thickness of the wall in comparison to where the cushion ended. Closing one eye, then opening it and closing the other, he did some mental calculations. Something about the space wasn't quite right.

He dove in. Prodding. Poking. Running his fingers along the edge of the seat, then the sides, searching for hidden levers or buttons. No good. He shoved his hand into the crack between the cushion and the wall. A tight fit, practically pinching his fingertips. A third of the way across, he hit a piece of metal—where no support ought to be. He pressed it. Nothing. Then pulled.

Something clicked. The back of the seat loosened.

Half a smile twitched his lips as he lifted the cushion, revealing a secret compartment large enough to smuggle a stash of guns, some stolen goods...or maybe an abducted man?

Bending closer, he scrutinized the area. No, stuffing an adult body into such a small space would never work, but clearly Joe had modified his cab in order to transport something he must hide. Which meant that the sort of clientele he dealt with needed to move items illegally. And if Joe had somehow crossed one of those brigands, well, that sort would have no qualms about harming him.

Jackson shoved the cushion back into place, mind whirring. Perhaps a trip to the docks was in order. Find out if anyone had seen who'd cleaned this vehicle so spotlessly.

But first, a visit to the Grouse & Gristle. Time to see what sort of *private people* Joe associated with.

Chapter Six

The Grouse & Gristle was a lonely soldier, claiming its ground between the bones of a burnt-out building on one side and a heap of rubble leftover from an underground railway excavation on the other. Soot blackened the scarred bricks. A greasy film coated the windows. Though afternoon sun slipped through a crack in the clouds, the brilliance did nothing to cheer the solemn old structure. How many wayward souls spent their hard-won pennies inside such a melancholy outpost?

Before shoving open the door, Jackson loosened his collar, then on second thought, he doubled back a few steps and swiped his thumb along the wall, collecting a good amount of grime on his fingertip. He smeared the grit across his forehead and, for good measure, added a dab to one cheek. There. The smudges—along with his civilian clothes—ought to lend credence to his factory worker facade. No one would give him a second glance.

But he couldn't have been more wrong. The instant his boot crossed the threshold, the low drone of chatter ceased and every eye in the taproom turned his way. Despite the wary looks, he forced a swagger to his steps and approached the counter.

The barkeep—who might've been a pirate at one time, guessing by the gold hoop earring and the nautical tattoo—lowered an eyebrow his direction.

Jackson glanced at the only other man bellied-up to the bar. Muscles bulged against the seams of his coat. He outweighed Jackson by at least five stone. The brute could be trouble should he wish to be. But the fellow merely ran his sleeve across his upper lip, wiping off the foamy remains of his ale, then he shoved away from the counter. In six long strides, he vanished out the door.

Jackson frowned. There went an opportunity.

"What'll you have?" The barkeep pulled a mug from beneath the counter.

"Information," Jackson said evenly.

A great chuckle rumbled in the man's chest. "Fresh out of that."

So. . .apparently the direct approach wouldn't be a go. "Cider, then," he conceded.

While the barkeep held the mug beneath a tap and filled it with a cloudy liquid, Jackson eyed the rest of the patrons. At a large table in the center of the room, two men nursed their mugs while chatting. Off in one corner, a solitary figure lurked in the shadows, leaning against the wall. In front of the window, three dockhands rolled dice, the stink of fish and sweat coming off them in waves. Not a particularly large crowd, but considering the time of day, not bad. He could always come back tonight when the day labourers were more likely to be swigging pints and swapping stories.

The barkeep shoved the mug across the counter, cider slopping over the rim. "A thruppence for your drink."

Jackson fished a coin from his pocket. "Thank you. Could you tell me if—"

The man turned his back before Jackson could finish the question.

"All right then," he breathed out. Perhaps he'd have better luck with some of the other patrons. Pirates were, after all, notoriously skittish.

Collecting his mug, he strolled over to the big table. Both men watched his approach.

"Afternoon, gents." Jackson nodded to the empty chair across from them. "May I join you?"

"*May I*, is it?" The smaller of the two men laughed and nudged the other with his elbow. "When's the last time a swell stumbled in here, Jimmy?"

Jimmy grinned up at Jackson. What few yellowed teeth he owned clung precariously to his gums. "Slummin' it, are ye, guv'ner? Or be ye lost? This here's the east side."

Jackson stifled a frown. So much for his factory worker disguise. "Just looking for a friend of mine. Thought perhaps you might have seen him."

"Are ye now?" Jimmy's gaze drifted to his friend. "You know any dandy toffs, Billy?"

"Why, course I do." Billy stood and sashayed in a circle with one hand on his hip. "I'm one meself. Say. . ." The man paused and waggled his wiry eyebrows. "Is it me yer looking for?"

This time Jackson did frown. The indirect approach was working about as well as the direct. "I am looking for Joseph Card, the jarvey," he ground out. "Have you seen him?"

The men exchanged a glance, but only Jimmy spoke up. "If I had an extra coin in me pocket, I'd slap it down for a pint o' ale, not a swirl about town in a hack. Same fer every man in here. Ye'll get nowhere asking questions about a cabby in this pub."

The truth of the man's words lit a fire of frustration in Jackson's gut. He *was* getting nowhere, and time was ticking away. Impatience overriding reason, he swung about and raised his voice. "Does anyone in this establishment have any idea where Joe Card is? I know you know him, every one of you. He is one of yours, and he may very well be in grave danger."

All mirth bled from Jimmy's and Billy's faces. Without a word, both grabbed their mugs and retreated. At the table by the window, the roll of the dice stopped. One of the dockhands rose and, after a nod to one of his friends, stalked over to Jackson and clamped a hand on his shoulder. Hard.

"The only one in grave danger right now, cully, is you." Cold grey eyes fastened on him. "So push off."

Jackson stared at the calloused fingers digging into his shoulder, then glowered at the man's face. If this slab of meat wanted a knuckle buster, who was he to deprive the fellow?

The man grunted and pulled back. A bluff charge, to be sure, but a warning nonetheless. There'd be no answers from this lot.

Jackson set down his cider and, bypassing the big bully, swaggered to the door. Just because he'd failed at gaining information didn't mean he had to slink out of here looking like a fool.

Outside, he released a defeated breath, reset his hat, then strode down the street. Maybe he'd swing by the station and get Mrs. Card's information, ask if Joe had any particular friends or enemies that might give him a lead. But first, he ought to stop by the Wapping Dockyard and poke around the waterfront where the cab had been abandoned.

Behind him, the pub's door opened and slammed, and the fine hairs on his neck rose. If that dockhand had decided to tangle further with him, he'd give him what for. Jackson reached for the truncheon tucked inside his coat and wheeled about.

Sure enough, the icy-eyed man stalked towards him, a smirk slashing across his face.

Jackson crouched, club at the ready. "I would not try anything, if I were you."

"Neither would I," a voice snarled at his back.

And the hard metal of a gun bored into his head.

The dockhand's smirk stretched into a wicked smile. "Drop the club, cully."

Thunderation! What to do? A quick move to take out the man behind him? A deadly maneuver if he weren't fast enough, but it might be worth a try. Or he could play along and see where they took him, for it could very well be where Joe Card had ended up.

Jackson splayed his fingers, and his truncheon fell to the cobbles.

Immediately, the man at his back wrenched both of Jackson's arms behind him. Rope bit into his wrists. Hopefully this would be worth it, for Joe's sake and his own.

"The boss don't take kindly to strangers asking questions." The man's hot breath blasted against Jackson's neck as he yanked the rope tight. "Ye'll be made to answer a few o' yer own. And was I you, I'd answer real quick like. Turner's not one to trifle with, especially not today."

The dockhand strolled past with a nod to the fellow behind him, just like he'd done earlier. Ahh. The same signal that he'd given in the pub. Clearly they'd done this before.

With a shove to Jackson's shoulder, the man propelled him forward, forcing him to follow the grey-eyed brute and trapping him between the two. For now. Jackson flattened his lips to keep from smiling. Once he found Joe, the knife in his boot and pistol in his pocket would change the order of things.

The men steered him to a door at the rear of the Grouse & Gristle. After three quick raps and two slow, it swung open.

"Fresh fish, eh?" Whoever spoke had a lisp, but Jackson couldn't see his face. The broad shoulders of the fellow in front of him blocked his view, nor could he lean sideways for a glimpse. The stairway they ascended was too narrow. Too dark. And entirely too rife with a sour stink. Compared to this, the cab manager's office was a field of blooming flowers.

"Aye," the dockhand ahead of him grunted. "This fish were asking about Joe."

"Was he now? Turner won't like that. Already in a collywomping temper over that one."

The stairs opened into a small room, barren and dimly lit by the lingering afternoon sun leaching in through a set of two windows. Three doors lined one wall. All were closed. Could the missing cab driver be behind one?

"Stop here," the man behind him rasped.

Jackson halted, but the lispy fellow and the grey-eyed dockhand advanced and pounded on the door farthest to the left. After a curt

"Enter," they vanished inside, leaving him with a muzzle still drilling into the back of his skull.

Sweat trickled between his shoulder blades. If he could make eye contact with the man, establish some sort of human connection, it would take more guts for the trigger to be pulled—and give him more time to figure a way out of this mess without any bloodshed.

"Lower your gun, man." He measured out the words calmly, slowly, as he might to a skittish colt. "I will not make a move."

"Hah! Ain't that the truth." The man's boots thudded against the wooden planks as he circled to the front of Jackson. He still gripped a gun—a beat-up double-barrel Lancaster pistol, likely pinched off a drunken infantryman—but at least now he held it at his side. Not that it removed the threat in his dark eyes. "Best you behave yerself, cully. Turner ain't been in a generous mood lately. You picked a bad time to come sniffin' round here."

Jackson's gaze slid to the door the dockhand had ducked through. Whoever this Turner fellow was, he clearly wielded a lot of power, leastwise in this parish. While he might be a good source of information, Jackson would have to be careful. This would take all the skill he'd learned in training and then some. Did he have what it took to interrogate the leader of a gang of cutthroat men?

The door at the far end creaked open. Jackson tensed. Second-guessing his skills was a moot point now. *A little help here, Lord, and...*

His prayer faded as the rustle of a skirt filled the room—a brown skirt. A bold step.

The thief of Blackfriars Lane.

She strode into the small space, her pert little nostrils flaring as she met his gaze. Recognition deepened the blue of her eyes and lightened the silver flecks.

Jackson clenched his jaw. What the deuce was she doing here? Ahh, yes. The day she'd worked the "dropped" wallet scheme, she'd teamed up with an old man and young boy. Likely all three worked for this Turner fellow. Jackson stored away the information. This could be a gang worth bringing down after he'd found the missing jarvey.

The woman stopped in front of him, practically toe to toe. "Well, well. . .we meet again, hmm?"

Without waiting for him to answer, she turned to the man with the pistol. "Did you check him for weapons?"

"This bumbler?" The man sneered. "All he carries is a big mouth and a club, one he dropped out on the street."

"Is that so?"

In two steps, she closed the distance between Jackson and herself then crouched. He tensed as her fingers lightly patted his leg. Did the woman possess no sense of propriety whatsoever? Her touch left a scorching trail, which burned all the hotter when she deftly ran her fingers down the other leg and retrieved the knife from his boot. Worse, she didn't stop there. She rose and felt along his ribs, over his chest, then plunged her hand into his coat pocket.

And there went his revolver.

Her lips quirked at him, then she waved the weapons in front of the other man. "Bumbler, eh? Takes one to know one, I suppose."

A dark flush crept up the man's neck, and he tucked his pointy chin to his chest. "My mistake."

"Your last." Her words struck like sharpened blades. "You are finished, Hanks. Do not show your face around here again."

Jackson's eyes widened. Apparently this woman was higher in rank than he credited her.

The flush erupted on Hanks's face, an angry red now. "Yer taking this too far! That man is nothing more than a loose-lipped half-wit—"

"That man is a constable," she cut in.

Hanks gasped and recoiled, as if Jackson might instantaneously produce a pair of cuffs.

The woman's brows lowered into a fierce scowl. "And now because of your blunder, we shall have to relocate. Again."

She stalked up to the man, steps clipped and skirt swirling, heedless of the fact that he bested her by at least a handspan in height and yet gripped his pistol.

"It could be worse, Hanks." She flipped the knife around, clutching the weapon as if it were a familiar friend. "Do not press your luck."

Hanks's gaze shot to the blade. Beads of perspiration sprouted on his forehead. Interesting. She hadn't aimed Jackson's revolver at the man. What sort of skill did the woman possess with a blade to make this thug quail while he yet held a weapon of his own?

"What about Duff?" Hanks shuffled back a step. "He were just as much to blame as me."

"Duff is not your concern." She tucked Jackson's revolver into her waistband yet kept the knife firmly gripped in her slim fingers. "Now leave, and do not show me your face ever again."

The man eased a few steps nearer the door, never once pulling his eyes off the knife in her hand. "Look, it don't have to be this way. I got five mouths to feed at home, and my wife, Janey, why, she's sick. I can't afford to go without." He lifted the pistol with a shaky hand, then aimed it at Jackson's head. "One shot will solve this problem. Just one. No one will be the wiser, and it'll never happen again. I swear it!"

Every muscle in Jackson coiled, prepared to tackle Hanks if his finger so much as twitched.

"Put it down, Hanks." The woman's voice was a winter wind, cutting to the bone. "That is not how business is done around here and you know it."

Hanks narrowed his eyes. "Then mebbe it's time for a change."

She grinned, but it wasn't so much a smile as a baring of teeth. "For once, you are right."

The words had barely made it past her lips when she threw the knife. Jackson ducked. True to the mark, the blade stabbed into the man's gun arm. The pistol clattered to the floor, the noise of it barely discernable past Hanks's cursing. Howling, he yanked out the blade, tossed it to the floor, and clutched his bleeding forearm.

"This ain't finished!" The threat bayed between sulfurous oaths as he fled down the stairs.

"It is now." She slammed the door.

Jackson rose from his crouch, wild energy coursing through his veins. The woman swiftly swiped up the knife and faced him. She'd saved his life—though they both knew she could just as easily take it now.

Pursing her lips, she circled him, a falcon on the hunt. "Well now, Mr. Constable. What am I to do with you?"

What was *she* to do with him? Had Turner entrusted so much power to this one slip of a woman that his fate rested in her small hands?

He met her stare. "I was told I am to see Turner, the boss."

She smirked. "You are looking at her."

Chapter Seven

Like the sharp grinding of a pebble in one's shoe, it used to irritate Kit Turner when men discounted her intelligence. Ignored her as being of no consequence. Or worse, falsely scorned her as a woman of ill repute. But years of sweat and toil to make something of herself had softened that visceral response. Their stupidity was now her advantage, and she laughed. Or it might be the astonishment rippling across the face of the constable that amused her so.

But just as quickly, her good humour faded. If this lawman had located her, it would be only a matter of time before her enemies did as well.

She planted her feet squarely in front of him. "How did you find me?"

He flushed red, glancing east and west of her before blowing a puff of air and finally locking onto her gaze with a steely stare. "I am not going to answer that question, Miss Turner."

She hid a smile. He had backbone, she'd give him that.

"Fair enough." She cocked her head and studied the man. He was a looker, with his brown hair dropping a careless curl on his forehead, just begging to be pushed back. His blue eyes were clear and deep as an August sky, lit with a healthy dose of ambition. He wore his moustache trimmed and side-whiskers neatly sheared, a man who either took his own hygiene to heart or actually cared about what others thought of him. Despite a smudge of grime marring his forehead and one cheekbone, such a handsome appearance was dangerous. For him, especially. Pretty bobbies didn't last long, leastwise not in Blackfriars. The temptation to carve up such a fresh face was too strong a pull for some.

Absently, she rubbed her thumb along the hilt of the knife—*his* knife—and a fine one at that. "I am told you were asking about Joe Card. Did you really come here for him or was that simply a convenient pretense?"

"Do you know where he is?" Zeal sparked in his gaze. Such passion would be this man's undoing. Not that she cared. One less constable on the streets would make her life better.

She tapped her lips for a moment before parrying his question. "Why should I tell you?"

"So you do know."

Fishing? Did this upstart lawman really think she'd fall for such a novice trick? She pointed the tip of the knife at him. "I did not say that."

He didn't so much as flinch. "But you have an idea of where he might be?"

Quite the tenacious fellow. Might have even made a good crew member were he not a man of the navy blue cloth.

"I am not going to answer that question, Mr. Constable." She tossed his own words right back at him. "I have a few secrets of my own, you see."

"Touché." He grinned, a full smile this time, one that sprouted a crescent dimple on the right side of his mouth. "We should work together, you and I. You help me find Joe, and I will see what I can do about lessening your sentence."

Hah! Again she laughed, then caught herself. Oh my. She hadn't been this entertained since young Frankie had let loose a bag of mice in Southwark Cathedral—then charged a fat purse of farthings to retrieve them all. Were the man in front of her not a constable, she just might take him up on his offer.

"That is a fine proposal coming from a man at my mercy." She flipped his knife around in her hand, driving home her point.

"But you are mistaken, Miss Turner." His grin disappeared, and his eyes narrowed. "It is you who are beholden to me."

"Intriguing. Enlighten me, sir."

"If you will remember, a fortnight ago I caught you red-handed with a pickpocketed wallet in your possession." He angled his chin to a smug tilt. "What say you to such an accusation?"

Sweet heavens. He'd have to do better than that if he hoped to bring her down. "Trivial hearsay." She shrugged. "Tittle-tattle. Nothing more than your word against mine."

"You mean an upstanding police officer's word against that of a known leader of a parish gang? Hmm. I wonder which way the magistrate will lean."

She fingered the knife hilt. He did have a point. Yet she'd not concede—a survival lesson she'd learned long ago. Those who appeared weak were weak. "You cannot prove it was me who you saw."

"Ahh, but I can."

Unbidden, her free hand flew to her neck, where once her token had hung on a chain, her single link to a past she'd rather not remember yet found impossible to forget. Her fingers met nothing but warm skin—and a hot fury burned in her belly. It was because of this man she'd lost her prized possession in the first place. Though she'd since returned several times to scour that particular stretch of Blackfriars Lane, she still had nothing to show for it. Had he, perhaps, found her pendant before she did?

No, ridiculous. He could have no idea her token was missing.

She lowered her hand carefully. "How so?"

"I think you already know."

A cold dread pumped through her veins, and the blade in her hand shook. He did have it! She'd bet on it. The man was naught but a conniving thief hiding behind a badge.

She tightened her grip on the knife. "What is it you want, Mr. Constable?" The question snipped through the air, sharp and direct, all her former amusement bleeding out in a rush.

A knowing twinkle sparked in his gaze. "The name is Jackson Forge, Miss Turner, and for starters, you can unbind me."

Kipes! He was a bold one. She was hard-pressed to decide if she should call for Duff to dispose of him or land a kiss on his smart mouth just to shut him up. Blast Hanks for dragging him in here!

She clipped out her steps, skirting the man, and after a few slices, undid the ropes on his wrists. They fell with a thud to the floor. Then she circled back to face him and shot out her hand, palm up. "I will allow you to walk out of here free and unharmed if you hand over my token. Now."

"Sorry." He rubbed the chafed skin just below his cuffs, never once pulling his gaze from hers. "You should know very well I do not have it on me, nor will I be returning it until you help me locate Joe Card."

"Pah!" she sputtered. Was there no end to the man's insolence? "Why on earth would I help you?"

"Because if you do not, I will turn you in for thievery."

"Pretty talk for a man who is under my control." She waved the blade in the air. "Besides, even if you do make it out of here unscathed, you'd have to catch me first. And I'm very good at disappearing."

"But you won't."

"What makes you think so?"

"You care too much about that token. I noticed the tremble in your hand when I first mentioned it. And you'd better believe I shall lock up that special trinket as evidence until I hunt you down." He spread out his hands. "So either you agree to my terms, or you can save us both the trouble and come with me to the station right now."

The tone of authority in his voice annoyed her. How dare this raw recruit of a constable threaten her in her own sanctuary? But it wasn't just her he endangered. Without her leadership, her cunning, the men beneath her would fold, as would their families, just like Hanks was soon to find out. The thought of it elbowed its way in, leaving behind a sickening twist in her gut.

She advanced, nose to nose, an intimidation tactic that usually sent men shuffling backwards. "You have no idea what the consequences of locking me away will put into motion, Mr. Forge. The lives you will upend. The families you will leave destitute."

He didn't budge. "Then tell me."

Of all the stubborn men! Whirling, she paced away from him. Had this fool approached a real criminal in such a fashion, he'd be flat on the floorboards with a slit throat.

She stared out the window, unseeing. Such an unfair twist of fate. Would that she'd quit this place, this bleeding-heart lifestyle of caring for those God seemed to ignore, long before things had gotten out of hand. Blowing out a disgusted sigh, she marched back to the overly keen constable.

"Here is my offer, Mr. Forge. I will help you find Joe Card—not because of your feeble coercion or association with the constabulary, but simply on the merit that I was about to go looking for the man myself. I will allow you to tag along, and in return, you will give me back my token and vow to leave me and my crew alone. There will be no arrests or any further harassment that will interrupt my business on Blackfriars Lane. When Joe is located, we part ways, never to cross paths again."

She tucked away the knife and spit in her hand, then held it out.

For a moment he stared at her palm, a buck in a daze. Would this lawman's black-and-white convictions of right and wrong stop him from taking the best offer he'd ever receive?

His blue gaze snapped up to hers, then he spit in his own hand and pressed his warm palm against hers. "You have a deal, Miss Turner. I will not haul you in for thievery."

Astonished, she shook on it. Yet a nagging doubt hovered over her, as disconcerting as the remnants of an off-key chord that'd been banged on a piano.

Had she just made a deal with the devil?

In less than an hour, Kit Turner blew to smithereens all the things Jackson thought he knew about women. Not that he had much experience. Still, he never expected a member of the fairer sex to handle a knife with as much finesse as himself—and his own knife at that.

Having left behind the Grouse & Gristle, he now stretched his legs to keep pace with Miss Turner. This time he wasn't chasing her, but it still felt like it. Did she always travel at such breakneck speed? He glanced sideways at her, attempting to determine if she was trying to lose him. She could very well be second-guessing the agreement she'd made with him.

He certainly was.

He gritted his teeth, swallowing a rising disgust for shaking hands on a deal with a known thief. What a horrible means to an end. But of one thing he was certain. Once this whole Joe Card affair was over, he *would* be back for Miss Turner. He'd promised not to arrest her for thievery, but that didn't mean he wouldn't haul her in for some other charge. If she broke one law, no doubt she broke others. He'd watch. He'd wait. And when the time came, he would see justice delivered, making Blackfriars Lane a safer place for all.

For now, though, he'd have to play the game her way—yet perhaps with a few rules of his own tossed in. The more he could get her to talk, the better.

He leaned closer to be heard above the din of a passing dray. "Tell me, Miss Turner, how long did you know Joe?"

"Long enough," she answered, without so much as a glance his way.

"Is he part of your operation?"

"No."

Interesting. So, not all of the patrons at the Grouse & Gristle belonged to her cutpurse crew. Unless, of course, she was lying. He eyed her carefully. "Then why do you care enough to hunt him down?"

She did look at him then, but not for long. They had to part ways when a costermonger rolled his cart between them, griping about the crowds who got in his way and something else about the queen's choice of hat—though how the two were related was anyone's guess.

When they met back up, Miss Turner frowned at him. "Not that it is any of your business, but Joe is my friend. He is everyone's friend. Many a time he ran an errand for me off the clock, delivering a food basket or taking one of my men to the hospital, just because it needed to be done, expecting nothing in return."

Jackson snorted. Did she really think him so gullible? "Quite the effort for someone who is merely a friend. And surely you do not expect me to believe you run a charitable organization, Miss Turner. That you are some sort of Robin Hood in a skirt."

"I do not care what you believe, sir. But you can bank on this. . ." Her frown deepened, and she stopped, earning her a sharp remark from a man in a blue serge coat who nearly toppled into her. But so fixed was her stare the rest of the world may as well not exist. "Whoever old Joe ran afoul of is a black-hearted snake who needs to be held accountable for any harm he has brought to the man, for a kinder soul never walked the face of this earth."

Jackson stared right back. "Are you so certain that Joe did not disappear of his own accord?"

"I am."

"And you aim to bring some accountability to whomever it was that abducted him?"

"I do."

He laughed. How absurd! Either the woman was insanely confident or just plain mad. Knife skills or not, Kit Turner could hardly take down a man on her own. Widening his stance, he crossed his arms. "A single, small woman against an unknown assailant? You do not stand a chance."

"We shall see about that." She pivoted and strode off at such a pace her dark hair slipped its pins and swung like a pony's tail off the back of her head.

Jackson darted ahead, catching up to her just as she turned into the underground rail station on Queen Victoria Street. Apparently they were to take a train the rest of the way, or at least part of the way. A boon, that. Easier to interrogate her while not having to dodge crowds.

They descended into the depths of the station, skirting the few suits waiting for the next run. With so few bystanders, a train must've recently pulled out. Miss Turner stopped at the farthest edge of the platform, nearest the black maw of the tunnel, where she proceeded to gather up the hem of her skirt. Shapely legs were tucked into those high-rising leather boots of hers, leastwise what he could see from the knee down. A scandalous act, yet she did so without blushing.

He glanced over his shoulder to see if the two gentlemen had noticed Miss Turner's brazen behaviour. One fellow stood with his back to them, facing the other, who pulled out a newspaper and pointed to something on the front page. A heated debate followed, their deep voices bouncing off the station walls.

Jackson returned his gaze to Miss Turner. "Is such a precaution really necessary? I hardly think your gown will get muddied inside the train."

She fumbled with something caught in the fabric of her skirts. "We are not going on the train."

"Then why are we down here?" He peered about. Was there a door hidden in the shadows or a grate large enough to pass through? But no. The only possible exit was back up the stairs. "Where are we going?"

"A place you will never find." She spun, flourishing a piece of dark material, and the world went black.

"What the deuce are you doing?" He grabbed the covering she'd flung over his head, but before he could yank the thing off completely, warm fingers pressed into his arm, staying his movement.

"Now, now, Mr. Forge. If you wish to continue with me, you will keep that sack on your head."

Of all the half-masted ideas! What kind of fool did she take him for? Wrenching away from her, he tugged the bag off the rest of the way. "I will not be led around like some blind beggar into who knows what kind of danger, especially since you have yet to turn over my weapons to me." He shook the sack in her face. "This was not part of our bargain."

She scowled right back. "Neither was the revealing of certain underground locations. I cannot have you doubling back here with your bobby friends in tow. If you want to find Joe Card, then you will abide by my policies. The question is, Mr. Forge, how badly do you want to find him? Enough to suffer a bit of humiliation and risk?"

Her pert little nose lifted in the air, adding to the challenge.

He gritted his teeth so hard, his jaw crackled. What choice did he have? Wherever she intended to take him was the only solid lead he had.

And time was ticking away.

"Fine!" He jammed on the hated fabric that smelled of a forgotten piece of Stilton.

"Good." Was that a gloat in her voice?

Her fingers wrapped around his. "Now stay quiet and try not to stumble. I will not be responsible for any injuries you may sustain."

With a tug, she led him forward. "Jump."

"What?"

She yanked. He flew. A breath later, his boots crunched into gravel. The acrid tang of creosote stung his nose. The ground beneath him vibrated, and dread punched him in the gut.

"By all that is holy, woman! Do not tell me we are on the tracks."

"Shh! Move quickly."

His arm practically wrenched from the socket when she dashed off, tugging him along. But as the great hissing of steam and rumble of an approaching train grew louder, he didn't need to be asked twice to keep up. Near as he could tell, his long strides ate up plenty of ground and spit it out in a spray of gravel from his pounding steps.

So did Miss Turner's.

But could they really outrun a train?

Thankfully, her grip pulled him sideways, away from certain death. "Crouch," she called. "Now!"

He ducked, but even so, the top of his skull scraped against a rough surface, nearly snagging the sack from his head. Miss Turner's grasp was relentless as they crouch-walked through some sort of connecting tunnel. His heavy breaths bounced back at him, echoing off the close walls, until finally the dank, hot air gave way to a blast of cold mustiness. The grip on his hand pulled him upward until finally he could stand.

But not stop.

"This way." Once again she tugged his hand.

He stumbled, his feet splashing in liquid—which grew in depth and stench the farther they traveled. Even so, he catalogued each twist and turn, every odour and drip-drip-dripping sound as they went. If he needed to make a hasty exit, he'd know which way to go.

Or not. By the time Miss Turner slowed, he'd lost track, so impossible was the route she'd taken.

"There. Not so bad, was it?" She swept the bag off his head.

Or did she? He blinked. Then rubbed his eyes. Neither did a thing to help him see. How in the world had the woman managed her way through such morbid blackness? Weren't females afraid of the dark? He'd hardly know she stood close to him if it weren't for the warmth of her breath feathering against his cheek.

"Stay near me, and for both of our sakes, let me do the talking. If Skaggs gets one whiff you are a constable, he will not hesitate to kill us both. No questions asked. Understand?"

He nodded—until he realized what a fruitless action that was. "Yes," he agreed, "but how exactly am I to stay close to you when I cannot even see you?"

A sigh whooshed in the murk, followed by the click of a latch. Seconds later, a wedge of light grew as she heaved open a door.

Jackson glanced around in the growing light. They stood in an egg-shaped, brick-lined passageway. Cold sweat ran in rivulets down the walls. Green slime crawled up from the greyish muck at their feet. No wonder Miss Turner had hiked her skirts.

He followed her into yet another passage, still shadowy, but not the black of a grave. It smelled of moist earth and stagnant water. A crypt? Some catacombs? Or could be an abandoned wine cellar. His chest tightened, craving fresh air. Hopefully this wasn't some forgotten plague pit.

Miss Turner rounded a corner and entered a chamber lit by oil lamps. Jackson's steps faltered. Shelves lined the walls with all sorts of products, from jewelry to pistols to a rack of fine furs hanging below one of them. Thick Turkish rugs carpeted the floor. A counter stood at center, with a man stationed behind it. Jackson pressed his lips flat to keep from gaping. For all the world, they might as well have stepped off the pavement and entered a merchant's on St. James.

He caught up to Miss Turner and, despite her admonition for him to remain silent, whispered, "What is this place?"

She shot him a look, clearly annoyed. "Skaggs Emporium, pawnbroker to the chancers and cheats in all of London."

He schooled his face, masking his surprise. He hadn't known such a place existed, but it made sense. This was where she must bring her stolen goods to sell.

"Well, well. If it isn't my dear girl Kit." The cocking of a gun accompanied the words.

Jackson snapped his gaze to the man at the counter, who aimed a barrel at Kit's head.

Chapter Eight

What was it with men and guns? Always flaunting their firepower as if no other weapon on earth ought to be more feared. Kit tossed back a loose hank of hair, using the motion to distract Skaggs as she reached for the knife tucked in her waistband. She'd trust a sharp blade any day over a pistol that could misfire. Still, she likely wouldn't need either. Skaggs wouldn't shoot her. Not really.

Would he?

Sudden doubt upped her pulse, and she gripped the hilt of the knife behind her back a bit tighter, ready for anything.

"Drop your weapon!" With one quick sidestep, Mr. Forge wedged in front of her, shielding her from harm.

She gaped. A brave move. A sweet gesture. But wholly ineffective. He was unarmed, and if Skaggs was intent on getting to her, he wouldn't think twice about shooting a stranger in his own place of business. If Mr. Forge were injured or worse, it would be her fault for leading him here. As much as she desired to get rid of her unwanted tail, her conscience—at least what was left of it—would not bear well another such mark against it. Sighing, she bypassed the gallant constable, intent on using her most powerful weapon against the pawnbroker.

Reason.

She planted her feet, disregarding the grumble in Mr. Forge's throat. "What is the problem, Skaggs?"

The pasty skin on the pawnbroker's brow pulled tight, stretching the blue veins that marked his face like a road map. Lord only knew how long it'd been since sunlight had touched that transparent flesh. "No problem a'tall," he said. "Not as long as you slap twenty quid on the counter right now."

She pursed her lips. She hadn't been down here for a good six months. How could she possibly owe him anything?

"I have hardly had time to shop yet." She shrugged one shoulder, an attempt at nonchalance belied by the clamminess of her palms. Despite her relative assurance that Skaggs wouldn't pull the trigger—and even if he did, the constable at her side just might lunge and take the bullet for her—her body wasn't convinced. "What exactly am I paying you for?"

"That vase." He tipped his head towards an alabaster urn sitting on a shelf to his left.

She eyed it critically. What in the world? "Very nice, but I do not need one."

"Neither do I," Skaggs snapped. "Not if it's a fake. Which it is."

"And how is this my concern?"

"It were yer man Hanks what sold it to me. Said it were Third Dynasty. Worth a fortune. And it would be, were it real." Curses belched out of him, mostly about Hanks. Not that she blamed him. Hanks had been nothing but trouble since the day she'd taken him on.

"It's an impressive replica, but I shoulda known better." Skaggs's fish-grey gaze drifted to hers, the aim of his gun steady and true on her head. "I trusted him because he were one o' yer men."

"Not anymore."

"That don't put the money back in my pocket."

"Yet neither will you lose more, because Hanks will never dupe you again."

Skaggs narrowed his eyes. "I want my money."

Mr. Forge edged closer to her, the tension in the room thick as a drift of fog off the Thames. If she didn't think of something fast, one of them would do something stupid.

"Listen, Skaggs." She blew out a breezy sigh, as if discussing nothing more than a change in the weather. "Truly you have no one to blame but yourself. Did you not think it a bit odd one of my crew members came in here to sell you a piece of stolen goods when you know we never steal anything?"

Next to her, Mr. Forge sucked in a slight, but audible, rush of air. Of course he assumed her to be a hack-about cutpurse. It was only natural. And though he wasn't the first—or last—man to think the worst of her, it still rankled.

"Besides, killing me here and now will scramble my crew, and without a leader, you will wait a good long time before you recoup that money. If ever. Not to mention ruining the resale value of these fine rugs with my bloodstains." She swept her hand slow and easy, indicating the carpet at her feet. "You shall have your money, the full twenty quid. I vow it, and you know my word is gold. When have I ever let you down?"

His lips rippled as he chewed on her words, his parchment skin stretching taut over his cheekbones. Slowly, he lowered the gun to the counter, but kept it within reach.

Kit eased the knife back into her waistband, keeping it easy to access as well. Something wasn't right. Skaggs's twitchiness. His sudden willingness to kill for money. Despite his notorious clientele, the man was a businessman, not a murderer.

She approached the counter, Mr. Forge mirroring her steps. The pawnbroker perched on his tall stool, as always, one leg dangling and the other with his trousers pinned up at the knee. An old injury, the lower half of his leg blown off on some obscure battlefield in the Crimean War. But other than that, he appeared hearty and hale. Well. . .as hearty as a man could be who never crawled from his hole to see the light of day.

Still, the odd twist in her belly could not be denied. "There is something bigger at play here than Hanks's short sale, is there not?

What is going on, Skaggs?"

Completely ignoring her question, the pawnbroker slid a chary gaze towards Mr. Forge. "You replacing Hanks?"

She tensed. One wrong reply and Skaggs could easily grab his gun and blast a hole through the constable.

But Forge merely stared the pawnbroker down. "Something like that."

Good answer—yet if Skaggs's curious stare was any indication, the longer they stayed here, the more chance that Mr. Forge's true identity would be discovered.

"We are here for information on Joe Card," she cut in. "Do you have anything? Did anyone bring in goods from his cab, something that could hint of his whereabouts?"

"It's not my policy to talk in front o' strangers." His head swiveled back to her in an unspoken challenge.

Flit! She should've known better than to allow Mr. Forge to tag along with her. Had there been any other way to get back her token, she'd have gladly done it. But this? This bordered on an outright lie— one that could get her killed.

"Do not worry about Mr. Forge, here." She angled her head at the constable, annoyed with his handsome face and the words she must push past her teeth. "I will vouch for him. He is one of mine now."

Surprise flashed in the constable's brilliant blue gaze, yet he remained silent.

Skaggs grunted. "Well. . .all right, then. Aye, I've got something on ol' Joe, but it'll cost you before I hand it over, a price you mightn't wish to pay."

She turned back to the pawnbroker. Again with the money? What kind of financial hurt was Skaggs in? "What do you want?"

A predatory smile stretched his lips, his teeth flashing like fangs in a wolf's mouth. "What I want is a trade. If you help me, then I'll help you."

This was new. Skaggs always had a cash value for his products, never an exchange of services.

"So, you *do* have bigger problems than simply being shorted by that greedy little goblin Hanks." She lifted her chin. "Let's have it, then. All of it. I want to know exactly what I am getting myself into before I agree."

"You mean what *we* are getting ourselves into," Mr. Forge grumbled beside her.

She rolled her eyes. "Yes, we."

Skaggs sniffed and leaned back on his stool, folding his arms. "Did you ever wonder how a cripple like me is able to run this place alone, allowing criminals of all sort to buy and sell, without ever once getting robbed blind by the blackguards I deal with?"

She cleared her throat, no longer able to deny the tickle induced by the dampness of the place. "I assume either you are well armed or you pay for protection."

"The latter. Reaper."

She blew out a low whistle.

Mr. Forge stepped closer. "Who is Reaper?"

His question was a thrown grenade, sucking the air from the room and leaving behind a silence that hurt the ears. For several beats, she and Skaggs stared at him. It took all her willpower and then some not to gape. Was he jesting?

Skaggs shook his head at the man, then finally faced her. "Where'd ye get this one?"

"You do not want to know." Once again, she shoved back some loose hair, hard-pressed to decide if she should be irritated by the constable's question, take pity on his lack of street acumen, or give in to the small amount of rising admiration for his forthrightness no matter the cost.

Lowering her hand, she settled on providing a simple education for the man. "Reaper runs all the flash houses on the east side. Keeps the women safe. Not a one gets roughed up lest the bully find himself sleeping at the bottom of the river."

Lesson over, she turned back to Skaggs. "No wonder no one touches you. They would be a fool to. . . Hold on." She narrowed her eyes. "Do not tell me you are in a tangle with Reaper."

"Not yet."

She threw up her hands. "What does that mean?"

"I pays him quarterly. Next drop is due tomorrow. Trouble is. . ." His Adam's apple bobbed on his long neck. "I don't have the money."

"Why not? You run a thriving business here."

He shifted on his stool, nearly toppling sideways with the movement. "A few months back, Gleason stopped by and we drank a bottle or two. Maybe more. Anyway, he let slip about an opportunity he'd invested in. Said he knew of a shipment of contraband soon to arrive. Smuggled brandy. Tobacco. Weapons. Quite the lot, one that could leave a man sitting fat and pretty for years to come."

"And you bought in?" Kit thought aloud.

"I wanted to, but turns out the whole deal were being run by a new player, and a skittish one at that, only passing money and goods through those he knew—and I was an unknown. So, I bargained with Gleason to put my money in under his name. He hedged, but I convinced him no one would be the wiser, and I'd be all the richer once the ship came in."

He drifted off then, the grey of his eyes going vacant, as if he had packed up his belongings and sailed off on the same sea where his ship rode the waves. It was a cold look. A dead one.

A shiver of sudden understanding rippled down Kit's back. "Your ship. . .it did not come in, did it?"

Skaggs inhaled, his thin chest stretching the fabric of his waistcoat. "Got word last week she sank off the coast o' Gibraltar. All were lost. I've got nothing to give Reaper when he comes, which means he'll take what I've got. Everything. And more."

Horror crawled up her throat. No one shortchanged Reaper. He would kill Skaggs with one strike of his beefy fist. "That is a tangle," she murmured—then frowned. "Wait a minute. You said Gleason let you in on this deal? *Bags* Gleason?"

Skaggs nodded. "The very same. Poor bloke lost all his money too."

"No, Skaggs. . ." She rubbed her palm along her skirt, thinking hard. "Something is not right with this. Bags has been skipping all over town in a shiny new barouche, sporting a woman on each arm, buying drinks, wearing a new suit every night. No one would grant him that much credit." She paused to let her meaning sink in.

A breath later, Skaggs's eyeballs bulged. "The scoundrel kiped me! What a bristle-backed son of a snake!" A few other blazing curses flew out of his mouth. "Always did want my business. Scads! But he played me like a well-tuned piano, and here I thought I was the one making him sing." He planted his face in his hands, the rest of his words coming out garbled. "I'm doomed."

The slumped sight of the one-legged pawnbroker, the despair wavering in his voice, broke Kit's heart and fisted her hands. "Not if I can help it—if *we* can help it."

She shot a glance at Mr. Forge.

Who promptly shook his head. "This Reaper fellow has nothing to do with the missing Joe Card, and that is our focus, remember?"

Planting her hands on the counter, she leaned forward, eager to somehow make things right for the poor fence despite Mr. Forge's objections. "Did you say you have something on old Joe?"

With a last shudder, Skaggs lifted his face. "Aye."

"So if Forge and I get your money back from Bags, you promise not to sell whatever it is you have to anyone else in the meantime and instead release it to us?"

An ember of hope added a shade of colour to the man's face. Not much, but it was something. "You get my money back, little lady, and I'll give you anything in this store that you want."

"Exactly how much money?" Mr. Forge asked.

"Nineteen hundred." Skaggs didn't so much as bat an eyelash.

Mr. Forge inhaled audibly. "But that is—"

"Deal!" Grinning, Kit spun on her heel and stalked to the door.

No matter the amount, bringing down Bags Gleason would be a pleasure, for he was the worst sort of criminal. The man would rob the shawl from the shoulders of his own dying mother.

But just as she passed through the emporium's door, a grip on her shoulder turned her around. Deep blue eyes bored into her own.

"If we must do this thing—which, for the record, I highly object to—then you are out of your mind if you think I am going into some criminal hornet's nest without my revolver." He shoved out his hand. "And while you are at it, I shall take my knife back as well."

Of course he was right. She wouldn't run headlong into danger without a sharp blade strapped to her leg either. But the constable could just as easily use his weapons against her as against Bags Gleason. Change his mind and haul her in.

She stared right back, desperately searching those blue depths for what sort of character lived and breathed behind that chiseled face. She'd never trusted a constable this much before. Hah! Who was she kidding? She'd never trusted one at all.

So why should she now?

Leftover light flickering from the emporium cast moving shadows on Kit Turner's face—a completely unreadable face. Jackson's gaze roamed from her stormy eyes to the smudge on her cheek and on to the dark swath of hair loose at her temple, searching for a twitch, a tic, any sort of clue of what she might be thinking. Nothing. She might as well be a carved sphinx, her stare fixed and unwavering. The woman was canny. Far too canny.

"Tell me, Mr. Forge." Her voice was as even as her stare. "Why do you carry a gun? It is rare they are issued. Most officers rely on their truncheons."

"It wasn't issued. The weapon is my own. Suffice it to say that being without was a lesson hard learned and leave it at that." And it was. Had he been armed that day when he and his brother had crossed paths with those black-hearted criminals, things would be different. James would be different. Jackson shoved his hand closer.

Without warning, Miss Turner snapped into action, retrieving his revolver and knife and dumping them both onto his upturned palm. "I trust you will use these as defense only, Mr. Forge, for if you come against me with them, you will never find out what happened to Joe Card. I am your best lead, and you know it."

"Actually, I would say Skaggs is."

"Flit! He would never talk to you without me. You are an unknown. Only because I vouched for you did he speak at all."

My, but she was a direct little thing. Tucking away his weapons, he stepped closer and lowered his voice. "So, why the sudden trust in me?"

Her fine nostrils flared for a moment, as if she smelled something rotten. "I do not have a choice. For now."

"Fair enough."

She fumbled with the extra fabric tucked into her waistband, then produced the head covering once again.

He shot out his hand, staying her arm. "I expect the same courtesy you required of Skaggs. If I am to help you with this Gleason fellow, I want to know exactly what I am getting myself into. And I cannot do that with a bag on my head."

Her arm hardened beneath his touch, but after only a slight hesitation, she wrenched from his grip and tucked away the hated thing. "Fine. We will take the long way out, then. One that you will never be able to retrace."

He smirked. "While I appreciate your gesture of goodwill, your confidence in my abilities is a bit underwhelming."

"Unless you have the abilities of a blind sewer rat, you shall never be able to manage the route I intend to use."

Narrowing his eyes, he glanced past her shoulder into the dark tunnel. She was right. "Am I allowed to know where the prize is at the end of this maze? Where exactly is this Gleason? Once we surface, I will need to round up some officers and direct—"

"Are you mad?" The question fired out loud and true, and after a glance at the emporium's open door, she retreated a few steps into the drip-drip-dripping of the tunnel and lowered her voice. "You cannot go after Bags with your bluecoats. He and his mates would scatter like cockroaches before you got anywhere near him. God is not on the side of the biggest battalions, but on the best shot—and I shall aim for where it will hurt Bags the most. Now—"

"Hold on." He closed the distance between them, making double sure she could read the resolution on his face. "I will not do anything illegal to get that fence his money back."

"Neither will I."

Hah! Both his brows shot up.

She popped a fist on her hip, adding an imperial tilt to her head. "I always stay within the bounds of the law, Mr. Forge."

"Really?" The skepticism in his tone hung heavily in the dank air.

She lowered her hand and folded both in front of her. "I admit, sometimes those boundaries are stretched a bit, but they are never broken. My crew and I merely present a picture of what might be and conclusions are drawn from there. Most people are happy to hand over their money when their heartstrings are pulled. There is no thievery in taking that which is freely given."

Balling his hands, he shoved them into his pockets. "But the way you go about it is all wrong."

A sharp look cut him off. "As wrong as watching a child starve to death? Or witnessing a man hauled off to the poorhouse to die? What about the mothers who work themselves into the grave at factories—those who are lucky enough to even hold a job? My schemes to help the needy of Blackfriars may be unorthodox, Mr. Forge, but sometimes they have little else. God knows you and your kind would not lend them a hand. I have learned that from experience."

The bitterness in her voice chilled him as much as the oppressive dampness soaking through his suit coat. What in her past fostered such resentment?

He blew out a long breath, exhaling all the unasked questions. Now was not the time to dissect Miss Turner's history. "Be that as it may, what is it you propose we do, then, in order to get Skaggs his money?"

She flashed a grin. "We swindle the swindler, of course."

He shook his head. "Honesty is always the best policy, Miss Turner. Deception has a way of doubling back and taking you out when you least expect it. But for the sake of expediency, I will hear you out. What scheme do you have in that crafty head of yours?"

She nibbled on her lower lip for a moment before answering, "I do not yet know."

Brilliant. He shoved down a growl. The longer they stood here without a plan, the more minutes ticked off of his deadline to find Joe Card. "So, if we are to beat Gleason at his own game," he thought aloud, "we must sell him on an investment and walk away with his money, the exact sum he siphoned from Skaggs."

"Of course!" She snapped her fingers. "A capital scheme if I ever heard one."

He cocked his head. Was the torpid air down here getting to her? "What scheme?"

Shoving past him, she trotted towards the emporium. "The one that involves the counterfeit vase."

Chapter Nine

Would it be considered murder to leave a man to fend for himself in the Gramble Street drainage tunnel? Pondering the morality of such a thing, Kit ignored yet one more of Mr. Forge's questions rumbling at her back and pressed on. The man could best a hot-sausage hawker any day in persistence. Though admittedly, were the tables turned, she'd likely be peppering him with as many queries. But that didn't mean she had to answer him.

Not now. Not here. Though maybe someday.

Bah! What was she thinking? There would be no someday. Raising her lantern higher, she kicked aside a rotted old boot, sending out ripples in the ankle-deep water. Stopping to chat in a brickwork tube with the chance of an incoming tide wouldn't be in either of their best interests. Neither was breathing in the stench of the meat market's runoff, which oozed from the connecting pipe near her elbow. She upped her pace, turned a corner—and came face-to-face with a one-eyed, pock-faced man in a greasy velveteen coat. Ridiculously enormous pockets hung low over his waxed canvas trousers. He carried a long pole with an iron hoe at the end of it, one that could easily bash in a head if the man had a mind to.

She smiled. "Evening, Jack."

"Turner?" The old tosher reached for the lens on the dark lantern strapped to his chest and widened the stream of light. "What the grey goose fat are you doin' down in my neck o' the netherworld?" He squinted past her. "And with a topsider no less?"

"Just passing through, aiming for Puddle Dock. Route clear?"

"Dunno. Din't come in that a'way. Been usin' the Upper Thames Street entrance. Easier grate to squeak through."

She narrowed her eyes. Did he really think she was that daft? With the way his pockets bulged, he'd never be able to *squeak* through any grate. "Modified it, did you?"

"I always said you were too smart fer yer own petticoats." He snorted and stepped aside. "Off with ye."

She dipped her head. "Godspeed, old friend."

Not long after she and Mr. Forge cleared the man, the constable caught up to her, speaking low. "Should I expect we'll run into more of your friends down here?"

She chuckled. "One-eyed Jack is not a friend, per se. More of an acquaintance. I know his wife far better. She is one of the families my crew and I deliver food to. As you can see, earning a living down here is thin pickings."

"Then why does he not find a different occupation? Surely there has got to be something more lucrative he can set his hand to."

"His hands, yes, but you saw his face." Though Mr. Forge couldn't see it, she frowned anyway, frustrated with the constable's glib sentiment. He had no idea how real a struggle it was to live in the City. "No one is willing to hire such a ghoulish visage, Mr. Forge. It would serve you well to get to know the people before you go ordering their lives about."

The constable's steps splashed behind her, muffling another question, especially since she upped her pace and didn't slow until they surfaced beneath the wooden-framed pier of Puddle Dock. The sun had set, leaving behind a world of darkness not much brighter than the tunnel from which they'd emerged. Nor did it smell any better, not on this stretch of sodden river embankment. After centuries of filth and waste, the Thames had leached its noxious odours permanently into the earth.

Arching her back, Kit worked out the kinks from walking

hunched over. After gently setting down the vase he'd been cradling, Mr. Forge did the same, grunting when his neck cracked loud enough for her to hear over the flowing current of the river.

"So, we got this thing out of there safe and sound." He nodded towards the fake antiquity resting on the black muck. "Now what?"

She blew out the lantern, then faced him in the shadows that rushed to fill the void. "Tell me, Mr. Forge, how are you at acting?"

Even in the lack of light, she could see the surprise registering on his face.

"Not that it signifies, but last Christmas, I played Joseph in a theatrical for children. Why?"

She huffed out a breath. Not much to work with, but it would have to do. "Can you pretend you are not a constable for an hour or two and perform the part of a prosperous dealer?"

His eyes narrowed. "What sort of dealer?"

"Smuggled goods." She retrieved the urn and held it out to him. "Rare antiquities, to be exact."

"Surely you are not asking a constable to become a thief like you?"

As always, the slur burned instant heat from her belly to her throat. A visceral reaction. One she couldn't stop, even though she'd been labeled a pickpocket since she'd returned a woman's dropped reticule as a young girl. She poked her finger into his chest. "I will have you know I am not a—"

"I know, I know." He pushed aside her hand. "But now is not the time to debate it, so let us agree to a truce on the matter."

Beyond Mr. Forge, a mist began to hover above the river. It would thicken. Rise. Cover them both if they didn't move soon. Though she hated to admit it, a ceasefire was a good idea. Why value what this man might think of her anyway?

"Very well," she agreed with a grudging nod. "I am not asking you to actually be a thief or a smuggler or anything of the sort. All you have to do is act the part, and they will believe it. Sketch a careful word picture, and the listener will see a full image of his own making."

His mouth twisted, taking his moustache for a ride. "If I concede—and that is a big *if*—then what is your plan to retrieve Skaggs's money?"

She hid a smile. Once a mark questioned with an *if*, she owned him. "I have a few ideas of where Bags hides out. When we locate him, I shall tell him that being it is no secret he has come into a bit of coin, I have a business opportunity for him. I will introduce you, so you do not have to lie about who you are, at which point you show him the vase."

Once again, she pushed the urn towards Mr. Forge, and this time he took it. "Inform Gleason you have a shipment of items such as that priceless beauty, all ready for market. Let slip you have a buyer lined up to purchase the lot in the morning, but I persuaded you to let Bags in on the action, make an offer of his own. And voilà. We walk away with Skaggs's money."

Mr. Forge shook his head. "It will never work."

Was he determined to be so obstinate or was that just his nature? Frustrated, she stamped her foot. "Why not?"

"Think about this from Gleason's perspective. He is going to wonder why you would cut him in on the deal and why I would go along with it. And if he is worth his salt as a criminal, he will question why he should pay more than what this fictional buyer of mine is offering."

She ground her teeth. He was right on all accounts, and that chafed. She should've thought of those questions herself. Even more disconcerting was the spark of admiration flaring in her chest for the man's quick and cunning thinking. Mr. Jackson Forge could prove to be a valuable ally.

Or a dangerous enemy.

She cocked her head. "I own a quick tongue, Mr. Forge. I am sure I shall think of something if Bags raises any concerns."

"Better we be prepared ahead of time." He widened his stance, the muck beneath his boots making a sucking noise. Clearly the man wouldn't move until she concocted her answers. Too bad she didn't have any—yet.

"Fine." She sharpened her tone to a challenge. "What are your thoughts on the matter?"

"I have one or two, but not here. I have had enough of this stink." He tucked the vase beneath his coat and offered her a hand. "Shall we?"

She stared at his outstretched fingers. A man offering her assistance, and a constable at that? Apparently, miracles did still happen. All the same, she turned on her heel and trudged up the embankment on her own. If she allowed his help, it could give him the edge, make him think he was in charge. And the last time she'd made that mistake, she'd been left with a bleeding lip and no money in her pockets.

Topside, ramshackle buildings perched along the narrow lane of Upper Thames Street, those that yet stood, anyway. Most were naught but charred skeletons from a recent fire. No one cared about this part of the City of London, which suited her purposes just fine. "Is this better?"

"Much." A grin flashed on his face. One that annoyed, mostly because it lured her closer just to admire the strong cut of his jaw and the attractive way his mouth lifted.

She shook off the odd feeling.

"So, you want to swindle the swindler." One-handed, he rubbed the back of his neck. "Then why not use the same tactics Gleason employed? Tell him you have heard of a lucrative deal you cannot pass up, but you will have to unless he goes in on it with you. Maybe even toss him a 40/60 split, being you are old pals and all. Wait a minute. . . are you?"

Pah! Her and that underhanded black heart? She'd sooner keep company with Spring-heeled Jack in the dark of an alley. "I have no love for Bags Gleason, but neither have I ever crossed him."

"Good enough." He shifted the vase higher on his hip. "Talk up the rarity of the shipment, the quality of the products, and the fellow you intend to undercut by buying out from under him—a purchaser who is coming for the load in the morning."

"And who exactly is that?"

"Good question." His gaze drifted to the night sky, then shot back to her face. "What enemies does Gleason have?"

"Too many to count. I am not the only one who does not care for the man."

"Anyone in particular?"

Hmm. Biting her lip, she mentally filed through the host of villains that plagued the area. "Got it. Jimmy Mullins—the Shark."

"There you have it. If Gleason is as underhanded as you and Skaggs say he is, he will jump at the chance to not only make some coin but take a jab at this Shark fellow as well."

"I like it." She truly did—which annoyed her beyond reason. *She* should've come up with such a crafty idea. Blast the man! She shoved back a loose wisp of hair, scratching her scalp in the process. "But you did not answer your last question. Why would you sell to Gleason and me if you already have the Shark set up as a buyer?"

"Because smugglers are cutthroat bargainers, are they not?" He shrugged. "You will offer me more than this Shark fellow has purported to pay."

Impressive. She narrowed her eyes. "You know, Mr. Forge, for a man of the law, especially one who clearly values honesty, you surely do think like a criminal."

"Is that an insult or a compliment?"

"I have not decided."

His pleasant chuckle lightened the darkness, altogether blithe, as if they were the best of friends out for an evening stroll. Easy enough for him to behave so now, but how would such a greenhorn hold up under pressure?

She'd soon find out. "Bags ought to be flashing his money over at the Rusty Lantern, this way." She turned.

He pulled her back. "Hold on. Though I hate to say it, I am afraid this is where we should part ways."

"What?" She scrunched her nose, wary. "Cold feet already?"

"Nothing of the sort. It will be more effective to portray a profitable load of stolen goods if we present a warehouse full of crates. Prying open a box in front of Gleason's eyes with this beauty"—he patted the bulge in his coat—"will be much more effective."

She pursed her lips. "True, but I—"

"There is no time for quibbling, Miss Turner. Just tell me where to go. I will hide the vase in a crate, and you bring Gleason to me."

If only it were that simple. But nothing in life was, especially of late. Hanks. Old Joe. And now Mr. Forge to deal with. The night air turned misty, the fog creeping upward from the bank, and she tugged her collar tight at the neck. "While I am flattered you think me so well connected, sir, I do not happen to have a warehouse full of goods at my disposal."

A shadow crossed his face, darker than the night sky. For a long while, he said nothing. Clearly he fought some sort of battle in his head. What?

Then just as quickly as it appeared, the shadow vanished, and he jutted his jaw as if he'd made a monumental decision. "I know of a place."

Jackson rummaged about in his pocket for the back door key of Hamstock's Storage. Nothing about this evening was right. Creeping about like a felon. Working with a known thief. The deception of it all, and to top it off, now breaking into the warehouse he'd earlier guarded. Thunderation, that seemed a lifetime ago. The information Skaggs had on Joe Card had better be worth this risk, or he'd have more to deal with than a dressing-down by the sergeant and the turning in of his uniform.

He'd be facing a jail sentence.

The door gave way, and he eased it shut behind him, closing him inside a blackness so thick it squeezed the air from his lungs. He felt about like a blind man, searching for a lantern. Surely there would be one nearby on a hook, or a shelf, or maybe a—

Ow!

His shin cracked into something hard, shooting pain up his leg. He flailed for balance, and his fingers smacked into the glass chimney of a lantern. A rather unorthodox victory, but a victory nonetheless.

Moments later, he located the matches and coaxed a flame to life. Glancing downwards, he snarled at the dog cage he'd run into—but at least the little rodent wasn't yapping on the velvet cushion inside of it. The terrier was probably lounging in satin pyjamas in front of a stoked fire at the Hamstocks' hearth.

Jackson lifted the lantern higher. Huge bolts of fabric, each one wrapped in an outer layer of burlap, were stacked and ready to fill the next day's orders. Not exactly the crates he'd originally planned, but it would do. And perhaps even better. What better way to smuggle fragile goods than swathed in layers of material?

He set down the vase and unbound the nearest bundle. While it would likely take Miss Turner some time to find Gleason, it wouldn't do to be caught unprepared—a lesson he and his brother would take with them to their graves.

Shoving away the morbid thought, he loosened the coil a bit. Not too much, or it'd be impossible to reroll. Just enough to work his arm down the middle, making enough space to slide in the urn and tighten it back up again. He worked his hand into the center, twisting his fist this way and that, when his knuckles hit something hard. What the devil? Did they use some sort of solid core in these bolts?

Wriggling his fingers, he clutched on to what felt like a knob and pulled, rotating back and forth as he did so, until finally he retrieved a bottle.

A what?

He lifted the thing to eye level. Sure enough, he held an amber bottle filled with liquid. Rum perhaps? French wine? Whichever, the guarding of this warehouse suddenly made sense. Not many would steal bolts of common fabric, but distilled spirits were a prized commodity, especially those that hadn't been taxed into oblivion. Did the sergeant know of his brother-in-law's dealings? Blowing out a long breath, Jackson set the bottle aside. Yet one more crime to look into. But for now, he had his own smuggling ring to set up.

Carefully, he wedged the counterfeit urn into the middle of the bolt, all the while wondering how Miss Turner fared. Hopefully he hadn't sent her into harm's way. He'd not be able to shake his guilt should she take a bullet he could've prevented. God only knew the load of guilt he already bore for the maiming of a loved one. One more person, a human soul and a woman at that, would be his undoing.

But surely Kit Turner could hold her own against this Bags Gleason fellow. Hah! The woman could hold her own facing a pack of wolves while wearing a pair of wrist cuffs. A small smile rippled across his lips. He'd never witnessed such boldness in a skirt before. The way she bartered with Skaggs. How, without flinching, she'd trudged through tunnels that could make a grown man faint. She was a feisty one, he'd give her that. A real fighter. He could appreciate such bravery and resourcefulness, especially when it came in such a comely package.

Heaven and earth! What was he thinking? He swiped a hand over his face. Now was not the time to admire a woman, particularly one who broke the law. . .or did she? By her own admission she and her crew weren't an orthodox gang of villains. She hadn't actually forced him to give her that sovereign when they'd first met. And if she truly didn't have any qualms about breaking the law, then why wasn't he already dead? Or left to wander lost in the tunnels? Either act would've ensured his silence.

He tugged at the bindings. Hard. Working out all his doubt and frustrations in the twist and tie of a thick piece of rope.

Footsteps approached the door. A single pair and heavy. Men's. Not Miss Turner's, which likely meant they didn't belong to Bags

Gleason either, since he'd be with her.

The doorknob jiggled. Jackson blew out the lamp and darted behind the roll of fabric. Blast! He should've thought to lock it! If Hamstock hired a daytime guard, of course he'd take on a night watchman as well.

Reaching for his knife, Jackson held his breath as the door swung open and lamplight washed away the darkness. He surely did not want to harm the man, but there was one thing he'd learned that day years ago as he'd watched his brother mercilessly beaten.

Sometimes you had to do whatever it took to survive.

Chapter Ten

Convincing a wily sharper addled by too much rum had taken far longer than Kit first estimated. Yet finally, she stood at the rear entrance to Hamstock's Storage with Bags Gleason breathing down her neck and two of his lackeys at her back.

Lifting her fist to rap out the code she'd agreed upon with Mr. Forge, she hesitated. Of all the things she loathed in this world—discrimination, poverty, injustice—she mostly hated what she now faced.

The unknown.

Had Mr. Forge done as he promised, or was he waiting inside with a squad of bluecoats? Would Bags fall for their charade, or might he sniff out their deceit and kill them on the spot? At the moment, she couldn't answer either and that rankled. Of only herself could she be certain, a lesson she'd learned the hard way as a foundling nobody wanted. More forcefully than necessary, she pounded a rhythm on the door, then shoved it open.

The muzzle of a gun and impossibly deep blue eyes greeted her.

Maybe Mr. Forge could play the part after all.

Behind her, two hammers cocked open. Kit shot her hand in the air, staying them. "We are all friends here, gentlemen. Put down your weapons."

Mr. Forge lowered his revolver, but no movement rustled at her back. Annoyed, she tossed a killer look over her shoulder. "Well?"

Bags flourished his fingers, signaling his henchmen to stand down. The excess skin of his jowls quivered with the movement. So did the drape of fabric hanging off his upper arm. Bags Gleason was a bloated affair of a man, excessive in every manner possible, from the bulb of his nose pitted by years of too much drink to the paunch of his belly that strained against the buttons on his dress coat.

Kit slid her gaze to Mr. Forge. "My associate here"—she hitched her thumb towards Bags—"would like to see the goods."

Mr. Forge held his ground. "Leave your guns outside."

"My men take orders from me alone," Bags grumbled.

Nonchalantly, Mr. Forge scratched the stubble on his chin, as if Bags were an inconvenience. "Then you tell them to disarm. I will not show anybody anything until I am assured a bullet will not nick me in the back."

Kit shot a cancerous look at Mr. Forge. Flit! The constable was adding in far too much bravado to his smuggler act.

Bags grunted. "This better be worth it." He pulled out a beauty of a double-barreled Lancaster from the waistband of his trousers and handed it to the larger of the men at his side. "Do as he says, boys." He listed like a schooner towards Mr. Forge. "But one wrong move from you, and my men will take you out, gun or no. Understood?"

"I would expect no less." Mr. Forge wheeled about and led them to a huge spool of fabric—not the crate she'd been expecting. A bit unconventional, but who was she to complain? She'd seen firsthand how that could serve an advantage.

Crouching, Mr. Forge pulled out his knife and sawed through the binding. After he loosened the enormous coil a bit, he worked his hand into the middle and eased out the urn, holding it up for Bags to inspect.

Bags blew a low whistle. "A real beauty. May I?" He held out his hand.

Mr. Forge passed off the vase and watched as Bags studied the artifact by the light of a nearby lantern. He turned it one way, then another, lips pursing into a fat pucker. The two men behind him stood silent, brooding, tense—ready for action.

Kit held her breath, all the while sliding her fingers to the knife at her back. Skaggs hadn't noticed the urn was a counterfeit. Would Bags?

He sucked in a deep breath, nostrils flaring to an obscene proportion, then lowered the vase and stared at her. "I must admit, missy, I didn't swallow your story at first, but now..." His gaze drifted to Mr. Forge. "A fabric warehouse is a genius front for your operation, yet that don't mean I trust you. How do I know this"—he shifted the urn from one hand to the other—"is real?"

A slow smile spread on Mr. Forge's face. "You do not."

Kit ground her teeth. Was the man mad? This was no way to negotiate with a sharper like Bags. After all the quick talking she'd had to do to get the fat fellow here in the first place, and now Mr. Forge would throw their scheme away with three little words? No. She would *not* have it.

She stepped between the two, blocking Mr. Forge. "You have known me for a long time, Bags. Do you really think I would buy into a scheme that I have not first thoroughly checked?"

Bags hunched his shoulders, a dark sulk spreading over his face. "Be that as it may, I want some proof, missy. Tangible proof."

"You are holding it in your hand." Mr. Forge's bass voice rumbled behind her. "Lift the urn to the light. See that yellowed vein running vertically from top to bottom? How it cants gently at first then drops straight down?"

Bags peered closely at the vase. So did Kit. Sure enough, a line ran jagged along the length of the piece.

"Aye, I see it." Bags narrowed his eyes at Mr. Forge. "What of it?"

"The alabaster used during the third century was of an impure nature. If you find a perfect piece, you know it is a counterfeit."

Kit pressed her lips flat to keep from gaping. How on earth did he know that? But when Bags once again studied the urn, Mr. Forge slipped her a quick wink. The scoundrel!

"I don't know. . . ," Bags mumbled, uncertainty thick in his voice—an uncertainty that needed to be squashed like a dung beetle.

Kit stepped closer. "Listen, Bags, a deal like this does not come along every day. You know that."

"And I already have a buyer lined up," Mr. Forge chimed in. "Either make me an offer worth listening to or get out."

Bags stiffened. "I don't take kindly to being pressured."

"And I do not take kindly to wasting my time." In one quick swipe, Mr. Forge grabbed the urn from Bags's grip. "It seems we do not have a deal after all, Turner." He nodded towards the door. "Take your mongrels outside and do not come back."

She gaped. This was no way to land a big fish like Gleason!

"Not so fast," Gleason rumbled, his podgy fingers trembling as he swept out his hand. "How many of these relics did you say you have?"

Mr. Forge swiveled a long glance around the warehouse floor, making a point. "Enough to make the buyer a very rich man."

"What's your markup?"

Anger snapped in the constable's gaze and his lip curled in a snarl. "My markup is my business. All you need know is that Mullins has offered me five thousand."

"We will pay you six," Kit cut in. Though Jackson had asked for more than they needed to supply wiggle room for negotiation, it couldn't hurt—hopefully—to inflate that number. If she pocketed extra funds after supplying Skaggs what he needed, she could have little Frankie's mother moved to the best hospital in all of London. Sweet heavens! With that amount she could move the entire family into better lodgings with enough left over to feed *all* the hungry mouths on Blackfriars Lane for months to come. Enough to open up a soup kitchen!

She shot a sideways glance at Bags for his reaction. Would he go for it?

His lips wrinkled as if the idea were a dram of vinegar to be swished about before spitting it out. Ever so slowly, his mouth evened into a thick line. "Like the lady says. Six. And not a ha' penny more."

She let out a breath.

Mr. Forge set down the vase and shot out his palm. "Then I will take your half now."

Bags grunted. "What of missy's here?"

"Not to worry." Jackson slipped her an evocative grin, one that nearly made her knees give way. "I shall be getting her payment when we are alone."

Sheesh. She rolled her eyes. If the man ever needed a second career, he could land a role on Drury Lane.

Next to her, Bags chuckled. "Fair enough, but what makes you think I have that kind of coin on me?"

Before either of Bags's henchmen could move, Jackson pulled his revolver and pressed the barrel against the man's forehead. "Pay me now or do not pay me at all. Your choice."

Silence fell loud and hard in the room. Fury lit a fire from Kit's gut to her throat. Was he trying to get them all killed? Mr. Forge was more dangerous than a loose cannon on wheels!

Bags scowled, the fleshy part of his brow pushing against the muzzle. "You've got brass, I'll give you that." Slowly, he retrieved a wad of bills from an inside pocket. "It's only two, but I'll bring the other grand when I return for the goods. And that's my final offer."

Kit clenched every muscle in her body. Bags's offering was less than Mr. Forge had asked but plenty enough to cover what Skaggs had lost and with leftover to help Martha and the families of Blackfriars. What would the constable-turned-fake-criminal say? Do? And how could she possibly counteract the man's foolish daring, especially with the two bullies at Gleason's back straining to pounce?

"Hmm." Mr. Forge's eyes narrowed to glittering slits, revealing nothing. His jaw hardened, and then he sucked in a breath, drawing it in slow, like the hiss of a snake. Finally, he tucked his revolver away and pocketed the money.

Bags cocked his head. "What'd you say your name was?"

"I did not say." Mr. Forge flashed a devilish smile.

Bags swung to her. "Quite the crowd yer running with, missy."

She stifled a relieved cry. He had no idea. "Not any more cut-throat than you. Listen, it will not be pretty when the Shark hears of our deal, so we should get these goods moved as soon as possible. I will wait here and keep an eye on the place while you get your men and the rest of your money." She turned to Mr. Forge. "I only think it fair, since Mr. Gleason here is fronting a fair bit of funds, that he be allowed to take the vase as collateral."

The constable nodded then narrowed his eyes at Bags. "Make sure to bring it back when you return with the money."

"Seems fair to me." Bags grabbed the urn then wheeled about and jabbed his finger into the smaller man's shoulder. "Butch, come with me. Carver, grab your gun and stay here with Turner."

The three of them stalked to the door. Once they ducked through it, Mr. Forge leaned close and whispered in her ear. "We cannot have that thug staying. Can you convince him to leave?"

She nodded, then, loosening a few buttons at the top of her bodice, she met Carver at the door. If Mr. Forge could play the part of a smuggler, she could do justice to that of a trollop. Reaching up, she ran her finger along the bristly edge of Carver's jaw. "Bags tells me you are his right-hand man. That true?"

His chest puffed out. "I like to think so."

"Understandable, a big strong fellow like you." She tweaked his nose. "Ever think of jumping ship?"

"Bags pays me good enough." He dipped his head, a dark fire lighting in his brown eyes. "But I'm open to offers."

"Are you?" She curved her lips into a seductive smile. "Would you like to see what I have to offer?"

"I would." The words were husky.

"Then how about we negotiate outside for a moment?"

Without a word, he flung open the door and stepped into the night, fast as a buck on the rut.

At the same time, Mr. Forge's fingers dug into her shoulder and pulled her back. "What are you doing?" he whispered.

"What I have to." Shrugging away from him, she crossed the threshold and reached for her knife.

Too late.

Before she could get a good grip on the blade, rough hands slammed her against the wall and the knife flew from her fingers.

Carver cocked his head to where the weapon clinked against a cobble, then swiveled his face to hers. "Like to play it rough, do you?" His gaze hardened and he rubbed his cheek against hers, harsh stubble chafing her skin. "So do I."

Pretend to be a smuggler. Pretend to be a harlot. What was next? Pretend to be a murderer? Jackson had not overlooked Miss Turner's slim hand reaching for her concealed knife.

Fuming, Jackson paced away, then doubled back. Kit Turner might be used to bossing her men around, but he wasn't one of them. And he'd be hanged if he'd let her beguile a man into lowering his guard just to drive a shank into his gut.

He pulled his own knife and shoved the door open, the bang of it hitting the wall like a gunshot in the night. Movement to his left. One big shadow pulled away from a smaller one. No time to think.

Flipping the knife around, he swung with all his might. The hilt cracked against bone, driving hard into a skull. A grunt. A gasp. The big shadow staggered one way, then the other, and finally dropped like a felled tree, landing not far from another knife lying on the ground. Light from the gas lamp overhead sliced over them both, reflecting a spark of ire in Miss Turner's storm-tossed blue eyes as she stepped up to him.

"I had this under control."

Bypassing her, he swiped up the woman's blade and dangled it in front of her. "Really?"

She snatched her weapon from his grip. "Let us get one thing straight here, Mr. Forge. I am not some damsel in distress who needs saving."

"I was not worried about you."

Her lips parted, but no sound came out. The tough Miss Turner rendered speechless? That was nearly as satisfying as the fat roll of money in his pocket—money they could spare no time in returning to Skaggs.

Tucking away his knife, he grabbed the passed-out Carver by the boots and nodded towards the door. "Open it."

She reached for the knob while casting a glance over her shoulder. "What are you doing with him?"

"I'll haul him in with the other fellow."

"What other fellow?"

He lugged the brute into the warehouse and over to a worktable off in the corner, hidden behind a row of fabric ready to move in the morning. Light footsteps followed.

"Who is he?"

The question curled over his shoulder as he dumped Carver next to the bound, gagged, and blindfolded night watchman, who now wriggled like a landed eel.

"Just a man in the wrong place at the wrong time." Jackson swept his hand towards the door. "Shall we?"

She turned. He followed. In no time, they dashed outside, rounded the corner onto the street, and took off.

Hardly a block later, a constable on night patrol stepped into their path from a shadowy alcove, forcing them to stop. The man pulled out his truncheon and slapped it against his palm. "You two are in quite a hurry. Where are you going, or better yet, where have you been?"

Jackson dipped his head, praying the man wouldn't recognize him. "The lady and I are just out for some night air, Constable."

"That so?" His tone sharpened. "Open your coat. There's been a rash o' burglaries around here and I won't be letting you slip by with stolen goods."

Jackson froze. Even in the night shadows, the bulge from the money roll would surely be noticeable without his coat to cover it.

"Oh Officer, my man here wouldn't rob the flea off a cat, so honest is he." Miss Turner's dialect changed to a street straggler, and a bawdy giggle slipped past her lips. Leaving his side, she approached the constable and lowered her voice. "We was just having a bit o' fun in the dark, is all. Surely you can understand that, a handsome man like yerself. Why, I bet all the ladies wish to shuffle you off to a quiet corner, eh?"

"Well. . ." The man cleared his throat.

Seriously? The constable would fall for such a flimsy bit of flattery? Careful to keep his face in the shadows, Jackson looked up—only to see the blunt end of a truncheon headed for his shoulder with a good jab. He stumbled back a step as the constable grumbled, "But like as not, I'll still see what you got beneath that wool."

He pressed his lips tight, stopping a sharp retort. Shouldn't the man be out looking for the missing men instead of bullying pedestrians? Keeping his chin tucked, Jackson slowly reached for the top button of his coat, scrambling to come up with some sort of excuse for the thick wad of bills he carried—but he didn't have to think long.

Miss Turner rammed her head into the constable's gut, knocking him backwards. "Run!"

He sprinted. So did she. The piercing shrill of a police whistle followed, and the constable's pounding footsteps. The man would be joined in no time by nearby officers, all of whom who could identify Jackson. How the devil would he explain this to the sergeant?

"This way!" Miss Turner's skirts disappeared down a narrow passage.

He shimmied after her, the brick snagging the fabric on both his shoulders as he tried to run sideways.

"Stop!" The constable's voice echoed down the passageway. "In the name of the—"

The words cut off as the long lane opened into a wider road and

Miss Turner swerved to the right. Fast as a whirlwind, she dove into yet another crevice, this one at gutter level, and disappeared feet first down an open grate.

Heaven and earth! The woman truly was as crafty as a field mouse—and as small as one too. But he wasn't. Jackson hesitated. If he were to get stuck in that hole, he'd be easy pickings for the constable, whose footsteps even now kicked up gravel in the narrow passageway not far behind him.

Nothing for it, then.

Jackson plummeted down the same rabbit hole as Miss Turner.

Chapter Eleven

If she had a farthing for each time her boots landed in wet sludge, Kit Turner would be wealthy enough never to set foot in a runoff channel again. She charged forward a few steps, lest Mr. Forge flatten her when he hit bottom, and used the remaining moments before his descent to hike her hem and tuck her skirt into her waistband. Damp boots were one thing. A sodden petticoat quite another, especially when she was trying to outrun a constable.

As soon as Mr. Forge splashed to the bottom, she took off down the dark tunnel. Intermittent shafts of light drifted in from other street-level openings, though she preferred the long stretches of nothing but black between them. The eerie remnants of aboveground gaslight looked far too much like ghosts hovering near the ceiling.

After covering a good distance, she stopped, a stitch needling her in the ribs. She could barely make out Mr. Forge's outline as he caught up to her.

"I think. . .whew." She inhaled deeply, then tried again. "I think we lost the constable."

But ahead, just beyond where the passage curved into a bend, the thud-splash of boots landed. Two times.

"I would not be so sure about that." Sarcasm ran thick in his tone.

"Well then, we shall simply go back." She pushed past him, only to hear a great rush of kicked up sludge coming from that direction as well.

Panic closed her throat. Trapped!

And this time young Frankie wasn't here to create a diversion.

Fingers wrapped around her arm, pulling her against Mr. Forge's side. His own heavy breaths warmed her ear as he whispered, "Are there any connecting shafts we can slip into?"

Were there? She rifled through the scant memories she had of this place and quickly came up shorthanded. If only they'd made it to one of the gutter openings and could climb out, fly free. . .wait a minute. Fly? That was it!

"Think like a bat, Mr. Forge," she whispered.

"Pardon?"

"There are handholds on the ceiling. Give me a lift then get yourself up. Hook your feet in one, grab hold of another, then belly up to the brick as best you can. And for pity's sake, make sure your coat flaps do not hang down."

He stared upward, slack-jawed, through the gloom.

The splashes grew closer, ending whatever objection swirled through his head. His big hands grabbed her hips, and up she went, flailing her arms to make purchase with an iron handle. As soon as her fingers clenched metal, she swung up her legs, kicking Mr. Forge in the head. He blew out a grunt, but no time to apologize now. Any minute and those officers would be on top of them. Or him, more like.

A small shiver of fear for the unwitting constable chilled her as much as the cold damp rung she clung to. He never should've gotten involved in this mess. Why didn't he simply stick to walking his beat instead of poking around after ol' Joe? Must every man try to prove himself through risk and danger?

Mr. Forge grunted as he positioned himself in front of her. Even if she wanted to, it was too dark to see him, so the officers shouldn't either. As long as they didn't look upward.

The splashing steps drew closer. Her muscles began to shake. If God was on her side, the men would keep right on going, run past, vanish down the tunnel. And they might have, had not another set of boots mucked up to meet them.

Stopping right beneath her and Mr. Forge.

She mashed her face against the slimy bricks, trying to ignore the mouldy stench and disregard the uncontrollable quivering in her arms and legs.

"Did you see them?" one man asked.

"No one made it past us," another answered.

A curse followed.

So did a tickle in Kit's throat. One cough, no, one little wheeze and she'd attract the men's attention. Yet if they didn't move on soon, that wouldn't matter, for she'd drop on their heads.

"Well then, they must've passed under your gutter before you entered, boys."

"You think they coulda made it that far before we dropped?"

Gah! Fire licked along every muscle, every nerve. Was Mr. Forge feeling as much strain?

"Clearly they are not here, and the longer we debate, the farther they'll get."

She held her breath, shoving down the tickle.

"Bah!" one of the men spit out. "Slippery blackguards."

At last, boots once again kicked up muck, blessedly moving away from them. She really ought to wait a few more moments, but no good. Her fingers gave. Her feet unhooked, and she dropped to the sludge.

"Not that I am complaining," Mr. Forge whispered, dropping down beside her, "but why are there handholds on the ceiling?"

She shook out the tension in her arms. "They are for flushers, in case they do not get out in time and the tunnels flood. Which they do. Provides for a bit of air—unless the whole thing fills. Which it has. But that is the least of our concerns right now."

She darted after the constables, taking care to keep her muck-splashing to a minimum. Yet she'd hardly reached the next gutter opening when Mr. Forge yanked her backwards, his words harsh and low in her ear.

"Are you insane?" His eyes burned an eerie cobalt in the grey light. "We are supposed to be evading those men, not running headlong after them. We need to go the other way."

She shook her head. "I am not familiar with the route from there."

"Then learn a new one. They are coming back."

At his words, she shut her mouth and listened.

Sure enough, splattering footsteps grew louder instead of softer. A disgusted sigh ripped out of her. What a night. She broke into a dead run, retracing their steps, passing the only entrance she'd ever used, and fleeing into twists and turns she'd never before navigated. She didn't stop until she reached a T.

And then her breathing stopped too.

Thin light filtered down either side of the passages, meeting in the middle to illuminate—barely—some words and arrows stenciled on the wall. Words she couldn't read. All the longing and shame she tried daily to keep locked up in a cage deep down in her soul rattled against the bars, squeezing her lungs. An ugly reminder that no matter how hard she tried to help the poor of Blackfriars, she'd never truly succeed until she could elevate their station by teaching them to read.

Tentatively, she ran her fingers along the painted letters, and suddenly she was a little girl again, standing outside on the streets, pressing her hand against a glass windowpane of a fine London townhome. Inside, a girl her own age with red ribbons in her hair perched on a plump cushion, a book in her lap, a glorious look of wonder widening the girl's eyes as she escaped into the rich world of words and story. *Oh Miss Lila, you had no reason to ever wish to escape.* Not like she did.

"Which way?" Mr. Forge rumbled behind her, breaking the spell. "Which street?"

Snapping to the present, she faced him. "There is an underground railway opening beneath Carthroat. We cannot be far."

"Of course not." His head angled like a curious raven, and he swept his hand towards the words on the wall. "It says Carthroat is to the left."

She dodged right.

"I said left," he cried, his voice a rasping stage whisper against the cobbled walls.

Ignoring him, she ripped off a swatch of cloth from her hem and snagged it on the rough edge of the wall, planting it just above ankle height, as if she'd run by and torn off the bit of telltale fabric. Then she doubled back, calling out as she passed Mr. Forge, "You coming?"

Twenty yards later, she halted near a round iron grate in the wall. She yanked. No good. The thing was wedged in tight.

"Let me." Mr. Forge flanked her, bent, and heaved. Without so much as a grunt or groan, the grill came away with ease. Admirable. Were he not a constable, she could actually use him on her crew.

"After I go in and you follow, put that grate back on as best you can before you crawl through." She hoisted herself up into the opening.

He stayed her by a touch to her shoulder. "Where does this lead?"

"The underground railway." She set off before her words could sink in, for surely he'd object. She objected herself. But there was no alternative, not with those officers on their tail. Her little scrap of skirt diversion wouldn't fool them for long.

The farther she crawled, the thicker the air. Her eyes watered. Her nose stung. Each breath scraped down her throat. A bruised knee and a cut palm later, she emerged into a tunnel reeking of creosote. Too bad that had been the easiest part of the route.

Mr. Forge shimmied out behind her, his feet barely landing before his anger touched down as well. "Do you have any idea how dangerous this is? If a train comes by now, no matter how much we flatten against the wall, we will be ripped to pieces. And hanging like a bat is no option here. We would be cooked like a shank of meat on a spit with one blast of steam. No, I will not have it. We turn right around and—"

The sound of a grate being removed and officers' shouts traveled down the crawl space.

"By all that is holy." Mr. Forge groaned, grabbed her hand, and yanked her into motion. And none too soon. A low thunder rumbled in the dark.

Headed their way.

Jackson pumped his legs hard, running like a madman—which *was* mad, because no one could outrun a train. Not even the fleet-footed woman keeping pace at his side.

Thin light from the engine's headlamps grew brighter with each passing breath. He kicked up gravel all the more, pushing him and Miss Turner to the limits of human speed. At least the constables wouldn't be catching them, a minute sort of consolation, that.

Sweat rained down his back, sticking his shirt to his skin. His lungs burned. His eyes. His thighs. Everything was afire. The heat of the oncoming train. The knowledge that he was about to meet his Maker in a spectacularly bloody way. The awful blaze of failure that he would not be locating Joe Card and, worst of all, that he was leading Kit Turner to her death—unless by some miracle God intervened.

Well, Lord? Will You?

The steam hissed hotter and the train growled angrier. Closer. Ever closer.

Miss Turner stumbled, pulling them both towards the middle of the rails. He tugged hard on her hand, yanking her body against his so violently that he staggered. He flailed his other hand, a desperate attempt to keep balance. Yet surprisingly his palm did not scrape against the brick wall.

He jerked his gaze aside.

Then jerked Miss Turner aside as well.

There, hidden by layers of soot and grime, was an alcove large enough for a body. But was there space enough for two?

Without any coaxing, Miss Turner flattened against the wall and pulled him close. As the ground vibrated and the roar deafened, he pressed into her, molding his body to hers. He clenched his jaw and every other muscle he owned, bracing, waiting.

A mighty rush of hot wind seared his back, flapping the legs of his trousers. His hair whipped sideways, following the gust. Thank God he'd never untucked the tails of his coat or he might very well have been dragged away from the small space. And he still might, if he didn't stay perfectly still until the entire length of train passed.

Miss Turner clung to him like a second skin. The world turned into nothing but ear-shattering noise, crawling in deep and shaking his bones. Strong enough to cleave soul from flesh.

A lifetime later, the thunder lessened. Maybe. Jackson stood resolute, unsure if he was fading from this world or the train was nearly past.

And then it was gone.

"Mr. Forge?" Miss Turner's voice muffled against his chest.

Unwrapping his arms from her, he retreated a step and blew out a shaky breath. Eerie red light from the back of the train painted the tunnel like Dante's Inferno.

Miss Turner peered up at him, worry creasing lines at the sides of her eyes. "Are you all right?"

He swiped the sweat from his forehead, then flashed her a smile. "Never better. You?"

"Of course." She grinned back. "I must say, sir, working with you is quite an adventure."

"It has been an interesting experience." He cracked his neck, working out the tension of the harrowing event. "One I do not wish to repeat." He angled his head towards the retreating train. "I assume this leads to a station, and hopefully sooner rather than later. Shall we?"

"Better than that," she called over her shoulder as she passed him. "It leads to a spur that will get us to Skaggs."

He caught up to her side. "Please tell me there are no more train tunnels or sewage channels involved."

She arched a brow at him. "Surely you are not turning squeamish now?"

He scoffed. Was this woman even real? What other female could possibly be so unflappable? But then a few more questions of a darker shade tagged quickly behind those. What sort of life had Kit Turner lived to make her so resourceful? So calm in the face of danger? His gut clenched when the answer hit him square in the chops. She'd had to learn at a tender age to look out for herself, something no little girl should ever have to experience.

A spark of protectiveness flared in his chest. Trains or sewers be hanged. He'd see her safely out of here, whether he knew the way or not.

Thankfully, there were no more close calls with trains. They traveled through air shafts, a series of old smuggler crannies, and finally looped their way back to the pawnbroker's underground haven.

Before they entered, Miss Turner stayed him with a touch to his arm. "I will take the money." She held out her hand.

He narrowed his eyes. After all they'd been through, she still didn't trust him?

Inside, one of the Emporium's clocks struck five bells. Five? Mercy! He didn't have time for a lengthy debate. The dimple set deep by her pinched lips left no quarter for discussion. He handed over the wad of bills.

"Thank you." She peeled off a few of the top banknotes and slipped them into her pocket.

The little thief! "You would rob the robbed?"

"Of course not. It is payment for our risk. Skaggs would expect as much." She shrugged one slim shoulder then sashayed into the pawnshop, where the one-legged pawnbroker yet perched on his stool.

The fellow's eyes burned with equal measures of hope and dread. "Well?"

"Did you really think I would let you down, my friend?" She slapped the money on the counter.

Wonder brightened the pawnbroker's face, easing the stark contrast of blue veins and white skin. "I'll be jiggered." He snatched the money.

"And so you have your payment." Miss Turner gave a toss of her head. "Now, our goods?"

"Like I said, weren't much to be found in Joe's cab, but I'll give you all I have." Bending sideways, Skaggs retrieved a small wooden box from beneath the counter.

So small? Jackson leaned in close. This had better be good after all the trouble they'd gone to.

"Thanks, Skaggs." Miss Turner whisked the container away and spun on her heel. "Best of luck to you with Reaper."

Jackson dashed after her, not catching up until halfway through the first tunnel. "Hey! I need to see what is in that box every bit as much as you do."

"You shall, Mr. Forge. But first there is something else we must take care of." Though it was hardly possible, she upped her pace, even taking the stairs of the station's exit two at a time. Was the woman part automaton?

And here he was again, chasing the little pixie through the streets of Blackfriars, this time in the shadows of a day on the cusp of breaking. He nearly lost her when she rounded a corner into a back alley, but once he swerved past the side of the building, she stood rosy cheeked and blocking his way.

"Wait here," she instructed.

"You are insane if you think I am letting you run free with that box of evidence. Let me have it." He shoved out his hand. "Now."

"Clearly you trust me as much as I trust you, which is why I have brought you here."

He cocked his head. What kind of swindle was she working? "I am not interested, nor do I have the time for this."

"Neither does Martha. But do not worry; you will be able to see me the entire time. I promise—and I do not give my word lightly. Ever."

The whites of her eyes shone stark in the grey dawn, earnest, almost pleading. Could he trust her? *Should* he? A known juggler of words with a keen intelligence always seeking to outwit? He rubbed his knuckles along his jaw, weighing the pros and cons—mostly cons. But curiosity was as alluring a siren as the woman herself.

"Very well." He stepped nearer and pulled out his most authoritative constable voice. "But the second you disappear from my sight is the second I shall turn in your token for an arrest warrant. Understood?"

Her only answer was a brief waft of breeze and sooty stench as she tore off. She stopped in front of a door and rapped, close enough he could see her, far enough he couldn't hear her exchange when the door opened. A few breaths later, a short figure emerged and trundled off down the opposite side of the narrow passage. Miss Turner waved Jackson forward.

So, she had kept her word after all—unless some sort of ambush waited for him inside.

And it did.

A host of noxious odours assailed him as he crossed the threshold. Soiled clouts. Damp rot. The same eerie spoiled meat stench that he'd smelled the day before his mother had passed. He left the door wide. The alley was a French perfume factory compared to this. Why bring him here?

On light feet, he crossed over to where Miss Turner knelt at the side of a pallet bed. His boots landed in a sticky substance as he leaned close and strained to hear her whispers over the whimper of a child and the heavy breathing of others. How many poor souls lived in this rat hole?

"Look what I have brought you, Martha." Miss Turner pulled out the banknotes. "No more fretting. No more fear. You shall have the best care and so will your children until you get well."

Jackson gaped. *That's* why she'd pocketed the extra bills? Not to spend on her own baubles or trinkets but to save a sickly woman and her offspring?

The skeletal woman on the bed fluttered eyes that were far too sunken in the sockets. As she took in the money, breath wheezed heavy in her lungs. "Oh miss! You are too good."

"Shh." Miss Turner stroked the lady's cheek. "Rest now. I shall have you moved this very morning." Tucking away the money, she brushed her lips against the woman's brow, then rose and beckoned for him.

In a daze, Jackson followed. Was Kit Turner a saint in disguise, then?

Lest he wake the children, he eased the door shut.

"And that, Mr. Forge"—she flicked her fingers at the hovel—"is why I do what I do. I care for the people of Blackfriars with money that is freely handed over to me, that is all."

He shook his head. "As much as I admire your compassion and convictions—and I truly do—swindling is not the way to go about helping these people."

She set her jaw, a sure sign her heels were even now digging into the muck on the cobbles. "I have no other means."

"Maybe not you, but God does."

"Of course He does." She rolled her eyes. "But God has bigger problems in the world than a sick woman who cannot feed her children."

"Ahh, but there is your folly, for God cares even for the sparrow."

"He has not cared for Martha. She has been ill a long time."

"Just because something has not happened yet does not mean it will not." The familiar words were like a letter from home. If he looked in a mirror right now, would his own father be staring back?

"You saw her." Miss Turner's voice grew throaty. "She does not have much time left."

What was he to say to that? Left untreated, Martha might take tea with her Maker this very afternoon. Jackson rubbed the back of his neck, silty grime thick against his fingers. Would that he could make things better for them both—but he wasn't God. And neither was she. "Miss Turner, you take on too much. The world is not yours to right."

Once past his lips, the sentiment boxed his ears. Wasn't that exactly what *he'd* been trying to do?

She lifted her pert little nose. "Maybe so, but that does not mean I cannot make the world a better place. Care for the needy. Love the unloved."

Of course. She was right. An unstoppable grin stretched his lips. "You are quite the enigma."

"Hopefully less so than before, since I have shown you what I really do." She cocked her head. "I do not suppose you will return my token now?"

"Tut-tut." He wagged his finger. "A deal is a deal, and we have yet to find Joe Card. Let us see what is in that box, shall we?"

Frowning, she untucked the small container and opened the lid. Inside was the bottom half of a broken pen, the back catch of a golden cuff link, and a torn bit of paper. They'd risked their lives for such rubbish?

With a sigh, Jackson reached for the paper. Miss Turner huddled close for a look as well. A smear of brownish blood marred the top corner, ripped in such a way that it'd clearly been yanked from whoever had been holding it. Joe Card, maybe?

Whatever had been written in ink was blurred into oblivion. Likely naught but a salutation. Perhaps a date. Too water stained to tell. But none of that mattered as much as the engraved printing at the top. A letterhead. In capital letters was the name Sir Robert Fowler, 1st Baronet. Jackson scrubbed a hand over his face. Not much to go on, but at least it was a lead. Someone he could question.

The trouble was, how exactly did one go about interrogating the newly installed Lord Mayor?

Chapter Twelve

Steps heavy, Jackson opened the station's door with five minutes to spare before the morning briefing. Fatigue draped over him like a sodden blanket, weighing him down. He'd hoped to catch at least a half hour of sleep before swapping his civilian clothes for his uniform, but it'd taken longer than he liked to spar with Miss Turner over the evidence they'd received from Skaggs. She'd wanted to pocket it all. So had he. Eventually, they settled on her retaining the cuff link catch and broken pen while he got to keep the tattered piece of letterhead. And they both agreed questioning the Lord Mayor was the next step in finding Joe Card. How they'd go about it, though, was still up for debate.

He tipped his head in greeting at Beanstaple right before an enormous yawn stretched his mouth—which wasn't missed by Officer Charles Baggett as he swung around the corner.

"Late one for you last night?" His new friend clouted him on the arm, but then as suddenly, Baggett's hand dropped, his nose lifted, and he sniffed the air with a curled upper lip. "Caw! What is that putrid stench?"

Frowning, Baggett lifted each of his shoes in turn, studying the bottoms. Jackson stiffened as a realization hit him sideways. He'd changed into his uniform but not had enough time for a thorough washing. After a long night of crawling through sewers and runoff channels, *he* was the one generating the stink.

But there was nothing to be done for it now. Once again a powerful yawn overtook him, and he covered his mouth with the back of his hand.

"So, what kept you up till all hours?" A knowing gleam twinkled in Baggett's eyes. "Out with a lady friend, were you?"

He stifled a snort. Kit didn't meet either of those requirements. "Something like that," he mumbled, then without giving Baggett the chance to travel that rabbit trail any further, he fired back a question of his own. "How goes it on the search for the missing lord and barrister?"

"A few leads." Baggett scratched his jaw. "Nothing worth chasing after, if you ask me."

"You think they are related, like Graybone says?"

"Hard to say. In a city this size, people go missing every day for all sorts of reasons. Could be those men wanted to disappear and we are doing them a disservice to hunt them down like common game birds. Speaking of which. . ." He angled his head. "I hear you have your own grouse hunt, tracking a lost jarvey. That's a step up from trotting around with a rat terrier, eh?" Baggett elbowed him—right in a tender spot on his bicep where the night watchman had walloped him with a truncheon.

Jackson bit back a wince. "Word sure travels fast."

"You know constables, bunch of old hens when it comes to gossip." He hitched his thumb at the door. "Shall we?"

Bypassing him, Baggett headed into the briefing room. Jackson slid onto his usual stool beside him and not a moment too soon. Up front, Sergeant Graybone entered from a side door, taking his place at the podium.

"Good morning, Officers." The sergeant greeted them without looking up from the stack of papers in his hands. "Another full slate today." He slapped down the documents with a *whack* and skimmed a dark gaze over the lot of constables. "We have yet to locate Lord Twickenham and Barrister Humphrey, but word is an innkeeper over on Bramble Street may have some information, at least about the barrister."

As the sergeant droned on, the man in front of Jackson turned on his seat, eyeing him with a wrinkled nose. Jackson gave a small nod towards Baggett, hopefully throwing the man off his scent. Literally.

"A few assorted burglaries last night," the sergeant continued, "and one break-in. Apparently nothing was taken, thank God. Still, I shall be sending an officer to check on the disturbance at Hamstock's Storage, since it involved the assault of a night watchman."

Jackson shifted uncomfortably. Apparently Gleason's man had run off, so no worries there. And the watchman wouldn't be able to identify him. But still, how would he tell Graybone his own brother-in-law might be tangled up in smuggling alcohol without incriminating himself?

Thankfully, the sergeant moved on to the day's assignments, divvying out all the tasks, and once again, Jackson's name came last.

"Forge," the sergeant clipped out.

Jackson approached the podium, and immediately Graybone tested the air with a few sniffs. He retreated a step. Too late.

Graybone's dark gaze skewered him. "Do not tell me that putrescent stink is coming off of you."

Sweet heavens! Could an odour earn him a demerit? Feigning innocence, he sniffed the air in several directions. "Pardon, sir, but I do not smell anything."

Just like Baggett, Graybone began checking his shoes.

"I have had a breakthrough in the Joe Card case, sir," Jackson interjected. Better to earn a verbal slap for interrupting the sergeant's efforts than gain his third and last mark.

The sergeant lifted his head. "That so?"

Jackson pulled out the bloody bit of letterhead and handed it over.

Raising the paper to eye level, Graybone studied the thing. "Where did you get this?"

He clenched his jaw. He couldn't very well tell the sergeant about Skaggs's underground emporium or about the partnership he'd struck with a thief in a skirt. But neither would he lie. He lifted his chin. "It came from the missing man's hackney."

"Interesting." Graybone lowered the paper to the podium and tapped a rhythm with one of his fingers on the document. "So, whoever rode in that cab clearly had some sort of relationship with the Lord Mayor."

"Or it may have even been Sir Robert Fowler himself, about to deliver a missive when something went awry."

The tapping stopped and instead the finger aimed at him. "Do not be daft. A baronet would not stoop to hiring a cab nor would he deliver his own correspondence."

"Unless he needed to do so incognito for nefarious reasons."

Despite the stench still lingering in the air, the sergeant's nostrils flared. "Are you seriously considering the newly installed Lord Mayor as a prime suspect in the disappearance of a common jarvey?"

His gut twisted. He knew that tone. Graybone had employed it during the banker debacle. "Only thinking out loud, sir."

"Well, don't. Hauling an innocent banker into the station is one thing. A politician—and a peer at that—quite another."

"Yes, sir."

The sergeant glanced up at the clock, then back to Jackson. "You have a little over twenty-four hours left, Forge. You had best make 'em count."

"I will, but, er. . .there is just one more thing." He cleared his throat. If he didn't tell Graybone about his brother-in-law now, he'd never do it. "About Mr. Hamstock, sir."

"Aye. Foul business last evening. My sister near to had the vapors." The sergeant stroked his beard. "That watchman was pathetic, first allowing himself to get caught and then not being able to identify the perpetrator. I suppose I shall have to send over a new night guard."

"You also might want to check into what your brother-in-law is shipping along with his fabric."

Graybone went deathly still. "What are you insinuating?"

He tugged his collar, desperate for air. One wrong word could slit his own throat. "It might be nothing, but I happened to notice when

I was there last that a bottle of Jamaican rum was hidden inside the middle of a bolt."

"Did you now?" the sergeant narrowed his eyes. "Were you not paid to patrol the *outside* perimeter?"

Jackson swallowed. Hard. "Yes, sir, but if you will recall, part of my duty was also to walk Mr. Hamstock's dog, which I could only accomplish by first going inside and retrieving the little rat—I mean, terrier."

"Hmm." Graybone's eyes blackened to coals, a fire burning deep within. Snatching his papers off the podium, he wheeled about. "Thank you. Dismissed, Forge."

Jackson took a step after him. "Sir, I only thought you should—"

"I said dismissed, Constable!"

Though the man couldn't see it, Jackson snapped a sharp salute at the sergeant's back then strode to the door, but as soon as he cleared the briefing room, his shoulders sagged. In hindsight, perhaps he ought to have held off on mentioning the sergeant's brother-in-law.

He blew out all his frustration and straightened his collar. Despite what the sergeant said, Sir Robert Fowler was his prime suspect, or at least the best man to cross-examine. There was only one thing to be done. He had to see the Lord Mayor.

And he had to do it today.

Yawning, Kit repositioned her back against the outside wall of the police station, keeping to the shadow cast by the awning snapping overhead. An old habit, this watching from a distance. Making herself invisible. Something she'd learned all too well as a child in the orphanage. Undoubtedly she'd be much more comfortable sitting on the bench near the station's front door, but it was probably a good thing the brick poked her shoulder blades. Were she comfortable, she'd fall asleep. And she still might if Mr. Forge didn't appear soon. What was taking him so long? Other constables had already come and gone, yet he'd been in there at least an hour.

As if conjured by her thoughts, the man himself finally strode out of the station and turned down the pavement, headed her way. Ahh, but he did cut a fine figure in his blue uniform with his long legs, his broad shoulders, and that strong chest she'd sheltered against when the train had blitzed by. He'd saved her life, this man. Risked his own for the likes of her. And she wasn't quite sure what to do with the way that warmed her heart.

He passed by without a glance. She remained still a moment longer, admiring his fine backside, then hurried to catch up on silent feet. "Where are you off to in such a hurry, Constable?"

His piercing blue gaze shot to hers, the flash of surprise on his face wholly satisfying. "Where did you come from?"

"If you can answer that, Mr. Forge, then I daresay you ought to be promoted to detective."

Without a word, he wrapped his big hand on her upper arm and guided her into a thin space between two buildings, blocking her from sight of any passing pedestrians. Her nose wrinkled in the close quarters. Obviously he'd not taken the time to wash away the reek of their nighttime intrigues.

"Why would you risk going so near a police station?" His question flew out harsher than a quayside fishwife's.

She grinned. A sincere rebuke, but toothless nonetheless. "Where else was I to find you? Besides, it is not the station per se that is a danger."

"Are you mad?" He flung out his arms. "With so many officers about, you could be picked up in a heartbeat for thievery."

"A baseless concern, I assure you." Then on second thought, she narrowed her eyes. "That is, of course, unless you have ratted me out?"

His head reared back as if she'd struck him with an open palm. "We made a bargain, Miss Turner, and I am a man of my word."

"I suppose time will tell on that account. But for now, that is neither here nor there. I have something for you." She reached inside her pocket and pulled out an envelope, and before she could even hand it over, his interrogation began.

"What is that?"

"An invitation to a charity event to reconstruct Westminster Hall. Tonight. You are my escort." She held it out.

He snatched it from her and waved it in front of her face. "We do not have time for this. Unless you have some intelligence that Joe Card will be in attendance?"

"No, but the Lord Mayor will."

His jaw dropped. "How could you possibly know that? Did you steal the guest list?"

"I did not have to." She shrugged. "It is at his residence. Mansion House."

"Mansion House?" He ran a finger beneath the wax seal, breaking it open. His blue gaze pinged back and forth as he read the length of the page, then slowly, he looked up at her, all former harshness in his tone replaced by wonder—*and* a trace of suspicion. "How the deuce did you manage an invitation to attend such a gala event?"

"It is probably better if you do not know." Truly, it was. She wouldn't stoop to crossing the line into lawlessness herself, but that didn't mean she wouldn't use her connections with those who did— and thankfully she knew the best forger in town.

His blue eyes bored into hers. "I am not certain, Miss Turner, if you and your skills are an answer to prayer, or if you are merely a temptress designed for my downfall."

"Oh? Find me tempting, do you?"

Without a word, he held her gaze a moment longer, then snapped his attention back to the invitation, flipping it over this time to study the front. "This is written out to me and Catherine Forge." He looked up. "Who the devil is she?"

"Your cousin."

He shook his head. "I do not have a cousin."

"You do now. Unless you prefer I pose as your wife?"

A deep shade of red crept up his neck, quite the contrast against the blue of his uniform. "Cousin will be just fine." He retreated a step.

"Good. I will meet you outside Mansion House at seven sharp. It is a gala event, so make sure to get some sleep, Cousin. You look a bit rough around the edges. I will see that a dress suit is delivered to the station for you, which ought to help. Even after moving Martha to a hospital and rehousing her children, there is plenty enough of Bags's money left over." She edged past him, returning to the pavement, then faced him once again with a quirk to her lips. "And for heaven's sake, take a bath. You smell as if you have been in the sewers all night."

Chapter Thirteen

Jackson walked the front portico at Mansion House several times before staking out his own piece of property near the third pillar. Though it wasn't proper etiquette, he loosened his cravat yet another notch. A stuffed goose couldn't feel more trussed. He'd never blend in with the gentry if he keeled over from lack of air. How did the wealthy stand wearing such garb so frequently? Christmas and Easter dinners, plus the occasional wedding celebration, were more than enough occasions in a year to starch and primp oneself into oblivion.

Breathing easier, he scanned the steady stream of silks and satins arriving for the gala. Miss Turner had yet to appear, and he wasn't quite sure what to look for. Would she go for an attention-grabbing scarlet skirt or a nondescript pale taffeta to fade into the woodwork? It could be either, knowing her. . .or actually, no. He didn't know the first thing about her other than her unpredictability. She might very well arrive in a pair of black trousers and a top hat just to snare a reaction.

While his gaze skimmed the gentry, he revisited the events of the day for possible missed details. After a few hours of sleep and then a thorough scrutiny of the torn letterhead, he'd visited several stationers before attaining a victory at Milton's Paper. Mr. Milton confirmed the scrolled *M* watermark belonged to him and that he was indeed the sanctioned provider of paper goods to the Lord Mayor's office—which left no question that someone with a connection to Sir Robert

Fowler had been in Joe Card's cab the night of his disappearance. But who? The deliverer or the recipient of the letter? Or perhaps the sender himself? The answer was as much out of his reach as the fleeting shadows cast by the portico torches.

And his inquiries into Kit Turner's true identity were no more solid, not that he really needed the information anymore. Still, Milton's Paper was conveniently located near the Wellington Barracks and had provided him with another opportunity to query the colonel of the regiment. Once again, the man was absent, but the visit hadn't been completely fruitless. He'd procured an appointment with the colonel—three weeks hence. Which would be too late. By then he'd have solved the whereabouts of the missing cabby and would be forced to return Miss Turner's token.

"Waiting for someone, Mr. Forge?" A playful voice drifted over his shoulder.

Blast! Would Kit Turner forever be sneaking up on him? He turned, poised to launch a snappy retort. But as soon as his gaze landed on her, his jaw went slack. He couldn't have put two words together if someone jammed a gun to his head. No man could. With her emerald gown clinging to such shapely curves, the woman would silence a raging battalion of hell-bent men.

A slow smile lifted her lips. "You are staring, Mr. Forge."

"I—" He cleared his throat. "Pardon. My mind was elsewhere."

Torchlight danced in her eyes. "And where might that be, I wonder?"

Gaff! The woman knew exactly the effect she'd have on him or any other man—and he'd fallen for it. Steeling himself against her charms, he threw back his shoulders. "About time you arrived. I can only hope you were busy uncovering information on the cuff link or the pen."

"I do have other matters to attend to, *Cousin*, but yes, I did some investigating." She glanced over her shoulder, then waited for a couple to pass before leaning close and speaking for his ears alone. "The pen was a dead end. The make is as common as a plum pudding at Christmas. But the cuff link, now that is quite another story. It came from J. C. Vickery over on Regent."

She jutted her jaw, as if she'd just explained the workings of the universe, but she may as well have been speaking Slovenian. He'd lived here for hardly a month and had yet to learn all the notable haunts of London, especially those outside the City limits.

"And?" he prompted.

"One needs a fair bit of coin for that high-hat shop." She pulled away a stray piece of hair that had drifted onto her cheek, the movement wafting lavender on the night air. The temptation to lean closer and inhale more of her fragrance was nearly enough to make him forget why he was there.

Giving himself a mental shake, he banished his baser instincts. "So...someone of wealth *did* take a ride in Joe's cab." He glanced over her shoulder at the opulent Mansion House. "Maybe even a Lord Mayor."

"That is what we are here to find out."

"Indeed." He crooked his elbow. "Ready for another adventure, Cousin?"

She grinned and planted her hand on his sleeve. "This one is bound to smell better, at least."

Leading her away from the pillar, he joined with the throng of other guests, and when it was their turn to stand in front of the footman, he plucked an envelope from his pocket and offered the invitation.

The man couldn't have been more primped and preened had he been a peacock. He gave the invitation a cursory glance before dipping his head at each of them in turn. "Mr. Forge, Miss Forge."

Jackson startled at the use of his surname in reference to the pretty scamp beside him, but he quickly schooled his face to a bored sort of distraction. That was how the rich appeared...didn't they?

Apparently, for the footman continued without missing a beat.

"You will find entertainment and refreshment throughout, culminating in a gathering in the Egyptian Hall at eleven o'clock for an address by the Lord Mayor."

"Thank you." Jackson brushed past him and entered a world of wealth he'd only read about.

"Keep a sharp eye," he whispered to Miss Turner as he led her into the first room off the hall. It was a lounge of sorts, with pale blue walls and garish red draperies bleeding off the windows. Plump matrons fanned themselves on even plumper settees. Several white-haired gentlemen swapped tales and sipped from tumblers near the mantel. Jackson's gaze darted from man to man.

No Lord Mayor here.

And so they moved on, sifting through the pampered princesses and starched gents, hoping to spy the lord of the mansion. Though Jackson had never personally seen Sir Robert Fowler, he'd garnered a great description from Baggett. The Lord Mayor was known to wear his salt-and-pepper hair slicked back and parted dead center. A beard covered his face from ear to ear with a curled moustache connecting the whole affair. His nose was rather long, somewhat nozzle-like, and his eyes were of such a deep hue that looking in them was like looking into the depths of a well. The biggest tell of all would be a silver medallion on a gold velvet sash. And though they wandered from room to room, the man was nowhere to be seen.

Yet it seemed every man in the mansion saw Miss Turner. Worse, Jackson knew those looks. Like starving men shown a juicy slab of meat. He tucked his arm close to his side, pulling her against him as he led her into the ballroom. Though he needn't have bothered. The crush of bodies forced them shoulder to shoulder anyway. With several "pardon me"s and one "I'm so sorry," he worked their way over to the punch table, then poured Miss Turner and himself a much-needed drink.

She peered at him over the rim of her glass. "With your height,

I am afraid you have the advantage over me in this crowd. Any sign of our man?"

"I do not have a clear line of sight to the other end of the room. Too many dancers blocking my view, but I think I have a solution." He set down his glass, then reached for hers and put it away as well. "Can you waltz, Miss Tur—I mean, Miss Forge?"

His own surname left a bitter aftertaste on his tongue. And no wonder. It was a flat-out lie. Father would be so disappointed with his recent behaviour. Even he could hardly stomach the deceptions he'd embraced. But with less than twenty-four hours to discover the cabby's whereabouts, he had no choice.

May God forgive him.

Tiny creases scrunched Miss Turner's brow. "I may live in a blighted part of town, sir, but that does not mean I do not live at all. Of course I can dance. Though that hardly signifies."

"Ah, but it does." Snagging her hand, he pulled her onto the dance floor. "This is a much better vantage point. We shall simply scan the suits while I guide us around the room."

It was a clever idea, or would have been. After only a partial sweep of the ring of guests, the feel of the lithe Miss Turner moving in time with his body derailed that effort. All he could think of was the warmth of her palm pressed flat against his, skin to skin. The way the small of her back rode beneath his hand. How well she fit against him.

Leaning close, he inhaled her sweet scent, all lavender and intrigue. "Clearly you have had experience on the dance floor."

"I could say the same for you." She flashed a mischievous smile. "How many hearts have you broken, I wonder?"

"None that I am aware of. The only love I have pursued is law and order." He studied her face, from the silvery blue of her eyes to the enticing red of her lips. "But I suspect you have a different tale to tell. What sort of body count have you left in your wake?"

She flashed a smile. "Broken hearts are not my specialty."

Hah! He nearly choked. She'd left at least ten casualties en route from the hall to the ballroom. He whirled her around, aware of the envious eyes upon them even now. Were she a true socialite, the woman could have her pick of any of these men.

Drawing her close again, he studied her carefully. "Do not tell me you have never been in love."

Her laugh was a sweet harmony to the music. "In my line of business, I do not have time for such pleasantries."

The reminder resurrected an awful image of the woman in the hovel, the one Kit so tenderly cared for. No wonder she didn't have time for flirting. She was too busy putting herself at risk to save the downtrodden.

"Speaking of which"—he guided them around a portly couple who listed to one side—"do you ever think of changing professions to something a little less dangerous? Surely a woman like you has other options."

"A woman like what?" Blue sparks ignited in the depths of her eyes, a cagey sort of wariness swimming just beneath the surface. What on earth did she think he was going to say?

"Resourceful. Resilient. Smart." He paused, unsure if he should continue, but wholly unable to stop the next word from slipping out. "Beautiful."

A pretty shade of scarlet warmed her cheeks, the skin of her hand heating against his. Apparently the resolute Miss Turner did have a feminine soft spot after all.

And then just like that, the blush faded, replaced with a steely clench of her jaw. "Unfortunately, Mr. Forge, therein lies the problem."

"What do you mean?"

She tossed her head, the move sweeping the curls from her shoulders. "Men scorn a female who can outthink them, especially one who is comely."

Maybe some. But not him. Not with her, at any rate. "I do not," he admitted aloud.

She sucked in a breath and for a long moment said nothing, just moved two-three, turned-two-three. God alone knew what might be going through her head.

"Have you any idea what a rare specimen you are, Mr. Forge?" she whispered.

He chuckled. He'd been called many things in his day, but this was a new one. "Call me Jackson. After all, we are cousins, are we not?"

His own words instantly sobered him. What the deuce was he thinking? Trifling with a known thief when he should be hunting down a missing cabby?

"Very well, Jackson. I suppose it follows that you should call me Kit."

"Kit." He'd thought it often enough that it rolled easily from his lips. "It suits you, you know."

"How so?"

"Direct. To the point. Full of mystery." Swinging her around, he pulled her in close and murmured into her ear. "Yet we both know that is not your true name."

She turned her head, her lips a breath away from his. "Been checking into me, have you?"

"Not nearly as much as I would like to."

Her nostrils flared, followed by a slow smile. "Then I shall have to make sure to keep my guard up when I am around you, hmm?"

Indeed. So would he.

Once again he twirled her, and when he drew her back, the feel of her body next to his pushed him past the breaking point.

She peered up at him. "Any sign of the Lord Mayor yet?"

"No." He forced himself to look anywhere but at her luminous eyes—and caught a glimpse of a sateen dress coat on a familiar shape. Good. An excuse. A flimsy one, but better than giving in to the urge to kiss Kit Turner's full lips in front of God and country.

He stopped dancing and pulled away. "Excuse me."

Deserted. In the middle of a dance floor, no less. And for what? Kit's gaze followed the broad-shouldered shape of Jackson Forge as he closed in on a flash of gold. But it was no official sash on a Lord Mayor's chest.

It was a redheaded temptress draped in golden moire with a plunging neckline.

Kit stomped her foot, a churlish action but wholly satisfying. She'd nearly fallen for it. What woman wouldn't? The intimate way Jackson had stared into her eyes. The spicy scent of his aftershave. The flattery. All of no consequence, of course. This was nothing but a job for him. As it should be for her.

"What is this? A beautiful woman without a partner?"

Kit clenched her teeth at the sound of a man's voice at her back. If she had to spend her time fending off lecherous males all night, she'd never get around to finding the Lord Mayor—which was exactly why she'd asked Jackson to accompany her in the first place. Yet there he was, chatting it up with some tart in a golden gown and the hunch-backed fellow beside her.

"May I be so bold as to offer my services?" the man behind her continued.

Blowing out a sigh, she turned, but her ready rejection scattered like a startled flock of martins.

The man himself, Sir Robert Fowler, Lord Mayor of the City of London, stood in front of her, offering his hand. "I know this is rather an unconventional way to go about requesting a dance, but it is, after all, my party. And besides, my good wife over there"—he tipped his head towards a portly woman in periwinkle tabinet near the punch table—"noticed your predicament and urged me to come to your rescue. So what do you say, Miss. . . ?"

"Forge. Catherine Forge." The name surged an unexplainable tingle in her belly as she placed her fingers in the Lord Mayor's.

Ignoring it, she reached for his shoulder with her other hand and rested it lightly on the wide golden sash. He smelled of cigar smoke and lots and lots of money. "Yes, my Lord Mayor." She smiled up at him. "I should be delighted to dance with you."

"Brilliant." With a light touch to her back, he set them both into motion. "I could not help but notice how abruptly your partner left you. Tell me, Miss Forge, was the gentleman causing you trouble?"

Pah! Jackson Forge had been nothing but trouble. For one devilish moment, she was tempted to admit such, but that would get them no further to finding Joe or to getting her token back. She smiled up at the Lord Mayor. "Not at all, sir. Cousins are sometimes changeable at events such as this. So many people to meet, you know."

"Ahh, so you and your cousin are new to town?"

"You could say that." And he could, though it wasn't true, for her leastwise. But who was she to stop him from saying such things? Plus, it provided an opening she couldn't refuse.

"A funny thing happened the other day as I explored the City with my dear aunt." The lie came out easily enough, but it left a sour aftertaste. A new sensation, that.

After a twirl, she continued. "I hired a cab and instructed the jarvey to show us about our new City, but he refused to take us into a particularly rough-and-tumble part of town. Which, I must say, was quite noble. I had no idea London cabbies would turn down coin for the sake of chivalry." She peered at his face, searching for any small tic or twinge at her mention of a jarvey.

Nothing flashed in those dark eyes. No quirk of his lips or tightening of his jaw. "I suppose there are good men in every profession."

"Oh, and he was truly good. Remarkable enough that I took his name for future use should I have need. Being that you are the Lord Mayor, maybe you have heard of the helpful and honest Joe Card?"

"Though I like to pride myself on keeping my finger on the pulse of the City, I cannot say I am familiar with that man in particular. But if you think him so worthy, Miss Forge, then I should be happy to summon him for a commendation. I look forward to meeting him, and there is someone I should like you to meet, as well. Someone with as kind a heart as obviously beats within your own breast."

In two swirls, he led her off the dance floor and delivered her to the woman in the periwinkle gown.

"Darling, meet Miss Catherine Forge. Miss Forge, my lady love, Mrs. Sarah Fowler." He winked at his wife. "I daresay the two of you are kindred spirits."

Kit coughed down a snort. What could she possibly have in common with a cossetted lady used to having her whims met before she even voiced them?

Mrs. Fowler squinted at her, then beamed—which only made the situation even more ridiculous. Had the woman known a Blackfriars street brat stood before her, she'd surely have turned up her nose. Or more likely had Kit thrown to the curb.

"Happy to meet you, my dear." Leaning close, Mrs. Fowler cupped her mouth, lowering her voice for Kit alone. "We women must stick together, hmm?"

"Indeed." Kit nodded. "I am grateful for your quick thinking."

"Darling?" The Lord Mayor tucked his wife's hand in his arm and patted her fingers. "Miss Forge is new to town, and as such, I think she would do well to meet the Gaffertys. Is there a dinner party or something next week?"

Mrs. Fowler's lips pursed for a moment, then once again broke into a smile, her green eyes sparkling as if they were the best of friends already. "Yes, indeed. As usual, my husband is correct, Miss Forge. I shall see to it that you are sent an invitation for next Tuesday's dinner party at Sir William and Lady Olivia Gafferty's town house. You simply must come. I will not take no for an answer. What do you say?"

Kit bit the inside of her cheek. So much time spent in the constable's presence must surely be affecting her. Not only did no quick answer come to mind, but she was suddenly tired of misleading people.

So, how was she to answer the woman swathed in pearls and determination?

Chapter Fourteen

The second Jackson pulled away from Kit, his arms felt the loss. Troubling, the way she managed to breach his walls of common sense, for there was no sense in getting attached to the woman. She was a means to an end, and he'd do well to remember such. Admittedly, it'd been boorish of him to leave her so abruptly, but it was either that or embarrass them both. Moving his body in time to hers had been far too dangerous an occupation.

He quickened his stride and focused on the man who'd stood up for him that awful day he'd hauled in the banker. "Excuse me, Mr. Poxley? I have been meaning to thank you."

The hunchbacked fellow turned, as did the lady next to him. Little creases at the sides of Mr. Poxley's eyes deepened then vanished as recognition seeped in. "Ahh, yes. Mr. Forge, is it not?" His gaze swept over Jackson from head to toe and back again. "It appears the sergeant not only kept you on but has given you quite the advancement." His features crinkled merrily. "I wonder what sort of foul play you expect is afoot here tonight."

"Foul play?" The woman in the golden gown slapped her hand to her chest. "I should hope not. There has been far too much of that already."

Mr. Poxley patted her arm. "Nothing to worry about, I am sure. Miss Shaw, please meet Constable Forge. Mr. Forge, Miss Shaw."

Shaw? Why was the name so familiar? He'd never met her. Had he crossed paths with her family or—that was it! The missing merchant.

Was she somehow related?

"Pleased to meet you, Mr. Forge." She sketched a small curtsy.

"The pleasure is mine, Miss Shaw." He dipped a bow.

"If you do not mind, gentlemen, I shall leave you to your own designs." She spun, her golden gown swirling with the movement.

"So," Poxley said as soon as she was out of earshot, "who is the blackguard to be shackled and hauled in tonight?"

Jackson chuckled. "Nothing so dramatic. I am simply gathering information."

"Information, eh? What sort? As the Lord Mayor's secretary, I attend all the grand functions in town. It may be I have the knowledge you need."

Hmm. This could be a mine to explore, especially since the man had such a close relationship with the Lord Mayor. "Perhaps you do, sir. As you will recall, a certain jarvey went missing."

Mr. Poxley snagged a flute of champagne from a passing server. "Yes." He took a sip. "That distraught woman came into the station. Tell me, have you found the poor devil yet?"

"No. But I am wondering if there happened to be an event the night before, one in which an inebriated gentleman might have felt the need to summon a cab?"

"Hmm," he hummed, then snapped his fingers. "Indeed there was. The Thompsons hosted a ball. Quite the gala. Everyone who is anyone attended."

"So, you were there?"

"Of course." Once again Mr. Poxley tipped his glass. "In the stead of my employer."

The music, the chatter, all faded in a rush of excitement. If the Lord Mayor wasn't where he should have been, then where had he gone? Jackson shifted to adopt a more casual posture. "Sounds like quite the party. Might I ask why the Lord Mayor was not in attendance?"

Mr. Poxley swirled the liquid in his glass. "Suffered from a headache that night, if I recall correctly."

Huh! An excuse as old as his grandfather's whiskers. . .unless it was true. "Does the Lord Mayor usually endure such afflictions?"

"Yes. But do not let word on that get out." Mr. Poxley leaned close and lowered his voice. "We cannot have the public getting skittish about the old boy's health, especially after the recent death of the previous Lord Mayor. There are already too many rumours floating about that perhaps Lord Mayor Nottage did not expire of natural causes."

Jackson gave him a sharp nod. "The secret is safe with me."

A slow smile stretched the man's lips, and he cuffed him on the arm. "I knew you were a good man, Forge. The sergeant is lucky to have you on the force. Now, if you will excuse me?"

"By all means." Jackson bowed. "And once again, my gratitude for your kind words to my sergeant."

"Think nothing of it. Good evening." Mr. Poxley downed the rest of his drink and turned away, his thin legs an anomaly to the rounded hump on his back.

Jackson searched the ballroom for an emerald skirt, guilt punching him in the gut. It had been caddish of him to abandon Kit, especially for such a base and selfish reason. As his gaze drifted from gown to gown, he rifled through various apologies he might offer if he had ruffled her feathers, though a woman with her tough skin likely hadn't given his departure a second thought.

And then a flash of green caught his eye, drawing his full attention. A thick ribbon hugged Kit's hips, cinching a lace panel that wound upward over her tiny waist to a ruffle at the plunge of her bodice. He tugged at his collar. Blast! Did she have to be so deuced distracting?

Refocusing, Jackson wove through the crowd to where Kit chatted with the Lord Mayor himself. How had the little vixen managed such a coup?

Beside her, the lady next to the mayor invited Kit to a dinner party with the express purpose of meeting some well-connected dandy by the name of Gafferty. It wasn't much to work with, but even a little bait could catch a large mackerel.

He draped his arm across Kit's shoulder. "Cousin, we met the Gaffertys at the Thompsons' ball just two days ago, do you not remember?"

Alarming how easily the deception flowed out of his mouth. Is this what came of keeping questionable company?

Kit shot him a sideways glance, clearly confused, then dipped her head towards the couple. "Please excuse my cousin's coarse manners, Lord Mayor, Mrs. Fowler, and allow me to introduce Mr. Jackson Forge."

Jackson pulled away from her, feigning surprise. "Why, I had no idea I was in such esteemed company." He snapped a sharp bow. "It is my deepest pleasure and honor to meet you both. I beg you to accept my apology for such rude conduct."

"I suppose one must." The woman narrowed her eyes at him. "You should be more attentive to your cousin, sir. Leaving a lady on the dance floor is quite the cut direct, relative or not."

Fighting the urge to loosen his cravat just a smidge more, he inhaled deeply and chose one of the many excuses he'd prepared. "You are quite right, madam. It was uncouth, but I assure you it could not have been helped. The lady near Mr. Poxley looked ready to swoon. I could not allow her to hit the floor." He flashed a sheepish smile at Kit. "Forgive me, Cousin?"

Her arched brow accused him as a liar. "Of course."

A storm brewed in the Lord Mayor's already dark eyes. "Why did my secretary not come to the woman's rescue? What the devil was Poxley thinking?"

"He is innocent, I assure you. His back was towards the lady at the time. Turns out she was merely trying to fix her shoe, not ready to collapse as I suspected. We all had a good laugh over the faux pas."

"I should think so," the Lord Mayor said. "Mr. Poxley dearly loves to laugh."

"Well, despite the circumstances, I am delighted to make your acquaintance, Sir Robert. I own I had hoped to meet you at the Thompsons' ball."

"Yes, well." The man cleared his throat. "I had business elsewhere." He turned to his wife. "Care for some punch, my dear?"

She shook her head. "Any more and I fear I shall float away."

Kit's fingers fluttered to her chest. "My, but you are a hard worker, Lord Mayor. Such a champion of the people. What sort of business would keep you from attending a social event?"

A nervous laugh gurgled in the man's throat. "Nothing a lady should interest herself in. It was not in the most fashionable part of town, you see."

"Oh, you would be surprised, sir." Jackson drifted his hand to the small of Kit's back and nudged her forward a bit. "My dear cousin has quite the business-minded head on her shoulders. Uncle often put off making decisions until he had consulted with her."

Appreciation radiated from Mrs. Fowler's eyes. "That is wonderful. Why, I was just telling my husband the other day how he would do well to listen to the women of the city. The only true innovators are those who dare to look at things from a different perspective."

"Well said, Mrs. Fowler." Kit beamed.

The Lord Mayor frowned. "Be that as it may, Miss Forge, my business was personal and far too delicate for the gentler sex."

"Gentler sex!" Mrs. Fowler harrumphed. "Women are stronger than they appear."

"Oh?" Her husband tilted his head in her direction. "Perhaps I should have sent you down to Blackfriars that night?"

Jackson stiffened. Beside him, Kit's shoulders straightened as well. That put the man exactly where Joe had been the night he disappeared.

"Blackfriars?" Mrs. Fowler's face paled. With a flick of her wrist, she opened a delicate gold fan and gave it a wave, averting her gaze. "Oh, there is Mrs. Spackle. I have been meaning to talk to her. If you will excuse me?" Without waiting for an answer, she dipped a quick curtsy and melted into the crowd.

Watching her go, the Lord Mayor chuckled. "Do not get me wrong. I love my wife. But the truth is her dainty foot would not so much as take one step into that part of town."

Jackson speared him with a pointed look. "I am surprised you took such a risk yourself."

All the man's humour bled away. "One cannot shirk the duties of office."

And there it was. A contradiction. The perfect opening. Jackson flattened his lips to keep from smiling. "I thought you said it was personal business."

"Yes, well. . .the line between the two is often hard to distinguish." Sir Robert looked past them, as if no longer interested in their conversation. "If you will excuse me. I really should attend to my other guests. Enjoy the evening." He nodded a bow to Kit, then scurried off.

Kit turned to Jackson, a hint of triumph quirking her lips. "That puts our man in the neighborhood the night of Joe's disappearance."

"It does." He nodded. "But I cannot arrest him merely for being in the same vicinity as a missing person."

"We need proof he made contact with Joe."

"And how do you propose we do that?"

"I have an idea." Mischief flashed like quicksilver in her eyes, the same gleam he'd witnessed last night before she dove into the runoff gutter.

Sweet blessed heavens! How many scrapes with death would this escapade involve?

Men stockpiled secrets, storing them like a cache of golden coins in a dragon's lair. So surely the grand serpent of this great mansion had a hoard of treasure tucked away somewhere. Kit shimmied through the crowded ballroom, determined to find it.

Jackson followed close behind, hissing, "Where are you going?"

She ignored him. If he knew, he'd stop her before she took another step.

Strolling into the adjoining hall, she slipped a glance around the area. Guests laughed and mingled here as well, but it was not nearly as thick a crowd as they'd just left. She kept to the wall, skirting them all, then stopped near a fat red velvet cord hooked between two posts, sectioning off a darkened passageway. Clearly the space was out of bounds to partygoers. With a last glance to make sure no one looked her way, she released one end.

Consternation rippled across Jackson's face. "What are you doing?"

"You said you needed proof," she whispered. "Either come with me or cover for me. Your choice, but make it fast."

Huffing out a long breath, he advanced, then snatched the cord from her to hook it behind them as if no one had ever passed through.

Kit peered into the gloom. Four doors lined the hallway, and with this proximity to the mansion's entrance, she'd bet her left shoe that one of them was the Lord Mayor's study. She shot towards the first door, which gave way into a library. A banked fire glowed on the hearth. The memory of leftover cigar smoke lingered on the air. Definitely a haunt of the Lord Mayor's, then, but not the one she'd hoped for. She retreated just as Jackson caught up to her, his scowl threatening enough to make a back alley ratter run the other way.

"What are you thinking?" His tone was as dark as the shadows. "What if we are caught back here?"

She bobbed one shoulder, unmindful of his concern. They were only snooping around, not committing high treason. "We have just as much chance of not getting caught, especially if we keep moving. Come on."

She scampered to the next door, but the knob wouldn't give. Perfect. Whatever was behind this door must be important. Her fingers flew to her chignon, and she worked out a hairpin.

"Do not tell me you are about to pick that lock," Jackson growled. She flashed him a cheeky grin then jiggled the pin in the keyhole. "I cannot believe this!"

While Jackson continued to seethe behind her, she angled the pin one way and another until the tip of it snagged against metal. One quick jerk, the lock clicked, and they entered a room that made her throat burn. So many cigars had been smoked in here that the acrid remnants were now part of the wallpaper and carpet. This was it.

The dragon's lair.

As soon as Jackson shut the door behind them, she turned up the gaslights. At the center of the chamber stood a massive cherrywood desk. On one corner sat a rather ornate humidor. An even fancier pen and ink set adorned the other. And near it lay a lady's lorgnette, the pooled chain casting a glimmer of gold.

But none of that mattered. Kit's gaze swept over the piles of documents and handwritten notes lying about on scraps of paper. A rush of excitement upped her pulse, then as suddenly dropped flat. She'd never be able to read what any of those papers said. As much as she despised the forced partnership with Jackson Forge, for this part of the search, she was glad to have him along.

Jackson, however, reached for the knob. "You have crossed a line from illegal into immoral, Miss Turner. I will not invade the Lord Mayor's privacy in such a rabid manner, nor will I allow you to. We are leaving at once."

His indictment crawled under her skin. Without further clues, she'd never find the man who'd taken her in and sheltered her from the harshness of the streets all those years ago. No, she had to stay, find something. She owed Joe and Natty too much for their years of kindness. She lifted her chin. "This is our best chance to discover if the Lord Mayor was involved with Joe's disappearance, and you know it. Sometimes unconventional behaviour is called for. Leave, if you like, but I will not give up on finding my friend."

She started rummaging through papers, keeping a keen ear for

Jackson's decision. If he turned away, she didn't stand a chance of figuring out what these documents said. Had she given the man enough rope to hang her efforts or just the right amount to lure him to her aid? Pah! How she hated having to depend on anyone but herself.

A few grumblings traveled on the air, but soon he joined her side. Hardly two breaths after that, he lifted a newspaper clipping and waved it in front of her. "I cannot believe I am doing this."

She bit back a retort and retrieved a handwritten piece of parchment. The letters themselves meant nothing, but the arrangement of the words did. Two by two, top to bottom. A list of names. And one of them was circled.

"Hmm," Jackson grumbled. "This may be bigger than we thought."

She slipped her gaze to his. "What do you mean?"

"Here is quite the scathing letter to the editor about the missing MP, penned by our very own Lord Mayor and published the same day as the baronet went missing." He nodded towards the list in her hand. "What do you have?"

She gripped the paper all the tighter, shame a sickening rock in her stomach. Only once had she admitted aloud that she couldn't read—and she still bore the scar to prove it. She shoved the paper at Jackson, forcing him to grab it. "See for yourself."

His eyes widened. "Jolly good find!"

She clenched her jaw to keep from gaping. Clearly that circled name was important, and important always meant a man. But who was it? And how could she find out without revealing her flaw?

"Indeed," she murmured. "Perhaps we could question him tonight."

Jackson arched a suspicious brow as he handed back the paper.

Immediately she bit the inside of her cheek, then set the list down and reached for something else—anything else—to detract from what had clearly been a blunder. A folded bit of paper with a drawn grid instead of words stuck out of a book near the lorgnette. A map, perhaps? Now *that* she could read.

Maybe.

She slid out the paper, relief loosening the tension in her shoulders, and held it up for Jackson to see. "Here is your proof. A map of Blackfriars. And look where someone has drawn an arrow." She tapped the spot with her finger.

Jackson squinted. "The Grouse & Gristle." His gaze drifted to hers, his eyes flashing like blue flames. "Well done."

"Is that enough evidence for you? Can you not arrest the Lord Mayor and question him more thoroughly about Joe? Clearly he knows something—something he will not spill at a gala surrounded by constituents."

Jackson shook his head. "This is not enough to bring him in, but I will present what we have found to Sergeant Graybone, which should buy me more time."

"Joe does not have time! Even now he could be in the hands of torturers, or worse, already dead." She slammed down the map and strode to the door. "Stay here and collect all the evidence you like, but I am going to confront Sir Robert on what we have found."

"Are you daft? Stop and think, woman. Going off on a hotheaded whim like that is only going to raise suspicions and possibly get you—or me—tossed in a cell."

She froze. Of course he was right. Pinching the bridge of her nose, she dipped her head and inhaled a few deep breaths.

Oh Joe. . .how do I find you?

She stared at the carpet, stuck, until her gaze focused on a forgotten ticket stub fallen behind a dustbin. Bending, she retrieved the thing and studied it. The paper was permanently rippled from having been wet and dried one too many times. Machine-printed letters were engraved across the top, along with numbers.

"What is it?" Jackson's breath warmed the back of her neck.

She handed over the receipt, surprised to see he'd drawn so close without her hearing. "Not only does the Lord Mayor use the public cab service but apparently water taxis as well. Maybe you ought to check if any river runners have gone missing."

"Or maybe this river runner is our next lead. Look here." He pointed to a handwritten date in the corner, ink smeared but clear enough to read. "That is the same night the barrister went missing. I would say, *Cousin*, that if this particular river runner can give us a positive identification of the purchaser of this ticket, we just might have enough to confront the Lord Mayor."

A smile twitched on her lips, then fell away. Footsteps clicked outside the door. Right outside. Before she could glance around for a place to hide, the knob turned.

There was nothing for it, then.

She launched herself into Jackson's arms and kissed him full on the mouth.

Chapter Fifteen

Jackson froze, arms stiff around the woman whose lips landed on his. Of course he'd kissed before. His Great-Aunt Agatha. That stolen dare of a smacker from Sissy Hawkins when he was seven years old. And even just two months ago, he'd exchanged a goodbye peck on the cheek with the girl next door when he departed for London.

But those were all child's play compared to the lightning jolt sizzling him to the core from Kit Turner's kiss. As her mouth moved against his, a single, fiery word thudded louder with each throb of his heart.

More.

He had to have more.

And that's exactly why he'd left her on the dance floor.

Wrapping his fingers in her hair, he groaned from the softness of it and kissed her back, so thoroughly, so deeply her body melted into his. All heat and breath and skin against skin. Fire surged through his veins. Kit clung closer. The world erupted into a frenzy of sparks, dangerous and irresistible. After tasting this forbidden fruit, he'd never be the same. He'd never want to be the same.

"Oh my!"

Somewhere near the door, a woman's voice buzzed like an annoying horsefly. The urge to shoo it away rose then fell when a small moan keened in Kit's throat, enticing him, heightening every heady sensation. He slid his hand down her back and locked her body against his.

"Pardon me, but guests are not allowed in this part of the... Miss Forge? Mr. Forge? Can it be?"

He stiffened.

So did Kit.

Then she planted her hands on his chest and shoved him backwards. A slap rang out; his head jerked sideways. His cheek stung sharp and raw.

"Jackson!" His name was venom on Kit's tongue. "How dare you?"

He blinked, stunned. How dare *he*? She was the one who'd flung herself against him in the first place!

"Mr. Forge, I am aghast, sir." The Lord Mayor's wife swept into the room and gripped Kit by the shoulders. "Miss Forge, are you all right?"

Sucking in a shaky breath, Kit lifted the back of her hand to her lips.

The first stab of shame cut into Jackson's gut. He'd taken things too far. Crossed a line he had no business stepping over. A ruse was one thing, but that kiss had been quite another.

Tears sprouted from Kit's eyes, and with a sob, she pulled away from Mrs. Fowler and fled the room.

Jackson stared, unable to move, to think.

In two steps, the Lord Mayor's wife closed the distance between them and poked him in the shoulder with a perfectly manicured finger. "You are, without a doubt, the lowest sort of snake, sir. Taking advantage of a defenseless female in such a ruinous fashion."

Defenseless? Hah! Even now, somewhere inside that silk gown of hers, Kit likely hid a concealed blade.

And he stifled a smile because of it.

"I assure you, Mrs. Fowler, this is not what it seems." He circled his hand towards the door Kit had vanished through.

"Oh really? Because it *seems* as if you lured an innocent woman— your cousin, no less—to a lonely part of the house in order to have your way. The indecency of it. The nerve! I can only thank the heavens above that I arrived when I did to save that poor woman from losing her virtue." She stormed past him and swiped up the lorgnette from the desk, aiming it at him like a gun. "Remove yourself from this house immediately, you lecherous beast, or I shall have you forcibly ejected."

That wouldn't do, especially not with Mr. Poxley as a possible witness. Graybone would hear about it in no time.

"I shall leave at once, madam." He dipped her a bow as he tucked away the water taxi receipt, for there'd be no way to leave the thing behind with Mrs. Fowler's eyes on him. "You are very gracious, and you have my sincere apologies."

"Tell that to your cousin, though I doubt she will ever forgive you. I know I would not. Now, be gone." She waved him off, the gold chain on her magnifying glass swinging wildly.

Without another word, he strode from the room, a hot mix of irritation, contrition, and a vague desire that he didn't quite know what to do with.

Blast that Kit Turner!

He stormed along the passageway, and just before it opened into the hall, a green gown stepped out of the shadows. Laughter bubbled from Kit's mouth—the same mouth he'd kissed well and hard—without one sign of the wronged miss that she'd so artfully portrayed for Mrs. Fowler.

She'd duped him. Again. He ground his teeth. "There is nothing funny about this. You ruined my reputation with that woman and with the Lord Mayor as well."

She looped her arm through his. "Better your reputation than your career. How long do you think you would remain on the force if you were caught pillaging Sir Robert's office? The way I see it, you ought to thank me. It was my quick thinking that got us out of there in one piece."

"It is your quick thinking that just may be the death of me," he grumbled as he wove her through the milling guests, annoyed more than anything that he could still feel the impossible softness of her lips against his.

"Come now." She grinned up at him. "Surely a small woman such as myself could not manage to bring down a strapping man like you."

He glanced at her, his gaze irresistibly drifting to her mouth—and a tremor settled low in his belly. "You, Miss Turner, could single-handedly bring down a charging bull."

Her grin grew. "I shall take that as a compliment."

"Take it any way you like. I do not care."

He ought not. He should not. But as soon as the words left his mouth, he knew them for what they were. A deception. Because in a shadowy crevice of his heart, admiration for her was beginning to kindle as brightly as his physical attraction to her. If he let the thing go, it could turn into a full-fledged fire.

And that would never do.

Upping his pace, he steered them around a marble statue in the front hall, towards the door. "The fact remains, Miss Turner, that I would not have been in such a compromising situation had you not suggested it in the first place. You are a bad influence."

"Me?" She blinked, all innocence and purity. "At least I am not a *lecherous beast*. After all, it was my virtue that was in danger, was it not?" Her merry laughter blended with the night air as they stepped from the door.

He pulled from her touch, wishing to God he could stalk away—far away—for good. Put this whole awful evening behind him and go on with his search for Joe Card on his own. Forget the woman. Forget the kiss. But that would not happen. Kit Turner knew Blackfriars. She knew Joe. Worst of all, she knew how to goad him.

And he'd never forget that kiss.

He set off across the portico, calling over his shoulder, "Come along."

She scurried to catch up. "Where are we going?"

"Somewhere where *my* virtue will not be damaged," he muttered under his breath. Then louder, "The wharf. There is a certain river runner we might like to talk to."

In one smooth move, she sidestepped him, effectively blocking his way. "I will do this part alone. Give me the ticket."

"Are you insane?" He snorted. "The riverbanks are no place for a lady on her own."

"I am not your average lady."

"Well said, but there is no way I'm allowing you to go alone." He bypassed her.

And once again she thwarted his passage. "You have no idea what you are getting into. Now hand over that ticket." She shot out her palm.

Dust and rot! The little spitfire was more adamant than Graybone himself. Jackson folded his arms. "I will not."

"Joe is just one of many missing men. He cannot mean anything in particular to you." She stepped nearer, outstretched arm unwavering. "Tell me, Mr. Forge, why is it you are so insistent on finding him? Is your job on the line, perhaps?"

His throat closed. She couldn't be more right, but it was so much more than that. He pushed back her hand. "It is complicated."

"How so?"

Because failure isn't an option ever again. He ground his teeth, stopping the words from any chance of escape.

He bullied past her, legs stretching long enough that she'd be hard-pressed to keep up, let alone block his way again.

Spring evenings were meant for lovers, especially early May, which usually Kit scorned. And she should now too. Gentle breezes and whispered promises were naught but frivolity. Intangible silliness for empty-headed geese. Nothing more.

But though she tried—hard—she had yet to shake that glorious moment in the Lord Mayor's study when she'd felt the magic. Given in to Jackson's strong arms and fervent kiss. Even now, as she kept pace at his side, she couldn't deny the leftover warmth tingling on her lips. Sweet blessed heavens, what a mistake that had been.

One she'd *never* make again.

She tossed back her head, flipping the hair out of her eyes. Of course he hadn't meant anything by his display of passion. Neither had she. All the same, she rubbed her thumb over her mouth, indelibly marked by the memory. A first kiss was bound to have such an effect. Not that he or anyone else would believe it of her. Blackfriars women weren't generally known for their innocence, and she made it a point to keep her virtue hidden from everyone, most of all herself. For it was a constant reminder of the wild, raging loneliness that lived inside her heart.

"Are you all right?"

Jackson's low voice rumbled beside her, pulling her back into the moment. "Of course." She forced a smile, stopping near the Stagg Street passage to Wapping Wharf. "Though I am allowing you to tag along, I must insist you let me do the talking." She held out her hand. "So, give me the ticket stub."

His head reared back. "Why are you so adamant about that?"

"It is complicated." She flung back his own words that had rankled her so. "Besides, you do not speak the language."

"What do you mean?"

"Just trust me."

"Trust you?" His voice ratcheted so tight it cracked. "The woman who nearly got me shot by a smuggler, killed by a train, and tongue-lashed by the Lord Mayor's wife?"

"You are still standing, are you not? Oh, and I will take a coin too, if you please."

A growl grumbled in his throat. Ahh, but it was fun to tease this man.

As soon as he placed the requested items in her hand, she whirled and scurried down the passageway, towards the river. The closer she drew to the ferry dock, the stronger the odour of muck and rot. Low tide. Good. That could work in their favor. Should the runner happen to be across the river, it wouldn't take as long for him to return.

But her concern was needless. Ahead, a man stood next to a dock that was hardly more than a collection of boards and hemp sitting cockeyed on the water. His flat cap drooped to the side and only one trouser leg was tucked into his boots. The other hung slip-hemmed to his heel. On a nearby pole a lantern hung from a hook, the light splaying over his bushy beard and snake-eyed squint. All in all, he was a formidable sight.

Not one she couldn't deal with, however. Kit planted one hand on her hip and slipped into her street persona. "Chub night, eh?"

His suspicious gaze traveled the length of her evening gown. "What would a skirt such as you know 'bout that?"

"Don't let the gown fool ye, luv." She curved her lips into a slow smile, making a point. "Nicked goods change the outside, not the in."

He laughed. "Ye mean to tell me ye left some poor swells a flappin' in the wind with only what God gave 'em?"

"You din't hear that from me." She held out the farthing. "And you ne'er seen me or my man if anyone should ask ye, aye?"

Jackson slipped her a sideways glance, eyes narrowing. She looped her arm through his and pulled him close.

The runner shoved the coin into his pocket, then once again shot out his palm. "Two more like that and I'll not only tuck my tongue, I'll skim ye and yer man there for a cut rate."

She shook her head. "Not skimmin', just wonderin' about this." She offered the ticket stub.

The man held the thing up to his face, lips soundlessly moving as he read. "Three week ago?" He shoved the ticket back to her, a dangerous chuckle rasping in his throat. "Ye may be able to gull a deep pocket but not me. No double backin'."

"What, think we'd do ye a cross?" She mixed in just the right amount of indignation and innocence into her voice. "No, luv. I'm needin' to know were you the runner what skimmed that night? Sold that fare? Lifted some gent?"

He turned aside and spit, then swiped a filthy hand across the remains on his beard. "Nah, weren't me. I toss the day run. Scudder's yer man."

Drat! She nibbled her lip. How late of a night would this be, chasing down a runner who was like as not downing a bottle at some back-alley gin joint?

"Where is he?" she asked.

"Skipped out o' town till tomorrow night's shift. He'll be back for slinging the six o'clock. And none too soon. Too many carps out in the dark for my likin'." His black gaze drifted to Jackson. "Carps like you. What's yer yap?"

Jackson rubbed his knuckles along his jaw, clearly confused. If he said one word, he'd give them away.

So she leaned in close to the runner, nearly gagging from his stink of sweat and sludgy river water. "Don't worry 'bout him none." She hitched her thumb towards Jackson. "Lost his tongue nigh on a year ago now, o'er at the Blackeye."

As she'd hoped, the runner sucked in a breath, squinty eyes widening as he took in Jackson with a new respect. "And ye lived to tell the tale?" He blew out a low whistle. "Ye e're need a skim during the day, mate, I'm yer man. And no charge a'tall."

Jackson gave a curt nod, thankfully saying nothing. A small action, hardly worth noting, yet because of it, her admiration grew. Oh, he could be stubborn and maddening at times, yet when it really mattered, he had an annoyingly endearing way of working with her instead of against.

She cuffed the runner on the shoulder. "Thanks for the bait. High and dry to ye."

The runner tugged his forelock. "High and dry to ye as well."

Gathering her hem, she headed back to Stagg Street, but at the opening of the passageway, Jackson stopped her with a touch to the shoulder.

"What on earth was that?" He flailed a hand back towards the water taxi.

"A bust, mostly." She shrugged. "We will have to come back tomorrow night."

He blew out a disgusted sigh. "That was the only part I understood."

"As I said, the language of the street—or river—is like none other."

"You never stop surprising me, Miss Turner." The moon peeked out from a cloud then, painting a swath of silver on his shoulders and lighting wonder in his eyes. Then he blinked, once again the constable focused on business alone. "But being that this was a bust, as you put it, I suppose you are right. We have no choice except to return. Still, that does not mean we stay idle in the meantime. With your obvious gift of speech, how about you question the editor at the *Daily Telegraph* tomorrow, see if the Lord Mayor has a habit of writing scathing letters or if the one we saw was an anomaly."

"All right, but what about you? What will you be doing?"

"I think I shall pay a visit to Mr. Poxley, try to find out why the Lord Mayor might be in need of a barrister."

"Good plan." And it was. But was it enough?

She leaned against the brick wall and stared past Jackson to the dark flow of the river. What hellfire had Natty Card been going through these past days, missing her husband? Worse, what sort of torture was Joe suffering. . .if he was still alive? No. Better not to think it. He *had* to be alive.

"I wish we had more to go on," she breathed. "Joe is out there somewhere, and it is taking too long to find him."

"We will find him." Warm fingers gripped her chin, gentle yet firm, and guided her face around to meet Jackson's intensely blue gaze. "Do not give up hope."

A sweet sentiment, especially coming from a fledgling constable who didn't have a clue of the workings of the London streets, yet a sentiment that was entirely misdirected. She pulled his hand away. "I am frustrated, not despairing. Of course I shall find him, for I have determined that I will."

The moonlight traced a smile on his lips—lips she had no business looking at or wishing to taste once again.

"You are a wonder, Miss Turner." A husky edge roughened his voice. "And when this is all over? When Joe is found, what will you do?"

She tossed her head, flipping back a loose strand of hair. "I shall return to the streets as always, helping the families of Blackfriars."

"Even with the extra funds Bags Gleason so freely handed over, I fear your help is nothing more than a short-term fix. A bandage, if you will."

The truth of his words squeezed her chest, and she turned away, unwilling that he witness the wild grimace that would not be stopped. He didn't need to tell her that her efforts were too little, too transient. That she was insufficient for the task. She shook her head, hating the way her voice wobbled as it came out. "It is all I know how to do."

He drew so near behind her that the heat of him soaked through the thin fabric of her dress. "Then let me help you."

She stiffened. Surely she hadn't heard correctly.

But more words came, stunning her further.

"Kit, please. I know I can help."

"You?" She whirled to face him. "How?"

"What if I taught you to read?"

She fisted her hands, fingernails digging half moons into her palms. How the devil had he discovered she couldn't read? No one knew save for Miss Lila, but that was a lifetime ago. She sidestepped him in a huff. Her girlhood dream of escaping into a story world was too precious, too fragile to discuss with a fresh-faced constable who didn't know a thing about want or need. "What makes you think I cannot read?"

"Because you suggested we question Mr. Artemus Humphrey, the barrister who has been missing for three weeks."

Shame cut into her heart. She'd slipped up. Revealed a piece of her that never should've been uncovered. A sob strangled in her throat, and she coughed to disguise it.

"Look, Kit, I do not know where you come from or what your childhood was like, but I do know this. . .you are beyond intelligent. Let me teach you to read. In exchange, you can educate me in the ways of the streets. I could use that in my line of work."

The offer drew her like a moth to a lantern, a powerful sort of wooing—but one that could burn. She already had a fine collection of broken promises. Why heap one more atop the pile? Slowly, she shook her head.

Jackson stepped closer. "Do not let pride stand in your way to become the woman I know you can be."

That prickled. She folded her arms. "Pride has nothing to do with it."

"Then what?"

She scowled, unwilling to expose her vulnerability. She *did* want him to teach her to read, though she'd never admit it. But how to say yes without revealing the strong desire welling in her chest?

"Well," she drawled. "I suppose reading could be useful, for the children of Blackfriars, that is."

"Hey." With a gentle touch, he brushed his thumb along her cheek. "It is perfectly all right for you to want to learn for yourself. To speak up for your own needs and desires."

Tenderness blazed in his eyes, and the strength of it nearly buckled her knees. No one had ever given such permission to her before. As much as she wanted to believe his bold words, dare she trust them as truth? Was this some sort of trick?

She stared deep into his eyes, measuring. Weighing. He might make good on his word, teach her to read with no expectations for anything more. But after only a few weeks, he'd fade away. Or she would, for his own good. No. She should and could only depend upon herself.

Yet was that not what the families of Blackfriars were doing as well?

She clenched her jaw so hard it hurt. This was too much, *far* too much to think about on a moonlit night with a handsome man standing a breath away, compassion glimmering in his eyes. "I make no promises. Perhaps when this business with Joe is all over, I shall consider it."

His teeth flashed white in the night. "I think you are scared."

"Of what?"

Arching a brow, he took another step, toe to toe, breath to breath. "Me."

One inch. Just one. Rise up to her toes and she'd feel those lips against hers one more time, melt into the warmth of his arms pulling her close and—white-hot anger flashed through her at the thought. She stormed around him. "I'll meet you here, six o'clock tomorrow night."

"No, earlier. Four o'clock at Southwark Cathedral."

She stopped, curious, but not enough to turn around. "Whatever for?"

"You will have to show up to find out."

Flit! She stomped away. The last time she'd set foot in that hallowed building, she'd barely escaped a pair of shackles.

Chapter Sixteen

This time of morning, just after the daily briefing, the station buzzed like a kicked hive. Constables dashed to their beats, replacing those who trotted in from the night shift, eager to get to their beds. Even Clerk Beanstaple appeared to be busy, slowly shuffling one paper then another about on the front desk. Jackson had hoped to snag Sergeant Graybone before he left the squad room, but no good. Before Jackson made it to the podium, the sergeant had slipped out and entered the fray.

So now Jackson elbowed his way through the uniforms, trying to catch the elusive man before he disappeared into his office. "Sir, a word please—oof!"

Jackson bounced off the broad chest of a quick-stepping officer, colliding headlong with Charles Baggett. His friend staggered as well, a good-natured laugh rumbling in his throat.

"Well now, you are in quite a rush." Baggett straightened his collar, humour lightening his tone.

"Sorry." Jackson brushed away his own wrinkles. It wouldn't do to face Graybone in a rumpled uniform. "But you are right; I am in a bit of a hurry."

Baggett held up his hand. "Hold on for just one moment, would you? I have been hoping to run into you, well, not literally, but seems it worked out that way. At any rate, some of the boys and I frequent the Four Sisters at the end of each day. You know, chuck back a pint and swap a few war stories. How about you come along?"

Of all the days to invite him, it had to be this one? "I would like that, but not today. Another time, perhaps?"

Baggett shrugged. "Of course. Think of it as a standing invitation."

"Thanks, Baggett. I will be sure to stop by sometime."

"Right, then. Good day." Baggett sidestepped him, whistling a tune as he went.

With a deep inhale, Jackson set off towards the sergeant's office. Would that Graybone owned such a cheery countenance. After a quick rap on the sergeant's door, a sour voice leached through the wood.

"Enter."

Jackson stepped inside, careful to stiffen every muscle to attention. "Reporting on the Card case, sir."

Graybone's dark eyes devoured him and spat him back out in one glance. "Being the man is not with you, it does not appear you have much to report." He swiveled his big head, taking in the clock on the wall. "And your time is up in an hour. You may drop off your badge and uniform with Beanstaple. Dismissed."

"But sir—"

"I said dismissed, Mr. Forge." The words clipped the air like scissor snips.

And dropped the full weight of failure on Jackson's head. He wouldn't even be given the chance to persuade the sergeant. Now he would never find Joe. How would he face his father. . .James. . .Kit?

"Sometimes unconventional behaviour is called for."

Jackson clenched his jaw as Kit's words echoed in his memory. She was right. He'd not slogged through sewers and barely escaped death just to be kicked to the curb like an unwanted pup. Breaking all protocol, he stalked forward and planted his hands on the sergeant's desk. "Hear me out, sir. If you do not think the evidence I present is compelling, then I will turn in my goods to Beanstaple."

Graybone stabbed a sharp look at Jackson's hands. "What evidence?"

Jackson pulled away and straightened. "I believe I have not found Joe Card yet because he is tangled up with the same person who is behind the other missing men."

"Is that so?" Graybone leaned back in his chair, springs squeaking a dissent. "What could a lowly jarvey possibly have in common with a member of parliament, a barrister, and an upstanding merchant?"

"The Lord Mayor."

"The Lord Mayor!" Graybone bounded forward in his seat, one fist coming down hard on the mahogany. "Are you daft, man?"

Sweat popped out on Jackson's forehead, but to swipe it away now would show weakness. If he didn't appear confident, didn't sound assertive, he would lose this battle. Worse, he could lose his whole career. . .and his only chance to be the protector his ten-year-old self couldn't be.

God, a little help here, if You please.

He threw back his shoulders. "In each instance there is a clear and direct tie from the missing men to Sir Robert Fowler. He wrote a scathing letter to the editor of the *Daily Telegraph* upbraiding the missing MP, published on the very day the man disappeared."

Graybone cut his hand through the air. "Naught but politics."

"The Lord Mayor was also in the vicinity the night Joe Card went missing."

"In Blackfriars after dark? A man of his stature?" A storm cloud darkened the sergeant's face. "I find that hard to believe."

"There is also definite proof that the Lord Mayor took a keen interest in the missing barrister, singling him out from a list of others."

"And how would you know?" The sergeant cocked his head like a vulture before the first peck. "What is your source?"

More sweat sprang out, trickling between his shoulder blades. Thunderation! He couldn't very well tell the sergeant he'd been rummaging in Sir Robert's home office. But what could he say?

Think. Think!

He'd been trained to deal with cullies and cutthroats, but nowhere in the police manual had it said how to. . .wait a minute. Maybe that was something he could use.

He pulled the small book out of his breast pocket and waved it about for validation. "Page thirty-two of the manual states a good constable develops his own network of informants."

"And who are yours exactly?"

Must the sergeant lob grenades at everything he said? Gritting his teeth, he tucked the manual away. "I cannot reveal that information, sir. It is a matter of confidence."

"Confidence does not stand up in a court of law." Graybone blew out a long breath and rose. Clasping his hands behind his back, he paced the length of his desk. A great black panther on a hunt, but for whom? The Lord Mayor? Or him?

"Even if these things are true, Forge, you have nothing but mere conjecture without tangible evidence. If you're even so much as toying with the idea of going up against the most powerful figure in the City, you would have to find one of those missing men to witness against him."

"Yes, sir."

The sergeant skewered Jackson with a malignant stare. "What do you mean, 'yes, sir'?"

"I will find one, sir." He lifted his chin. "I am close. I know it. A bit more time is all I ask."

Graybone grunted, then sank into his chair. "Well, you are persistent, if nothing else. Like as not I shall regret this, but two more days, Forge. That is all. Bring in your man by then or you are finished."

The tightness in his jaw loosened. Thank God. And the sergeant.

"Thank you, sir," he voiced aloud. "I will make you proud."

Graybone shook his head. "I sincerely hope so."

Jackson swallowed hard. So did he.

Gunmetal clouds hung low, dripping a steady, irksome rain. The sort that seeped through seams and leaked into the very fabric of the soul. But it wasn't annoying enough to force Kit to shelter inside Southwark Cathedral. It would take more than a good soaking for such a drastic measure. And even then she'd choose the threat of lung fever over stepping foot into that church.

So she paced. Back and forth, from one column to another, then pivoted to do it all over again. Each time she passed the ornate front door, she flinched. Of all the places to meet, Jackson had to pick this one?

Tugging her collar tighter, she rounded the column for another lap, trying to forget that horrid day she'd nearly been arrested. And for what? The satisfaction of a fat reverend? She'd only been trying to help that lady with the stack of prayer books, not kipe one. It'd been by God's grace alone she'd slipped away from the reverend's grasp just as the police entered. Even now a shiver skittered down her spine at the near miss.

"You look like a caged tiger."

Jackson's voice rumbled at her back, and she turned.

He advanced, holding out his big black umbrella and sheltering them both. "A drowned one at that. Why did you not wait inside?"

She frowned up at him. "Why were you not on time?"

His blue eyes searched her face. A knowing gleam hinted he knew her question was a parry, but was he curious enough to ask about it? Let him. She was up for a good skirmish with the way her sodden petticoats irritated.

Rain pattered on the umbrella for a few moments before he finally answered. "I did a little digging on that missing barrister, visited his office. Turns out the Lord Mayor's secretary paid him a call on the very day he went missing."

"Hmm," she murmured. "Could be happenstance."

He smirked, his moustache riding high on one side of his mouth. "Do you really think so?"

"I suppose the coincidences are starting to pile up."

"They are. Hopefully this river runner, Scudder, or whatever he is called, will give us a definitive answer tonight and direct us to some hard evidence. In the meantime, we have a stop to make first. Shall we?" He crooked his arm.

She tensed. If they stepped past that cathedral door, would the same reverend be inside? Would he still remember her? And if he did, would Jackson be forced to haul her in?

His arm dropped. "What is wrong?"

"What makes you think something is?"

"Your tone. Your stiff posture. The way your nose scrunches as if you smell trouble."

She stamped her foot, tempted to grind her heel into his toes as she did so. "My nose does not scrunch!"

"And now your nostrils are flaring." Jackson laughed. "But I did not mean to offend, Miss Turner. Both traits are quite endearing, actually." His smile faded. "Yet that does not answer my question. So, what is it you fear right now?"

"If you must know"—she flapped her arms, not caring in the least that rain seeped into her sleeve from off the umbrella's edge—"there is a certain reverend inside who accused me of thievery—a theft I did not commit."

She jerked a loose piece of hair behind her ear, snagging her nail against the tender flesh. How many times must she defend herself? Speak up for her innocence when all she sought to do was help others? Fat lot of good it did her anyway. Completely unstoppable, a bitter grumble rose up. "Not that it would surprise me if neither you nor God would believe my word. Not against that of a reverend."

"Oh Kit. Anytime you speak truth to God, He hears *and* believes, for He sees the heart of any matter." Compassion thickened Jackson's voice. His arm draped around her shoulder and he gave a little squeeze before releasing her. "Measuring God by how people—even godly people—have mistreated you is not a good measuring stick. Man will always betray, forget, malign, misjudge, abandon—but God remains steady and dependable. Of course that requires you depend upon Him to begin with. Do you?"

He could have no idea how deeply his words sank into her heart, filling cracks, healing wounds. She peered up at him. "I am no heathen, Mr. Forge. I was taught scripture at a young age."

"Then you also know that perfect love casts out fear. Bidden or unbidden, God is with you always. And though I daresay it is a small consolation, I shall be with you the whole way as well. So, shall we?" Once again, he crooked his arm.

Though a remnant of trepidation still clung to her soul, she rested her fingers on Jackson's sleeve. Weakness was for cowards, and she'd vowed a long time ago to never—ever—appear vulnerable.

But he steered them away from the cathedral's front door and turned onto the street.

Mouth agape, she stared at him, trying not to notice how they stepped in unison, so close their shoulders touched. "Why did we meet at the cathedral if we were not to go in?"

"Because I knew you would not have met me at the place where I plan to take you."

"Intriguing. Should I be frightened?"

He peered down at her, one brow lifted. "I doubt there is anything I can do that would scare you, Miss Turner."

Oh, he couldn't be more wrong. The strange twist in her belly whenever she stood near him alarmed her in all sorts of ways.

"Look out!"

A shout turned them both, and a breath later, she was yanked aside and cradled in Jackson's arms. A runaway barrel fallen from a dray scudded past where she'd been strolling only a moment before. Without Jackson's quick thinking, she'd be facedown in the lane and likely sporting a turned ankle by now.

She peered up at him, focusing on the virility in his eyes instead of the full lips that only yesterday she'd tasted. "Quite the habit of yours, this sheltering me from danger."

"Perhaps the true habit is the way trouble seems to find you." The words were low, intimate, and far too correct. There was nothing but trouble to be found here in his arms.

Even so, she leaned into him. Blasted traitorous body! She had no business savouring the feel of him pressed against her.

"We, uh—" Her voice cracked, forcing her to try again. "We should go."

"Actually, we are here." He tipped his head towards the nearest door.

She followed his gaze, then immediately pulled away. As if meeting at a cathedral weren't bad enough, now he expected her to frequent a bookstore?

She popped her hands onto her hips. "I am not amused, sir."

"Yet you are amusing when your feathers are ruffled." He chuckled. "I did not mean this to be a cruel jest. I mean to make good on my offer to teach you to read. Come on." In two steps, he approached the door and held it open with one hand. "Unless, of course, your courage is flagging?"

The tilt of his head was an outright challenge, and she pressed her lips tight to keep from telling him to shove off. Such a retort would be a dead giveaway, for indeed, a skittish desire to turn tail and run quivered in her legs.

With an upturn of her nose, she sashayed past him, yet she didn't get far before the scent of ink and leather slapped her in the face. Instantly the scar by her eye began to ache. She flung out her hand against a stand in the window display for balance.

Jackson leaned his umbrella against the doorframe then strode past her, rubbing his hands together with zeal. "Just take a whiff of that. There is nothing quite like the smell of a bookstore, is there?"

When she didn't answer, he turned back, a bewildered tilt to his head. "Well, are you not coming? I thought we would pick something out together."

"Go right ahead. I, uh. . ." She chewed the inside of her cheek. What could she possibly say? That her feet wouldn't move? That the scar by her eye was a chain tethering her to the door and a past she'd rather forget? That his knack for dredging up memories she did not wish to face was impeccable?

Scrambling for a more plausible excuse, she snatched a small book off the window stand and waved it in the air. "Something has caught my eye here. I will be along shortly."

He brooded a moment more, then at last he conceded with a nod of his head and disappeared into the maze of shelving.

Kit sagged against the doorframe, absently rubbing her finger over the tooled leather book cover in her hand. As a child, just such a book had been chucked at her head, cutting the skin by her eye when she'd angered the young master of the house she'd served in. She never should have been in the library that day, but Miss Lila had been insistent, and one should never refuse the master's daughter. Perhaps if she'd not confided to the girl that she couldn't read, Miss Lila wouldn't have been so adamant.

"Excuse me, madam, but that is a first edition of Byron." A harsh voice and an even harsher face shoved into hers. With one quick swipe, the bookseller snatched the book from her hand. "I doubt a woman like you has the coin for such a purchase."

"A woman like what?" She jutted her jaw.

"Well, look at you." He fluttered his fingers in the air, indicating her gown. "A proper lady would not be dripping all over my floor."

Anger flared in her belly. Flit! But she was sick to death of propriety and all its inherent prejudice. She plucked the book from his grasp and aimed it like a gun. "You of all people should know not to judge a book by its binding."

Cradling the hardback to her chest, she whirled and was satisfied to hear the slap of her wet hem hitting his leg. She stalked off to find Jackson, which took a fair amount of twists and turns, for the building was crammed with bookshelves scattered harum-scarum.

"There you are." Jackson smiled at her approach and held up two books. "I am trying to decide. Which of these catches your fancy?"

She set the collector's item on the shelf and gathered Jackson's offering. One was a fat tome, rather pretentious, with bulging pages that were ragged at the edges. The other was smaller, only as thick as her pinky finger, with a pretty green broadcloth cover and gold ink letters. Though she'd accused the bookseller of such, she had no choice but to judge by binding alone.

"I like this one." She clutched the green book and shoved the ugly one onto the shelf.

Jackson held out his palm. "That one it is, then."

She handed over the book and followed him to the front desk, where the bookseller eyed her before facing Jackson. "Can I help you, sir?"

"Yes. I will take this one." He set the book down on the counter. "But I would like to leave it here and pick it up tomorrow, if that is not a problem?"

"No problem at all, sir. Name?"

"Forge. Jackson Forge."

The man scribbled down Jackson's name and tucked the paper inside the cover. Turning, he set the thing on a shelf behind him, then once again faced Jackson. "That will be one bob, unless your lady friend is adding to the total?" He shot a cancerous eye at Kit.

Of all the hog-dribble! Did he seriously think she'd buy anything from him after his insults? It took all her restraint not to bare her teeth as she spoke. "I do not intend to purchase anything here."

"There you have it, then." Jackson fished in his pocket and pulled out a coin.

And that's when the absurdity of the whole thing hit her. Kit widened her stance to keep from staggering. Why would a constable spend his own money to buy a book for her—a woman who had swindled him? She'd never met such a selfless man. She never even knew one existed.

"Thank you." Jackson nodded at the merchant. "I shall return in the morning."

"Very good, sir."

Jackson led her outside. The rain was more of a mist now, leaving a wet dog sort of smell in the air, and the cathedral bells were just finishing the strike of six.

"Well"—Jackson angled his head at her—"shall we go have a *chub* night with Scudder?"

She chuckled at his blunder, then laughed all the harder at the flash of little boy innocence rippling across his forehead.

"What?" He spread his hands. "That is exactly how you greeted the river runner last night."

"That is because it was a pleasant evening. *Chub* means fair weather. There is nothing remotely pleasant about this miserable rain. And so, you have learned your first bit of cant."

"Cant?" he repeated.

"Slang. Jargon." She shrugged. "Strect talk, as you put it. Needless to say, I will be doing the talking again tonight, hmm?"

She strode off, and hardly two steps later, he caught up to her, umbrella once again held stalwartly overhead, sheltering them both.

"Very well," he blew out. "But try to word things so I can at least understand a little of the conversation this time, would you? And I would prefer not to be a mute."

"Where is the fun in that?" She grinned.

Yet her smile quickly faded as her own words doubled back and hit her square in the belly. She *was* having fun, having entirely too good of a time with this man, time that would be better spent in helping the families of Blackfriars. Guilt suddenly tasted sour in her mouth, and she swallowed. The sooner this escapade was over, the better. Find Joe, say goodbye to Jackson, and go back to life as normal.

Still, deep down, in a crevice she'd rather not explore, a niggling feeling lingered that life might never be the same without tromping about town next to the handsome constable at her side.

Chapter Seventeen

Did life get any better than this? Walking in the rain with a beautiful woman at his side? On his way to garner a clue that could lead him to finding not only Joe Card but perhaps the other missing men? Jackson inhaled deeply, content with how things were working out. Gentle drops pattered against the umbrella as Kit nudged him to turn the corner. An innocuous enough gesture. One she'd made several times already as they worked their way to the riverbank. But this time, on this street, all his good humour seeped away into the gutter, replaced with a rising foreboding.

Why?

He scanned the road. Shops lined both sides, all tightly closed for the night. A single horse clopped down the cobbles, pulling a two-wheeled trap with a figure hunched against the rain. Down the block, a cluster of three men debated beneath an awning, the red glow of cigarillos bouncing like tiny balls in the shadows as they gestured. Jackson frowned. Why the sudden clenching of his gut? Nothing was out of the ordinary.

Five strides later, a crevice opened up between two buildings, a narrow bit of an alcove. One a young boy could dodge into and never be seen. His pulse soared, pounding loud and hard in his ears. He tugged Kit across the street at a breakneck pace.

She wrinkled her brow. "Something wrong with that side of the street?"

"No, just. . ." Cold sweat stuck his shirt to his skin, and though he tried, he couldn't prevent a tremor from shaking through him. "Are we nearly there?"

Grabbing his arm, she stopped, forcing him to stop as well. Her blue eyes were impossibly large as she searched his face, then suddenly they narrowed. "Ahh. . .you are having a cathedral moment as well, are you not?"

"A what?"

"A bad memory, like I had back at the church." She glanced over her shoulder at the narrow passage next to the butcher's. "Something happened there, am I right?"

"It does not matter. The past is the past. We should move on."

A fierce frown darkened her face. "The past is not the past if it presently causes you to cross the street."

Like the squeezing of a great bellows, all air fled his lungs. This time, she couldn't be more wrong. He deserved every bit of God's vengeance for his failure. Deserved the very fires of hell for his offense. He turned away.

She pulled him back. "I will not be so easily put off, sir."

His knuckles whitened on the umbrella handle. She had no idea what sort of monstrous box she was prying the lid from. "Unlike you, I am guilty of my crime. Let us leave it at that."

"I will not." She popped a fist on her hip. "Tell me what happened."

Scads! Kit Turner would not be refused, not with that tilt of her head. Had his tongue been removed, she'd require him to write his confession. . .in his own blood, no less.

"Fine," he spit out, frustrated beyond measure with the irksome woman. "When I was a lad, barely ten years old, Father brought me and my elder brother along on his annual business venture to London, because Mother had been ailing. My father tasked James with keeping an eye on me at the inn while he conducted meetings over several long days."

He turned his back to the street. Revisiting the horrid event in words was one thing. Visualizing it all over again, quite another.

Instead, he focused on Kit's silvery blue eyes. "But staring out the window is no occupation for a boy, so I suggested to James we go on a grand adventure, promising we would return by supper. Father would not be the wiser. Hah! Stupid words from a stupid boy. My brother never should have listened, but at only fourteen, he was as eager to explore as I."

And what a glorious afternoon it had been. Licking peppermint sticks bought with James's hard-earned pennies from working in Father's shop. Pressing their noses against the bakery's glass panes, picking out sweets they'd buy on their way back to the inn. Playing kick-a-rock down endless London streets, leaving a flock of squawking pedestrians in their wake. And all the while James's endless jesting, his laughter bright as an August sun. Two brothers prancing about like young bucks without a care in the world.

Until Jackson's world crashed facedown in a bloody heap, kicked to a pulp by thieves angered at his brother's lack of money.

"Jackson?"

He sucked in a breath, startled by the light touch on his sleeve.

"Then what?" Kit squeezed his arm.

"We got lost. The sun set, and. . ." Words fled. So did reason. All that remained was a raw, open wound that never did quit bleeding.

Keen intelligence flashed in Kit's gaze. "And so the two country boys were waylaid by street scum."

He shook his head. "No. I hid like a coward while two men beat my brother senseless—and he lives as such to this very day, with all the intellect of a potato."

"Oh Jackson." A little cry moaned in her throat. "Surely you know a young lad could not have stopped cutthroats bent on devilry."

"Maybe not. But I could have run for help. At the very least I could have called for it. But I did nothing. Nothing!" His voice rang harsh in the gathering dark, drawing the glances of the men beneath the awning. And he didn't care. Let them look! Let the entire world see what an inglorious fiend he was.

His head sank to his chest. "I failed him that night. I failed my brother."

"You were a child. You were not responsible for your brother's injuries." She stepped toe to toe, her face a breath away from his. Real. Soft. Anchoring him to the now instead of an ugly past. Tears glimmered in her eyes. "I am sorry for what happened, but cruel tragedies happen every day. Such is the world we live in. Yet it is often in tragedy where we find our life's purpose, and that purpose is to love God and man. I do so by bringing aid to the people of Blackfriars. You, well. . .you are living it out."

"How so?"

"You are keen to make safe the streets of London, protect people from harm, are you not?"

Slowly, he nodded, trying to grasp where she was going. "I am."

"And therein you have turned an ugly tragedy into a beautiful purpose. Next time you walk down that pavement"—she tipped her head across the street—"do not skip to the other side. Let the memory strengthen your resolve."

Despite the gravity of the topic, a grudging smile stretched his lips. "You know, Miss Turner, you own a surprising wealth of wisdom for one who rooks coins on a street corner all day."

"Not all day." She laughed. "Now and then I venture off at night to the riverbank. So, are you ready to question another ferryman?"

Inhaling, he glanced across to the alcove where all those years ago his life—and his brother's—changed course. She was right. He *would* make something good come of James's misfortune. And of Joe Card's.

He repositioned the umbrella over their heads. "What are we waiting for?"

Four blocks more and a few jig-jaggedy trails between some warehouses, and they finally reached the slime-covered stairs leading down to the Thames. A low line of fog hovered over the river, like a gathering of unmoored ghosts. With careful steps, Jackson guided Kit to the water taxi dock, but this time no unkempt runner waited by a boat. The place was empty. Nothing but black water lapped against pilings that jutted like grave markings.

Unwilling to test the strength of the rickety jetty, Jackson stopped shy of the stand. "Looks like we wait."

She pursed her lips. "There is no sense in both of us staying out here for who knows how long." She tipped her head back towards the city. "I can manage on my own. Go. I will find you and let you know what Scudder says."

"What? And miss all the fun?"

"Fun? Ahh, yes. I see your point." She swept her hand at the nonexistent horizon. "Who would want to miss out on this drizzling damp and cold grey, not to mention the stink of the river and the coming of night?"

"It is a step above sludging through drainage pipes."

A grudging smile worked its way across her lips, and she nudged her shoulder against his. "Truly. Go. I give you my word I will not run off and find old Joe on my own." She stepped away from him.

He followed, shoving the umbrella squarely over her head. She may be good with a knife, but that didn't mean he'd leave her untended on this deserted stretch of foreshore. "Joe Card had better appreciate your persistence on such a miserable night. Most folks I know would not go to the lengths you have to find a mere acquaintance."

Her blue eyes flashed up at him, sparking as if he'd hit a nerve. "Joe is more than that."

Hmm. So much passion for a man more than twice her age? "He is a bit old for you. Not to mention he has a wife."

She rolled her eyes. "Of all the mad conclusions. It is nothing of the sort."

"Then what is it?" Curious, he dared a step closer. "Come now, I have already shared with you one of my secrets. Will you not trust me with one of yours?"

"There is no secret. Joe and Natty took me in when I was in need, provided food and a roof, that is all."

"How did you come to be in such dire need in the first place?"

"You already know." Her lips flattened to a sharp-edged grimace. "You have my token."

"True, I know you were a foundling." He rubbed his jaw a moment, confused. At least her parents had cared enough to leave her at an institution instead of selling her on the black market. "But it is my understanding those children are given good care, taught a trade or put into service, not tossed out on their ear to fend for themselves."

The silvery flecks in her blue eyes turned to steel. "Oh, I was put into service, all right. But no matter how well one serves, how faithful one is, an orphan is never seen as anything but a thief. I was twelve when I was let go for no fault of my own."

"Another wrongful accusation?"

"Would it matter to you if I said yes?"

Her voice chilled him to the bone. "Of course it would. You matter. Everyone deserves justice."

"You are a singular man, Mr. Forge, for you honestly have no idea how rare that sentiment is, do you?" Her jaw hardened. "The fact of the matter is I have never and *will* never be seen as anything but a thief. You have called me so yourself."

He shook his head. "Look, Kit, I am sorry for what has happened in your past and in mine, but as you have already hinted at tonight, that does not need to define your future. Your station in life is not fixed any more than mine is. You do not have to play the part of a thief just because others assume you to be one. Things can change. *You* can change. God can make all things new."

She stepped so close the heat of her anger radiated past the dampness of his coat. "If God were going to change my situation, then why has He not done so?"

A hurt little girl stared out of her eyes, desperate for an answer. So that was it. The ugly core of what ate at her. Contrary to all her bluster, Kit Turner truly was a damsel in distress—but not one he could save. Not from this.

On impulse, he cupped her cheek with his palm. "I cannot fathom why God has not changed things for you, but I do know this. His work is not yet finished, and, though I struggle with it myself, I am learning that His timing is impeccable. Mine is not, and I would venture to guess neither is yours. Perhaps the real question is, will you trust Him despite your circumstances? Will you depend on Him rather than yourself? For in the end, everyone else will fail you—including yourself."

Her lower lip quivered, hardly a ripple, but for the streetwise Miss Turner, the movement was monumental. She whipped away from him and tromped closer to the water, hugging her arms tight about her. Back rigid. A solitary pillar standing against the world. Against God.

And the forlorn sight cut straight to his heart.

In three quick strides, he closed the distance and reached for her shoulder. "Kit."

She flinched away. "The boat is here. We have work to do."

In the distance, lantern light emerged out of the fog. The splash of oars cutting through the water blended with Kit's footsteps towards the dock. Jackson watched her go, unnerved by the rare glimpse he'd had of the real Kit Turner. He lifted up a prayer as he followed.

Grace, Lord. Grant Kit Turner the grace to know You are in control.

Infuriating man! Kit stopped where the dock met the water and planted her feet, shoulders stiff against the footsteps grinding into the foreshore behind her. Why, oh why, had she said so much? Given Jackson Forge a peek into her true thoughts. Exposed the underbelly of her doubts and fears. She'd done stupid things before, but none quite so reckless as this. Worse, she never should have listened with open ears when he planted those stunningly awful questions that would surely haunt her in the blackest hours of the night.

"Will you trust Him despite your circumstances?"

"Will you depend on Him rather than yourself?"

She ground her teeth, not wanting to know the answers, for to do so meant she'd be forced to give up control. And that was something she simply couldn't do, for she had no one else to depend upon. Her parents had deserted her. Miss Lila had refused to defend her. Even the Cards, though they'd tried, had not filled her craving for love. *"In the end, everyone else will fail you—including yourself."* No. If she didn't survive by her own wits, she'd die. Plain and simple.

Thankfully, Jackson waited silently behind her as the few passengers from the water taxi scooted past them into the thickening fog. If he said one more thing, asked her any more personal questions, she'd swing around and pop him a good one on the jaw.

When the boat was empty, she stepped onto the warped boards of the dock and faced the great toad humped at the back of the boat. A single, unnatural growth bulbed out at the side of the river runner's nose, purplish and pitted. A great gash of a mouth cut across the bottom half of his face, and who knew if he had eyes, his cap sagged so low. No wonder he worked the night shift. With a visage like that, he'd scare off customers by the light of day.

She stared him down with a tilt to her head. "You Scudder?"

"Who's askin'?" he croaked.

"I am."

He lifted the front of his cap, and instantly she understood why he wore it so low. His eyes bulged even more than the warty growth on his nose. "A farthing fer a skippin' and another fer a gob-waggin'." He shoved out his hand.

This was the man, all right. She'd bet on it. She arched a brow at Jackson.

Without a word, he retrieved the coins. He paid the runner, then offered her a hand into the boat. He followed after she settled, bumping up against her as he sat at her side.

"Pardon." He flashed her a smile. "Don't have my sea legs yet, apparently."

Scudder's face darkened, and her breath caught in her throat.

Jackson sounded like a green-bowed gentleman, which would not grease the jaws of a jaded runner. She'd have to do some silvery talking to put the man at ease.

She faced Scudder with a wink. "Just need a piece o' bait, luv. A few, actually. And this fish here is willing to sweeten yer pocket for it." She hitched her thumb at Jackson then pulled out the ticket stub, handing it over to the runner before he could push off from the dock.

Scudder studied the thing, sniffing as he did so, the growth on his nose bobbing along for a ride. Then he shoved the stub back to her and grabbed the oars, putting them into motion. His big eyes drifted from her to Jackson, then back again.

"Ahh," he said at length. "I get yer what-for now." He cocked his head at Jackson. "Like to play with rough skirts, aye?"

"Sorry?" Jackson cut her a sideways glance, clearly confused.

Scudder laughed. "Why, yer nothing but a—"

"The stub, luv," Kit cut in. Jackson may not know street cant, but there'd be no mistaking what Scudder thought of him or her despite the language. "Did you take a swell fer a skippin' three weeks ago? One with a long nozzle, scrub of a face bush, and willing to pay to still yer tongue?"

"Aye, but his pockets din't open wide enough to keep me shut for good. Maybe they weren't as deep as yer man's there." He tipped his head at Jackson. "Bet ye pays quite a slice for a fine piece like that." His big head swiveled towards her. "Say, what do ye charge, anyhow? Got me a few bits I could part with."

Jackson's hands curled into fists on his thighs. "Now see here, you have been paid for information, not for insulting the lady."

"Lady?" A great guffaw rolled past the man's big lips. "More like a ladybird. With a gob like that, she's a rum doxy fer sure, and that's the truth of it."

Jackson half rose off the seat, rocking the boat.

Kit snagged his arm and spoke under her breath. "Leave it be." Then louder for Scudder, "This ain't about me, luv. It's about this." She waved the ticket in the air.

Letting the oars go slack, he leaned close, bringing the stink of brine and old cheese along with him. "It could be about ye. Once yer gent there is finished, come back round and see ol' Scudder. I'll give ye the romp o' yer life."

"Enough!" Jackson rose, swinging back his fist.

Kit groaned and clutched the side of the wobbling boat. If these two fools sparred like roosters, the skiff could very easily capsize.

And she couldn't swim.

"Stop!" She grabbed Jackson's leg, hoping to guide him down to the seat. "Please, just sit."

But the muscles beneath her touch coiled all the harder. "I will not stand for such crude innuendo against this woman. You will apologize at once, man!"

Scudder ripped out a belly-busting laugh. "A fish like you telling me what to do, and on my own tub no less?" His laughter drained, leaving behind nothing but water sluicing eerie against the hull.

"I'll not have it." Scudder grabbed an oar.

Then swung.

Jackson ducked and swerved, tipping the boat to a dangerous angle.

Kit scrambled for a hold, fingers slipping on wet wood. Slivers dug under her nails. But no good. She flew overboard. Cold shocked her. Water filled her eyes, her nose, her mouth. She flailed. Kicked. Wriggled. Yet none of that stopped the blackness from closing over her head.

And she was sucked down to a murky grave.

Chapter Eighteen

"Kit!" Jackson roared, the sound freakishly muffled by the fog. He shoved his arm over the gunwale, ready to snag her as she bobbed back up.

But not even a bubble of air surfaced.

God, no!

"Now see what ye've done!" Scudder belched out a curse. "That were yer fault, ye hotheaded skivvy."

Ignoring the man, Jackson peeled off his coat and dove into the water. An icy chill penetrated to the bone. Inky darkness swallowed the pale light from the boat's lantern. Jackson cut strong strokes with the current. Scudder was right. This was his fault. Just like the day his brother had been beaten to within a hair of his life.

God, please. Not again. Let me find her. Let me help.

Two strokes later, his hand met flesh. Cold as the water. Stiff as a corpse. His heart seized. Had her lungs already filled?

Bypassing her fingers, he grabbed hold of her arm and pulled upward. The faster he got her to the shore, the more chance he could pump the water from her chest.

She didn't budge. Not one bit. Were her feet stuck? The hem of her gown caught? Willing every bit of strength he owned into his muscles, he yanked with all his might.

Her arm didn't give. Her body didn't move. His own lungs burned with need. He'd have to dive deeper and untangle her from whatever tethered her in place, but he just didn't have the air.

Yet.

Though it killed him to do so, he released her and kicked like a madman, shooting upward. One gulp of air. Just one. Then he'd dive back down and rip the very gown from her if that's what it took to free her.

Hold on, Kit. Hold on!

The second his head broke the surface, he inhaled until his ribs ached—then jerked his head towards the sound of wild thrashing. A body length away, a brown-haired head popped up, spitting and gurgling before sinking once again.

Kit?

Then whose arm had he been tugging on?

No time. No choice.

Jackson dove after Kit, praying to God to catch her before the current yanked her in a different direction. Silky hair brushed against his fingertips, and he forced his way deeper. With a crazed swipe, he caught her just beneath the armpit, stopping her descent, then kicked until his thighs cramped, lifting them both.

What seemed a black eternity later, he finally emerged into the grey world of fog and life, gasping for breath. The woman in his grasp didn't. Kit floated deathly still.

"Help!" He squinted into the gloom for any sign of Scudder's boat, straining with his whole body to listen.

The faint glow of the lantern drifted farther and farther away.

"Scudder!"

The muted slap of oars against water was the man's only reply.

Blast! Just like that awful day years ago, there was no one to help him. It was up to him alone. Yet this time, even if it meant the loss of his own life, he would *not* fail.

Readjusting his hold, Jackson looped his arms beneath both of Kit's armpits and pulled her back against his chest. Then he poured everything he had into kicking against the current. Mouthfuls of filthy water choked him. The strain of keeping Kit's head above the surface sapped his strength. But stroke by stroke, breath by laboured breath, they advanced, until finally his feet hit bottom.

He rose on shaky legs, heaving Kit up along with him. Half the water of the Thames must've soaked into her gown, so heavy was she. Grunting, he staggered the rest of the way to shore, spent. But not finished.

He laid her down, then dropped to his knees beside her. "Kit!"

She didn't move. Not even an eyelash flutter.

Gut twisting, he shoved his ear to her nose. No breath warmed his cheek. Had her lungs filled with water?

God, no!

Jerking back, he planted his hands on her chest then pressed. Sharp. Strong. Praying to God he'd be able to push out the water.

Nothing happened.

"Come on. Come on!" He pushed again, harder this time. He'd give anything to hear her upbraid him. Scold him. Tell him to shove off and be hanged.

Yet no water came out. Her lips didn't so much as twitch.

"Do not do this. Do not die! Kit, please." His voice howled ragged into the mist. He couldn't lose her without losing part of himself.

One more time he pressed. Surely this would do it. *God, let this do it!*

Nothing changed.

He sank back on his haunches, hands falling useless to his sides. He'd failed. All over again. Just like that horrid day when his brother was crippled for life. Only this was worse.

This time someone was dead.

"Do not do this."

A warning? Some sort of plea? Sweet heavens. Was she in trouble again? The screaming agony in her chest said so.

"Do not die!"

Someone was dying? Her heart broke, not for the poor soul who was about to expire, but for the wrenching anguish weighing heavy in the words. Whoever spoke was clearly tormented by the thought of losing someone dear.

"Kit, please."

Wait.

What?

She was dying?

Everything exploded then. Pain. Light. Sound and water. She convulsed, body arching. Streams gushed up her throat and spewed out her mouth. Strong arms wrapped around her, flipping her over, holding, supporting, while half the Thames ejected past her lips. She coughed and choked and gurgled until nothing more came.

Then heaved some more. Stomach in knots. Everything burning.

Finally, the awful retching stopped. A blessed nothingness descended. Her body turned to jelly, and she collapsed.

"Kit!"

Her name swirled around somewhere overhead. Ethereal. Just a vibrato of a note that shouldn't still be heard so long after the musician walked off stage.

More notes followed. "No. I will not lose you. Not after all this."

Like a rag doll, she was yanked up to her feet. A stinging slap jerked her face aside, and the world came into focus. Or more like a pair of electric blue eyes did. *Jackson* struck her?

A burst of anger surged, and she pushed away from him. "What are you doing?"

He flung out his hands. "Trying to save your life!"

"I. . ." Whatever words had intended to come out packed up their bags and left. All that remained was the fire in her chest and the cramp in her belly as she glanced into the darkness gathering over the river. Then it all came rushing back, and she staggered. "The boat. The water. I told you to sit down."

"And I should have listened." His strong hands grabbed her by the shoulders, shoring her up. "Are you all right?"

Her fingers fluttered to her throat, pressing against the ache. "I have a sharp pain in my ribs and it hurts like a firebrand to breathe, but I have seen worse."

Dropping her hand, she looked at Jackson. *Really* looked. From his drooping wet curls, to the rivulets dripping along the curve of his face, down to the soaked shirtsleeves and trousers plastered against his muscles. And all because he'd risked his life to jump in after her and pull her out.

Her. A nobody. Him, a constable.

Slowly, she shook her head, trying to make sense of it all. "You saved me?"

"I did. But. . ." He rubbed his hands along her arms, brow folding. "There is still a body out there."

Her jaw dropped. "You killed Scudder?"

"No. I think I just may have found my hard evidence the sergeant wanted. We will speak of it later, though. For now, I must get you home. I will not have you taking a chill." He wrapped his arm around her shoulder and led her into the oncoming night, away from the lap of water. Away from what could've been her grave.

She peered up at him as they turned onto a cobbled lane. "Do you think that it is. . .Joe? Back there, under the water?"

"Hard to say." He steered her around a rain barrel blocking part of the pavement. "But with Scudder confirming he gave some gent a ride and admitting the man paid him to stay quiet, whoever it is— or was—under that water could be tied up in some sort of political intrigue."

Sorrow tasted as acrid as the leftover bile at the back of her mouth, and for a long while, she said nothing. *Oh Joe.* What a horrid way for the old fellow to have gone. . .if it was him.

"As much as I do not want it to be Joe," she murmured at last, "at least I would know what happened to him." A tremor rippled through her.

Jackson pulled her closer. "Sorry, being I am as wet as you, I am not much warmth. I would give you my coat if I still had it."

"No need." She'd take his arm about her any day over a bit of cloth and button.

The closer they drew to her home, the more hesitation lagged her steps. Revealing where she lived was an exposure she'd not even allowed to little Frankie. She peered up at Jackson, and her inner debate heaved a final breath as a stunning realization hit her broadside. She trusted him.

Wonder of wonders! She actually trusted this strong-armed, handsome-faced constable.

She bit back a smile. "Turn left at the next corner."

He cut her a sideways glance. "I thought you lived above the Grouse & Gristle."

"That hovel?" She'd snort if it wouldn't hurt. "No. It is a convenient place to meet with the crew, but the stink of ale would drive me mad."

He chuckled. "You never stop surprising me."

Several blocks later, she stopped in front of a narrow brick building squeezed into a row of identical flats. Only the painted placard above the door differentiated it. "I live here." She tipped her head towards the door.

"Mistress Mayhew's Boarding and School of Deportment," Jackson read aloud, then faced her with a scrunched brow.

Too spent to smile in full, she curved her lips halfheartedly. "Where do you think I learned to waltz or speak properly?"

"Does the matron of the house know of, em, your career choices?"

"Of course not. She thinks I work at a milliner's over on State Street."

He shook his head. "Though I have said it before, it still bears repeating. You are a wonder, Miss Turner."

"Back to such formality, are we?"

"Well"—he hitched his thumb at the building—"we are standing in front of a deportment school."

She laughed—then immediately regretted it. Grabbing her belly, she pressed her arm tight against a cramp.

All mirth fled from Jackson's face. "Are you going to be all right? And I will have the truth of it, if you please. No more deception."

She licked her lips, surprisingly warmed by the idea of no lies, no pretext whatsoever between them. "Like I said, I am a little sore. And it still burns to breathe. But a good night's sleep ought to do me right." She peeked up at him. "I, uh, I suppose I should thank you, for what you did back there."

"No need. Part of the job." He flashed a smile. "But I am thinking I ought to add swimming lessons to your reading instruction."

Maybe it was the humour. Or perhaps the way he looked at her as if she were special, cherished, not an annoyance to be gotten rid of like yesterday's trash. Still, it could just be the leftover foggy haze of having swallowed so much of the river. Whatever the reason, she leaned close to him, relishing the way his nearness wrapped around her like a warm embrace even without touching.

"You know, I could get used to you, Jackson Forge. You are not so bad."

He chuckled. "Quite the ringing endorsement of my character."

"Considering you are a constable, I would say so."

He stepped closer, toe to toe, his blue eyes searching hers so thoroughly she shivered.

"You are not so bad yourself." He buffed his thumb across her chin. "Go on. Get some sleep. We have a busy day tomorrow, uncovering that body. Good night, Kit."

She swallowed, throat raw, unsure if she could even form a word.

"Good night," she rasped. Pivoting, she headed towards the back entrance, aware of Jackson's gaze following her until she cleared the building, but even more aware of a sinister foreboding adding to the pain in her chest.

As much as she wanted to find Joe, she did *not* want to find him at the bottom of the Thames.

Chapter Nineteen

The midafternoon sun was an abomination. Such brilliance ought not shine so merrily on the three men bobbing in the river near the police boat. One by one they alternated dives into the black water, working to free the corpse. Shading his eyes, Jackson watched from the mucky shore. This was no simple recovery. But they were getting close. They *had* to be getting close. He'd been standing here since morning.

Stifling in his woolen officer's coat, he loosened his collar. Hardly mid-May and already summer knocked at the door. How different from last night, when Kit had shivered in his arms and his own soul had been chilled by the thought of losing her. He frowned. Of course such a feeling was strictly business. He'd have been as unsettled at the thought of losing any coworker. . .wouldn't he?

He shifted his gaze to the horizon. At least three, maybe four hours of light left. It had been just after daybreak when he'd stopped by Miss Mayhew's boardinghouse and been told Kit was still abed. To be expected, naturally, since suffering a near-drowning experience, but after this long, she should've been here.

"Thought they'd be done by now."

The grumbly voice announced Sergeant Graybone, tromping down to the river's edge. Jackson snapped to attention. "The men ran into a snag, sir. Literally. Whoever put that body in the river wanted to make sure it would stay there. They have been having a dickens of a time cutting through the chain."

Graybone grunted. "Why do they not just hitch up some horses and drag the body out?"

"Apparently there is a fair amount of Portland cement involved as well."

"Is there, now?" The sergeant scratched his jaw, nails bristling against his whiskers. "Quite a bit of trouble for a mere jarvey. Seems to me you are putting an awful lot of stock into this find. If that corpse is not your missing cabby, then you have only twenty-four hours remaining to uncover him."

Graybone was right, of course. If that body turned out to be anyone other than Joe Card, he'd have thrown away nearly an entire day of searching. Jackson exhaled, long and low. "I know that, sir, but perhaps you could see fit to give me a bit more time if need be."

The sergeant scrubbed his meaty hand over his face, ending by a smoothing of his beard. "Look, Forge. I have been more than generous with you. I realize my ways may seem harsh and unyielding, but I have lost too many good men to risk losing more. It is my experience that if a new recruit cannot prove himself capable within the first fortnight of service, he will eventually become a liability to himself and the squad. I do not expect you to understand this, just to accept it."

Slowly, Jackson nodded. "I do understand, sir. And I appreciate your leniency with me."

"There is nothing lenient about it. These are desperate times, what with the rumours about the previous Lord Mayor's demise and the rash of notable missing persons." With one big swipe, he cuffed Jackson on the back. "I hope you can pull this off, Forge. I really do."

"Thank you, sir. I—"

"Heave!" A shout from the river drew both of their gazes. The boat canted as a grey body thwunked over the gunwale. This was it, but what, exactly? A moment of glory?

Or defeat?

Jackson's pulse banged hard in his chest as the boat made for shore and the dead man was unloaded. The body landed with a sickening thud facedown onto the mucky bank. A shock of rust-coloured hair spread like seaweed over the head, far too much to be naught but "a fluff o' hair about his ears" and "bald on top," as Joe Card's wife had said.

Swallowing down a rising sense of failure, Jackson dipped his head at the recovery team. "Turn him over, lads."

Two of the men flipped the body while the other two set about hauling the boat the rest of the way onto the foreshore. Jackson crouched near the corpse's head, trying hard to ignore the grey flesh and the churning in his gut. He couldn't afford to show weakness now, not in front of the sergeant. Sucking in a breath, he shoved his fingers into the bloated lips and spread them open, only to see a full set of teeth. Not one missing. Not Joe Card.

Blast!

He sank back to his haunches, purposely averting his gaze from Sergeant Graybone's. Another failure. With no further leads to find Joe. He might as well turn in his uniform now. He pinched his nose. No, he still had twenty-four hours. More than enough time for God to provide a miracle. . .if only He would do so.

"Hmm, what have we here?" Opposite him, the sergeant lifted the man's hand, tugging at a golden band on the pinky finger. It didn't budge, so Graybone leaned closer, examining the thing and murmuring as he did so. "Whoever dumped this fellow was in a slip-slap hurry, not taking the time to remove what could have easily brought a coin or two. Even on the battlefield the bodies are picked over."

At length, the sergeant let go of the hand and stood to full height. "Well done, Forge."

Well done? "Sir?"

A hint of a smile ruffled the sergeant's black moustache. "See for yourself." He tipped his head towards the corpse's hand.

Steeling himself for the touch of cold flesh, Jackson grabbed the fingers and eyed the gold band. The sergeant was right. Skaggs would've paid a tidy sum for such a fine signet ring. A tiny engraving of the scales of justice decorated the center, but more interesting were the ornate letters before and after it. "A.H.," Jackson whispered as he rubbed his thumb over the metal.

And then it hit him.

Artemus Humphrey.

He dropped the hand and shot to his feet. "This is the missing barrister, sir! This is the hard evidence you asked for."

Graybone rubbed the back of his neck, staring hard at the corpse. "Apparently so."

"We must bring the Lord Mayor in for questioning at once, sir. He is the key to unlock the whereabouts of Joe Card, and I still have the time to do it." He tipped his hat at the sergeant as he strode past him. He knew God would not let him fail!

"Hold up there, Forge." Graybone snagged his shoulder, turning him back around. "I will not have you firing into Mansion House like a misaimed musket. A person of the Lord Mayor's status must be treated with the utmost care. I will bring the man in myself."

Anger flashed through him, from gut to gill. This was not to be borne. This was *his* investigation. "But sir, I—"

"But what, Constable?" The words boomed like a cannon. Beneath the black scruff on Graybone's face, a lethal red spread up his neck to his ears.

Jackson widened his stance, unwilling to bend but knowing he must. If he didn't give in, he'd be sacked and might never know what had happened to poor ol' Joe. Finally, he tipped his head. "Of course, sir. You are right."

Graybone grumbled a response, too low for Jackson to hear, then squinted at his pocket watch. With a sharp snap of the lid, he tucked the thing away. "Stop by the station at eight o'clock tonight. By then I will have finished with a preliminary round of questions and let you have a go at it with the Lord Mayor—but only under my supervision, mind you. Understood?"

He stiffened to attention. "Yes, sir."

Behind them, canvas riffled in the air. Jackson glanced over to see the men wrapping the barrister in sailcloth. "What of Mr. Humphrey's body, sir? Notifying his family and such?"

"Have Baggett help out."

Jackson nodded. "Thank you, sir."

Graybone strode off, and after a last glance at the lifeless barrister, Jackson did too. Finding the fellow was a victory, albeit a bittersweet one considering the circumstances. . .but somehow it seemed a bit hollow without Kit to share it with. He upped his pace and turned onto the cobbled lane. As soon as he finished talking with Baggett, he'd find her. Tell her all their hard work had not been in vain. And what better way to do that than over a quick victory dinner before he interrogated the Lord Mayor?

Yes indeed, this would be a banner evening.

Despite the afternoon sun streaming long fingers between buildings, Kit shivered. Clammy sweat dotted her forehead as she strode down King Street. She swiped it away with the back of her hand, annoyed. She didn't have time to be ill. Didn't have one spare moment to give in to the cramps that'd plagued her since coughing up half the river last evening. A full night and half a morning of sleep ought to have set her to rights, yet she couldn't have been more wrong. If anything, her muscles ached all the more. But why? She'd fallen into water, not landed on a slab of granite.

Dodging a hawker selling candied nuts, she pressed two fingers against the throb in her temple. As much as she'd like to blame her headache on her swim in the Thames, the pounding probably had more to do with the crew meeting she'd just finished. Flit. One would think she'd dropped off the face of the earth instead of merely been absent for the last several days. How could grown men get so sidetracked without her guidance? Two hours—*two!*—of reordering duties then reissuing assignments. Which had meant two hours lost, hours in which she could have been looking for Joe.

Or finding out if he had been dredged from the bottom of the river.

Shoving down that thought, she sidestepped a fat splat of tobacco spit and sped towards the riverbank. The sooner she joined Jackson, the sooner she'd discover what he'd found out. Her errands today had taken much too long—but been well worth it. A quick stop at hospital had revealed that Martha was on the mend, and for that Kit truly was glad.

Her stomach twinged again, but this time not from sickness. Footsteps. Mirroring hers. Close. Drawing closer. Hand covering the hilt of her concealed knife, she spun, ready for anything.

Anything except nothing. A pedestrian swerved around her, but it was only a washerwoman with chapped skin, smelling of lye and charcoal. A man with a newspaper hailed a hackney. Across the street, another fellow strolled the opposite direction. And two doors down, a woman in a long blue apron swept the stoop in front of an apothecary shop.

Nothing out of the ordinary. No whiff of danger. She bit her lip. What was wrong with her? Had that dip in the river skewed her usual sense of peril? And if it had, how would she ever function when she did go back to work on Blackfriars Lane? Disturbed by the troubling prospect, she chewed her lip a moment more then turned around.

Only to face a pointy-chinned pile of muscle. Hanks. Of all the things she didn't want to have to deal with today. Her stomach churned afresh, mostly with disgust. "What part of 'do not show me your face ever again' did you not grasp, Hanks?"

His tiny eyes shrank to two black dots. "Someone wants to talk to ye."

"Who?"

"My new boss."

"You mean to tell me you found someone who is willing to put up with you?" She rolled her eyes. "I do not have time now. Make an appointment with Duff."

In three quick steps, she bypassed him.

"*No* weren't an option," he grumbled behind her. Close behind.

But no closer than the two men who suddenly flanked her on each side, herding her towards a choke point between two buildings. If nothing else, at least Hanks had learned a trick or two since leaving her employ.

Yet he should've learned one more. On this populated of a street, all she need do was issue a cry for help. She opened her mouth.

And the sharp point of a knife poked into her ribs. On both sides. Double flit!

Her belly cramped all the harder as she was roughly herded into the wedge between two buildings, just wide enough for a cart to pass through. Not that one would. The narrow lane was a dead end, with a fat blodgett of a man waiting halfway down, wearing a ridiculous yellow sateen dress coat and smoking a cigar.

The men stopped her in front of Bags Gleason, then pulled back, no doubt lining up behind her in case she bolted. She'd known this moment would come, but did it have to be now, when she was on the cusp of finding Joe?

A small laugh bubbled out of her. "Why am I not surprised?"

"Because you know we have unfinished business." Bags twiddled his cigar between thumb and forefinger, flicking ash to the ground. "And since your associate apparently skipped town—along with my goods—you're the one what's gonna finish the deal."

She shrugged a shoulder, then wished she hadn't. The ache in her ribs cut like a knife. "As you say, that man is gone, skipped out on us both. I do not have your money."

"Don't care what you have." He took a long drag of his cigar, then blew out a chimney of smoke. "What I'll take is my two thousand."

Of course he would. He'd take it and squander it then steal more and start the whole process over again. It was blackguards like this that gave swindling a bad name. She lifted her chin, trying hard to discount the roiling in her gut. "Even if I had that kind of money on me, I would never give it to you."

He aimed the fiery end of the cigar at her. "Big words for a little scoundrel outnumbered four to one."

It hit then. A spasm she couldn't ignore. She pressed a fist into her gut, barely managing to eke out, "I am going to be sick."

Bags chuckled. "Such a ploy might work on one of your street marks, but it won't work with me, missy."

Doubling over, she vomited on his shoes.

Bags roared. "Take her down, boys!"

Spewing out the last of her sickness, she grabbed her knife and dodged to the right, putting the safety of a wall behind her. Not an ideal spot, but better than having that big swine Bags behind her.

Hanks shoved past the other two fellows, holding out his arms to keep them at bay. "Let me have her."

Kit shook her head. Stupid, stupid man. "You truly did learn nothing when you were with me, did you?"

"What I learnt is yer the worst sort o' woman in this world, taking on a man's role when ye ought to be hearthside with a passel o' younglings." A scowl slashed across his face. "Then again, this world don't need more o' yer kind."

White-hot anger filled her now-voided gut. She'd always known that's what he'd thought of her. That's what most men thought of her. Refusing to let her be anything but marginalized as a woman, an orphan, a nobody. She worked up a wad of spit and let it fly, inordinately satisfied when it splatted onto his cheek.

Hanks flicked it away, blade flashing in his other hand as he lifted it. "Been waitin' a long time for this pleasure."

"Me too." She lunged, yanking free her knife. In three lightning slashes, she cut through his braces, dropping his trousers, and slashed a thick line along his knife arm. As his blade clattered to the ground, she pulled back. "You always were a bumbler when it came to checking for weapons."

Then once again she crouched, muscles shaking. Sweat beading. No time for any more gloating. The other two menaces advanced towards her, blades in their hands and murder in their eyes. She'd had just enough stamina to fend off Hanks, but with her reserves empty, how would she ever stay standing against these men?

Chapter Twenty

Jackson squinted as the late afternoon sun glinted off a King Street milliner's window and lanced him in the eyes. Striding at his side, Charles Baggett adjusted his hat, no doubt fighting off the same enemy.

"With the barrister's body on the way to the morgue, the gruesome part is finished." Baggett paused at the corner—as did he—waiting for a slow-moving wagon to pass. "Now to contact the family, which I can do on my own."

Jackson peered over at his friend as they crossed the street. One day he'd have to perform the same heart-tugging task, but thankfully, not today. "Best of luck with that."

"Part of the job." Baggett sniffed as if the duty were no more unpleasant than directing traffic, then shifted his brown eyes to Jackson. "You really think the Lord Mayor is behind all this?"

"I have harboured suspicions for several days now, but I will know for sure once I have questioned the man. Graybone says I shall have my go at it later tonight."

"And in the meantime?"

He hitched his thumb at the Tin Whistle pub across the street. "I am hoping to dine there with a certain lady."

No sooner had the words passed his lips than farther down the block the swirl of a brown skirt caught his eye. He craned his neck, scanning past the few pedestrians dotting the pavement. "Say, there she is. Halfway down the block. See her? The woman in the brown gown with her hair done up and no bonnet."

Baggett shaded his eyes, then blew out a low whistle. "Quite the looker, that one. Leastwise what I can see from here. Where did you meet. . .hold up." Baggett rose to his toes. "Is she being flanked?"

Jackson tensed, his eyes narrowing in reflex. Sure enough, the second Kit continued on her way, one man closed in behind her. Another crossed the street and pulled up on her side while yet another exited a doorway and sandwiched her on the other. The hairs at the nape of Jackson's neck lifted like a dog's hackles. "She is being funneled into that passageway. Come on!"

Unwilling to wait for Baggett's response, he took off at a dead run, pulling his revolver as he did so. Must trouble always walk hand in hand with Kit Turner?

He and Baggett cleared the mouth of the alley in time to see the flash of Kit's blade. A breath later, a man hunched over, gripping a bleeding arm. His trousers drooped around his knees. Comical—were it not for the other two men advancing on her with blades drawn.

"Stop in the name of the Crown!" Jackson bellowed.

One of the men glanced his way. The other lunged, striking Kit's knife arm and planting a kick to her gut. Her blade flew as she doubled over.

Baggett cocked his gun. "Aim for the legs. Sarge frowns upon corpses at the station."

Jackson pulled his trigger in unison with Baggett, the shots cracking loud in the close quarters.

The men dropped, each howling. One clutched a thigh, the other grabbed his knee, both as effectively out of the game as the one Kit had maimed. She turned towards Jackson, relief evident in the sag of her shoulders.

But then a fourth fellow stepped out of the shadows and aimed a muzzle at her back.

"Stop right there, missy, and put your hands where I can see them." The man's voice was a tin of shaken gravel, all too familiar. So was the jiggle of his jowls as he stretched his neck to peer past Kit. "Back off, ye slimin' bobbies. This is between the woman and me."

Jackson gripped his revolver all the tighter. "Listen, Gleason, there is no possible way this ends well if you harm her."

"And how would you know my name, you bluecoated blighter?" The man cocked his head, his black gaze devouring Jackson's face until a spark of recognition flared. "You," he spat out. "I knew something was off about you."

"Friend of yours, eh?" Baggett grumbled.

Jackson ignored him. "Put the gun down. Now!"

A toothy smile spread like a cancer across Gleason's face. "You're not going to shoot, not with the woman betwixt us."

Jackson's chest squeezed. The man was right. He could not risk hitting Kit. His gaze shot to hers, and when their eyes met, a cold sweat broke out on his forehead. He knew that slight lift of her brow. The gleam of mischief arcing in her eyes like a flash of electricity.

"Kit, no—!"

Too late.

In a lightning move, she pivoted and grabbed Gleason's gun arm with one hand, then drove home her other elbow into the man's neck. Before he could respond, the little she-devil kneed him in the groin and slid the pistol from his grasp. Gleason wheezed hard, doubling over. Kit backed away, towards Jackson, towards safety, but not without first swiping up her dropped knife.

She stopped just shy of him and Baggett. "There. Problem solved."

Baggett sucked in a breath.

Jackson reached for her, guiding her behind him with one hand, never once taking his eyes off Gleason. "We will leave you and your men be for now, Gleason. But if you ever touch this woman again, if you so much as go near her, I shall have you tossed into the deepest, darkest cell at Newgate and personally throw away the key. Am I clear?"

Gleason groaned, barely eking out an answer. "Perfectly."

"You are letting him off?"

Baggett's question hissed in his ear, as venomous as the bite of Jackson's own conscience. Allowing Gleason to roam free didn't make the streets any safer. But neither could he risk what the man might say to the sergeant about that night Jackson had posed as a smuggler. As much as he hated to let the man go, it was better to earn the sergeant's goodwill with the Lord Mayor's arrest and the discovery of the other missing men before hauling in Gleason.

Though it cost him in ways that cut deep, Jackson gave Baggett a curt nod.

"And what about you?" Baggett snapped his face Kit's way. "Do you not want us to press charges against that lot?"

"Leave the rats in the alley where they belong, but you can take this into custody." She handed over Gleason's pistol.

Jackson tucked away his own revolver. "I suggest we move before those rats recover. Gleason is agreeable for now, but who knows how long that will last."

Three abreast, with Kit in the middle, they made their way to the pavement. Baggett shook his head at her. "That was quite an impressive move, Miss Turner, especially for a lady."

Jackson couldn't help but grin. Baggett had no idea what Kit was capable of, and oddly enough, it warmed his gut that he did. "Indeed. She is quite an impressive lady."

Surprise flickered in her gaze before a smirk masked her true emotion. "Your timing was impeccable. Thank you for coming to my aid." She swung her face towards Baggett. "You as well. Not that I couldn't have managed on my own, mind you, but you did make things a lot easier."

"It is our job, miss." Baggett tipped his hat, then nodded at Jackson. "And with that I bid you both goodbye. Duty calls." Before another carriage could rumble in front of him, Baggett stepped off the pavement and crossed the street.

With his friend gone, Jackson pulled Kit aside, out of the way of pedestrians. "How are you faring?" He frowned at his own stupid question, for clearly her skin was pallid. He flattened his palm against her forehead. "Are you feverish?"

"Pah!" She wrenched away from his touch. "I could conquer the world if I had to."

Vexing woman! She'd go to her grave with fists raised if it meant hiding a vulnerability. A sudden urge welled—to be the one to tame her. But with the way the tilt of her head challenged, that taming wouldn't be tonight. . .nor likely anytime soon.

He clicked his tongue. "Well then, would you settle for vanquishing some supper instead?"

She lifted her pert little nose. "Is that an invitation?"

Hmm. If he said it was, in her current mood, she might easily turn him down. Better to leave a trail of crumbs for her to follow. He turned on his heel. "There is a pub just down the street. How about you come along and find out?"

Absently, Kit rubbed the pain in her forearm where a bruise was no doubt already purpling. Her belly still cramped, though not nearly as much as before. Her lungs yet felt thick and heavy. But despite all her aches and pains, more than anything, she truly did wish to dine with the handsome Jackson Forge.

But she'd be trussed up and cooked over a spit before she'd admit to any such weakness.

She narrowed her eyes, watching the broad-shouldered constable stride away, scrambling for a reason—*any* reason—to dine with the man other than sheer desire. A cab rumbled by, so close to the curb that the grinding wheels reverberated in her chest. . .and then she knew. For Joe! That was it. Of course she must accept Jackson's invitation or she'd never find out if it was Joe that had been buried at the bottom of the Thames. Gathering her hem, she scurried after the man.

"So," she panted as she caught up to him, pressing a hand against a stitch in her side. "Who did you dredge up from the river?"

"Is that your way of saying you will dine with me?" He winked.

Tenacious man! She rolled her eyes. "Yes."

A grin spread wide and brilliant. "Good. And for your information, it was not Joe Card we uncovered, but one of the other missing men. The barrister, Artemus Humphrey. Hence the reason for a victory dinner." He shoved open the door to the pub and stepped aside.

"Hmm," she murmured as she passed him. "He was the one on the Lord Mayor's list."

"The very same." He hailed the barkeep with a snap of his fingers. "Two ciders and two of your finest steak and ale pies, please. We will take the window table."

The man dipped his head. "Right away, Constable."

At the mention of food, her stomach rebelled once again. Not to the extent of earlier in the alley, but enough that she knew eating a steak and ale pie wouldn't be the best decision of her life. Still, how could she refuse the bright-eyed man who'd so proudly ordered for her?

With a light touch to the small of her back, Jackson led her to a table and held out a chair. "For you, miss."

"My, but you are in a good mood." She fluffed out her skirt as she sat, hiding a wince as her elbow brushed against her ribs. "Not that I blame you, mind. The barrister was quite a find. So, what happens next? Clap the Lord Mayor in irons and torture him until he squeals?"

Jackson chuckled while the barkeep set down mugs of cider in front of them. "No, next is a toast." He held up his cup. "To you and me, an unlikely pairing but a very efficient one, if I do say so myself."

"Is that so?" His smile was contagious, and she grinned, then clinked mugs with him. "To us. Unlikely and unstoppable."

Sweet cider filled her tummy, quieting the leftover cramps.

"In answer to your question." Jackson swiped the back of his hand across his mouth. "You are somewhat correct. By now our prominent politician is likely already being interrogated—sans torture—by the sergeant. I shall have my go at him in an hour or so, and with any luck, I will discover Joe Card's whereabouts."

"Brilliant." She shot out her hand across the small table, palm up. "Then I will take my token back now, if you please."

His warm fingers wrapped around hers, pressing her hand closed. "Not yet."

"Why not?"

"I am not finished with it." He rubbed his thumb across her knuckles, slow, gentle. Entirely too distracting. She could get used to that touch—to Jackson's touch. Jackson's face. His voice, his smell, his—

Gah! What was she thinking? She cocked her head. "What do you mean you are not finished with it? What *is* your intent, sir?"

For a moment, he said nothing, his gaze drifting to their hands entwined on the tabletop. His smile slipped when he spoke. "I am not sure you would like the answer to that."

"How cryptic of you." She pulled away, eyeing him. "You have developed quite a skill at evading questions. You know, if this constable thing doesn't work out, you might consider becoming a member of my crew."

A good-natured laugh rumbled in his throat, and he shoved back the same rogue curl that had a habit of flopping onto his brow. "Can't get enough of me, can you?"

"Let's just say it is a case of keeping my enemy close."

"Is that what I am? Your enemy?" He leaned forward, blue gaze drilling deep into hers, all humour fading. "Is that what you truly think?"

Her throat closed, her usual snappy retorts drying to bone dust. Who could think with those blue eyes regarding her so earnestly? As if his life hung on her opinion of him. Did he truly care so much for what she thought?

"Jackson." The taste of his name on her tongue was far too sweet.

She was treading onto dangerous ground. Much too revealing and intimate. Dare she be honest with him? With herself?

She shifted on her seat. This would be a good time to run. Leave this place. Forget about the striking constable with all his probing questions. But his eyes held her in place, allowing for nothing more than a slight squirm.

"Truthfully, I am not at all certain of what you are or what you want to be." She took a deep breath, wholly unprepared yet compelled to go deeper with this man. "Are you someone who cares for me in a way I cannot explain, or someone who only pretends a sincere regard in order to get what you want?"

She leaned across the table, spearing him with an intense stare, equal parts fearful and eager. "Do you wish our relationship to be strictly business or something more?"

The lines on his face softened, the blue of his eyes smouldering to a shade she'd never witnessed before. "Kit, I—"

"Would that be Miss Kit Turner?" a bass voice rumbled at her back.

Bother! Of all the inopportune moments to get interrupted.

She glanced over her shoulder, where two brass-buttoned constables stood, feet planted and shoulders stiffened to beams. "Who wants to know?"

"Briggs. Hammerlund." Jackson nodded at the men. "Can I help you?"

The officer nearest her shook his head. "No need. We've got this."

She glanced between Jackson and the men. "Got what?"

"You." In one swift movement, the constable dug his fingers in beneath her arm and hoisted her to her feet. "Kit Turner, you are under arrest."

Chapter Twenty-One

Arrest? The word whipped around in the air, and every time it circled back, Jackson tried to grab it and strangle the thing. But it would not be caught, and it certainly would not be understood, not any more than the sight of the lithe woman in a brown skirt kicking and scratching like a mad hen tucked beneath Constable Briggs's thick arm.

"This is a mistake. Release her at once!" Jackson tagged their heels out the door. "Miss Turner is with me."

"Not anymore." Briggs grunted as he adjusted his grip on the squirming Kit.

"You will have to take it up with the sergeant, Forge." Officer Hammerlund swung open the door of the Black Maria, skeleton key at the ready to lock up the old prison cart once Kit was deposited. "We are just obeying orders."

Kit wrenched sideways with a feral cry, her wild eyes boring into Jackson's. The betrayal in her gaze knocked the air from his lungs.

"You played me!" Her voice was savage. "No wonder you did not return my token. It is already tendered as evidence against me, is it not?" Her tone grew shrill. "I never should have trusted you. Never!"

"Kit, listen." He advanced a step, careful, easy, as if walking on a plate of glass that might shatter at any moment. "I swear I—"

"No!" She lunged against Briggs's blue sleeve. "I am done listening to you. You are the worst sort of swindler there is, pretending to be a friend when all along you were sharpening a knife to stab me in the back."

"Enough." Grunting, Briggs patted her down, confiscated her boot knife, then hoisted her into the back of the cart, all the while ignoring every objection Jackson hurled at him.

The instant Briggs released her, Hammerlund slammed the door shut, the click of the lock sharp as bone on bone. For a moment, Kit's blue eyes blazed between the bars, accusing Jackson in ways that cut deep. Then with no more words, no tears, no anything, she turned her head and refused to look at him.

"Kit! Please." He strode to the bars and grabbed hold. "Believe me, I had nothing to do with this, but I will make things right. I swear it! I will not rest until I do."

His pulse thudded sickeningly loud in his ears. She didn't move. Not a whit. She sat there, spine stiff, refusing to glance his way. If she wasn't certain before, she was now. She truly did think he was her enemy.

Which was the last thing he wanted to be.

The cart lurched into motion, pulling from his grasp. For a moment, he stood gaping as the woman who did strange things to his heart rumbled off in a cart for criminals and cutthroats.

Then he ran.

Each judder of the police cart's wheels rattled Kit's teeth, and she clenched the worn edge of the wooden seat, desperate for a solid grip to shore her up. Hah! What a farce. Her entire world had been turned upside down and inside out. Nothing could right her, least of all a pathetic grip on a jiggling slab of wood. Here she was. Locked in a cage, hurtling towards jail. Just like Miss Lila's father had prophesied all those years ago.

"You are a thief, girl. A light finger. The worst sort of stain on human-ity. I spare you the hell of a prison cell now, but I wonder if you will not

end up a jailbird in years to come despite my great mercy. *Time will tell, I suppose.*"

Gritting her teeth, she closed her eyes. She had no one to blame but herself for this nightmare, falling victim to a constable's honeyed words, false assurances, handsome looks.

"I will not haul you in for thievery."

Liar!

Her hands balled into fists. The second Jackson had gotten what he wanted, taken into custody the one responsible for Joe's disappearance, he'd turned her in. Pretended all was well, nay, victorious! Making toasts, smiling into her face, husky voiced and soft eyed, all the while knowing her doom was about to burst through those pub doors. The injustice of it all roared out of her. God only knew what those on the street thought of the mad cry tearing past her lips, but there was nothing to be done for it. This was what came of depending upon someone other than herself.

The cart lurched, her teeth coming down hard on the skin inside her cheek. Blood tasted brassy. Good. She relished the flavour, the pain. Anything but give in to the gnawing ache that would surely consume her if she dwelled on Jackson's treachery. For it wasn't only her he'd hurt. What would become of the families on Blackfriars Lane? Duff and Blake. Skims and little Frankie. Oh, they'd operate fine for a while, but it wouldn't take long before people got wise to them. None of the men on her crew had the smarts to hatch a new swindle that teetered on the lawful edge of honesty. They'd cross the line. Revert to their former ways of outright theft. And then where would their families be? The workhouse. The poorhouse. Dead of starvation or disease. All because of an overeager recruit who thought he was doing the world a favor by having her arrested. Bullheaded, ignorant man!

An eternity of black thoughts later, the cart grumbled to a stop. Bracing her back against the wall, she readied to kick. A sharp jab to the first guard's head. Jump down. Strike an elbow into the other man's windpipe. Run fast. Run far. It could work, if only she didn't feel so blasted weary.

Bootsteps clopped near the door. Keys jangled. Kit tensed. The lock slid and hinges creaked. The second a helmeted man reached inside to pull her out, she'd launch. Yet nothing happened. No head appeared. Only night shadows crept in the door, save for the sharp clicks of two guns cocking.

"Come on out, missy," the deeper-voiced officer bellowed. Briggs, according to Jackson. "And keep your hands over your head or we will shoot you in the leg."

Flit!

Heaving a sigh, she climbed down and lifted her hands. Moments later, one of her arms was wrenched back and secured in a steely grip. "Now walk."

Torches flickered in iron sconces on each side of the door. Newgate. A hulk of brick and despair tormenting souls for centuries, and now it was her turn. The stench of guilty men slapped her in the face as soon as she crossed the threshold.

The constables shuffled her down the hall, but not far. Not yet. Just to a small room off the side of the main passage. At center, a clerk perched on a stool in front of a tall desk. He looked up at their entrance, yawned, then retrieved a pen. "Name?"

"Turner," Briggs answered from behind. "Kit."

"Offense?"

"The suspect's been accused of thievery."

A flash of hot rage surged up from her belly. Though she'd known all along what the charge would be, it still burned afresh to hear it echo off the prison's stone walls.

The clerk set down his pen, his watery gaze drifting to the officers at her back. "Holding cell two. No, wait. Make that three. The other two are full. Been a bit of a backup at the Old Bailey what with Judge Wherry laid up and all."

Kit stumbled as the officers guided her down the hall, then

ascended a short flight of steps. A holding cell was a small mercy. For now. One she'd best enjoy. After her trial, she'd be shoved into the bowels and forgotten, or so she'd been told by past inmates, those lucky enough to survive.

Briggs snagged a key off a hook, bypassed the first two doors, then opened the third. "In you go." He stepped aside and the other officer nudged her forward.

Panic clenched her gut. This was it.

Before the door slammed and the brilliance of the outside torches disappeared, she glimpsed two other women inside the cell. One sat in the corner, legs sprawled beneath a patched skirt, with a tatty yellow shawl draped over her shoulders. Her lips moved. Words mumbled. Hard to tell what she was talking about though, for it appeared she only owned one tooth.

The other woman stood at the center of the chamber, her arms folded about her for warmth, and no wonder. A golden gown dipped low off her shoulders, red hair done mostly up in what had once been a magnificent chignon. Kit's jaw dropped in recognition as the door banged shut behind her. The woman from the Lord Mayor's party two nights back, still in her evening gown.

What in the world was she doing here?

Winded and weary, Jackson swung onto Old Jewry and trotted towards the station, just in time to see a man in a well-tailored suit stepping into a coach with the Lord Mayor's insignia emblazoned in gold on the door. His step faltered. What the deuce? Was the Lord Mayor making a break for it right in front of the public eye? How had he managed to slip past the officers at the station?

First Kit. Now this. What else could go wrong?

"Stop!" Jackson sprinted ahead.

But the horses already stepped lively, carrying the man he had yet to question off into the night. Anger flowing hot and fast, Jackson punched open the station door and flew past Beanstaple's desk.

"Mr. Forge," the clerk called after him. "You ought not—"

He dashed into the sergeant's office and snapped a salute. "Pardon the intrusion, sir, but the Lord Mayor is getting away. He must be pursued at once."

Graybone looked up from a stack of papers, eerily quiet. Surely the man had heard him.

But on the off chance he hadn't, Jackson upped his volume. "Sir, I said—"

"Sit down, Forge." The words fired like grapeshot. A command, not a suggestion.

Jackson lowered into the hard wooden chair in front of Graybone's desk, a chill creeping up his spine.

The sergeant rolled a pen between two of his massive fingers. "Mistakes were made, Forge. Errors that could have been prevented."

"Errors, sir?" Jackson's gut clenched, especially since Graybone didn't so much as glance at him.

"Your first mistake was accusing my brother-in-law of illegal activity. Turns out that bottle of rum was his personal supply, tucked away from my sister's prying eyes."

In hindsight, perhaps it had been a rash accusation, one he should have checked into further before mentioning it to the sergeant. He swallowed. *Should haves* far too often paved the way to the gallows. "Sir, I had no idea—"

"Secondly, about that letter to the editor." Graybone's dark eyes followed the roll of the pen, back and forth, back and forth. "Scathing, as you said, but it was not without provocation."

Why wouldn't Graybone look at him? Had he truly missed something that scandalous? "Such as, sir?"

The rolling stopped. The sergeant's gaze lifted to his—and Jackson recanted his wish to read the man's face, so fierce were the sparks in Graybone's eyes. "The missing MP to whom the letter was directed led a faction against Sir Robert, greasing the wheel of the rumour mill. While the Lord Mayor vehemently disagreed with the man, which he took no pains to hide, he also denies any sort of collusion in the MP's disappearance and, in fact, has been a champion of the man's family by providing financial support during his absence."

Jackson fisted his hands to keep from tugging at his collar. Was it getting hot in here?

"And as for our waterlogged barrister," Graybone continued. "The connection with the Lord Mayor is innocuous. Sir Robert's secretary, Mr. Poxley, had asked for a legal recommendation on a private, familial matter that had nothing whatsoever to do with the Lord Mayor."

No, it wasn't hot. There was no air. None whatsoever. He swallowed against the tightness in his throat. But surely God would not let him hang now after the requested miracle that He provided only a few hours ago. "Sir, I—"

"I am not finished, Mr. Forge." The pen snapped. The sergeant dropped the pieces. Each ping like nails in Jackson's coffin.

Graybone shoved back his chair, legs scraping against the wooden planks and Jackson's nerves. But the man didn't stand. Didn't pace. Just folded his arms and stared down the length of his nose at Jackson, a falcon perched on a precipice, ready to swoop. "The water taxi ticket did not even belong to the Lord Mayor but to his secretary, Mr. Poxley. And the map of Blackfriars was in the Lord Mayor's possession because he met someone at that pub, but not the jarvey."

Jackson mentally rifled through the pub's occupants on that auspicious day he'd stepped through the door. Unsavory characters, all. "Then who did he meet?"

"A reporter for the *Times*, one with a misguided urge to run a story that would vindicate Sir Robert and stop the rumours about his involvement in the former Lord Mayor's death. A story Sir Robert had no desire to see printed." The sergeant scrubbed a hand over his face, whiskers bristling at the touch. "So he met with the reporter, who due to fear of his enemies, asked to meet at a place that would not attract attention, where men do not ask questions or tell tales, and if they do, don't live long enough to make the same mistake twice."

"Politicians lie all the time, sir. These could be false excuses. Some sort of fabricated alibi."

"The reporter verified it, Forge, with this." Graybone yanked open a drawer and shoved a paper across the desk with a stab of his finger.

A black-and-white image of a young boy stared back at him. Raven hair slicked at an angle just above his eyebrows. Below that, pale eyes haunted, like a soul caught unaware. Just a portrait. Head only. The edges silhouetted by a hazy dark shadow.

He set down the photograph, thoroughly confused. What sort of verification was this? "Sir?"

"You are looking at the Lord Mayor's illegitimate son, a son he very much wants to keep out of the public eye. Sir Robert had been in Shropshire visiting the boy during the entire duration of the former Lord Mayor's illness. He did not—*could* not—have had anything to do with his predecessor's death, proving the rabble-rousing naysayers wrong."

Jackson shook his head, which did nothing to straighten out the rapid-fire information being launched at him. "If this is all true, then why does the Lord Mayor not go public with the information? End the speculations once and for all?"

Graybone reached his meaty paw across the tabletop and snatched back the image. "The boy was born with a debilitating defect, one that will soon take his life. Sir Robert would rather face the innuendo of foul play than see his son's final days besmirched in the papers. And if you breathe one word of this to anyone, I'll see you locked in the cell you would have thrown the Lord Mayor into."

"Of course, sir. Not a word." He rubbed his eyes, a growing

headache behind them. Not only had he failed to find Joe, he had nearly had the wrong man locked up. A man, apparently, as innocent as his own brother. A hangman's knot of failure constricted around his throat so that he could only croak out, "I had no idea."

"As I said, errors were made. Sir Robert had nothing to do with the murder of that barrister or the demise of the former Lord Mayor." Once again Graybone leaned forward, this time planting his elbows and resting his chin on steepled fingers. "But do you want to know the biggest mistake of all?"

No. He didn't. Because whatever it was would be worse than all the damning evidence already put forth. Despite propriety, Jackson loosened his collar. "And what would that be, sir?"

Graybone's hands dropped. So did his tone. "I trusted you."

Jackson clenched his jaw, fighting a wince. A punch to the kidney couldn't have hurt more. "I—" He choked, remorse thick in his throat. "I am sorry, sir. I only wished to find Joe Card. To bring to justice the one responsible for his and the other disappearances. I was so sure. I mean, all indications pointed to the Lord Mayor." He had tried so hard to do what was right. How had it all gone so horribly wrong?

A huge sigh ruffled the sergeant's moustache, his big chest deflating with the long, low breath. "Well, I suppose your heart is in the right place, Forge."

The noose loosened a fraction. Jackson let out his own breath. The sergeant wasn't going to dismiss him? Even after all his failures? Maybe he would survive this after all. "Thank you, sir."

"But." Graybone let the word hover in the air. "There is more to being a good officer than heartfelt intentions." The sergeant pushed to his feet, pacing as he spoke. "It takes bravery, brawn, and most importantly, the brains not to go off half-cocked, no matter how eager or how right you think you may be." He faced Jackson, his dark eyes sharp enough to bore holes, driving home his next point. "Unless a criminal is caught in the act of breaking a law, you must present evidence that cannot be broken. Do you understand?"

"Yes, sir. Of course, sir. I will strive to never make such mistakes again."

Graybone eyed him a moment longer, then sank into his chair. "I am sure you will not."

"Thank you, sir."

And thank You, God.

All the tension in Jackson's shoulders slowly unwound, like a great spool of wire unrolling down a hill, then stopped short.

Kit.

She'd be hauled into Newgate any minute now.

His spine straightened to a ramrod. "Pardon me, sir, but there is another matter I must discuss, concerning the arrest of a Miss Kit Turner."

Graybone shook his big head. "Our discussion is over." His face hardened. "Turn in your uniform."

Jackson stiffened. Surely he hadn't heard right. He pressed on. "There is a woman, sir, who is even now being taken to a holding cell at Newgate. I have no doubt there has been a mistake and I urge you to immediately look into the matter. If you would but—"

"Mr. Forge!" The sergeant shot from his chair and slammed his hands down on the desk. "I will not tolerate another word from you. Effective this moment, you are not only fired but banished. On behalf of the Lord Mayor, his secretary has issued a restraining order against you for harassment, and if you step foot into the City of London again, I shall have to arrest you. In short, Forge, you have failed."

Chapter Twenty-Two

Things should be different. *He* was different. An officially confirmed failure. But the back stairs Jackson had trotted down for years still creaked in exactly the same spots. His boot still hit the dip in the last step with a loud *scritch*. And as always, the door to the finest watch-making shop in Haywards Heath yawned open, the tick-tick-ticking inside counting away the minutes and hours of his life.

He paused in the entryway, caught between present and past on the stoop that his mother had swept clean every day until her death of the dropsy five years ago. To her final breath she'd said she loved him, forgave him even, but deep in his heart he knew he'd let her down the day those ruffians had forever changed their lives.

Just like he'd let down Kit by leaving her to rot in jail.

Stomach churning, Jackson crossed the threshold into the work-shop. James sat in his usual spot, hunched on a stool, his brown hair cascading over his eyes, a box of broken gears and springs on his lap. Humming a tuneless ditty, he swirled his finger aimlessly through the mix, the same action he'd be doing for the next eight hours.

With a lump in his throat, Jackson approached him, a physical reminder of his own cowardice. "I see you are hard at it this morning, Brother."

A crooked smile lifted the old misshapen scar that crawled from James's chin to his scalp, cutting through his left eye. Words came out garbled but cheerful, stabbing Jackson in the heart.

He clapped his brother on the shoulder. "Keep up the good work."

After a nod, James dipped his head and went back to mindlessly shoving about scraps of metal.

Jackson wound his way past the long center counter to where his father sat at a worktable near the window. Daylight poured in, bathing his father's white head in brilliance. Fitting. The man deserved a halo even on this side of eternity. Not only did he provide for his broken son, but he had taken in Jackson without a single question when he'd shown up with bag in hand. Had he gotten even one thing right in his short stint as a constable? If so, he couldn't recall it now. Maybe God had been trying to tell him from the beginning he wasn't suited for the job.

He stopped near his father's elbow. After two days of licking his wounds, it was time for him to do what he could to repay his father's generosity. "How can I be of service, Father?"

For a moment, his father didn't say anything, just kept on squinting through a magnifier while tightening a miniscule screw on a pocket watch. At length, he set down the timepiece and lifted his face. "Oh Son."

Two words. Just two. But his father's faded brown eyes were so loud with unspoken pity that Jackson fisted his hands to keep from stopping up his ears.

"Do not worry, Father. I may have been a great muck-up as a constable, but I can at least attach a fob without fouling it into oblivion."

Laughter shook his father's shoulders. "Just because you can be a watchmaker does not mean you should be."

"What else am I to do?" He snatched a wire snipper off the worktable and fiddled with it, unwilling to face the man he'd sorely disappointed. Not that his father would ever admit to it. But it had to be true. Jackson could hardly stand himself. "I have no other options at the moment."

"It has been two days." Father pulled the tool from Jackson's hands, then leaned back in his chair. "Is it not time you told me what happened?"

Jackson shook his head. "There is nothing to tell. I went, I blundered, it is over."

"It cannot be all that bad."

Hah! A magnificent smirk twisted his lips. "It is worse than you can possibly imagine."

"I don't know about that. I have a very vivid imagination." His father winked. "Look, Son, you shall always have a place here, but the truth is you are not a watchmaker. You do not love the craft. I have no idea what happened in London, but I do know this. . .it is far better to be a failure at what you love than a success at what you hate."

"It is too late." Blowing out a long breath, Jackson worked out a kink in his neck. "Mistakes were made, errors I could have—*should* have—prevented, and now my reputation is ruined."

"Bah! A reputation is only what others think of you. Character is what matters. That is who you really are." His father leaned forward and peered up at him. "And I am proud of the man you are. Be sure your mother smiles down at you from heaven as well. You are a good man, Jackson. An honest one. Compassionate and determined. Your heart beats for justice, not springs and wires."

Well-meant words, but just that. Nothing but air moving past vocal cords. "There is more to being a good officer than heartfelt intentions. I had my chance and failed." He bit back an *again*, his gaze sliding over to James, who poked and prodded at the same box of parts as he did every blessed day. Because of him.

"Oh Son, failure is fatal only to those who refuse to learn from it, for only One has lived who was perfect. The question is not *if* you will fail. Rather, will you let God redeem your failure for good, turning your end into His beginning?"

Jackson snapped his gaze back to his father, anger rushing hot through his veins. "You do not understand. There is no way to begin again, for I cannot go back."

His father sniffed as if he smelled something rotten. "Cannot or will not?"

Pah! If only it were that easy of a choice. But there was no choice at all. No say whatsoever, though he had been over and over the sergeant's last words, vainly trying to figure out a way to go back and save Kit.

Weary, he leaned against the worktable, letting the strong structure shore him up. "It is complicated, Father. I was on the hunt for a missing man, a jarvey, who did not merit a full search squad, what with the other officers busy trying to find a barrister, a wealthy merchant, and an MP. I crossed paths with a woman who was also looking for the cabby, a very well-connected woman. After a thorough investigation, it seemed we had found the culprit." He raked his hand through his hair, grazing his scalp and relishing the pain. "But it turns out we could not have been more wrong. Now she is in jail, which is where I will be if I ever show my face in the City of London again."

He pushed away from the table so forcefully the clock workings rattled. "I cannot help but feel that somehow I was the cause for her arrest. That had I never walked into her life, she would still be free. And that the jarvey will never be found because no one is looking for him."

Father folded his arms, head bobbing a slow rhythm to the low "hmm" reverberating in his throat. He stared out the window, but judging by the way his eyes didn't track the parade of passing pedestrians—especially the outrageous matron in a chartreuse gown with an ostrich feather waving off the top of her hat—the man was miles away.

At length, Father slapped his hands on his thighs and looked up. "Well then, I suppose you shall have to go in disguise."

Jackson's jaw dropped. Who was this imposter staring at him through his father's brown eyes? "You cannot be serious."

Father chuckled. "I am neither a newborn nor a saint. I have lived long enough to know that most of life dwells in the murky grey between right and wrong. Misfortunes will come and go, but through it all, our main duty is to keep loving God and keep loving man."

Jackson flattened his lips as Kit's own words barreled back.

"It is often in tragedy where we find our life's purpose, and that purpose is to love God and man."

"Besides, my boy, your heart is already there. I see it in your eyes. You care about that poor man, you loved your work, and if I do not miss my mark, you love that woman as well."

Jackson stiffened. How the deuce could his father know that? Even more stunning, a niggling suspicion wormed its way up from his gut to confirm his father's intimations. He had loved his work. The thrill. The mystery. But part of that—most of it, if he were honest—stemmed from loving the woman he'd worked alongside.

Joints and chair creaking, Father clapped him on the back. "As much as you are welcome here, the only true failure in life is refusing to do what God has asked of you. Is it not time for you to return and make right whatever wrongs you left behind?"

The words lingered long after Father had gone, resurrecting what Kit had told him after visiting Martha. *Perhaps I cannot save the world. But that doesn't mean I cannot make it a better place.* And at the end of the day, isn't that what he really wanted? Not a job with the constabulary, but to leave the world a better place? So while there was no way for him to earn back his job, and he would most certainly never be a constable again, that did not excuse him from doing what he could do.

But how would he free Kit from jail and find the still-missing jarvey without landing behind bars himself?

Kit sat on the cold flagstones, hugging her knees, watching the lady in the golden gown pace circles in the small cell. And no wonder. Grace Shaw's father was the missing merchant. If Kit actually had a father who'd been mysteriously taken, she'd do more than pace. She'd climb the walls and shimmy out the slit window or die in the trying.

She tightened the grip on her knees, the pervasive chill seeping into her bones. In spite of the discomfort of the cell, her nausea had faded away, replaced by a cold pit in her stomach as one day and then another ticked by. It was just her and Grace now, the other woman having been taken out yesterday, and none too soon for Kit's liking. The old woman's mumbling had only grown more growlish the longer she rambled. Not that Kit blamed her. After two days of skilly and brackish water, she felt like grumbling herself.

Sighing, she looked up as Grace's golden skirt swished near her. "You will wear a rut into the floor."

Grace slowly gathered her hem and slid down beside Kit. "How can you just sit here, doing nothing?"

"What makes you think I am not doing anything?"

Her new friend cut her a sideways glance. "I hardly think scheming against the constable who put you in here is productive."

"Do not tell me you have not done your fair share of scheming with each turn about the cell." Kit nudged her shoulder with her own.

"Lot of good it will do me." A fleeting smile wavered on Grace's lips then vanished. "Or my father."

Sorrow thickened her voice, cutting straight to Kit's heart. It was hard enough to be fretting over Joe's disappearance. How much more painful would be the mysterious loss of a father?

"Well"—Kit shifted to face Grace—"how about we scheme together? Sort through your facts one more time and perhaps something new will come to light."

Grace nodded, then tipped her head back against the wall. "I suppose we could."

"That's the spirit." It would be far better to dwell on Grace's problems than her own.

"As I have already said," Grace began, "when my father did not come home several weeks ago, I paid an unannounced visit to his warehouse at the Wapping Dockyard and was rudely turned away by some man claiming to be his new foreman." A sour look pinched her brow as if she were reliving the horrid experience all over again. "The man said Father had traveled to Southampton on a business matter and the warehouse was closed until his return. But Father did not return, nor were my continued inquiries into the matter satisfied."

Kit studied the woman. Was Grace making too much of this? The man might well and truly be down in Southampton.

But that didn't explain the crates Grace claimed to have seen.

"And you are certain, absolutely certain, that you glimpsed cargo inside your father's warehouse, despite the foreman's claims of it being shut down?"

Grace nodded. "So I checked with the harbour master, who confirmed that indeed there was a bill of lading for a load of cargo from Birmingham that had recently been delivered to the warehouse."

Kit shifted again, the cobbled floor shooting pains into her hips. "So," she thought aloud, "clearly the warehouse is in operation. But what was that cargo and where is it going?"

"I tried to find that out as well, which is why I went to the harbour master's supervisor, then moved up the ranks when he could not help me. Every shipment going in and out of the City of London has to be cleared and documented, and ultimately, that clearance and documentation can either be approved or denied by the Lord Mayor's office. Someone knows about those crates in my father's warehouse, and I suspect it is the Lord Mayor himself." Grace's green eyes blazed. "And I am certain he is the one who put me in here. He planted that guest's bracelet in my reticule because I got too close to the truth that night at his party. Far too close. I just know it."

"If so, then you have nothing to worry about." Kit gave her friend's hand a little squeeze. "The Lord Mayor is likely even now in one of the men's holding cells awaiting trial. The truth will come out."

"But will it come out before I am falsely convicted?" Worry quivered in Grace's voice. "Oh, how I wish my father were here!"

Kit opened her mouth, hoping some words of wisdom and comfort would magically appear, but the scrape of a key in the lock turned their heads.

A moment later, a thick-bodied guard stood on the threshold. "Out you go, Miss Shaw."

They both rose, Grace never once loosening her hold on Kit's hand. Hope warbled in her voice. "I am free to go?"

"Aye." The guard chuckled. "Free to go to the Old Bailey for trial. Come now. Judge don't like to be kept waiting."

Panic flashed in Grace's eyes, her fingers clamping on to Kit's in a death grip.

"Do not lose heart," Kit whispered. "Truth will prevail."

Grace sucked in a shuddering breath, then threw back her shoulders and marched towards the doorway like a soldier to battle. Brave woman.

The door slammed shut, leaving Kit alone in the semishadows with questions she'd staved off by focusing on Grace's problems. If truth really did prevail, then what was to become of her?

A chill shivered through her, and she rubbed her arms. Perhaps Jackson had been right all along. She'd played too fast and loose with the truth, twisting it to suit her needs, allowing people to believe falsehoods. Grace Shaw didn't deserve to be incarcerated, but she surely did. Perhaps Jackson didn't merit her scorn after all. A bitter laugh bubbled up to her throat and out her mouth. Easy to think so now, but when she was locked down in the guts of Newgate, would she still believe the same?

"Will you trust Him despite your circumstances? Will you depend on Him rather than yourself?"

The truth of Jackson's former words dropped her to her knees. Were she honest, she'd have to admit that, no, she hadn't been trusting God. Always coming up with her own designs, her own way to provide for the people of Blackfriars and herself. . .and look where that had landed her.

"In the end, everyone else will fail you—including yourself."

Indeed. She had. And the knowledge sank like bad beef to her gut.

Clenching one arm to her stomach, she bowed her head. "Well,

God, it seems You have given me the perfect opportunity to give this trust thing a try. Men have failed me, time and again, and doing things my own way has led me here. So. . ." She screwed her eyes shut and sucked in a shaky breath. Standing at the edge of a precipice was notoriously breathtaking. Was she ready for this?

How could she not be?

"I surrender, God," she whispered. "I leave my fate, whatever that may be, in Your hands."

Her eyes sprang open, and she lifted her face to the ceiling. "But I am really hoping it is not a lengthy stay in a cold, dark cell."

Chapter Twenty-Three

It was dark. But not evil. This blackness was the sort one could rely on, lean back against and rest in as securely as if in a mother's arms. That is, Jackson could if his muscles weren't so coiled and ready to spring. If word got out to Sergeant Graybone that he was in the City once again, he'd be joining Kit at Newgate.

So he waited, tense, in the thin space between a violin shop and the Four Sisters taproom, where Baggett and the other constables took a pint after their shift. Each time the door scraped open and bootsteps hit the pavement, he pressed his back against the wall, praying to God Baggett would exit alone. There'd be no approaching him if the man chummed along with another officer. And even if his friend strolled unaccompanied, soliciting his help could still blow up in Jackson's face.

Once again, he turned to counting the bricks in the wall. Over and over. Anything but speculate on his friend's reaction to helping him in light of the sergeant's threat. Or think on how much he missed Kit. Because he did. He missed every little thing about the sprite. Her lively banter. The way her nose crinkled as she figured out how to solve a problem. How tender she could be despite the hard life she'd endured. Her companionship fit him as well as a bespoke pair of gloves.

In the distance, the bonging of Big Ben tolled the hour, adding to Jackson's counting. Nine chimes. So late? Didn't Baggett have to work in the morning?

Finally, his friend's familiar chuckle exited the pub, along with the bass laughter of another man. Blast! Jackson ground his teeth. Had all this covert standing about been for naught?

Thankfully, the bass voice drifted the other way, and footsteps thudded towards his dark cranny. A moment later, the thick outline of Baggett's shoulders passed by.

"Baggett!" he whispered.

Immediately, the man wheeled about, slipping his hand to the grip of his revolver.

"Just me, Forge," Jackson whispered, louder this time. Hopefully his friend would identify his voice.

Baggett edged a step closer and peered into the narrow passage. "Forge?" The whites of his eyes grew as his gaze locked onto Jackson. After casting a glance about, he stepped fully into the shadowy corridor. "What in the name of queen and country are you doing here? Graybone has yet to cool off from your Lord Mayor debacle."

"Hence this clandestine meeting."

Baggett snorted. "I cannot say I am surprised, not since hearing about your Miss Turner."

"What have you heard?" Jackson closed the distance between them, as if by nearness alone he might glean everything there was to know about Kit's incarceration. "Why was she arrested?"

"Some bookseller over on Trounce Street claims she lifted a copy of Byron."

"That is ridiculous. She cannot even read. Why would the man think. . .oh." He smacked the heel of his hand to his head. "Of course. I should have thought of it then."

"What are you going on about?"

"Come. There is no time to spare." Jackson edged past Baggett. "The man could be closing shop any minute now—if he has not already."

"Are you mad? You cannot go tromping along the streets for all to see. If a night constable comes along, you are done for."

Jackson upped his pace, leaving Baggett's mutterings behind. True, it was a risk to speed along so unconcealed, but worth it if it freed Kit. *Anything* to free Kit. This late in the evening, it would be a stretch to find the bookseller still in his shop, but trotting along the pavement by daylight really would be a danger. This had to work. He had waited too long to return to London as it was.

Ahead, golden light glowed from the shop's front window. Jackson dashed onwards, thanking God the whole way, until his silent prayer shattered on the ground in front of the bookseller's door. Behind the glass, the man himself flipped the OPEN sign to CLOSED. Jackson rapped on the frame.

The shopkeeper squinted at him, then aimed a stubby finger at the placard.

As the man turned away, Jackson knocked harder, rattling the windowpanes. "Open up!"

He turned back, a glower deeply etched into his face. "I am closed, you big oaf!" Though muffled, the words were easy to distinguish, especially the oaf part.

"The man said open up." Baggett's voice rumbled next to Jackson's ear, drawing the bookseller's gaze.

As the man took in Baggett's uniform, his nostrils flared. Yanking the key from his pocket, he unlocked the door then aimed an evil eye at Jackson. "Your book has been sitting here nigh on five days, and now you decide to come calling for it the very second I close?"

Jackson darted past him. "Follow me."

He wound through the narrow stacks, stopping at the row where he'd stood days ago with Kit. Days? Seemed like forever. He pulled down the big brown book that Kit had rejected, and there behind it stood a small leather copy, the one she'd been carrying. The one that'd landed her in jail.

"What is this about?" the shopkeeper's voice bludgeoned from behind. "Why rummage on my shelves at this late hour?"

Jackson wheeled about and handed over the missing book.

Baggett's dark eyes narrowed on the shopkeeper, who blew out a reverent breath as he turned the small volume over in his hands.

"Well, I'll be a hedgehog's harpy," the bookseller murmured.

"As you see, your book has been here safe and sound all along." Jackson looked down his nose at the man. "You must drop the charges on Miss Turner at once."

The man lifted his face, confusion wrinkling his brow. "So, she was not a thief after all, eh?"

"No, she is not." He blinked. Had he really just said that aloud? And yet, as his father had pointed out, much of the world was indeed murky, and he had seen with his own eyes that Kit acted out of nothing but compassion for others. Perhaps she hadn't acted rightly, but maybe she hadn't acted as wrongly as he had first judged either.

Baggett's gaze bounced between the two of them, finally landing on the bookseller. "Stop by the station in the morning, and I will personally oversee the paperwork."

Shaking his head, the wide-eyed bookseller gazed at his beloved copy of Byron. "Aye, Constable."

Relief loosened the knots in Jackson's shoulders, and for the first time in several days, he breathed easier. Thank God this misunderstanding had been cleared up. But had it been cleared up soon enough, or was Kit already locked away in some deep, dark cell?

"Time to go." Baggett tugged on Jackson's arm, leading him away. "Now that you have cleared your lady friend's name, you are done here. And you are done in London. Get out, Forge, before Graybone gets wind you are still around."

"Done? No, not quite yet. I have one more thing to take care of." He peered up at the strip of night between the dark buildings. He'd promised to find Joe, and God willing, that's what he would do.

The longer Kit stared into the semidarkness, the more the walls closed in on her. She rubbed her eyes with the heels of her hands, weary beyond measure. This solitude was getting to her.

Her hands fell away and she sighed. Near as she could tell, Grace had been gone twenty-four hours. A full day and night with nothing but her own company, and already she was thoroughly sick of herself. Still, was this not better than doubling or tripling up with the hardened criminals in the long-term cells?

She picked at a thread on the hem of her bodice, frustrated. Anger still flared now and then against Jackson for putting her in here, but were she honest, she'd have to admit that her ire had as much to do with the achy part of her heart that yet longed for his company. His ready smile. The curiosity and intelligence behind his deep blue eyes. How rousing of a challenge he'd been, matching her wit for wit.

Outside the door, boots thudded up the stairs. She cocked her head. A key jangled, and the door skrudged open.

A breath later, the same thick-bodied guard who'd called on Grace Shaw yesterday now stood at the threshold for her. "Out you go, Miss Turner."

The words spidered down Kit's spine. This was it. The last time for who knew how many years that she'd breathe fresh air on the short walk from the prison to the neighboring courthouse. She rose, every nerve taut, and strode stiff legged out the door.

The guard tipped his head towards the stairway. "After you."

Kit blinked. Was he not going to cuff her? Drive her like a stupid sheep with the tip of his truncheon? And why weren't there two guards to prevent her from tearing off once her feet hit the outside world? A small hope kindled in her belly as she picked her way down the stairs. Maybe she could make a break for it. She just might actually get away before the man could catch her.

But as quickly as thoughts of escape arose, she tamped them down. Would that not be taking things back into her own hands?

Forgive me, God. I said I surrender, and if nothing else, I am a woman of my word. And so, would You go before me?

Setting her chin, she descended the stairs then marched along the wide corridor, ever closer to the front entry. If God could prevent lions from eating Daniel, He could get her through whatever horrors were to come. Was that not what Jackson meant with all his talk about trusting God?

Bracing herself, she stopped near the scarred front door and held out her wrists. Surely now the guard would clamp on the cuffs, and the sooner this part was over, the better.

Without so much as a glance, he strode past her and unlocked the big door. Light rain pattered outside, the air washed clean with each tender drip. Kit drank in the fresh scent, memorizing every blessed nuance of it to revisit in the cold, dark days to come.

"Right then, out you go." The guard handed her a small paper and stepped aside, allowing her free passage. "Sorry for the mix-up. Give that pass to the gatekeeper and Godspeed to you."

What was this? A wicked trick? Setting her up to run off so yet another charge could be added to her list of crimes? No. She'd not fall for such a swindle.

She balled up the paper and shoved it into her pocket, then once again stiffened her arms out in front of her, this time all the straighter. "Go ahead and do your duty."

He chuckled. "My duty, miss, is to see you off. You're free to go."

"I am free?" But even in her own voice the words didn't make sense. "You mean I can walk out that door and you will not hunt me down as a dodger?"

"That's right. All charges against you were dropped this morning."

Stunned, she let her arms fall to her sides. Questions popped up, one after another, but she'd be a fool to demand answers on this side of the jail's walls. Mumbling a thank-you, she gathered her hem and dashed out into the beautiful murk of a drizzly May day. Not even the ugly stone walls could crush the joy spreading through her. She stopped at the gate guard's hut and shoved the crumpled note at him, then held her breath. If this was some sort of swindle, now would be the time to find out.

He held the paper practically to his nose, squinted, then jammed the thing onto a spindle of other papers and ducked out into the rain to unlock the gate. "Good day." He gave her a sharp nod.

Kit hesitated, then strode past him, half expecting a long arm to reach out and yank her back. But as soon as she cleared the iron gate, it swung shut and the lock clicked behind her. What in the world? Shading her eyes from the falling rain, she glanced heavenward, astounded.

Thank You, God, she silently mouthed.

"Kit."

Her jaw dropped. Did surrender mean God would talk to her as well as listen to her prayers?

"Kit, over here. Please, come out of the rain."

She snapped her gaze to the side, where a broad-shouldered, blue-eyed man stood with an outstretched umbrella. Jackson. Her heart skipped a beat at the sight of him, and she wasn't entirely pleased with the base response. Traitorous body.

Traitorous man.

She should not give him one more minute of her time. Gathering her hem, she poised to leave him behind forever.

His other hand shot out, palm up, bearing her token. What sort of dupe was this?

"Walk with me a ways?" His blue gaze bored into hers. "I can explain everything."

Wary, she advanced, ready to flee if need be. Would he snatch the thing back once she got close? Chuck it into the air like a mean boy playing a cruel game of keep-away?

Yet his hand didn't waver as she drew nearer, nor did he pull away when she made a swipe for her precious button. Her fingers wrapped around the metal, still warm from being on Jackson's person. Instinctively, she held it to her breast, reclaiming all she had of who she was.

"As you see, I never turned in your token." Jackson's low voice blended softly with the falling rain. "I had nothing to do with your arrest. It was all a misunderstanding from that bookseller we visited. He thought you had lifted that copy of Byron."

She peered up at him. "You did not betray me?"

"I would never betray you, Kit." Slowly, he cupped her cheek. "Not in a million years."

Time stopped, then. Right there. On a busy London street just outside the ugly grey stones of Newgate prison, his touch warming her in places that'd been cold and lonely since the day she'd been discarded at the foundling hospital. *"Everyone else will fail you."* Except Jackson hadn't. He had kept his promise. Dependable. Just like God. Maybe—just maybe—this was a man worth giving her heart to. But the way the thing pounded inside her ribs and the longer he stared deep into her eyes, it was too late to even consider such a thing.

He already owned her heart.

Sorrow deepened the blue in his eyes. "I am only sorry that it took me so long to get you out. I should have realized sooner, should have—"

"You were right."

His jaw sagged.

"The last few days have been horrible, yes, but they showed me you were right, that I needed to trust God, not myself. And for that, I thank you."

Air chuffed past his lips. "You, Kit Turner, never cease to surprise me."

Heat crawled up her face, so many strong emotions swirling in her belly that she hardly knew what to do with them. She pulled away. "So, have you found Joe, then?"

Glancing about, he tipped his hat lower then angled his head. Curious. It was almost as if he didn't want to be seen. "How about we walk while we talk, hmm?" With a sweep of his hand, he guided her beneath the umbrella and led her to a side street where few carts passed and even fewer pedestrians trod. "As for Joe, I am afraid we are back to the starting gate."

"What do you mean? What about the Lord Mayor?"

"He was a dead end." Jackson lowered his head as if ashamed. "We were wrong."

"Wrong?" The word tasted foreign on her tongue. "No, the man *is* tied up in all the disappearances. Grace Shaw, the missing merchant's daughter, was my cellmate, wrongfully imprisoned by Sir Robert when she got too close to the truth that night at the party."

Again Jackson darted a glance before and behind them, then led her over to the side of a building, his back to the street. An intimate sort of stance the way he faced her alone, but she got the distinct impression there was more to it than that. Something that threatened—but whom? Her? Or him?

"Explain, please," he said simply.

Shoving down the foreboding feeling, she lifted her face. "Miss Shaw's father recently hired a new foreman who told her that he had gone off on business, that the warehouse was closed. But Grace saw merchandise in the supposedly empty building, and the harbour master confirmed it. She thought if she could find out what the cargo was and where it was going, it might open up new avenues to finding her father. She inquired all the way up to the Lord Mayor's office yet no one seems able to help her, nor are they willing to look into the matter. And for her questions, she ended up wrongfully accused and imprisoned. Seems to me like someone is keeping that cargo a secret and making sure it stays that way."

"Hmm," Jackson grumbled, then once again glanced about.

Kit frowned. What had him on edge? Who was he expecting to show up?

But as suddenly, his blue eyes once again focused on her. "Perhaps we ought to pay that warehouse a visit ourselves. Confirm the truth of Miss Shaw's words. That is, if you can find a place on your crew for a hunted man."

She gnawed the inside of her cheek, chewing on Jackson's impossible implication. Surely he didn't mean himself, but what other option was there? "You?"

"Afraid so. I am no longer a constable and no longer welcome inside the City limits. It will be a race to find the one responsible for the missing men before I am discovered by the police."

"You mean I will be the one hiding your identity?" She chuckled. What a brilliant turnabout! "I wonder, Mr. Forge, how many more surprises you have in store for me."

Chapter Twenty-Four

With a last look over his shoulder, Jackson eased away from the shadow of a fishmonger's shop and darted down the damp stretch of pavement to the doorway of the next black building. He gulped in night air, then wished he hadn't. The lingering fresh scent of the earlier rain didn't reach into this part of town. The stink of the Wapping Dockyard could choke a horse with its noxious combination of brine-soaked wood, dead seaweed, and something peculiarly like the breath of a man with rotted teeth.

Three buildings later, the weathered sign of Shaw's Stowage screeched on rusty hinges. Good. Almost there. Winded and weary, he crouch-ran the rest of the way and ducked behind a man-sized spool of thick chain near the side of the east wall.

Ahead of him, a whisper shot out of the dark. "Over here."

Rising to his toes, he craned his neck and peered past the spool. Stationed behind a huge coil of rope, Kit's pale hand beckoned in the moonlight. Leaving behind the safety of the chain, he crept to her side.

Though it was dark, amusement twinkled in her eyes. "You are fashionably late, sir."

"Took me longer than I expected to zigzag around all the night patrols." Lifting his cap with one hand, he swiped the sweat off his forehead with the other. "Did I miss anything?"

"Quite a bit, actually." She hitched her thumb towards the front loading bay of Shaw's Stowage. "Three wagons unloaded crates of various sizes about an hour ago."

His gaze drifted across the road to the black outlines of ships bobbing, then strayed down the empty lane where the rest of the warehouses hunkered dark and silent. "Strange time of night for a delivery." Resetting his cap, he faced Kit. "But it does confirm the information you received from Miss Shaw. Speaking of which, I asked Baggett to see what can be done about getting her released from Newgate. He agreed to check into it."

An enigmatic smile ghosted Kit's lips. Disbelief? Or dared he hope, admiration?

He cocked his head. "What?"

"I did not ask for such a favor, yet I am grateful for it, as I am sure Miss Shaw will be also." She leaned closer, her whisper feathering warm across his cheek. "You have quite the soft heart, you know."

Simple words. Likely tossed as carelessly as bread crumbs to a flock of seagulls. But even so, he gobbled them down eagerly. Ahh, but she was a sight, with moonlight bathing her tipped-up face, her dark hair pulled hastily back to a loose tail. The outline of her full lips begged a kiss. If he edged a bit nearer—

Wheels rumbled against cobbles, growing louder, breaking the spell of the moment. Kit snapped into action, tugging at his arm. "There is a better vantage point closer to the door."

She scurried ahead, hem hitched up like the night they'd ventured through the underground tunnels, freeing her shapely legs for quick movement. Jackson grinned as he followed the feisty woman. Was it her fearlessness that attracted him so or her love of adventure?

Just a yard before the end of the building, she crouched behind a rain barrel with barely enough room for him to squeeze in at her side. Not that he minded the way her body pressed against his. Quite the contrary.

A brougham pulled to a stop, its dark silhouette overly large against the warehouse's slatted sides. From this angle, naught but the back half could be seen. No running lights? Curious. Traveling unmarked on London streets in the dark of night was asking for a collision. Even more strange, the driver did not appear to open the door. The carriage simply sat like a gravestone in the shadows. Why would someone take the trouble to drive here then remain inside their carriage?

Jackson glanced at Kit, who merely shrugged. Clearly, she entertained the same questions.

Moments later, a door scraped open and footsteps scuffed the cobbles. The silhouette of a man approached the carriage, then stopped at the door.

After the click of window locks and shush of glass being lowered, a deep voice wafted out of the brougham. "Everything going as planned?"

Jackson angled his head. There was something about that tone. That unique accent. Hard to decipher from this distance, but he'd swear he'd heard it somewhere before.

The other man's voice squeaked like a hinge in comparison. "Yes, sir. One more delivery tomorrow, then we're set for the dark ship the following night. That is, as long as you have the bill of lading on you?"

"Do you question my proficiency, Mr. Griffen?" The question boomed out sharp as mortar fire.

"No, sir." Griffen's rusty words grew considerably raspier. "Not at all, sir. It's just that. . ."

An eerie silence followed. Griffen's arm lifted, and if Jackson didn't miss his mark, the man was loosening the knot of his neckcloth.

"You were about to say, Mr. Griffen?"

Griffen's hand fell useless to his side. "Without that paper, sir, we're sitting ducks should someone come sniffing about like that Shaw woman did."

"I told you she has been taken care of."

"That don't stop what she might've set in motion. Without that document, were a bluecoat to come nosing in, it's our heads on a pike, that's what."

More words followed, but so low it was hard to hear. Should they edge closer? He turned to Kit, about to suggest it, but too late. Already she dodged around the rain barrel and flattened against the wall at the edge of the building. Jackson trailed her, then pulled her back with a grip on her shoulder and eased her behind him. If anyone was going to get caught, it ought to be him. Lord only knew what these scoundrels would do to a woman.

A heated protest tickled low in his ear, but when the voices started up again, Kit quickly quieted.

"You are being compensated well enough for the risk, Mr. Griffen. Once that shipment arrives in Morocco, you will never have to work again."

Jackson whispered over his shoulder. "That is quite a sum of money they expect to make. You think Bags is wrapped up in this somehow?"

"Maybe." She stood so close her lips brushed his ear. "Maybe not."

"But to quiet your mewling. . ." The deep voice from the carriage was followed by the click of a door handle. Griffen retreated a step as a dark figure descended and held out some sort of paper. "Here you are. Now, show me the goods."

Paper in hand, Griffen pivoted and stalked towards the warehouse. The other man followed. Jackson leaned forward, blinking. Then rubbed his eyes and looked again. Sure enough, a great hump of a back marred the fellow's form as he trailed Griffen.

Poxley. The Lord Mayor's secretary.

Jackson pulled back and faced Kit. "So, we were right," he whispered. "The Lord Mayor's office is behind this scheme, but all along it was the secretary. Quite the well-played game."

"There you have it. Get your friend Baggett to haul in Poxley and perhaps the fate of the missing men will finally be revealed."

She was right. That's exactly what he would've done before Sergeant Graybone's words had lodged deep in his mind like a great strike of a pickaxe.

"Unless a criminal is caught in the act of breaking a law, you must present evidence that cannot be broken."

Kit edged away from the barrel.

Jackson pulled her back. "It is not that simple. We have to catch Poxley in the act of committing a felony, not just visiting a warehouse."

"Hmm. Well then, I suppose it would help to have one of us on the inside to orchestrate such a delinquency."

No, she couldn't be serious. Could she? But judging by the slow grin spreading on her lips, the little rabble-rouser fully intended mischief. The sort that could get them killed.

"Kit, do not even think about—"

Before he could grab her arm, she darted off, towards the very same door through which Poxley and his henchman had disappeared. Blast the crazy woman!

Her streak of headstrong fearlessness may very well end up costing them both their lives.

Kit shoved open the warehouse's side door, ignoring Jackson's harshly whispered protests stabbing her between the shoulder blades. She'd learned long ago to face fear rather than skirt it, but that didn't stop a cold sweat from making her palms clammy. There was no denying it. This *was* a risk. One that would be well worth it as long as neither of them was killed. She smoothed her hands along her skirt. Was she running ahead of God again? Or had He provided this opportunity for a reason?

She stopped just inside the door, Jackson practically stumbling into her as he caught up. Gun hammers clicked behind them. Flit! Perhaps she'd overestimated how easy this would be.

"I told you this was a bad idea," Jackson whisper-growled at her back.

Ahead, the hunchbacked Mr. Poxley turned their way. So did Mr. Griffen, though he stood in a shadow so it was hard to see his face.

Kit squared her shoulders. Despite the threat of gunfire, it was better to take charge than show fear—a lesson gleaned from years on the streets. "Good evening, Mr. Poxley. I would like to have a word with you, preferably without a gun to my head."

His eyebrows arched, and judging by Jackson's sharp inhale behind her, his did too.

Mr. Poxley angled his head, his dragon-green eyes glowing. Amusement? Or irritation? "Then you should have made an appointment at my office, miss."

"My mistake. I did not realize you met publicly with reputed thieves."

"A thief? How intriguing. And who might you be, I wonder?" He advanced, his shiny leather shoes clacking on the floor planks as he studied her. His gaze drifted past her, and as he took in Jackson's face, his eyes widened. "Forge? Huh. What do you know." Lifting a hand, he snapped his fingers in the air. "Stand down, men. For now."

Clicks sounded again, followed by the rustle of cloth as arms lowered.

Mr. Poxley stepped nearer to her, smelling of bergamot and ginger drops. "What is it you want, Miss. . . ?"

"Turner." She lifted her chin. "Kit Turner."

A curse ripped out of the shadows behind Mr. Poxley, followed by the dark shape of Mr. Griffen. "She's naught but street trash, Mr. Poxley. Not worth the time it would take to crush her under yer heel."

Jackson sidestepped so fast, Kit was forced to shoot out her arm to hold him back. Now that Mr. Griffen stood in a swath of lantern light, she eyed him. Scruffy dishwater-coloured hair poked out shaggy beneath his cap. A scar rippled over the bulb of his nose. But most telling of all was a big brown mole protruding from the side of his chin. No wonder the man's whiny voice had seemed familiar.

She quirked her lips. "Taken on a new skin just like the snake you are, eh Grimes? I heard there was a price on your head after the way you rolled ol' Rook and ran off with his money."

A purply-red flush rose up the man's neck, spreading over his face like an angry bruise.

Satisfied her arrow had hit home, Kit swung her gaze back to Mr. Poxley. "But I am certain you have done your due diligence and already knew about the Rook affair before you hired Mr. Grimes. Even so, it is all the more reason for you to consider my proposition."

Mr. Poxley cut a sideways glance at Grimes before facing her. "I do love a good proposition, especially from a comely lady such as yourself." He advanced a step closer, examining her in a way that burrowed under her skin. "I cannot help but feel I know you from somewhere. Have we met before, Miss Turner?"

"Surely you would remember if we had." Reaching out, she ran a finger down the length of his lapel. "I would certainly remember if I had met you."

A grumble rumbled at her back.

"Your watchdog is quite protective." Mr. Poxley caught her hand and lowered it, then snapped his gaze to Jackson. "I believe there is a restraining order against you."

"You ought to know. You issued it yourself."

His thin lips slowly spread into a smile. "Yet it appears you are ignoring it, which is interesting. A man once given to upholding the law is now breaking it? What sway does this little vixen have over you, I wonder?"

Kit smiled. Perfect. She could use the man's own words to her advantage. "Much, which is why Forge is now a member of my crew. You should consider my proposal, sir. These goods are to be moved two nights hence, are they not?" She arced her hand in the air, indicating the many crates stacked around them.

Mr. Poxley's smile faded.

But Kit's grin grew. "Two full days is a long time to avoid detection. It would be a shame to be discovered now that you are so near to closing your deal. Mr. Forge here, as you well know, is the keenest eye around for spotting trouble. I could lend him to you for a price."

"Price!" Grimes spat out a curse. "More like a bloodletting, knowing you."

Mr. Poxley shook his head. "While I appreciate your offer, Miss Turner, I have all the security I need."

"I beg to differ, being that both Mr. Forge and I walked freely in here tonight. What is to stop the bluecoats from doing the same?"

"I assure you," Mr. Poxley's bass voice deepened to a threat as he slipped his gaze to the men behind her and Jackson, "that problem will never happen again."

And neither would this chance. She scrambled for words, for reason, for anything to get Jackson on the inside of this operation. "Your security notwithstanding, sir, Mr. Forge knows the routes and routines of every constable in this area. Plus, he has a friend on the force. Someone who can tip him off should the police decide to investigate this warehouse."

Poxley's face hardened to steel.

Oops. Wrong reasoning.

Once again, the man snapped his fingers. Guns clicked. Poxley's eyes darkened to a swampy green. "And how would the police know anything about my operation unless you told them, Miss Turner?"

Beside her, Jackson widened his stance.

Kit didn't blame him. They might have to fight their way out of here if she didn't come up with something. *Think. Think!*

"Do not be ridiculous." She forced a small laugh. "Why, I was only just released this morning from Newgate myself. Do you really think I would hand over such a juicy bone to my captors?"

"Perhaps, if you thought to blackmail me."

She fluttered her fingers at Jackson, making a point. "Why would I resort to such a dangerous game when I can simply profit by hiring out my best crew member? A benefit to you and to me. This is a business deal, Mr. Poxley. Nothing more. But if you would rather trust the obvious deficiencies in your current team and in the jaded past of your foreman there"—she tipped her head towards Grimes—"then I suppose we have nothing more to say on the matter."

She folded her arms, an exclamation mark to her willingness to end the deal.

Mr. Poxley jutted his sharp chin, equally as stubborn. "What is to stop me from having you killed here and now? Especially since you have seen and heard far too much."

She curved her lips into a slow smile. Theatrics had saved her many a time. Would to God that it might do so again. "Because, sir, the rest of my men are waiting outside for my departure. If I do not reappear in a timely fashion, they have their orders."

Curiosity flashed in his eyes. "For what?"

"To go directly to the police and inform them." She didn't move, not an inch, and lowered her voice to a silky purr. "The incarceration of the Lord Mayor's secretary would be quite the spectacle, I should think, especially if I am correct in my suspicions that these crates are full of contraband armaments."

"You are bluffing," he puffed, but his gaze flicked to the door.

"Do you want to take that risk, or would you rather avail yourself of my generous offer?" She cast the question like a sharpened hook. Would the fish bite or not?

His lips pursed, and for a moment he rubbed the back of his neck. Finally, he let out a long sigh. "If I happened to be interested—and I am not saying that I am—what is your fee?"

And there it was. Victory. Once a mark asked a price, the deal was already made. She hid a smile. "Ten percent of your take."

"Five," he countered. "But only after the ship is loaded and safely out of the City limits."

"Done." Kit shot out her hand, all the while feeling as if she might be making a deal with the devil.

And if so, what sort of hellfire had she just gotten Jackson into?

Chapter Twenty-Five

Trouble never came alone, that's what Jackson's father had always said. And he was right. From the day Jackson first met Kit, he'd walked hand in hand with one difficulty after another. But this time? He huffed as he approached Shaw's Stowage. This predicament might just be the thorniest of them all.

He reached for the doorknob of the loading bay entry, still unsure if the plan he and Kit had cobbled together was genius or idiocy. The next step would be for him to provoke Grimes to run off to Poxley, which wouldn't be easy and just might be deadly. With more force than necessary, he twisted the knob, but it didn't give. Not like last night. Apparently, Grimes had taken his lacking security to heart. Out of fear? Or out of pride? Actually, either could work. Cheered for the first time all morning, Jackson rapped on the door with his fist. It swung open and he stared down the barrel of an Adams revolver, held steady in the hand of a scar-faced mug. Grimes.

Jackson smiled. "I see you have upped some of your security. Good for you, man." Shoving aside the tip of the revolver, Jackson strolled past him.

Grimes grumbled as he slammed the door shut and locked it. Tucking his revolver away, he wheeled sharply about. "Do whatever it is you do, Forge, but stay outta my way while yer doin' it."

"Well, well." Jackson scratched his jaw. "That is quite the novel method of teamwork. Before I get to my duties, however, an assessment is in order."

"Scat! I got no time for you."

"How about intruders? Have you time for them?"

Grimes narrowed his eyes just as a short man in a brown flat cap darted up to him with a paper clutched in his fingers. "Pardon, sir, but this stock count don't figure right."

Grimes held up a hand, quieting the fellow without so much as a glance at him. "What're you goin' on about, Forge? What intruders?"

"Those who are craftier than you." Jackson hid a grin. Judging by the sour twist of Grimes's lips, provoking him might not prove to be as hard as he'd feared. "But to your credit, I noticed you put a man on the street who actually did stop me and ask about my business. Still, how did he know I am who I said I was? And were I not, how would he have warned you?"

The fellow next to Grimes edged closer, a curious tilt to his head. "Yeah. How 'bout that?"

Grimes puffed out his chest and thumped it with his thumb. "My man Puggs has direct orders from me to leave his post and come running if he smells anything fishlike."

"Hmm," Jackson drawled. "This Puggs fellow may be a record-breaking sprinter, but even so, sound travels faster. I suggest you institute a warning whistle."

The fellow next to Grimes widened his eyes. "Say, that's a gem-crackin' idea." His gaze drifted to Grimes. "How come you din't think o' that?"

"Been too busy managin' yer mistakes." He yanked the paper from the man's hand and hitched his thumb towards the door. "Go figure out some sort of signal with Puggs. Now!"

The man scurried to the entry before Grimes finished bellowing.

Jackson lifted his chin. "Excellent. Now, join me on the roof. I should like to see what your setup is there."

"What setup?" Once again Grimes narrowed his eyes. The perpetual squint didn't do much for the scar splitting his nose; in fact, it made the purple line all the more prominent.

Without a word, Jackson stalked along a row of crates to the wooden staircase on a side wall. Let Grimes wonder. Let him squirm. Keeping the upper hand was simply a matter of putting the other person on the defensive. Leastwise, that's what he'd gleaned from working with Kit.

On the second floor, just ahead of him, a ladder of sorts was nailed to an outer wall, leading to a trap door in the ceiling. After a climb and a heave, Jackson broke through to the sooty air of a city morn. From this height, rooftops spread out in a checkerboard fashion. Shading his eyes with one hand, he scanned the entire perimeter, then swung about to face Grimes as soon as he emerged. "Why is no one manning this area?"

"Yer mad!" Grimes turned aside and spat, then swiped his mouth with the back of his hand. "Ain't no one gonna bust in from up here."

Jackson shook his head, adding just the right amount of pity to the twist of his lips. Beckoning for Grimes to follow, he sauntered to the edge of the roof. Below them, the road snaked along the dockyard before crawling into the maze of city streets. "One man with a gun on this perch can take out three or four blackguards before they even know what hit them. Post another man in that corner"—he aimed his finger parallel with the roofline—"and you will not only double your firepower but your range. No, make that four men. One in each corner."

A January wind couldn't freeze any colder than the chill of Grimes's gaze. "No one tells me what to do."

"Oh? Not even Poxley?"

The muscles on the sides of Grimes's neck bulged.

Jackson pivoted and retraced his steps down to the lowest level, then leaned against a crate and folded his arms. A few more nudges, and Grimes would bolt to Poxley's office, though he might pop Jackson in the nose first. A risk, that, but one well worth it.

Finally, Grimes stomped down the last stair.

"Oh, by the way." Jackson swept a dramatic look around. "Where are your dogs?"

Grimes cursed. "This ain't no scabbin' menagerie. We got crates. We move crates. That's all. Don't need no dogs."

Jackson straightened and poked the man in the chest. "That is where you are wrong, my friend. Even just one dog will not only alert you but be a first line of defense against an intruder."

The front door opened once again, and in stepped the short man with the flat cap. Perfect. Jackson crooked a finger at him, summoning him over. "You. Run down to Bolivar Street and see if there are any bull terriers to be had. Price out a few, then report back to me. Go. Now."

The man's gaze swerved from Jackson to Grimes, wavered a moment, and then swung back. "Aye, sir."

As he took off, Jackson turned to Grimes, only to see him lunging. Grimes grabbed him by the collar and shoved him up against the stack of crates.

"Who do ye think ye are, comin' in here with all yer swagger and fancy ideas." With each word, specks of spittle flew from Grimes's mouth, landing wet and noxious on Jackson's cheek. "Don't be tellin' my men what to do!"

Jackson gritted his teeth, keenly aware that every workman's eyes in the warehouse were pinned on them, hungry for a fight. But brawling with Grimes wasn't the goal, and in fact just might get him kicked out by Poxley. So he kept his tone placid. "The blame does not lie with me. Had you issued the order for a dog earlier, then I would not have had to direct your crewman elsewhere."

"Bah!" Grimes loosened his grip. "I'm done with you."

"Maybe, but I am not quite finished with you." Jackson tugged down his suit coat and tipped his head towards the side door. "Over there."

"What?" Though he asked, Grimes didn't make a move to look.

Jackson strode along the aisle and stopped in front of the door.

Nearby, a man in rolled-up shirtsleeves slipped him a glance while he bent over an open crate.

Jackson cocked his head at him. "Are you merely doing inventory or also guarding this door?"

As Grimes's footsteps thudded closer, the man jerked his face downwards and mumbled, "Just countin'. Tha's what I were told to do."

"Let me guess," Grimes groused at Jackson's side. "You want to station Rigsby at this post."

"Not at all." Jackson faced the other man once again. "You. Rigsby, is it?"

He straightened, avoiding eye contact with Grimes as if the man were a basilisk. "Aye. That's me."

"We are going to need to fortify this door"—he jutted his jaw to the entryway near his shoulder—"and you are just the man to do it. A few brackets from the smithy. A thick post from the lumberyard. That ought to suit. Are you up for the task?"

Rigsby threw back his shoulders, as proud as if he'd just been handed the keys to the kingdom. "Yes, sir. I'm yer man."

"Good." Jackson turned to Grimes. "Give Rigsby here some money for the supplies."

"No. I'll not have it!" Grimes roared. "First ye shame me, then ye tell me what to do and order about one o' my men. Now you think to pick my pocket? Out!" With one slick movement, he yanked open the door. "Get your ugly backside outta here and don't come sniffin' around 'ere again. Rigsby, back to countin', if you can even do that right."

Jackson smiled. Triumph was at hand. He could practically taste it. "Mr. Poxley hired me, Grimes. It is not up to you to fire me."

"Oh, you wanna play it like that, do you? Fine!" His voice ratcheted to a bowstring about to break. "Poxley will make you disappear once he's heard of this, and don't think he won't."

Grimes marched out the door.

Jackson grinned, then darted outside as well. Truly, the morning couldn't have gone any better, but this was only half the plan. Would that the rest of the scheme ran as smoothly. Lifting up a prayer for such, he skirted to the rear of the building, then pulled out a small mirror and caught the sun, aiming the beam far down the lane. In return, a flash of light several blocks away answered. Good. Kit's boy, Frankie, had seen and would take off with fleet-footed speed to signal her.

Jackson pulled out his revolver and checked its load. Then did the same with the other revolver he'd gotten from Kit—or more like one of her men—before taking off at a dead run. Timing for this part would have to be perfect or Kit could be in grave danger.

Hopefully he wouldn't cross paths with any constables who knew him on the way.

Kit smoothed her skirts as she entered the front hall of Mansion House. How different it looked without the dazzle of lit chandeliers and the press of partygoers.

Stationed near the door, the security guard on duty tipped his hat. "Can I direct you, miss?"

"Yes, I should like to see Mr. Poxley."

"The appointment clerk is over there." He tipped his head towards a thin man seated at a desk.

"Thank you." She approached the fellow, who appeared to be dozing, so squinty were his eyes.

"Can I help you, miss?"

"Yes. I have an appointment to see Mr. Poxley." The lie really did taste greasy this time. "Miss Turner. Nine o'clock."

The clerk flipped open a ledger and ran his finger down the column, then looked up, puzzled. "Are you certain you've got the correct date, miss?"

"Absolutely—oh! Dear. Perhaps not." She shook her head, hand flailing to her chest, then heaved a great sigh. "Whatever shall I do?

After I've traveled all this way today, leaving my sick mother unattended." She leaned close, adding an extra measure of trembling to her voice. "Is there any possible way you could get me in this morning? I'd hate to have to return tomorrow and leave my poor mother all alone again. I'm sure a man of your power has the authority to get me in a day early."

"Well, I. . ." He glanced again at the schedule, then nodded. "It appears Mr. Poxley is free at the moment, so I suppose it wouldn't hurt to allow you in today. Just go right up the stairs, Miss Turner." He swept his hand towards the grand staircase, beyond a life-sized statue of a man on a horse. "First door on the left."

"Thank you." Fighting the urge to run, she put one foot in front of the other as fast as she dared. Drawing attention wouldn't do, but neither would getting caught here by Grimes before she could plant the proper amount of doubt in Mr. Poxley's mind.

With a last tuck-up of a stray piece of hair, she sashayed into Mr. Poxley's office. The first thing that hit her was the cloying scent of ginger drops and far too much bergamot oil. The second, how luxurious the plush carpet, the velvet draperies, the flocked walls. Quite impressive for a mere secretary. How much more opulent was the Lord Mayor's official office?

A dark scowl pulled Mr. Poxley's brows into a thick slash where he sat ensconced behind a massive desk. "Miss Turner." He set down his pen with a sharp *thwack*, clearly annoyed. "Your visit had better be of the utmost importance. I expect the Lord Mayor to return at any moment."

"I assure you, it is." She wandered over to the large window at the far end of the office—the preappointed stage for the next act. Glancing across the road, she peered up at the roof. No Jackson-shaped man yet appeared with guns in hand. She chewed the inside of her cheek. Timing, as usual, would be everything. But first to get the secretary to join her.

She traced an imaginary pattern on the glass with one finger.

"Curious, is it not? Despite how Londoners pride themselves on being a savvy people, they are easy to deceive, especially when one presents a picture that is painted with broad-stroke lies."

Footsteps shushed on the rug, growing closer. "I find it hard to believe you came all this way to discuss the sheepish predilections of city folk."

"No, I did not." She turned, then retreated a step, allowing space for Mr. Poxley to stand centered in the window. "My man Forge sent word there is a mole in your operation. Apparently, Grimes has been feeding information to the police. It would not be the first time. How do you think he managed to make off with Rook's money?"

Poxley's eyes narrowed to green slits. "What sort of information?"

She forced her gaze to remain on those lizard eyes, fighting the urge to glance out and see if Jackson was in place yet. "That you are about to make an assassination attempt on the Lord Mayor."

"Preposterous!" Grumbling, he flicked his hand in the air as if batting away an annoying horsefly. "A complete falsehood."

She hid a smile. Seed planted. Deep, judging by the vehemence roughening his voice. "Surely you know that an accusation does not need to be true as long as it detains you for the next several days. And once you are gone, who do you think will take over and make off with the money for that shipment tomorrow?"

Footsteps pounded up the stairs just outside the door. As Poxley turned to the sound, Kit glanced out the window. There. Across the road, Jackson peered over the roof's edge, guns in hand.

Catty-corner from where she and Poxley stood, Grimes darted in the door, then stopped short as his gaze landed on her. The glower on his face could sever flesh from bone. "What are you doing here?"

"Rather a bold move, Grimes. You showing up here when. . .ahh. Setting the stage yourself, are you? Making sure the players are all in the right place. Too bad the Lord Mayor is not in at the moment. Quite the mistake on your part. Tell me, though, after the shot was made by your assassin, how did you intend to pin the blame on Mr. Poxley here?" In a dramatic move, she spread her arms wide, then gathered them at her back as if clasping her hands.

But instead of clasping, she pulled a red bit of cloth from her waist and waved it in the window, then quickly tucked it back. Had Jackson seen? Her pulse beat wild.

Grimes sneered. "I don't know what you're talking about." He faced Mr. Poxley. "Nor do I know what sort of jibbity-jab she's fillin' yer head with—"

Two shots exploded, showering glass over her and the secretary as they dropped to the ground. Belly-crawling out of the line of fire, Kit did a quick assessment. Nothing bleeding on her or Poxley, as far as she could tell. Jackson hadn't been jesting when he'd said he was handy with a gun. It took a good marksman to hit someone, but an even better one to closely miss.

She pushed up to sit—more unnerved than she liked to admit from the near bloodshed—and aimed a shaky finger at Grimes, who peeked out from behind the top of a high-back chair. "You snake! Trying to take me out as well!"

Grimes opened his mouth, but a voice thundered from the door. "No one move!"

Gun drawn, the guard from downstairs edged inside on high alert, sweeping the entire room with a steady glance. Another guard followed, wearing the same livery and sporting an identical pistol. "Mr. Poxley? Are you hurt? Stay away from the window, sir. We've sent another man to locate the shooter."

The secretary shook shards of glass from his arm then extended his hand to Kit, drawing them both to their feet. "No, the lady and I are fine."

"That's no lady!" Grimes spit out. "That's a—"

"Enough!" Poxley boomed. With a flick of his fingers, he motioned the guards towards Grimes. "Lock him away in one of the holding cells. I shall have him questioned later."

The guards trained their guns on Grimes. The one who'd been at the front door cut a glance at the secretary. "On what charges, sir?"

"An assassination attempt."

Curses flew from Grimes, loud and ugly, crude enough to heat Kit's cheeks.

"I don't even have a gun on me!" Grimes roared.

"No, but your marksman out there did." Mr. Poxley angled his head at the broken window. "Though I cannot say much for his eyesight. Not only did he miss his target, but I am a full head shorter than the Lord Mayor."

"You think I'd be fool enough to order a shooting while I were bloody well in the same room?"

Kit leapt in. "Hah! Why not? It's the perfect alibi. And would that not be just like you, watching to see that the deed was finished? Next time you should pay for a better deadeye and—"

"There will not be a next time," Mr. Poxley cut her off. "As I said, lock him up at once!"

"Right, bind him, mate." The guard kept his gun trained on Grimes, while the other snapped into action. Retrieving a length of rope coiled on his belt, he ducked a flying fist from the purple-faced Grimes. It took a tussle to the floor before the guard finally tied the man's wrists behind his back and hauled him to his feet.

"This isn't the end. You hear me? This isn't the end!" Grimes's voice screeched like fingernails on slate all the way out the door and down the stairs.

Mr. Poxley shook his head, then faced her. "Are you quite all right, Miss Turner?"

Flit! She was better than he could possibly imagine. Thus far, their plan had worked out smashingly well.

But she wasn't finished yet.

She dipped her head in an appropriately solemn nod. "I am fine, but I admit I am sorry you had to find out about Grimes's character the hard way. He always was one to watch as his mark was stabbed in the back—or shot, as the case was here. It is an ugly betrayal, one I have experienced several times of my own. Had you come to me first and hired my crew, this whole mess could have been avoided."

"Yes, well. . ." The secretary guided her away from the breeze now freely flowing through the broken window. "Hiring criminals is always an iffy proposition. I had checked most thoroughly into Grimes's background, but apparently the blackguard must have paid well to hide his nefarious dealings. Humph. And he seemed so loyal."

"Do not be too hard on yourself, sir. Fidelity is a rare thing in our line of work. But Grimes is gone, so there should be no more issues with the rest of your operation. Your ship will sail. The profit made. End of story. Though I suppose you will have to replace Mr. Grimes, and in light of that, I shall leave you to your work." She dipped him a bow. "Good day, Mr. Poxley."

"Good day, Miss Turner," he murmured, clearly distracted.

She pivoted, measuring each step to the door. This was the key moment, as crucial as Jackson's aim. But by the time she passed the threshold, still Mr. Poxley had not called her back. Had she miscalculated? Did he have another felon already standing in the wings to replace Grimes? Maybe one of his other warehouse men?

Defeat sank like leaden slag to the bottom of her belly. Now what to do? How could Jackson summon Poxley to the warehouse if he wasn't in charge? Pah! They'd have to come up with an entirely new scheme. With heavy steps, she approached the top of the stairs.

"Miss Turner."

Poxley's voice turned her around. "Yes, sir?"

The secretary stood grim-faced in his office doorframe. "Let your man Forge know he is my new foreman."

Chapter Twenty-Six

Not knowing was the worst. Like walking alone at midnight past a narrow passage and wondering if something in the darkness might reach out and pull you in. An impossible feeling to shake, clammy as a night sweat, one that had stuck to Jackson every step of the way back to the warehouse along with a barrage of unrelenting questions.

Had his shots fired true and missed Kit? Had he avoided Poxley? Did Kit have time enough to plant doubt in Poxley's mind before Grimes arrived? Or had Poxley detected her swindle and ordered her arrest? And if such was the case, would the next person strolling through the warehouse door be the grim reaper, handing his calling card to Jackson?

Ignoring the men buzzing about, resealing crates that he'd had double-counted for accuracy, Jackson pressed the heel of his hand to the ache between his eyes. He'd been wrong. Kit wouldn't be the death of him. All the wondering and waiting would.

A deep whistle from outside leached through the warehouse walls, followed by two shrill notes. The warning signal charged through Jackson like an electric current. He reached for one of his revolvers and strode to the front bay entry while calling over his shoulder, "To your places, men."

Sucking in a breath, he turned the lock then eased open the door. Better to face an enemy head-on than cower in a corner like a trapped hare.

A brown skirt swished down the road and a chuckle rumbled in his throat. Kit. Completely unhurt. Strolling along as casually as if she promenaded through a field of daffodils—all while Puggs stared down the barrel of a Snider-Enfield rifle aimed straight at her back. Jackson waved the man off, relief washing through him, and for the first time all morning, the tight muscles in his shoulders loosened.

"Quite the welcome." Kit's gaze lowered to the revolver in his hand. "But I bet you treat all the girls that way, hmm?"

"No, only you." He grinned while he tucked away the revolver.

She smiled back. "I feel special."

"You are." The telling words escaped before he could retrieve them, exposing his true feelings in a way that made him feel naked. Heat crawling up his neck, he wheeled about and shoved open the warehouse door. As soon as they cleared the threshold, he lifted his voice. "Stand down, men. False alarm."

Around him, the crew returned to their previous posts, and he closed the door behind Kit. Her hair was disheveled, a few brown strands straggling to her neck and several specks of broken glass still glinting at the crown. But other than that, she appeared as spritely as ever with both hands fisted on her hips.

"Well." Her nose crinkled up at him. "I see you have taken charge here quite seamlessly."

"And I see you are unscathed. I am assuming things went well."

After a quick glance around, she lowered her voice. "Thanks to your marksmanship, yes. Grimes is out of the way and you, sir, are the official foreman of this operation."

"The outcome we wanted, but is it a curse or a blessing, I wonder?" He heaved a sigh and led her over to the nearby receiving desk. Papers littered the surface, a legitimate cover should the harbour master happen by and get too curious. Jackson did a perimeter scan to be sure no crewmen paid them any mind, then picked up a bill of lading and rummaged about in a drawer with a false bottom to pull out an identical document. Both bore Poxley's signature, but one was fabricated. He held them both for Kit to see.

"These crates of guns were a covert operation originating with the Home Office, destined for the Metropolitan Police. Being that firearms are generally frowned upon by the public, the Home Office had hoped to have these distributed quietly. Naturally, Poxley got wind of it and decided to conduct his own secretive plot. Look here and here." He pointed to the destination line on both bills of lading.

Kit squinted. "One has more letters in it than the other."

"Correct. Because this cargo is supposed to be delivered to the Home Office here in London, not to Morocco, which is where Poxley intends to divert it. Yet both are signed by him."

"Then we've got him!" She grinned.

Leaning close to her, he lowered his voice. "If I am to persuade Baggett to go to the sergeant, I will need all the solid information I can get, which is why I've got the men busy taking a final tally of the goods." He shoved the paper back into the drawer.

"But even then, do you really think Mr. Baggett will listen? Will he help? I mean, you are still a man on the run."

A valid question. Would he? "Let us hope so."

"Hmm," Kit murmured. "I fear you have the harder sell than I." With a brush of her fingers, she tucked away one of her wayward locks. "Speaking of which, I have already asked Frankie to round up my crew. I am assuming we move forward with our original plan?"

"I see no reason not to." He crossed to the front of the desk and leaned back against it, thinking through their scheme, then satisfied himself with one more scan of the place to make sure no one was listening. "Have your men arrive at the wharf by nine tomorrow when the ship docks. I'll pass them off as extra hands hired by Poxley. As they load, have them slowly stow away on board. When the task is nearly finished, I will summon Poxley then convince him to personally attend the shipment until it is out of the city proper. Of course, with the help of Baggett and your crew, the ship will never make it that far. Poxley will be arrested. Questioned. And with any luck, we will discover the whereabouts of Joe and the other missing men."

"I still think we should just have Baggett and a squad here on hand to arrest him as he arrives."

"Too risky for a snake like that. He'd slither out of such a loose snare, simply saying the false bill was forged. No, I need him on that ship with the document in his pocket for the noose to tighten around his neck. The sergeant clearly impressed upon me, and I quote, 'Unless a criminal is caught in the act of breaking a law, you must present evidence that cannot be broken.' And my plan is shatterproof."

"But what if it's not?" Kit stepped close, the silvery flecks in her eyes as troubled as the North Sea. "What if Poxley will not talk? Or is as bad a lead as the Lord Mayor was? What if none of this has any bearing whatsoever on finding Joe?"

"Then we work another angle, for you see"—reaching out, he tweaked her cheek—"I am as tenacious as you."

Her lips curved. "Well, I suppose I should be off, then. We both have work to do."

She turned—just as the front door crashed open and in stormed a bloodied, limp-stepped figure.

Shock flashed cold through Jackson's veins as Grimes swung a pistol barrel their way.

"Thought you were rid of me, aye?" Grimes chuckled, then turned aside and spat out a mouthful of blood. "Fools, as were those security guards who thought to turn me over to the police. No one crosses me and lives to tell about it."

Immediately, Jackson sidestepped Kit, blocking her from the hot-headed scoundrel. If Grimes was out for blood, may it be his. "Leave Miss Turner out of this. Your fight is with me."

"My fight is with whoever I say it is. This is my job. These are my men. And you and the woman are fish bait, just like that lawyer what I sank to the river bottom."

A shot cracked.

Jackson dove one way, reaching to pull Kit along with him. Too late. She lunged the other direction. Thank God so many crates filled the place. She sheltered behind one on the opposite side of the aisle. Before Grimes pulled off another round, Jackson whipped out a revolver and pushed it across the floor to Kit, then he yanked out the other. Her wide eyes met his, and when she nodded, they both rose and aimed at Grimes.

"Give it up, man," Jackson boomed. "You are outnumbered."

"Now there's where yer wrong." A macabre smile sliced across Grimes's face. "Rigsby! Sparks! Flank 'em."

Jackson swung a wild glance behind him and spied two of the warehouse men obediently pulling out pistols. Blast! He and Kit could only take out two, maybe even three or four of Grimes's men before the rest of the crew swarmed them. Defeat bludgeoned him in the gut. Was this how he'd go out, as unable to protect Kit as he had his brother?

God, no! Not again.

"Listen, men," Kit's voice rang strong. "Do you know how Grimes has treated his mates in the past? Unless you have a direct deal with Poxley, you will not see one ha'penny from Grimes when this job is done. He will skip off with your wages before you know he is gone. If you are that loyal to a backstabber, then so be it. But if you really want to make a coin, then take Grimes down and deliver him to Rooks, who has a fat bounty on his head. You could make twice the price."

A murderous flush spread over Grimes's face. "I shoulda killed you that first day you strolled in here."

While he spoke, Jackson dared another glance back at Rigsby and Sparks. The men exchanged a look, then after a sharp nod by Rigsby, both muzzles swiveled towards Grimes.

The steel bands in Jackson's chest loosened. Sweet heavens! That had been a close call. Once again, Kit's silver tongue proved lifesaving. Grinning, he faced Grimes.

But then a shot rang out.

Kit flew backwards.

And Jackson's world, all that was right and wrong, what should be and shouldn't, shattered to a million pieces, leaving nothing but a red rage rushing through his veins. Sound receded, save for a queer buzzing in his head.

If Grimes had killed her, Jackson would personally send the man to his grave.

∞

"Kit!"

Jackson's ragged shout blended with a scuffle of boots. Some grunts and groans. An explosion of curses, one of them possibly hers. But all that paled in comparison to the cry rising up Kit's throat and ripping past her lips.

White-hot agony burned through her upper arm as she stumbled and crashed heavily into a stack of crates. Shoring herself against them, she pressed her hand against the pain—which only made it worse. She gasped as her fingers came away bloody. Her stomach heaved, and she bent double, fighting nausea. Battling the wildfire in her arm. Scrunching her eyes so tight that white sparkles flashed on the black background.

"Kit! Speak to me." Strong arms guided her upright.

She blinked open to a worried blue gaze scanning the length of her from head to toe. The fear in Jackson's eyes stole her breath every bit as much as the bullet that had torn through her arm.

"I—" Her voice cracked, and she cleared her throat. "I am fine."

"Blast it, woman! You are not. Your sleeve is drenched in blood." In one swift movement, he swept her off her feet and cradled her against his chest as if she were naught but a babe in arms. "Rigsby!" he ordered as the world blurred by. "Get a wagon brought round, and for heaven's sake, shut that man up."

Her head jostled against Jackson's waistcoat, somewhat muffling the roar of Grimes's expletives. She snuck a peek over his shoulder as they passed the blackguard. One warehouse man planted a boot on Grimes's back, pinning him to the floor. The other finished binding his feet then yanked the stained kerchief from his neck and stuffed it in the man's mouth. Despite the nearly unbearable pain radiating in her entire left arm, her lips quirked into a small smirk. Christmas would be early for Rook. Grimes would've been safer locked behind the merciless walls at Newgate.

Gently, Jackson eased her onto the stool behind the receiving desk, but before he pulled away, he peered deep into her eyes. "Are you able to balance on your own, do you think?"

She jutted her jaw, hiding a wince. "I will not fall and break."

But even as he released her, she wished she could take the words back. Without Jackson's solid strength, she gripped the edge of the stool until her knuckles cracked just to remain upright. Biting her lip, she dared a glance at her injured arm. Sweet mercy. No wonder she felt a bit light-headed. Red soaked the fabric nearly down to her wrist. Flit!

Jackson stripped off his coat and waistcoat, then untucked his shirt and proceeded to rip the hem into strips. "What happened with this Rook fellow that he's willing to pay for Grimes?"

"He—" She swallowed back a wave of pain and tried again. "He ran a cockfighting ring in Whitechapel. Grimes and one other man kept his books." Gritting her teeth, she sucked in a breath as Jackson gently maneuvered her arm for inspection.

"Let me guess. Grimes cooked the books."

She nodded, clinging to the conversation instead of the agony in her arm. "And then he blamed it on the other man, which gave him enough time to run off with the money."

Jackson pulled back and knotted the strips into one big bandage. "How did that involve you?"

"The man he blamed was one of my crew."

He met her gaze. "And you wouldn't leave a man wrongly accused to suffer unjustly. I wonder that Rook doesn't have a price out on *your* head."

"We came to an agreement."

"An agreement with the tip of your blade, no doubt. But enough of that. Getting this bleeding to stop is more important." He tucked the hair that had fallen in her eyes behind her ear with an infinitely tender touch. "As near as I can tell, the bullet grazed the outer side of your arm, so at least you will be spared the torture of having the ball fished out. You will still need to see a doctor, though, for it must be sewn up. But first, I intend to stop the bleeding. I hate to hurt you, but I fear I must, so brace yourself. Ready?"

She dug her fingers into the stool and gave him a sharp nod. But she was wrong. She'd never be ready for the gut-wrenching blaze that burned out of control as he wrapped the fabric tightly around her arm. Again and again. Sweat popped out on her forehead. Between her shoulder blades. Drenched and dripped as she gritted her teeth.

A fiery eternity later, he stepped back, keeping one hand on her good arm. "There. How are you faring?"

She swallowed hard, tamping down a leftover scream that yet begged release. "Well enough. A few stitches and I will be ready to bring down Mr. Poxley tomorrow."

"Absolutely not." The words were tight, as if squeezed through a clenched fist. "Your crew will have to operate without you."

She shook her head, then wished she hadn't. Dizziness swirled, and she inhaled until the queasy feeling went away. "You worry too much." She forced a smile. Hopefully, a convincing one. "I will be fine."

"Are you mad?" He reared back his head. "First you nearly drown. Then you are almost killed in a knife fight. And now this? No! I will not take the chance of losing you. Do you hear me? I *cannot* lose you."

She blinked. From the vehemence in his voice or the thick worry in his eyes? She shifted on the stool, studying his face. Was he truly that concerned about her? "Watch it, Constable. You are starting to sound as if you care."

He bent, leaning close, and tenderly cupped her face in his

palms, the touch of which nearly made her forget about the throbbing in her arm.

"I do care. Very much."

His lips brushed against hers, soft, warm. So gentle, so nurturing, it breathed life into places in her heart that had long lain fallow and empty. She could live here in this moment, ignoring the pain in her arm, in her life, in the world. Safe and loved in Jackson's sweet kiss.

But the *thwack* of the front door pulled Jackson away.

"Wagon's just outside the door, sir."

"Good." Jackson nodded at the brawny man on the threshold. "Take Miss Turner to a doctor at once." He swung his gaze back to her, and he lowered his voice for her alone. "And you, get yourself patched up, send word to your men with directions for tomorrow night, then lay low. I will see that Grimes is delivered to Rook and that Poxley is arrested. You, rest and heal. Agreed?"

Hah! Did he really think she'd consent to missing out on all that? Even so, she dipped her head in compliance. "I hear you loud and clear, Jackson."

She averted her gaze as he helped her to her feet. She may have agreed to resting and healing, but she'd never said for how long she'd do so.

Chapter Twenty-Seven

And here he was. Waiting. Again.

Jackson leaned against the wall in the dark passage, scorning the permeating stink of urine. An arm's length away, the same number of bricks he'd counted last week still held up the Four Sisters. He ought to know. He'd tallied them five times already this evening. But earlier, when Big Ben faithfully struck nine bells, no Baggett had appeared. And even now, when the last bong of ten hung in the air like a left-over note in an empty cathedral, still no constable. Jackson shifted his weight to his other foot. Blast! Where was the man? *Everything* hinged on this meeting.

The pub door shushed open. Footsteps thudded, hitched a step, then shuffled a bit before regaining a regular rhythm. Whoever it was clearly had tippled one pint too many. Jackson eased closer to the passage opening and peered out from the shadows. Convincing a sober Baggett to help him would be hard enough, but a muddle-headed one?

A round blob of a silhouette teetered past Jackson's hideaway, far too stout to be Baggett. Jackson sank back against the wall. Was he waiting for nothing? Had his friend simply gone home after his shift? He pinched the bridge of his nose, worrying about a hundred different details that were completely out of his control. Hah! As if he ever really had control to begin with. Dropping his hand, he bowed his head.

Forgive me, God. Your will be done with this whole snarled mess.

Your justice go forth. Your—

He jerked up his face as once again the door swooshed open and boots hit the pavement. This time square shoulders on a tall figure ambled his way. Triumph. He leaned close to the opening and blew out a "Hsst! Baggett."

The man stopped but didn't turn. Didn't move. Just stood there, taut as a sail in the wind.

"Baggett, please," Jackson tried again. If Charles didn't help, there'd be no catching Poxley. "Just a word."

A disgusted sigh traveled into the passageway. Baggett swiveled his head, scanning behind him, then ducked into the narrow space next to Jackson. "What the blazes are you still doing here?" His ragged whisper indicted harsher than a hanging judge bent on swift justice. "I told you to get out of London. If we are seen, I will be forced to arrest you on the spot."

"Then I shall make this fast." Jackson drew in a breath, fishing out the words he'd rehearsed in his mind over the past several hours. "I need you to go to Sergeant Graybone in the morning and have him authorize you to lead a squadron of river police to the waters just off the Bankside Pier, late tomorrow night. Around midnight."

"Thunderation, man!" Baggett whisper-yelled. "What on earth for?"

"Because this time I believe I have found the true culprit behind the missing men."

"Look where your belief got you last time, kicked off the force and banished from the City." Baggett snorted. "And now you want to drag me into your next bubble-headed scheme? No thanks." He wheeled about.

Jackson snagged him by the sleeve and tugged him back. "This is different, I swear. No conjecture. No false evidence. There is absolutely no chance for an alibi to let this one slip away, either true or concocted. You *will* catch the man I suspect in the act of committing a crime."

He let go of Baggett's arm and waited. It wouldn't do any good to drive him away with over-the-top theatrics. Care was needed. Space and breath. But too much and his friend might walk away.

"Even if that much is true," Baggett rumbled low, "what if you are wrong? What if this fellow is not the one responsible for those missing?"

"Then you will still have arrested a felon perpetrating an offense against the Crown."

Baggett's huff filled the space between them. "Are you certain?"

"Of that much, yes."

"Hmm." Lifting his hat, Baggett ran his fingers through his hair several times over. "Convincing Graybone to make use of the river police is no small thing. He will need the inspector's permission, and there is no love lost between the two. What sort of crime are we talking about?"

"A full shipment of smuggled guns and ammunition—a thousand pounds' worth and then some."

"Well, well. . .that is quite a find. Who is responsible?"

The answer languished on his tongue. Revealing such a high-profile perpetrator wouldn't go over well, especially since he'd been wrong before. But hang it all! Mr. Poxley was guiltier than a demon.

Lifting his chin, Jackson stared Baggett down. "The Lord Mayor's secretary is behind it all."

"Poxley!" Baggett boomed, then shot a look over his shoulder.

Jackson craned his neck as well, glancing past Baggett. If anyone was out there, they'd have heard such a roar.

But no boots thumped their way. No curious heads peeked in.

Baggett turned back, his voice lowering to a deadly hiss. "Are you out of your mind? You expect me to waltz into Graybone's office and ask for men to help arrest the sergeant's personal friend with nothing but the word of a hunted man to back me up?"

"Look, I know it is a risk." And he did. More of a danger than he even dared consider. Thank God Kit would be out of the way. But this time it wasn't only her well-being that could be damaged. If things were to go wrong, Baggett would be the one to bear the brunt of Graybone's wrath.

He squeezed a hand on Baggett's shoulder. "Trust me, I do not take your involvement lightly. But it is not just my word. Look for yourself."

Jackson fished about in his pocket and pulled out the bills of lading—the real and the faked—both with Poxley's signature flourished across the bottom.

Baggett held the documents up to eye level, squinting in the dark, and scrutinized the writing as best as one could in such poor light. Eventually, he shoved them back at Jackson. "Even so, Forge, while two different destinations may persuade me—and I am not saying it does, so do not get your hopes up—it will take more than invoices to convince Graybone."

"Then do not say Poxley is involved. Just tell him you got a solid tip about the whole deal." He tucked away the bills. "You have been on the force a long time. The sergeant trusts you."

"And it is exactly that trust I do not wish to cast to the wind."

"For the sake of your job security, you would let a crime slip by under your nose? What sort of officer does that?" He stepped toe to toe with Baggett and lowered his voice. "I thought you were a man of integrity."

Silence fell. Hard. Heavy. Save for the faint drunken laughter leaching out from the pub and the slight wheeze of Baggett's laboured breaths.

"Fine," Baggett grumbled. "But if this thing goes sideways"—he shoved his face into Jackson's—"it will be more than the sergeant who is out for your blood."

A full night. An entire day. And now, nearing the stroke of midnight, shouldn't the pain in her arm have subsided? Kit winced as she crouch-walked to a barrel nearer the road in front of Shaw's Stowage. With the vessel close to being fully loaded, Duff ought to be sneaking off here soon for final instructions. Thus far, the plan had run smoothly. No one questioned Jackson's explanation that Poxley had hired on extra men for the loading. What did it matter if the unknown man next to you sweated and grunted with as much gusto as yourself?

She hunkered in the shadows, waiting, wondering. How much had Mr. Poxley paid the night harbour master to look the other way? Once Poxley arrived—*if* he arrived—would Jackson be successful in convincing him to board the ship? Would the police rendezvous in time to arrest the man and, in the process, vindicate Jackson? She bit her lip. Most importantly, once Poxley was behind bars, would he reveal the whereabouts of Joe and the other missing men?

What if she and Jackson were wrong about the Lord Mayor's secretary being the mastermind and Joe still wasn't found?

Blowing out a long breath, she readjusted the arm strap on her sling, fighting a whimper, both from the pain and the unanswered questions. There were far too many loose ends in this affair, swinging about like little nooses in the breeze. Any one of them could be fatal.

Horse hooves clopped in the distance, and she turned her head towards the sound. A carriage approached, the ground vibrating the closer it drew. No one should be arriving except for Poxley. Leaning sideways, she peeked around the side of the barrel.

The coach stopped. The driver jumped down to open the door, and a humpbacked man emerged, shoes clacking onto the cobbles. Kit gasped, not caring in the least about the well-tailored suit disappearing into the warehouse. Her eyes trained on the driver as he rounded the back of the coach, mere yards in front of her. He walked with a slight limp. Left leg. And in his hat, though it was too dark to differentiate colours, the round shape of a fabric poppy with a speared leaf bobbed along the band. Could it be?

Her heart pounded hard against her ribs as she took off running, snubbing the searing ache in her arm. She pulled up next to the carriage just as the man sank onto the driver's seat above her. "Joe! I can hardly believe it. Are you all right?"

The man's face swiveled down to hers, his eyes squinching nearly to slits. And no wonder. For the sake of blending in tonight, she'd donned an old pair of Duff's breeches that she'd cut short and hemmed to fit her. The waistcoat, though, she'd left large and floppy on purpose, better to hide the curves that no man would have beneath his shirt.

"Kitty? Ith that you?"

His pet name for her slid out sideways, his front tooth long since missing. But lisp or not, the sound of it wrapped around her like a warm woolen jumper. He was safe. Thank God, he was safe!

Emotion squeezed her throat, making it difficult to eke out words. "Yes, it is me. Your Kitty."

He stared a moment more, then raised his whip. "Get out o' here, then. Off with ye!"

She blinked, no more able to comprehend the sudden vehemence rasping in his voice than she could the confusing shapes of letters on a page. A load of hurt avalanched over her. Of all people, why would he turn on her so violently? Unless. . .

She dug in her heels. "I am not leaving unless you come with me."

The dark shape of the whip wavered in his grip. "Can't," he spat out.

"Why? What keeps you? What has made you hole up for the past three weeks and. . .wait a minute." She stepped closer, peering up into the shadows of his face. "Perhaps it is not a what but a who. . . Poxley. Come away now, Joe, while he is inside. I will hide you. Give you protection. As soon as this thing blows over, and I promise you it will, I shall—"

"Don't need yer help. Don't want it. Go!"

The whip cracked near her head, and she jerked backwards.

Stunned, she turned aside, cradling the wound on her arm and slice in her heart. Had she really spent all this time looking for a man who didn't want to be found? Risked her life several times over for naught? Surely God hadn't brought her this far, hadn't revealed Joe's presence to her, only for her to walk away. Whether Joe liked it or not, was it not in his best interest—and Natty's—that he go home?

Or was that just her trying to orchestrate things on her own again?

Her shoulders sagged, zinging instant pain through her arm, and she breathed out her failure in a prayer. "Forgive me, God. Looks like You are the One to sort this out. You and Jackson. Not me."

Kitty.

She stopped and glanced over her shoulder. Was Joe calling her back?

But no, he hunched on the seat, purposely looking the other way.

Kitty.

Again the name came, and with it all the emotion she thought she'd first heard when Joe had spoken it. Kit sucked in a breath with the sudden realization. Joe would never have used such a term of endearment if he hadn't truly still cared for her. He was trying to protect her by sending her away!

She pivoted and marched right back. "Come on down, Joe. Whip me all you like, but I am not going anywhere till you do."

A growl ripped out of him. "I said—"

"Oy! You there." Behind her, heavy bootsteps pounded. "Get a move on. No slacking this close to being done."

She froze. Joe's eyes snapped from her to the man at her back.

If the fellow saw her arm in a sling, he'd know she was an imposter. She lowered her voice, putting every ounce of compliance she owned into one single word. "Aye."

Had it worked? Would the fellow shove off, thinking she'd follow him, giving her the chance to dart the other way?

"Now!" The man roared, grabbing her shoulder and spinning her around.

A cry flew past her lips as she staggered, the pain in her arm too great to deny and her hat flying off in the process, revealing a thick ponytail of hair dropping low.

The man peered closely at her. "Say, yer not one o' the crew. Yer not even a man." He snagged her by the good arm, wrenching it painfully behind her back, and propelled her towards the warehouse bay doors. "Let's see what the boss has to say about this."

Chapter Twenty-Eight

Jackson eyed the last four crates sitting like a giant set of toy blocks near the open bay doors. Fifteen more minutes, twenty at most, for the men to load them, then with or without Poxley, that ship would be ready to sail. Jackson yanked out his watch and glanced at the time, then shoved the thing back into his pocket. Where was he? He'd sent for the man nigh on an hour ago now.

And if Poxley didn't show, this whole thing would implode.

He strode towards the stairs, boots hitting the planks harder than necessary. From the roof, he'd see the approach of a carriage sooner than gawking down the street from the loading dock. With any luck, he'd spy the man turning onto the road near the last streetlamp at the end of the dockyard and—

"Forge!"

He wheeled about.

Poxley stalked through the door, his dark cape fluttering behind like bat wings. "What is so dire I must be summoned from my bed?" The man's green gaze swept the perimeter of the warehouse, then locked onto Jackson. "Everything appears to be running smoothly. What is the problem?"

Jackson clenched his jaw. This was it. Show time. Drawing on everything he'd learned about swindling from Kit, he beckoned Poxley closer with a flourish of his hand.

"Sketch a careful word picture, and the listener will see a full image of his own making."

Kit's words hovered at the back of his mind as he cherry-picked a handful of precise words. "There is a problem, sir. Grimes was not the only one out to double-cross you."

True enough. He and Kit were as well.

Poxley cocked his head, morbid curiosity furrowing his brow. "Is that so?"

"Indeed, sir. I suspect the captain of that ship"—Jackson hitched his thumb over his shoulder—"the one in charge of delivering your valuable shipment, is planning on off-loading several of those crates for his own profit before he reaches Morocco."

"The devil you say!" Clenching his hands behind his back, Poxley stomped about in a tight circle, muttering all the while. "I shall have the man horsewhipped. No, better yet, keel-hauled. Blast him!" He stopped midcircle and pivoted to Jackson. "But there is no time for finding a new captain now. The cargo must arrive on the appointed day or my buyer will walk. Why did you not send for me sooner?"

"One does not cry wolf with the Lord Mayor's secretary. First, I had to be certain. But all is not lost. I believe I have a solution." He rocked back on his heels, taking his solution with him. Feeding the man too much at once would only cause him to lose his appetite, and he dearly needed Poxley to swallow this story, mouthful by mouthful.

"Well?" Poxley flailed his hands. "Spit it out man!"

He bit back a smile. A beggar holding out a cup for alms couldn't look more eager. "I propose you board the ship to keep an eye on things, and as you do so, I will send word to Miss Turner. As you know, she has quite an intricate web of associates throughout London. By the time you reach the Bankside Pier, she ought to have a new captain there, ready and waiting to swap out with yours. A trustworthy one."

Poxley leaned forward, eyes narrowing. "Why would she go to such efforts for me? What is in it for her?"

"If you lose money on this deal, Miss Turner and I lose out as well." Though tempted to say more, Jackson shut his mouth. Too many excuses and he'd appear grasping. He had to trust the process, bank on the fact that Poxley understood greed well enough. But even secure in that knowledge, the muscles in his shoulders tightened to steel bars.

From the bay door, men grunted as they heaved. Crates creaked. Wood scraped. The ship's tackle jingled in the distance, an urgent reminder that time was running out to get Poxley aboard.

And still the man said nothing. He just stood there, one bony hand rubbing the back of his neck. At long last, he peered at Jackson. "Hmm. I suppose there is no other way."

Relief flooded Jackson in a great rush, and he couldn't stop a small smile from curving his lips. "I believe it is the only way, sir."

A man's curse belched from the door, followed by a woman's angry "Let. Me. Go!"

The hair at the nape of Jackson's neck popped out like wires. He knew that voice—and it shouldn't be here. He and Poxley spun to the sound.

One man shoved another man through the door, a smaller one who stumbled past the threshold. Hips filled out those trousers, and a long brown ponytail tumbled past a pair of slim shoulders. Jackson's hands coiled into fists. Thunder and turf! Kit had promised to lie low, rest and heal, yet there she was in all her feisty glory.

"Miss Turner?" Poxley advanced. "What are you doing here, and dressed like a dockhand no less?"

She wrenched from the man's hold, no doubt slackened now that he'd gotten her where he'd wanted, then lifted her pert little chin, avoiding Jackson's gaze.

"I have been lying in wait for Forge." At last her blue eyes darted to him. "He has duped us all."

Sparks kindled in his gut, flaming hot. Spreading like a wild-fire and colouring the world an angry red. Had she been acting a part all this time? Sketched for him a careful word picture? After all they'd been through, all they'd shared, was Kit Turner double-crossing him?

∞

The pain in Kit's arm stabbed but didn't cut nearly as sharp as the doubt darkening a thundercloud on Jackson's face. While she hated to be the one to put it there, raising such suspicion was a necessary evil. If she didn't do some slippery talking, neither of them would make it out of here alive.

She snapped her gaze back to Poxley. "I was wrong about Forge. He is not to be trusted."

"Interesting." Poxley crept closer, the hump on his back adding to the chilling image of a man-sized spider coming at her. "You trusted him yesterday. What has changed?"

Jackson stomped over to them both. "This woman is out of her mind, looking for a demon behind every bush. You do not have the time, sir, to listen to such folderol. That ship is about to leave the dock, and if you are not on it—"

"Enough!" Poxley shot up a hand towards Jackson, never once pulling his gaze from her. "Miss Turner, I asked you a question."

"I did believe in Forge, enough to recommend him to you, but then this happened." She pointed at the sling cradling her bandaged arm. "I narrowly missed getting arrested last night, me and my crew."

True enough, for she and her men were always perilously close to being hauled in by a constable, but this time the sideways words scraped her throat as they came out. A new sensation, that. One that quickened an ever-growing pulse in her faint conscience. She frowned. What horrible timing for Jackson's morality to have taken root in her soul.

In three strides, she closed the distance between her and Jackson, breathing out for his ears alone, "Play along."

Then she poked her finger into his chest and raised her voice. "You have been out to get me since the day I swindled a few coins from your wallet. I hurt your pride, did I not, Constable? A bit of a woman like me besting a man sworn to uphold the law. Admit it! You would have done anything I asked of you just to infiltrate my crew long enough to catch us in the act of a felony and have us arrested."

She held her breath, pleading with her eyes. Would he take her bait?

"And why would I not do so?" He shoved his face into hers. "You are a disgrace to womanhood. Look at you, strutting about in trousers. Swindling honest, hardworking people out of their money, a worse crime than selling contraband goods like Mr. Poxley here. You are the one who deserves to be locked up, foul creature that you are."

She whirled, blinking back the sudden hot tears stinging her eyes. He'd done it. Played along exactly as she'd asked, and more convincingly than one of her seasoned crew members. But all the same, his words had pierced straight to her heart.

Fighting against the lump in her throat, she faced Poxley. "There you have it. Forge's involvement here has been nothing but a ploy to get to me. I beg your pardon for having disrupted your operation, Mr. Poxley, but I assure you that Forge will no longer be a problem. My crew stands at the ready outside. I will take care of him."

Poxley shook his head, an eerie smile stretching his mouth to an unnatural length. "I think not, Miss Turner. Rather, it is I who shall take care of him *and* you."

Alarm churned in her belly. What was the old man up to? "You need not bother, sir." She forced a small chuckle, hating how tight it sounded in her own ears. "I have this under control."

At her back, several sets of boots pounded in from the loading dock. A disturbing sound, but not nearly as unsettling as the sudden sharp applause clapping out from Mr. Poxley's hands.

"Well, well. That was quite a performance, all the way around, would you not say so, men?" He peered past her and Jackson, where gruff laughter scuffed harshly on the night air.

Kit's tongue went slack. Something was wrong. Horribly wrong.

Jackson stepped beside her, shoulder to shoulder, and while his proximity ought to comfort, she felt anything but safe.

Especially when Poxley's gaze swung back to hers. "I knew it was not Grimes who ordered those shots yesterday, Miss Turner, though I thank you for orchestrating such a ploy. The situation played very nicely into my hand, giving me a convenient way to rid myself of that hotheaded Grimes and thus increase my profit."

A rash of pinpricks spread beneath her skin. How the bluff-wankle had he known?

His face swiveled to Jackson. "Furthermore, I also know there is a squadron of river police lying in wait for me near Bankside Pier. Oh, do not look so surprised, Mr. Forge. Of course I have ears inside your former precinct. How do you think Clerk Beanstaple remains in his position? Certainly not for his work ethic."

Jackson edged in front of her, a protective stance, but one she couldn't allow. Not yet. If she didn't get answers before fists started flying, she might not get them at all.

She stepped even with him, eyeing Poxley. "If you knew all this, then why let us carry on with such a charade? Why did you not finish us off that first night we stumbled in here?"

A discordant chuckle shook his shoulders. "Because, my dear, as you well know, it is always better to keep an enemy close, especially until your shipment is about to sail." He leaned sideways, peering past her shoulder. "The load is ready to go, is it not?"

"Aye, sir."

"Good. Have the captain prepare to sail towards the Shadwell Fish Market." Amusement flashed in Poxley's eyes. "That is right, Mr. Forge. It is a rather inconvenient detour, but one well worth the effort. I am afraid your officers will have a long night waiting in the dark for nothing. But enough of these dramatics, eh? Bind them up, men!"

She and Jackson swung in unison, her good elbow catching an approaching man in the gut and his fist cracking into someone's jaw with a loud *thwack*.

Before she could reach for her boot knife, another man lunged, knocking her sideways. Pain exploded in her injured arm as she went down. By the time her free hand was tied tight at her waist and she was hauled to her feet, Jackson had taken down three of Poxley's thugs.

But he was no match for five or six. He hit the ground hard, blood dripping from his nose onto his lips, all the while beseeching Poxley to take him and let her go.

Poxley's shiny shoes clicked on the floor as he neared them. "I think it is about time you two discover what happens to those who poke their nose into my business. Sergeant Graybone's missing persons list is about to have two more names added to it."

Chapter Twenty-Nine

The barouche juddered over uneven cobbles, swaying like a one-footed drunkard on a slack line. Jackson leaned hard into the carriage wall, trying to keep from banging into Kit's injured arm. Despite his effort, she grunted with each lurch, and the sound punched him in the gut every time. He had to get her out of here—get *them* out of here—and fast. God only knew how many breaths remained until Poxley tired of this cat-and-mouse game.

Disregarding the raw skin on his wrists, Jackson strained to loosen the knot. Because he'd purposely put his wrists side by side while getting bound—a trick learned as a lad with an older brother—the move had afforded him extra space when he jerked his palms heel to heel. It wasn't much wiggle room, but it would have to do. What he needed more was time. He'd been wrangling with the blasted bindings since the carriage jolted into motion and still had nothing to show for it but scraped flesh and an aching jaw from clenching his teeth so hard.

Across from Kit, Poxley cocked his head at Jackson, taking a sudden and unwelcome interest in him—one he couldn't afford right now.

Jackson leaned forward, meeting his gaze. Sometimes offense was the best defense. "Do you actually think you will get away with murdering us?"

Poxley chuckled, and next to him his henchman—Rigsby—flashed a toothy smile. Jackson jiggered with the rope all the faster. He had hoped Rigsby would be on his side, just as the man had been when Grimes had challenged him. But when Rigsby had thrust him headfirst into the coach with a merciless kick, Jackson realized the man's true loyalty was to Poxley.

"Oh please, Mr. Forge." Poxley brushed imaginary dust from his sleeve. "I would not stoop to getting blood on my hands."

"Of course not." Kit tipped her head at Rigsby. "Your pile of muscles does it for you."

"Really, Miss Turner." Poxley shook his head, and while his attention was on Kit, Jackson contorted his fingers all the more. "Killing is so overvalued. The inconvenience. The mess. I prefer less barbaric methods of doing away with my enemies."

Jackson sneered. "I daresay the barrister Mr. Humphrey would attest otherwise, were he still alive. Drowning is not a particularly civilized way to go."

"His demise was never my intention." Poxley shrugged in time to the sway of the coach. "Grimes acted without my knowledge or consent. Humphrey was on retainer by Lloyds Bank, insurer of Shaw's Stowage. That gadabout Miss Shaw raised one too many questions and that piqued his interest. He went nosing about the warehouse, which inflamed Mr. Grimes, especially when the barrister began interrogating him. He panicked and, in the process of throwing the man out, accidentally killed him. Or so he says. Humphrey has only himself to blame, though. Had he not angered my foreman, he would even now be in the fine fellowship of our missing member of parliament and the industrious Mr. Shaw on the last leg of their excruciatingly slow voyage to China."

Kit leaned her head against the wall, huffing out a sigh. "So that is why we are going to the East India Dock."

"I do hope you are not averse to a tight confinement, my dear. Rigsby here will make sure a berth—if you can call it that—is properly arranged for you and your companion, though I daresay Forge might take up most of the space. After eight to ten weeks, you will arrive in, well. . .actually I do not know where. Somewhere over there." He fluttered his fingers at the dark horizon outside the window. "At any rate, by the time you make it back to England or even should you manage to send word of my dealings ahead of your arrival, I shall be happily living in an undisclosed paradise. That is if you survive the voyage."

"I thought you did not abide murder?" Jackson gritted his teeth as his fingernail ripped. Just a few more contortions, and he'd be free.

Poxley sniffed in the dark. "It is not murder if one expires from natural causes."

"It is if you arrange for those causes," Kit grumbled.

"I hardly think it worth my time to argue semantics with a known swindler."

The rope gave. So did Kit's anger. She let loose a volley of scathing retorts, educating Poxley on exactly where and how he could do the world a favor by his own disappearance. Jackson waited for her to calm down, for the wheels to hit a hole, the carriage to bounce upward and—

He slid his hand behind Kit's back and squeezed her fingers. She stiffened, but didn't turn her head his way. Good girl.

"Oof!" Poxley exclaimed as the rear wheels once again hit ground, then he banged on the wall with his fist. "Have a care, Mr. Card!"

Jackson dared a sideways glance at Kit. Clearly she now knew he was free, but did she know he needed her to provide a distraction if he was to take out these two men? Especially Rigsby. That pistol in his lap could be a problem.

The press of Jackson's fingers against Kit's skin zinged a charge up her arm. How on earth had he slipped out of his bindings? An unbidden smile twitched her lips. Apparently the man possessed skills she didn't know about, skills she'd very much like to discover—but now was not the time.

She could feel Jackson's eyes on her as the carriage jostled along. A quick glance. Nothing more. Yet she didn't chance a look at him.

Tipping off a mark too early ended in disaster. If Rigsby or Poxley suspected Jackson was no longer bound, that pistol would go off despite Poxley's lofty talk of disliking blood.

But what to do now? There was no way she'd be able to twist out of her ropes, not with a useless arm. And Jackson couldn't very well help her without giving away his own newly found freedom. He'd have to attack on his own, but in such close quarters, any attempt would be short-lived. She nibbled her lower lip, thinking hard. Thinking fast. She had to separate them. Give Jackson time and space to fight one man at a time.

The carriage jolted again, knocking her sideways, the movement straining the stitches in her arm. She groaned, the sharp pain sickening her all the way to her stomach—which gave her a horribly wonderful idea. Being sick had worked to her advantage in her last skirmish with Bags Gleason. Why not here?

"Ooh," she moaned, adding just the right amount of pitiable raggedness to her tone. "I do not feel so well."

Jackson snapped his gaze to her, his eyes widening a moment before narrowing. "You do not look so well either."

Good. He'd taken the bait. Now for Poxley to snap his jaws over her hook.

She hunched forward, hovering just above his shoes. "I am going to be sick."

Beside her Jackson bellowed, "Let her out!"

Poxley huffed. "This carriage is not stopping until—"

Putting to use all her street dramatics, Kit coughed a few dry heaves. Loud. Forceful. Arching her back like a cat.

"Stop the coach!" Poxley pounded on the wall. "Take her outside, Rigsby, and make it quick."

"Aye, sir," Rigsby gruffed.

He shoved his pistol to Poxley right before he grabbed her shoulders and hauled her off the seat. Sharp pain stabbed in her arm, and this time she really did feel like casting her accounts. She gritted her teeth against a cry as the man toted her out of the carriage.

Jackson tensed. Poxley wasted no time in leveling the muzzle on him the second Rigsby handed it over. No resting it on his lap. No taking any chances whatsoever. Smart man. Jackson outweighed him by at least two stone.

The door flapped shut, somewhat muffling the sounds of Kit's retching and Rigsby's disgusted curses. Whether she was acting or not, it was a brilliant diversion. But one that wouldn't last long.

Jackson dipped his head at the pistol. "You will need more than that to take me down."

"Pshaw." A crooked smile curled Poxley's lips. "You are but a mere mortal, Mr. Forge, and an incompetent one at that."

"If you truly believe so, then why did you persuade Graybone to keep me on the force?"

"Did you honestly think me your champion?" He chuckled. "Why, you were nothing but an amusement. Something to keep Graybone occupied while I finished arranging the final details of the most lucrative deal I have ever made."

"And yet you shall never see one penny of it." Ever so carefully, Jackson edged his hands from behind his back, the fabric of his coat chafing roughly against the torn skin on his wrists.

"Such bravado." Poxley shook his head like a scolding schoolmaster. "Though I will say as misguided as your boldness is, you do have a certain amount of daring about you."

He smiled. "I am glad you think so."

Poxley angled his head like a curious tot.

And Jackson lunged.

Kit bent double on the pavement, straining out groans and gasps. Adding in a few coughs for good measure. And all the while, she staggered her way on the uneven cobbles towards the front of the coach. Once Jackson disabled Mr. Poxley, he'd need the space to leap out the door and take down Rigsby, hopefully before the man even knew what hit him.

"Hack it out already, woman!" Rigsby swore. "A bleedin' cat could've yacked up a hairball the size o' Brighton by now."

The cab light on the front of the coach flickered inside the glass sconce, blinding her momentarily as she dared a glance up at Joe. Would he help her? Or had he become a full-fledged member of Poxley's crew? Hard to say, the way he sat like a black lump on the driver's seat with one hand clutching the horsewhip, his hat pulled low over his face. Would he really turn on her?

Yet had he not already abandoned his wife of thirty-odd years without so much as a goodbye?

"Come along, now," Rigsby barked. "Ye're wastin' my time."

She dodged the man's swiping reach. Perhaps she would truly have to lose her dinner to buy a little more time. Gritting her teeth, she eyed the side of the carriage. One good smack of her injured arm against it ought to sicken her good. Bracing herself, she—

A gunshot cracked inside the carriage.

Kit swung about, heart hammering. Had Jackson taken control of the pistol?

Or had he been hit?

She squinted, desperate to see who would duck out the door and poised to bolt away if she must.

But then the sharp snap of the whip cut through the air.

Jackson's ears rang. The shot tore wild through the carriage wall. Still gripping Poxley's wrist, he cracked the heel of his other hand into the man's forearm.

Poxley hollered. His fingers splayed.

Jackson grabbed the pistol and flipped it around, the barrel hot against his palm. Then he struck fast, the butt of the weapon coming down hard on Poxley's skull. The man crumpled beneath the blow, collapsing back against the seat.

Chest heaving, Jackson leapt for the door. Now for Rigsby.

Outside, a whip whirred then snapped. His breath hitched.

Sweet mercy! Was Kit having to stave off the driver as well?

∞

Kit flinched as the zing of the whip whooshed past her ear. Two paces away, Rigsby roared. His coat sleeve flapped open in tatters, and even in the shadows she could see the pain twisting his mouth.

Gaping, she glanced back at Joe, just as he struck again. This time the lash sliced along Rigsby's face, tearing open a line from chin to ear. He reeled, instinctively slapping his palm against the wound. A primal howl keened out of him.

Joe's boots smacked the pavement behind her. "Move!"

She jumped back, the cruel whip snaking out one more time, taking Rigsby in the knees. The man wobbled, rubber legged—and Jackson flew from the carriage door, knocking him flat to the ground.

Bootsteps thudded behind her, followed by a familiar lisping voice in her ear. "How now, Kitty? Ye holdin' up? I'll cut ye free."

Blessed relief sagged her shoulders as he worked a knife against her bindings. "I am fine, my friend, thanks to you."

The second her wrist sprang loose and the rope dropped to the ground, she rubbed the chafed skin.

Jackson strode over to her and nudged up her chin, searching her eyes. "Are you all right?"

"I am now that this is over."

"This part, anyway." He buffed his thumb over her cheek then dropped his hand. "Are you ready for the finale?"

Hah! She'd been ready for this since the moment Natty had waylaid her back on Angel Lane. "More than anything."

Sidestepping her, Jackson offered his hand to Joe. "Mr. Card, it is a pleasure to meet you at long last. For the sake of expediency, however, I must cut my greeting short, and we will also have to leave that one here." He tipped his head to where Rigsby lay in a discarded heap. "Better to lose a small fish than to let the big shark go, and that big shark shall be waking up soon. Tell me, Mr. Card, can you make haste to drive us and the incapacitated Mr. Poxley to 12 Trimble Street?"

Joe gave him a sharp nod. "Aye, sir."

Kit narrowed her eyes. "Should we not get Poxley on board the ship and sailing before your Constable Baggett and his men call it quits?"

"I fear it is too late for that. While Poxley is out, we must go directly to Sergeant Graybone."

"Graybone!" Though she said it aloud, it still didn't sound right in her ears. "Is he not the one who banished you from London?"

Jackson's left eye twitched, confirming her suspicion without a single word.

She blew out a low whistle. Risks were a necessary part of any good swindle, but this? She peered up at him, fighting the urge to shove back the dark curl of hair drooping on his forehead. How much mercy would the sergeant show after being called out of his bed, especially when discovering the man pounding on his door was one he'd exiled? Would Graybone even listen to him?

She shook her head. "I hope you know what you are doing."

He grimaced as he swung about and called over his shoulder, "So do I."

Chapter Thirty

Jackson's fist hovered in the air. Showing up on Sergeant Graybone's stoop was bad enough, but rousing the man from his bed? He may as well be knocking on the gates of hell. Defying the damp chill of night, hot sweat made his shirt cling to his skin. This was it. The last moment to back down before summoning a demon. A desperate move, but wholly necessary.

He rapped his fist against the wood. Then waited.

No answer.

"Sergeant?" He hammered louder.

Behind him, one of the carriage horses nickered. A cat screeched down the street, either startled or kicked by the drunkard zigzagging along the pavement. But no footsteps pounded inside the redbrick row house. Jackson scowled. He didn't have time for this. Poxley would be stirring soon, and though Kit held a pistol in her lap, the blasted thing was out of shots.

He pummeled the door for all he was worth, which at this point wasn't much. "Sergeant Graybone!"

Muttered oaths rumbled inside. A low "This'd better be good" leached through the door just before it swung open.

"Forge?" Graybone's mouth hung in a perfect O, a gaping hole in a face full of whiskers. His hair smashed flat on one side, the other stood on end. Half his nightshirt spilled out of his trousers. All innocuous enough. Disheveled. Sleepy. Not a hint of menace or threat.

But then a deep, deep stain darkened the sergeant's face. "Of all the cod-wangled nerve! Showing up in London, and on my doorstep no less? You may as well have gone straight to Newgate, man, and saved me the trouble."

"Sir, please. Hear me out. Better yet. . ." He yanked the two bills of lading from his pocket and shoved them at Graybone.

"What the scarpin' nag is this about?" Graybone snatched the papers, turned aside to a vigil lantern on an entry table, and bent to study them.

Jackson stood rigid, every muscle clenched, not daring to move so much as a hair. The sergeant was a ticking time bomb. Anything could set him off, and that would be a disaster if it happened before the man fully dissected and compared each document.

At long last, Graybone swung back, spearing him with an evil eye. "Where did you come by these?" His voice was cold as a grave.

Widening his stance, Jackson forced out his words strong and even. "It does not matter. What *is* pertinent is that there is a huge discrepancy between those bills of lading. One is real, the other fake. Both signed by Mr. Poxley and designed to transfer a large shipment of arms to a buyer in Morocco. *His* buyer."

"Thunderation!" the sergeant barked. "Are you seriously accusing the Lord Mayor's secretary of gun smuggling?"

He nodded towards the papers clutched in Graybone's big paws. "You hold the proof in your hands, sir."

"For all I know these documents are fabricated." He crumpled the bills into one big ball and threw it to the floor. "You just don't listen, do you, Forge? I told you the only sure way of convicting a criminal is to catch him in the act." He lunged and snagged Jackson's arm, fingers digging in like iron spikes. "Just as I have caught you breaking your restraining order."

With a mighty wrench, Jackson jerked away and scooped up the papers, then shook the wad in the air. "This *is* valid evidence, but the real proof is down at the Wapping Dockyard. If that ship is not there as I say, then you can toss me in Newgate and throw away the key."

"Wapping? The dock next to Bankside?" His eyes popped wide. "*You* are Baggett's informant? Blast! I should have known. The man was far too cagey when I pressed him."

Jackson jammed the papers into his pocket and spread out his hands. "At least Baggett was willing to give me a chance."

"Baggett is a bleeding heart!" Graybone roared.

Next door, a sash groaned open, wood scraping wood, window glass rattling. A nightcapped pale face poked out through the opening. "For snipe's sake! Shut yer gobs. We're tryin' to sleep over here!"

The window crashed down. Jackson winced, fully expecting the glass to shatter, but it held.

"In the name of all that is right and just, sir," he lowered his voice to a dull drone, "I implore you to see for yourself that what I say is true. Not only will you apprehend a load of guns already bought and paid for by the Crown, you will have the man responsible for the illegal movement of that cargo, the very same man who is behind all the recent disappearances. I know what happened to the MP and the merchant, and I can pin the blame on Poxley."

Despite the neighbor's grousing, Graybone bellowed once again. "The devil you say!"

Jackson swung his arm towards the carriage driver's seat. "And there, sir, is Joe Card. The missing jarvey."

Graybone inhaled sharply.

"Well, sir?" Jackson pressed the sudden advantage. "Will you come?"

A tiger's growl reverberated in Graybone's throat. Exasperation? Repudiation?

Or—dare he hope—resignation?

Kit shifted on the leather seat, propping her back in the corner of the carriage closest to the door. A better angle should Poxley awaken. Much easier to launch an attack with the butt of the pistol or flee if that didn't work. Thankfully, it didn't appear to be a problem for now. The man slumped catty-corner from her, head tipped against the wall, mouth hanging open with little wheezes on the exhale.

Men's voices drew near—Jackson's familiar tone and a deeper one. The sort that forced attention whether you wanted to give it or not. So, the sergeant decided to listen to Jackson after all. A relief, that. Taking down Poxley on her own and then having to figure out how to get Jackson out of jail would've been a headache and a half, or worse...impossible.

The door opened, and the coach listed to the side as a dark figure climbed in. Without so much as a glance her way, a man as broad-shouldered as Jackson bypassed her legs. As he lowered next to her, he suddenly froze, staring hard at Mr. Poxley.

Before Jackson could sink on the seat across from her, the sergeant boomed, "Are you out of your mind, Forge? You assaulted *and* abducted the Lord Mayor's secretary? This time you have taken things too far!"

The carriage lurched into motion, canting hard to the right as Joe turned the thing around. Kit counterbalanced with a swift lean sideways, but when the wheel hit a pothole, the accompanying jolt bumped her into the air. Her injured arm crashed against the wall when she landed, and an unstoppable cry flew past her lips.

Sergeant Graybone's head swiveled to her face, the whites of his eyes flashing wide. His sudden intake of air hissed louder than the grind of the wheels. Though it was nearly impossible to tell, she'd swear to a galleried jury that the man's face paled to a deathly grey. A haunted look, thoroughly disturbing, as if he stared at a lost loved one risen from the grave.

"Who are you?" His question cut like a blade.

While she was happy Jackson was no longer the focus of the man's ire, neither did she particularly want those dark eyes staring into her soul. She shifted uncomfortably on the seat. "I work with Mr. Forge."

His head snapped back. "You are a woman."

She bit her tongue, annoyed that her voice had given her away. "Despite the trousers, yes."

"Most curious," he breathed, then after a long look at her face, he turned to Jackson. "Well, what have you to say for yourself?"

"I did not kidnap Mr. Poxley, sir. Quite the contrary. He abducted us with the intent to mete out the same fate given to his other victims, Mr. Shaw and Lord Twickenham, the merchant and the parliamentarian."

"And that fate is?"

"They were subdued and put on a ship to China. Poxley himself plans to flee the country within the week."

The sergeant stroked his beard, a passing streetlamp washing light over his brooding face. "They are not dead?"

Kit snorted, crude but completely irresistible. "That depends on whether or not they survive the voyage."

For a long while, Sergeant Graybone said nothing. He simply sat across from Poxley, studying the man, every now and then casting her a glance. His big hand rubbed along the length of his thigh, back and forth. Back and forth.

She peered over at Jackson. He knew the man better than she did. Was Graybone crediting them with telling the truth. . .or even now condemning them, particularly her?

Jackson's blue eyes held her gaze, and he gave a little shake of his head, as clueless as she.

The seat creaked as the sergeant shifted, her own side of the cushion propelling her upward with the movement. "If what you say is true—and that is a big *if*—then why did Poxley want to get rid of those men in particular?"

Jackson leaned forward, and Kit hid a smile at his enthusiasm. Badge or not, he was a fine constable. Always striving to right wrongs and serve justice, even to his own detriment. And then a smile truly did break free as she remembered the day he'd stood magnificently defiant on her own turf, outnumbered and outgunned.

"Lord Twickenham," Jackson began, "was drawing too much attention to the Lord Mayor's office with his crusade to attach Sir Robert Fowler to the death of the previous Lord Mayor—which of course would have been damning to Poxley if the workings of the office were overly scrutinized. As for Mr. Shaw, his warehouse was the most convenient to use, being the Wapping harbour master was put into place by Poxley himself. However, Mr. Shaw was not so cooperative and thus was eliminated until Poxley's grand and glorious arms transaction was finished."

"And what of the barrister?" Graybone cocked his head. "Was he part of this affair?"

Kit winced as Jackson answered, the ache in her arm growing with each bump of the coach.

"Mr. Poxley hired a rather hotheaded foreman to manage the warehouse end of things, as you can see by the sling on my associate's arm." Jackson's gaze drifted to her, his blue eyes darkening to the shadows around them, then he snapped his focus back to the sergeant. "Mr. Humphrey ought never to have called at the dockyard himself, nor would he have had not Miss Shaw posed too many questions to too many people. Poxley said his death was an accident. Seems Grimes got too rough while ejecting him from the premises. Poxley wasn't happy about it, but the deed had already been done, and Grimes made short work of disposing of the body."

The sergeant folded his arms, clearly digesting all he'd been served. The grind of the wheels changed timbre as cobbles gave way to wooden planks. Kit glanced out the window. Beyond the road, the Thames was a thick black snake. Soon, then, this would be over. . .but what would be the outcome?

Sergeant Graybone grunted. "That accounts for all save our jarvey, Mr. Card. What is his part in this affair?"

At the mention of Joe's name, Kit jerked her gaze back inside the coach. "That is what I intend to find out."

A moan escaped Poxley, luring all their attention. His eyes

fluttered, then sealed again. Not quite awake yet, but he was definitely coming around.

The sergeant turned to her and Jackson, his bushy brows gathering into a line. "I have yet to believe one word from either of you without definitive proof."

"And so you shall have it."

The carriage stopped. Jackson opened the door, and the moment his feet hit the dockyard, he offered up his hand.

For a fleeting moment, Kit met the sergeant's stare, then grabbed hold of Jackson's warm fingers, allowing him to help her out as she puzzled over Graybone. Why did the man keep dissecting her as if she were a moth pinned to a board? Had she swindled him in the past? Tricked a loved one out of a coin or two?

Joe had judiciously stopped them near the gangplank, where a barrel-chested man with a mariner's cap paced. The captain, no doubt. He circled like a baited bear tethered on a short chain. Kit glanced past him, up to the ship's gunwale, where at least ten sets of eyes stared down. The crew...but whose? Had her men been successful in—

"You!" The captain's booming voice drew her and everyone else's notice as he pounded over to Jackson and poked him in the chest. "Where the flying sampson is my paperwork? I should've been on the water by now."

A noxious blend of fish and rage wafted off the man. Kit retreated a step, yet Jackson—God love him—not only held his ground; he squared his shoulders. He opened his mouth, but a voice behind them spoke.

"Give it to him, Forge." Mr. Poxley's shoes clacked onto the wooden walkway with an uneven beat. And no wonder. After taking such a wallop to the head, it was a wonder he walked at all. He teetered over to Sergeant Graybone. "And as soon as he does, arrest him and Miss Turner on the spot."

Kit gaped. "For what?"

Poxley's green eyes glowed unnaturally bright in the darkness.

"Defamation of character."

"Flit!" She fisted her hand at her waist. "It is not slander if it is true, you underhanded, black-hearted cully."

"Kit," Jackson warned under his breath while shooting her a sideways glance. "Leave this to me."

Poxley turned his back on them both, facing the sergeant alone. "Will you believe the word of a known Blackfriars swindler and a man who even now is breaking the law by being here in the City? One who speaks against me, your friend? Come now, Henry. We both know this man is a washed-up failure."

Graybone grunted.

Jackson advanced, stepping abreast of Mr. Poxley. "Look, Sergeant, all you need do is board that ship to see the truth for yourself."

"A ridiculous waste of time." Poxley turned on Jackson like a demon dog. "Hand over that bill of lading, Forge, and let the sergeant be about his duty of hauling in you and the woman."

"Calm down, my friend." Graybone laid his big hand on Poxley's shoulder. "I assure you there will be arrests carried out this night, but I must do my due diligence." He turned to the captain. "I would have you show me that cargo now."

"Think twice about that, Graybone." Poxley's tone was a deadly shiver in the air. "You would not want your name besmirched at the Home Office."

The sergeant's head swiveled his way. "Is that a threat?"

Poxley eyed him steadily, the power play bouncing between them twisting Kit's gut. She hadn't witnessed a standoff this tense since old one-eyed Tayborn had pulled a knife on Grub McCoy. A bloody day, that. One she didn't wish to live through again.

With a sneer, Sergeant Graybone wheeled about and strode towards the gangway.

Jackson chuckled. "Well, Poxley, looks like you will be the one sleeping at Newgate tonight."

Kit snapped her gaze to the ship, scanning the men's eyes that peered at the scene with interest.

Poxley fumed. "Take him down, men!"

The sergeant stopped in his tracks, his broad back a stanchion in the night. "You do not want to do this, Mr. Poxley."

"He is right, but I do." Kit cupped her hand and yelled up at the crew. "You heard him, men. Bind him up!" She shot out her hand.

And pointed at Poxley.

Chapter Thirty-One

Pandemonium broke out. Men shouted. Footsteps thundered. A few spare lunatics leapt over the gunwale and plummeted to the dock, landing on their boots like overgrown cats. But the only set of shoes Jackson cared about were the shiny patent-leathers darting the opposite way.

He sprang after Poxley—just as Kit stuck out her foot and tripped the man. The hunchbacked fellow went down hard. Jackson yanked him up even harder, digging his fingers into the soft flesh under Poxley's arm.

"You will pay for this, Forge." Blood dripped from the man's lip. "You too, Turner! Nothing will stop me from having my revenge."

"Now, now, Poxley, that is more than enough threats for one night." Sergeant Graybone pulled alongside Jackson, a leering semicircle of Kit's crewmen behind him.

Poxley wrenched and wriggled. Jackson planted his feet, holding strong.

Graybone's dark gaze shot to him, a strange light in his eyes. "See Mr. Poxley to his carriage while I check that cargo, eh Constable Forge?"

Constable?

Jackson froze. Surely he hadn't heard right.

But the flash of surprise in Kit's eyes and the way she suddenly smiled at him confirmed the message drummed by the wild beat of his heart.

He snapped a salute with his free hand. "Yes, sir!"

The sergeant wheeled about.

Kit nodded at her crew. "Help the sergeant out, men, and pry open some of those crates." Then her blue gaze sought his. "Congratulations, Constable."

Poxley turned aside and spat a mouthful of stringy blood. "You are no lawman, Forge. You are a disgrace. A failure."

The accusation greeted him like an old friend, offering a hand, an embrace, then a choke hold. But this time, by God's great mercy and the shine in Kit's eyes, the condemnation didn't sink into his soul. It rolled right off his shoulders and into the night.

He lifted his chin and stared down Poxley. "Failure is but an instructor, not an undertaker."

"What a load of mawkish claptrap!" Poxley sneered.

Kit sniffed. "I would say Mr. Forge here is the real champion and *you* are the one who has failed."

Though she likely meant it as a swipe at Poxley, Kit's praise lit a fire in his belly, kindling a foreign hunger he'd never before tasted. . . respect from the woman he loved. He craved it. Needed it.

Needed her.

But clutching a criminal in one hand was not the most opportune moment to let her know.

He tugged on Poxley's arm. "Come along. You have a short ride ahead of you to your 'paradise,' though I do not think it will be what you imagined."

"I'll see you to the door." Kit strode ahead of them.

As they neared the carriage, Jackson called over to Joe, who stood calming one of the horses. "Have you anything with which I can bind this man?"

"Aye, guv'nor." Joe tipped his head. "I can do ye."

By the time Joe tossed a rope and Jackson tied Poxley's hands behind his back, Kit stood ready and waiting for them.

"In you go." Jackson hefted the man up, ignoring the curses and slurs streaking the air.

Kit slammed the door behind Poxley and then smiled sweetly up at Jackson. "You did it."

"No, *we* did it."

One of her brows arched in that beguiling way only a swindler like Kit could manage. "I will not argue that point."

"Heave it open, boys!" The sergeant's voice bellowed from the ship's deck.

Soon this would all be over—and the thought punched Jackson in the lungs. There'd be no more working with Kit on a day-to-day basis now that Joe Card had been found. The ugly truth was there'd be no need to work with her at all.

On impulse, he grabbed her hand and led her away from the carriage, out of earshot of Poxley or Joe. "Kit, about what I said back in the warehouse, I want you to know I did not mean it. Not a word. Even in trousers, you are no disgrace to womanhood. On the contrary, you are more beautiful than any woman I know."

"Oh?" She peered up at him, mischief curving her lips. "And just how many women do you know, sir?"

He lifted her hand, her fingers entwined with his, and brushed a light kiss over her knuckles. "The only one I want to know is you."

For one blessed moment, she leaned closer, rising to her toes as if she just might kiss him.

But then her smile faded, and she pulled back. "Of course you cannot mean that. I am nothing but a Blackfriars street brat. You could do so much better than—"

He shot his finger to her mouth, and the softness there nearly drove him to his knees. "There is no better fit for me than you. And if you would consider it, I would ask you to be my—"

"Forge!"

A sigh ripped out of him. Of all the rotten timing! His hand fell away as he retreated a step. "Duty beckons. And I am afraid a mountain of paperwork does as well. May I call on you tomorrow?"

Her teeth flashed white in the night. "If you can find me."

He grinned. He'd hunt her down to the farthest corner of the earth if he had to.

Kit watched Jackson stride over to the sergeant, admiring how his coat stretched across his shoulders as he faced the man who could've easily locked him up instead of listening to him. Jackson Forge was a rare find. Honorable. Virtuous. Completely unlike any man she'd ever known.

She brushed her knuckles across her mouth. She may have swindled him out of a few coins that first day they'd met, but he'd hoodwinked her into giving him something far more valuable.

Her heart.

She dropped her hand. My, how she'd underestimated that raw recruit.

Footsteps shuffled on the dock behind her, and she turned.

Joe approached, hat in hand, fingering it round and round. "Thorry I had to turn on ye like that, Kitty, with the whip and all. I'd hoped ye'd a'scurried away. Just wanted to see ye safe."

She couldn't help but grin. "I thought as much." But then as quickly, her smile faded, and she peered deep into his grey eyes. "Oh Joe, how did you get twisted up in such a mess? Natty's near torn apart from worry."

"I feel awful 'bout that." Shaking his head, he stared into the distance, miles away from a damp dockyard in the middle of a smuggling deal gone bad. Then his gaze jolted back to her, face hardening. "But it were all fer her sake, and tha's the truth o' it."

She stepped closer, shutting out the drone of Jackson and the sergeant's nearby conversation. "What happened the night you disappeared?"

With a last turn of his hat, he popped it back onto his head. "There were an ill wind a'blowin' that night. Felt it in my bones.

Shoulda gone home sooner 'n what I did, but ye know, the promise o' a coin, it do have a shiny lure to it. Nursed me pint just a'waitin' on a fare that never showed. I were one of the last to leave the Grouse & Gristle, and tha's when I crossed paths with that villain." He hiked his thumb at the carriage.

Her gaze followed the movement to Poxley's temporary cell on wheels. "What was he doing outside a Blackfriars pub?"

Joe shook his head. "He weren't. I were on my way to Forder's to drop off my cab when I comes across a dandy o' a coach stopped flat in the middle o' the road. I carped at the driver, but the blasted man didn't move. So, I hopped on down to give the pop-headed bloke a good what for when I sees he's a'danglin' by one foot off the seat. Throat slit. Looked like the work o' Skully Weaver, that no-good free-booter. Always lookin' for a wealthy sow to roll. The coach door were open but no one be inside. I backs away to my own trap, but tha's where my real trouble began."

Thinking hard, she narrowed her eyes. "That coach belonged to Mr. Poxley, didn't it?"

"Aye, and the very same devil were a'standin' pretty by my cab door, though he weren't so dandy when I first laid eyes on him. Skully or whatever blackguard cut down his driver took a few swings at Poxley as well. He were sportin' a gash near his eye, bleedin' all over the kingdom. Din't run off fraidy-cat, though." Pursing his lips, Joe scratched the whiskers on his chin. "And that's when I knew he weren't no regular gent."

She rolled her eyes. "You can say that again. So, he had you take him where? To the police station? Or home perhaps?"

"Neither, which I thought were odd. Most folks would run for help or hide 'neath their bed. Bold as daylight he ignored his poor bled-out driver and said he had some important-like document to be delivered to the harbour master at Wapping. Funny time o' night to be doin' business, I says, but a coin's a coin." His hand flew into the air, thumb and forefinger rubbing together. "I tell the man I'll get his precious paper delivered if he'll just hand it over. Oh, he huffed and puffed 'bout that, I tell ye, but the old duff knew I had him o'er a barrel, so he gave in. I stuffs the thing into my hidey-hole, keepin' it real safe-like lest some other thievin' cully come along. Then I takes my usual side routes to get him and his blessed paper to Wapping in one piece."

"Hmm." Kit paced a few steps, mind awhirl. That document must've been what she and Jackson had gotten from Skaggs, the one with only a letterhead. And the broken cuff link? Joe had said Mr. Poxley wasn't in the best of shape when he'd found him. Could've been it simply fell off in Joe's cab after his tussle with the anonymous street thief.

She turned back to Joe. "What was on that paper?"

"Even if I could read, it were too dark inside the coach when I pulled it out o' the hole. Blasted thing teared on a nail I'd been meanin' to pound back in, and Poxley weren't too happy about it when I finally got out and gave it to him. Puffed right up and stomped off." Joe edged closer, tucking his head with a smile. "But I did listen real keen-like outside the cracked-open window of the harbour master's hut. Something about power of attorney over Mr. Shaw's holdings, namely of Shaw's Stowage."

"Ahh." She smiled. "So that is why the place wasn't scrutinized."

"Don't rightly know. What I do know is by the time I got Poxley safely back to his fancy town house, he made me an offer." Joe sucked in air through the gap in his teeth. "One I was forced to accept."

"And that was?"

"Poxley needed a new driver, what with the other 'un a'bled out like a stuck pig. Stupid man shoulda seen that lurker comin' for him. Pish!" He turned aside and spat. "Poxley said he'd pay me a queen's ransom to tote him about for the next month, just till he was to leave the country. The snag was I couldn't see my Natty nor anyone. Had to be at Poxley's. . .now what was that he said?" Joe's face screwed up. "*Disposal.* That were it. I were to be at his disposal day and night, with nary a snipe about it to anyone."

A sour taste rose up in Kit's throat. For all his wily ways, why hadn't Joe at least tried a double cross on Poxley? "Could you not have somehow sent word just to Natty? She has fretted herself half to death."

Joe pushed out his lower lip and folded his arms. "Couldn't risk it. Poxley said if he got wind I told anyone about anything—anything at all—he'd have me tossed in jail on false charges, and that'd mean the poorhouse for Natty. The old girl's got too many years on her for that, and ye know it."

She did. Every bit as much as Joe did. Natty scraped by only on the fares Joe brought home. Blast that Poxley!

Slowly, she nodded. "A sorry business, all of it."

"Aye, that it was," Joe breathed. He unfolded his arms and reached out, pressing a palm as leathery as one of the reins he gripped against her cheek. His grey gaze sought hers. "I knew ye'd hunt me down sooner or later, Kitty. Knew it right from the start, and I feared it."

"You need not have worried." She smiled. "I can take care of myself."

He grunted. "Bein' apart from Natty, well, it got me to thinkin'. It ain't good to be alone. Not fer me. Not fer you neither." He pulled away and stared down his nose. "Time you settled, Kitty. Time you left yer street swindlin' and found yerself a good man to care for. One who'll care fer you right back."

Unbidden, her gaze drifted to Jackson.

Perhaps Joe was right.

Chapter Thirty-Two

Late. Again.

Fighting a yawn, Jackson dashed up the front stairs of the Wellington Barracks, the home of the 1st Infantry Brigade Headquarters. After last evening's excitement, combined with not leaving the station until just before daybreak, he'd slept like a corpse—and nearly missed his interview with the colonel. Though it wouldn't have mattered. He didn't possess Kit's token anymore, so what was the point other than the stain on his name for shirking a scheduled appointment? Still, a commitment was a commitment.

Inside the spacious lobby, the corporal on duty directed him to an overstuffed leather settee, where he waited to be called. How different things were from the first time he'd sat here, nigh on a month ago, keen to discover exactly who Kit Turner was. Or had it been longer than that? Doffing his hat, he scrubbed a hand over his face, willing the movement to banish his sluggish thinking. Oh to sink back, just for a moment, and slip into the blessed darkness of sleep.

Hah! Who was he kidding? He dropped his hand. Even given the chance to stretch out on the cushions beneath him, he wouldn't, not when he'd promised a visit to a certain lady—the one who'd swindled the heart from his chest. It didn't matter a fig who her father was. He'd love her should the man turn out to be a deserter hung for high treason.

"Mr. Forge?"

He rose and faced a magnificent flowing moustache, so full

and billowy it compelled one to completely ignore the man behind it. Which was a mistake. Anyone who snubbed the set of muscles stretching the fabric of that scarlet uniform might very well find himself laid out on the floor.

"Good morning, Colonel." Jackson dipped his head.

The colonel swept his hand to the open door at his right. "My office awaits."

Jackson followed the crisp-stepping fellow, a gait no doubt honed from years of active duty, countless musters, and probably a parade or two. The chamber was small but immaculately kept, from the rows of shelved books standing at perfect attention to the sharp lines of the green draperies. Even the desk the colonel sank behind was polished so vigorously that the silver pen and ink stand cast a reflection as if in a mirror. Clearly, he was a man of order.

Not wishing to offend, Jackson sat stiff as a fire poker. "Thank you for seeing me today, Colonel."

"What is it I can do for you, Mr. Forge?" With each word, the man's moustache waved like a banner in the wind.

It took all of Jackson's concentration not to stare. "Originally, I had hoped you might identify a token, one that had been given as an identifier for a child placed in the foundling home. Since then, I have had to return the item, but being that I still had this appointment and we are both here, may I borrow your pen and a sheet of paper?"

The man hesitated, then pulled out a drawer and retrieved a sheet of linen paper and pushed it across the desk. "Have at it."

Rising, Jackson paced the few steps to claim a pen, dip it in ink, and, to the best of his memory, sketch both sides of Kit's button. When finished, he handed over the sheet. "Does this look familiar?"

The colonel's eagle eyes dissected the drawing. "It appears to be a Coldstream Guard button, design of some years ago, dating to Crimea. Third company, if I do not miss my mark." He leaned back in his chair, a low whistle ruffling his facial hair. "The Battle of the Alma, now that was a real kick in the pants. Lost a lot of good men in that one. I have that to thank for this." With one hand, he lifted the left side of his moustache, revealing a hideous scar that cut jagged off the side of his mouth. No wonder the man wore such a thick fringe on his face.

Jackson lowered into his seat. "Is there any way to tell who this button belonged to?"

The colonel shook his head. "Not usually, though some men carved their initials on the back side of their buttons, hoping to be identified by a loved one if they fell. Like here. This H.G." He tapped his index finger on Jackson's drawing.

His head perked up. Perhaps even without the token, he would discover who Kit's father really was. He edged forward in his seat. "Did you know this man?"

The colonel chuckled. "Sorry, not familiar with any H.G., then again, one can hardly be expected to know every soldier in an entire battalion."

Though he tried to hide it, Jackson's shoulders sagged. The defeat felt like a drayload of bricks pressing down on him. Forcing a smile, Jackson rose. "Well then, I thank you for your time, Colonel."

"Not so fast there, Mr. Forge." The colonel rose as well. "While I may not be able to identify your button owner, that does not mean I cannot tell you who it is."

Jackson's brow scrunched. "Sir?"

With precise steps, the colonel marched over to one of several bookshelves, ran his finger along the spines of identical blue cloth-bounds, and pulled down a ledger. Returning to the desk, he opened the thick book and paged through, eventually landing on something of interest, for he leaned close and squinted.

Then he straightened, turned the book around, and pointed half-way down the page. "There you are, sir. More than likely, that button came from this man."

Jackson advanced and bent over the sheet. A column of dates came first. Then regiment. Followed by company. And last was a name.

Air whooshed out of his lungs, leaving behind an empty cavern. Of all the queen's men!

That's who Kit's father was?

The hamper on Kit's arm swung with each of her strides down the street. Early afternoon sun shone overhead, but the rays didn't dare reach down into Blackfriars. Just as well. Her quick pace already trickled dampness between her shoulder blades. She'd promised to send a basket of bread and cheese to the Cards when she'd parted ways with Joe last night, and it wouldn't do to keep them waiting. With essentially no income for weeks, they had to be hurting for food.

"Kit!"

She turned at the sound of her name, her heart skipping a beat at the familiar tone. Jackson skidded sideways across the street, narrowly missing a collision with a loaded omnibus. His brown cravat had come loose, the ends flying over one shoulder as he dashed up to her. Wild hair curled onto his forehead, his hat who knew where. He planted his hands on his thighs and heaved in great breaths.

"My, but you are in a hurry."

"You," he huffed, "are a hard one...to track down."

"Truly? Why did you not think to look where you first found me, here on Blackfriars Lane?"

After a last big exhale, he straightened, and an impish smile appeared. "Come. I have something to tell you."

He tugged her towards the grimy window of a cobbler's shop. Shoes? What could he possibly have to say about half boots or slippers? She pulled from his grip, the basket on her arm swinging wildly. "Can you not tell me on the way to Joe and Natty's? They are expecting me."

He shook his head. "This will not take long. Give me your hand." He stretched out his own, palm up.

She stared. What in the world had gotten into him?

But the pull of him was too strong. The beguiling scent of his sandalwood aftershave. The almost schoolboy gleam in his blue eyes. The chance to press her skin against his. She set the basket down at her feet and laid her hand in his.

He angled, gently tucking her in front of him, so that she faced the window with him at her back.

"Hold out your pointer finger." His warm breath tickled in her ear, making it hard to do anything but stand there weak in the knees.

Somehow, though, she obeyed, and he guided her hand in sweeping strokes against the grimy film on the window. Three lines. One straight. Two angled. Connecting in the middle.

She turned her head, just a bit, any farther and her mouth would brush against his. "Pardon, but what exactly are we doing?"

The edge of his moustache tickled the top of her ear as he spoke. "We are learning to spell your name. That is a *K*. It sounds like *kuh*."

She blinked, confused. Even were she not so muddled from sharing body heat with the handsome Jackson Forge, she still wouldn't understand why the sudden urgency to teach her to read and write. They'd already suffered a few "would you look at that"s and a "well I never" from passersby.

"While I appreciate your effort," she murmured, "I hardly think this is the time or place for a lesson."

But Jackson merely forced her finger to retrace the lines she'd made. "*K*. Try it. *Kuh*."

She knew that tone, the one that said he'd not be moved until she yielded. Stubborn man. Though he couldn't see it, she rolled her eyes anyway. "Kuh."

"Good. Next letter."

Moving her hand slightly to the right of the *K*, he guided her finger once again.

"That's an *I*. It sounds like *ihh*."

"Ihh," she breathed while leaning against his strong chest. She'd never remember anything but the solid feel of him. The warmth. How strange little tingles fired low in her belly.

"Perfect. Now, fortunately your Christian name is short. One more letter, and it is an easy one."

Her arm moved in unison with his. As if they were one body. Her following his lead. Was that what it was like for a husband and wife? A floodgate opened, this time blazing heat clear out to her fingers and toes. Any coherent thought she'd had up to this point flew from her head.

"Kit?"

The censure in Jackson's voice jolted her back to reality. "What was that?"

"I said that letter is *T. Tuh.*" He bent so close, his lips feathered against her ear, and a wicked playfulness ran husky in his voice. "Are you listening to me?"

Hah! What woman in all of London could possibly pay attention to meaningless letters when the only thing that mattered was the man she loved standing so close that one little shift of the head would bring her mouth against his? She clenched her jaw so hard it ached. Admitting such a base response to herself was one thing. Confessing it to Jackson?

No. Absolutely not.

"Of course I am listening," she snapped.

"Good." He pulled back just a bit. "Then try it all together, *Kuh-ihh-tuh.* Then faster, Kit."

She pushed out the sounds while her gaze followed the foreign markings on the glass. "Kuh-ihh-tuh. Kit."

And then a brand-new sensation swept through her, every bit as heady as the nearness of Jackson. The lines on the window, the sounds, all came together. "Kit!" she said again, this time pulling free of Jackson's hold and whirling to face him. "I did it!"

"You did." His teeth flashed white against his dark moustache. "But we are not quite finished." He guided her back around. "Now for your surname. Ready?"

She nodded, this time shooting her finger to the glass before he even wrapped his hand around it.

He pushed her finger in a circular pattern. Almost. Before closing the loop, he stopped and connected a straight line to it. "That is a *G*. It sounds like *guh*."

"Guh?" She shook her head. "No, that cannot be right. Kit ends in *tuh* and my last name starts with the same. Tuh-turner."

"No, my sweet." He turned her to face him, his brown gaze delving deep into hers. "And that is why I was in such a hurry to find you. I have discovered who—"

"Forge! Miss Turner! There you are, at long last."

They both turned as a sweaty Officer Baggett jogged up to them.

Kit smirked. "There appears to be a plague of shortness of breath today."

"The sergeant," Baggett panted, his cheeks puffing into round balls with each exhale. "Wants to see you. Like a half hour ago."

Jackson frowned. "What for?"

"Don't know." Lifting his cap, the constable swiped his arm across his forehead. "He stormed into the station after an early meeting at the Home Office."

A small groan rumbled in Jackson's chest. "That cannot be good."

Baggett reset his cap, lips flattening to a grim line. "Honestly, I have no idea."

Kit peered up at Jackson, hating the worry pinching his lips. "I am sure it is nothing. Perhaps just a forgotten form you did not sign last night or maybe a question about Mr. Poxley's operation that was not yet answered."

"I am afraid you will be finding that out for yourself, Miss Turner," Baggett cut in. "The sergeant has asked for you too."

Chapter Thirty-Three

Jackson yanked open the door of the station, allowed Kit to pass, then followed her in with Baggett at his heels. He'd hoped to have a moment alone with her, to tell her about her father before this meeting, but blast it! His friend had accompanied them every step of the way. And while he appreciated Baggett's integrity, this was something meant only for Kit's ears.

He clenched his jaw. Of all the inopportune times to meet with the sergeant. A necessity he'd known was coming, but oh that he'd had a minute more with Kit.

Just past the threshold, Baggett tipped his head. "Good luck."

"Thanks." Though trepidation twisted his gut, he turned to Kit with a smile. "Follow me."

As they neared the clerk's desk, he did a double take. Where Beanstaple had once drooped like a worn hound, a new fellow perched on the stool, bright eyed and with a pen gripped in his hand, poised above a ledger. "Your names? Purpose of visit? Officer you wish to see?"

Jackson blinked at the rapid-fire questions. This was quite an alteration from the former slothful clerk—and no doubt was a big change for Beanstaple as well, who even now warmed a holding cell alongside Mr. Poxley.

"I am Constable Forge and this is Miss Turner." Jackson nodded at Kit, who looked positively green being inside a police station. "The sergeant summoned us."

The man's pen flew so fast he finished writing at the same time Jackson's last word left his tongue. "Yes, yes. He's waiting for you. Off you go, then."

Jackson reached out and grabbed the basket in Kit's hand, then entwined his fingers with hers. Though she stood tall and lifted her chin as they neared the sergeant's door, her palm was clammy against his. Or was that his own angst seeping out? He'd rehearsed a hundred scenarios in his head as to why he and Kit had been called here, but they all ended with the same conjecture...

The sergeant had discovered Kit's real identity and was furious with Jackson for not telling him sooner. Which meant dismissal for him.

And possible heartache for Kit.

Oh God, have mercy.

Kit peered up at him as he rapped on the door. "No matter what happens, I think you are a fine officer."

His heart swelled at the admiration in her gaze. Sweet heavens but he'd never tire of that look.

"Enter!" the sergeant's voice bellowed.

Sucking in a deep breath, he pushed open the door and led Kit inside, ushering her to one of the two chairs in front of the sergeant's desk.

Jackson, however, scorned the empty seat and snapped a crisp salute. "Reporting as requested, sir."

But the sergeant's stare was fixed on Kit, much the same as last night in the carriage. Did he, perhaps, recognize her?

"Sir," Jackson began. "I believe there is something that must be said."

At last the sergeant's big head turned his way. "Do sit down, Forge. This is not a roll call nor a drill."

"But, sir, I—"

"Now!"

He sat but did not loosen so much as one muscle.

Graybone pushed up from his desk and twined his hands behind his back—a familiar stance now, though every bit as intimidating as the first time Jackson had warmed this seat. "This whole Poxley affair has come to the attention of the Home Office, as naturally it would. It is not every day the Lord Mayor's right-hand man is found to be an arms smuggler."

The sergeant stared down his nose. "Though I disagree with the commissioner's decision, there was nothing I could do to change his mind."

Jackson shifted on the hard chair. It was generous of the sergeant to have stood up for them against his superior, but apparently even the man's favorable word had done him and Kit no good. What sort of reprimand had the commissioner meted out? And why? He slipped a sideways glance at her, but Kit—the brave, beautiful girl—sat unflinching.

Graybone widened his stance. "It is my duty to inform you both that—"

"No." Jackson shot to his feet, refusing to hear even so much as the possibility of any reprisal against them without first spilling what he knew. "Do as you will with me, sir, but go lenient with the lady. She is your flesh and blood."

Two sets of eyes drilled into him. One blue and impossibly wide. The other so brown it was nearly black. Doubt hit him in the gut like a thrown brick. Had the colonel been wrong? Glancing between Kit and the sergeant, he ground his teeth. They looked *nothing* alike.

"What in the hot blazes are you talking about?" the sergeant roared.

Jackson turned to Kit, praying to God he'd not been fed false intelligence. Though he hated to ask it of her, there was only one way to know for sure. "Show him your token."

At the mention, she clutched her neck. "Are you out of your mind?"

Perhaps, but it was too late now to change tack. He softened his tone. "Please, Kit. Just do it."

"This is ridiculous," the sergeant grumbled, but all the same, his eyes locked on the button Kit pulled from her bodice. She unfastened the chain and held out the worn token on her palm.

Graybone aged a decade as he sank heavily in his chair. Slowly, he reached and took the offering. "I can hardly believe it."

Kit's gaze bounced between him and Jackson. "Would someone tell me what is going on here?"

"Sir?" Jackson nudged.

But the man didn't speak. Didn't move. Didn't anything.

Kit peered at him. "Jackson?"

He blew out a long breath. The answer really should come from the bushy-haired man behind the desk. Why the deuce did the sergeant not tell her? Was he that nervous? Frightened? Or was it guilt that held his tongue—remorse at having abandoned a child and her mother?

A horde of unanswered questions welled in Kit's eyes, and the pitiful sight of it burned in Jackson's chest. He crouched at Kit's side and pulled her hand into his, wrapping the other atop it and squeezing what he hoped to be a measure of some comfort. "Kit, Sergeant Graybone is your father."

How did one stand in a world that flipped like an overturned boat? How did one even breathe? Kit clenched Jackson's hand, grateful for the anchor his strong touch provided. All these years, she'd wondered whom she belonged to. Had spent decades craving to know if her mother or father yet walked the earth or gave her the smallest thought.

She stiffened. And now to find out that the man who'd sired her lived but a stone's throw from Blackfriars. Hounds and fairies! Why had he not sought her out? Was this nothing but a cruel jest?

Yanking from Jackson's grip, she shot to her feet and searched the face of the man seated behind the desk. "Is it true? Are you my father?"

Shoulders slumped, he rubbed endless circles over the button with his thumb. "I have been wondering that myself since I saw you last night."

Never once did he pull his gaze from the token. *Her* token. The one she'd worn next to her heart until the day Jackson upended her life—and still upended it! She curled her fingers, stifling the urge to snatch the button back.

The sergeant's big head lifted, his dark eyes red rimmed and growing redder the longer he stared at her. "You—" His voice cracked, and he cleared his throat. "You are the very image of your mother."

Unbidden, her hand flew to her face, feeling the curve of her cheek, the hollow just below the bone, the prominent jaw she frequently jutted. Had her mother done the same? Had she been as spirited? Had Kit nothing to do but look in a mirror to see the woman she'd longed for all these years? Trembling, she lowered her fingers, so many emotions slamming into her she could hardly hang on to one. But as they passed, in their wake, a single burning sentiment remained.

Rage.

She slammed her fist onto the desk. "Why did she abandon me?"

"Kit, please." Jackson rested a light touch on her shoulder. "Have a seat."

"I will not." She leaned over the desk, scowling at the man who should have been there for her. Protected her. Loved her! "Why did you not come for me? Why forsake your own flesh and blood? What kind of a craven, spineless man does that?"

"Kit!" Jackson warned.

"No, Forge. Let her be. She has every right to her fury." The sergeant—dare she think of him as her father?—shook his head like a withering old man. "I had no idea Isabella was with child, or that you had been born. Yet that would account for. . ."

His gravelly voice ground to dust, and he wilted in his seat as if his lifeblood drained in a great pool at his feet.

Kit straightened at the sober sight, anger momentarily quelled. "Account for what?" she asked.

He sucked in a breath, chest swelling against his uniform. "By the time I made it back from the war, eager to make Bella my wife, she was gone." The raw anguish in the black pools of his eyes lifted gooseflesh on her arms. "Your mother took her own life."

Suicide? The word was a leaf caught in an eddy of wind. Round and round it went. Swirling like a wild dervish, evading any attempt she made to crush it beneath her heel.

Reaching back, Kit grabbed the arm of the chair and lowered to the seat. Of course she understood how desperation could push one to extremes, for had she not felt the same countless times? But this? Self-destruction made no sense.

"Why would she do such a thing?" Her shivery question hung on the air like the last note of a dirge.

For a long moment, her father—a word she still could not quite grasp—pinched the bridge of his nose, not speaking until after a shuddering breath.

"Your mother and I were an ill-fated match from the start. We both knew it, yet neither of us could accept it. Ahh, but I loved her. More than the beat of my own heart. She was—and ever will be—my grandest, brightest passion."

His gaze drifted to some undisclosed place in the past only he could see. "But her father would not have me as a suitor. A soldier was not good enough for his angel."

A sigh deflated him. "Not that I blame him. A fighting man can have his life snatched away in an instant. So, Bella and I made our goodbyes when I shipped out for the peninsula, intending to respect her father's wishes and never see each other again. I left her with a poorly engraved button from my uniform, for I could offer her nothing else. But the whole time I was over there, guns blazing, mortars blasting, I lived and breathed for her. For my sweet, sweet Bella. And the very instant my feet once again touched English soil, I sought her out. But it was too late."

His eyes narrowed. "Her father told me she had disappeared shortly after I shipped off. He heard nothing from her until the day a constable showed up on his stoop and asked him to identify a corpse. I never understood what drove Isabella to such desperation that night on Westminster Bridge, but now I think I do."

Kit's heart stopped midbeat. It took several tries before she could push out the awful words singeing her soul. "Are you saying *I* am the cause of my mother's death?"

"No, child. I would never!" The big man pushed up from his chair and circled the desk with speed that belied his great frame. He crouched before her, just as Jackson had done moments before. "Blame me, if you must. But never—*ever*—blame yourself or your mother. She must have concluded she could not care for you on her own and that you would be better off without her." He reached out a huge hand, but inches from her face, he pulled back, sorrow welling liquid in his eyes. "Had I known you were alive, I swear I would have come for you. You were conceived in love, never doubt that for a moment."

Her throat closed, making it hard to breathe. Her little-girl heart throbbed from the tenderness in his voice. The emotion in his gaze. This was no swindle. He meant every word. And every word did much to begin the arduous task of healing the anguish of all the lonely years.

She nodded, barely whispering a "Thank you."

He pressed his lips so tight, his bushy side-whiskers trembled. Then with a final sniff, he returned to his seat.

"And now." Drawing in a big breath, he eyed them both, once again the composed sergeant of the station. "I am doubly glad I stood against the commissioner, though he refused to listen."

Jackson edged forward on his chair. "So, what did he have to say, sir? What exactly is to become of us?"

"You, Mr. Forge, have been promoted to inspector. Your dogged perseverance in the Poxley case impressed the Home Office immensely." He swung his gaze to Kit. "And you, my dear, are hired as his partner—off the books, mind. We cannot have the public knowing a woman is on the payroll of the Metropolitan Police."

She gaped, mind frozen for one second, the next charging through potential plans. Ways she could use such a position for those on Blackfriars Lane. A ready-made network of spies and informants if there was one. Oh, there might be a few that would balk, but with a little bit of talking and the promise of coin, she could probably persuade most of them...

Jackson's voice sliced into her vision. "But that is *good* news. Why would you argue the point with the commissioner?"

"Because you are too much like me, Forge. Or rather like I was. Overeager. Expecting to solve the world's problems with naught but a bit of will and some chewing gum." Her father's face darkened. "Look at the both of you. Bah! Callow as spring lambs. I had hoped to spare you the ugly underside of the City. The threat. All the dangers. Leastwise till you have more experience."

Hah! She bit the inside of her cheek to keep from spouting an unladylike oath. This man—this father of hers—had no idea of her experiences.

He planted his arms on his desk and leaned forward, as if by proximity alone he might persuade them. "Kit, Jackson, you do not have to do this. I will tell the commissioner you have decided to hold off a few years before taking on such a responsibility."

She exchanged a look with Jackson. The shock on his face surely mirrored hers. But why? Was it the sudden use of their Christian names? The fact that her newly found father wished to keep them from harm's way? His willingness to stand before the commissioner and turn him down on their behalf?

Jackson threw back his shoulders and faced the sergeant. "I cannot speak for the lady, sir, but I am not afraid of a challenge. While I appreciate your caution, I wholeheartedly accept the position."

"I was afraid of that," her father grumbled, then focused on her.

"But you. . ." His chest heaved. "After all these years on your own, I would not fault you for knowing your own mind on the matter. Still, I have only just learned of your existence. New as the knowledge is, I am strongly inclined to do everything in my power to prevent you from accepting the offer." He swiped all emotion from his face with a wave of his hand. "Even so, I leave the decision to you."

Warmth flickered in her heart. Not love, exactly. Too soon for that. But she couldn't deny the small kindling of admiration that he'd not bully her into refusing a position she'd very much like to take on. "I do not discount your counsel so lightly, sir, but if Jackson is in, then I am too. After all"—she jutted her jaw towards Jackson—"we are partners, are we not?"

"Well then," her father grumbled. "If neither of you is to be deterred, you are to report to the Home Office tomorrow morning. Nine sharp. Do not be late." He speared Jackson with a pointed stare.

Jackson snapped a salute. "Yes, sir."

She and her father stood as well, but before she could leave, the man once again crossed to the front of his desk, this time with open arms. "If it is not too forward, may I?"

He stopped, just paces from her, the hope flickering on his face as uncertain as the flutter of her heart. But what girl could resist the embrace of a father, even one she'd scarce known for ten minutes?

She took one hesitant step, then another, closing the distance he'd left between them, then melted as his arms pulled her gently to him, a chaste kiss buffing the top of her head. "I look forward to getting to know you, Daughter."

She smiled up at him. "Me too."

He released her with a sigh, then glowered at Jackson. "And Mr. Forge, if I hear of so much as one hair of my daughter's head being harmed in any of your half-baked hijinks, I will come for you. Is that fully understood?"

"I would expect no less, sir. But trust me." He gathered her hand and tucked it into the crook of his arm and, turning his head, winked for her alone. "I will treat her as if she is my own."

Somehow Jackson led her from her father's office, through the station, and onto the street with her feet hardly touching the ground. How could they? That gleam of passion in Jackson's eyes would surely keep her floating for days.

Content beyond belief, she smiled up at him. "Well then, what now, Inspector?"

"A word, I think." He guided her off the pavement to an alcove near a bookseller's window, then planted his hands on each side of her, effectively penning her in place. "About our pending partnership."

She cocked her head. "There is nothing pending about it. You heard what my father said, though I can still scarce believe any of it is true."

He bent his head close, murmuring low, "I am not talking about our professional ties."

Her pulse took off at a gallop. "Then what are you taking about?"

"Kit Graybone, it is my intention to pursue you for a more lasting partnership—of the matrimonial kind, if you will have me."

A thrill arced through her, tingling way down to her toes. Not that she'd let him know, though. Instead, she arched a brow. "A pursuit, hmm? As you must know by now, I dearly love a good chase. But do you really think you can catch me?"

His moustache lifted on one side as he pointedly glanced at his arms on each side of her. "It appears I already have."

"Ahh, but you should have learned by now that looks can be deceiving." Laughing, she rose to her toes and kissed him full on the mouth, then ducked out of his reach and called over her shoulder, "But by all means, let the chase begin."

Historical Notes

City of London vs. London

Essentially, there are two Londons. The City of London is a city inside a city, often referred to as simply *the City*, the *Square Mile*, or historically as the *Corporation*. London itself is the far wider area that includes all the boroughs in addition to the City of London. This district owes its origin to the fortified Roman settlement of Londinium, which was settled on the northern bank of the River Thames and encompassed one square mile within its walls (hence the *Square Mile* moniker). Today, it covers two miles. The boundaries are marked with cast-iron dragons at each corner.

The Lord Mayors of the City of London

This politically powerful position has been around since the 1300s. The Lord Mayor heads the City of London Corporation, the governing body of the Square Mile. Only the sovereign wields more command over the City than the Lord Mayor. Sir Robert Fowler was the last Lord Mayor to have served more than once, in 1883 and again in 1885, after George Nottage died in office. Mansion House, built between 1739 and 1752, where Kit and Jackson have their first dance and kiss, is to this day the official residence of the Lord Mayor.

The Metropolitan Police Force

The Metropolitan Police (founded in 1829 by Robert Peel) was composed mostly of young men, many of whom were recruited from rural areas. Few were from London, the philosophy being that they would thus be free from local patronage and influence.

It is a bit of an anomaly that hero Jackson Forge and his friend Officer Baggett carry a sidearm. Some did, but most relied on truncheons. It was up to the officer. Revolvers were usually only supplied after the death of a police officer by an armed criminal, at the discretion of the Divisional Officer, or if a constable requested to use one during night duty. In 1884, after the deaths of several police officers, the Home Office ordered nearly a thousand revolvers from Webley & Scott to be issued to branches of the London police...which is where I got the idea of a shipment of guns for Poxley to attempt to steal.

Police detectives were recruited from within the ranks of existing uniformed officers. There were actually women on the force at the time, employed as police matrons. But these were behind-the-scenes workers, tasked with guarding women and children. If Kit were to be out in public, serving as Jackson's assistant, she'd have to keep her job secret. The first female police officer wasn't seen on the streets until 1919.

The Foundling Hospital

Unwanted babies are unfortunately always a reality, and that's why the Foundling Hospital began in the eighteenth century. Children under two months were admitted then sent to the country to be wet-nursed (away from the diseases of the city) before returning to London for schooling and apprenticeships. Mothers were asked to leave a distinguishing token with their child so that they could be retrieved in the future if so desired. Many of these tokens can still be seen today at the Foundling Museum in London. Eventually that custom changed into simply receiving a receipt, which is what the custom was in Kit's day. I took a bit of artistic license with that. The Foundling Hospital was in operation until the 1950s, when it was replaced by in-home foster care.

Flushers and Toshers
It wasn't only trainmen and passengers who frequented the underground tunnels beneath London. Some people worked there.

Flushers were men employed by the city to free the sewers of debris and maintain them in good repair. They also kept down the brown rat population. Besides the obvious dangers of disease and bodily injury, drowning was a very real possibility. When a rainstorm began, an aboveground worker would raise the nearest manhole cover six inches then let it drop, the echo reverberating as a warning to those toiling down in the tunnels to beware of flash floods. Lest you think these valiant men are of bygone days, think again. Today there is still a team that goes underground every day to ensure things keep flowing.

A tosher was a scavenger, like the mudlarks on the banks of the Thames. They made their living by trolling through runoff pipes and sewers, picking up whatever they could find. And they did find things, usually to the tune of six shillings a day (about fifty dollars in today's money). They were colorful characters with colorful names: Lanky Bill, Short-armed Jack, One-eyed George. Usually they wore a long velveteen coat with enormous pockets and a canvas apron, and they carried a bag on their back and an eight-foot-long pole in their hand. After 1840 it was illegal to enter the sewers without permission, and there was a five pound reward for anyone who snitched on them, so usually toshing was done secretly at night with a lantern.

The Underground Railway
The idea of an underground railway to ease London street traffic was first proposed in 1830. By 1863, the Metropolitan Railway was opened between Paddington and Farringdon, carrying 38,000 passengers that first day. Steam locomotives hauled gas-lit wooden carriages, making ventilation a huge problem for drivers and passengers alike. Attempts to build smokeless locomotives were unsuccessful, so something else

needed to be done. All that steam needed a place to escape, so in some places airholes were cut into the street, allowing sooty hot air to discharge aboveground. But times changed, as did technology, and eventually those airholes were no longer needed. Neither were many of the stations that had been built over the years. Today there are forty-some lost underground stations known as ghost stations.

Spring-heeled Jack
English folklore of the Victorian era is steeped with tales of a creature called Spring-heeled Jack. The first reported sighting was in London in 1837 and carried on right up through 1904. There are several conflicting accounts of the villain. Some describe him as having clawed hands and eyes that resemble red balls of fire. Others claim this man-like figure wore a helmet and a skintight oilskin garment. A few even say he had the appearance of a gentleman, being tall and thin. But all agree that this entity is devil-like with a penchant for ripping out throats.

Black Maria
Americans know this vehicle as a "paddy wagon," but Black Maria is the proper name for the quintessential black police carriage used for transporting prisoners. The name is pronounced mah-RYE-ah, *not* mah-REE-ah, and the term is still used today in parts of Britain.

Bibliography

Flanders, Judith. *The Victorian City: Everyday Life in Dickens' London.* New York: St. Martin's Press, 2012.

Haliday, Gaynor. *Victorian Policing.* Barnsley: Pen and Sword Books, 2017.

Smith, Philip Thurmond. *Policing Victorian London: Political Policing, Public Order, and the London Metropolitan Police.* Westport: Greenwood Press, 1985.

Barrie, David G., and Susan Broomhall. *A History of Police and Masculinities 1700-2010.* New York: Routledge, 2012.

Bailey, Victor. *Policing and Punishment in Nineteenth Century Britain.* New Jersey: Rutgers University Press, 1981.

Ackroyd, Peter. *London Under: The Secret History beneath the Streets.* New York: Doubleday, 2011.

Mayhew, Henry. *London Labour and the London Poor.* New York: Viking Penguin, 1985.

Howson, H. F. *London's Underground.* Surrey: Ian Allan, 1981.

Trench, Richard, and Ellis Hillman. *London under London: A Subterranean Guide.* London: John Murray Publishers, 1996.

Emmerson, Andrew. *The Underground Pioneers*. Middlesex: Capital Transport Publishing, 2000.

Howell, Caro. *The Foundling Museum: An Illustrated Guide*. Berkshire: Lamport Gilbert, 2018.

Acknowledgments

The names rarely change, but my grateful sentiment does—it grows. A huge thank-you to the many who sacrifice their own time for the sake of making my books possible...

My critique buddies who hold my feet to the fire despite my squealing like a stuck pig: Lisa Ludwig, Tara Johnson, Ane Mulligan, Shannon McNear, Kelly Klepfer, MaryLu Tyndall, Sharon Hinck, and Dani Snyder.

My plot and plausibility wizard who deserves mention all on her own—Chawna Schroeder.

Kudos to Julie Klassen, who faithfully keeps me in the historically accurate lane no matter how often I veer off the road.

Editor Annie Tipton and all the awesome staff at Barbour. Shout-out to Reagen Reed as well, who whipped my manuscript into tip-top shape, and my agent, Wendy Lawton, at Books & Such Literary Agency.

There are so many readers who deserve the spotlight but there are too many to name, so here is a random smattering of just a few of the faithful: Brenda Dokey Lauridsen, Elisabeth Espinoza, Perianne Askew, Susan Snodgrass, Judith Hicks Wellbaum, Stacey Ulferts, and Jeanne Alfveby Crea.

And, as always, a huge thank-you to my long-suffering husband who puts up with listening to my crazy ideas and frequently helps me out of plot pickles.

About the Author

Michelle Griep's been writing since she first discovered blank wall space and Crayolas. She is the Christy Award–winning author of historical romances: *The House at the End of the Moor*, *The Noble Guardian*, *A Tale of Two Hearts*, *The Captured Bride*, *The Innkeeper's Daughter*, *12 Days at Bleakly Manor*, *The Captive Heart*, *Brentwood's Ward*, *A Heart Deceived*, and *Gallimore*, but also leaped the historical fence into the realm of contemporary with the zany romantic mystery *Out of the Frying Pan*. If you'd like to keep up with her escapades, find her at www.michellegriep.com or stalk her on Facebook, Twitter, and Pinterest.

And guess what? She loves to hear from readers! Feel free to drop her a note at michellegriep@gmail.com.

Other Books by Michelle

The House at the End of the Moor
Brentwood's Ward
The Innkeeper's Daughter
The Noble Guardian
A Tale of Two Hearts
A Heart Deceived
Gallimore
The Captive Heart
The Captured Bride
Once Upon a Dickens Christmas
Out of the Frying Pan

More Romantic Intrigue. . .

The House at the End of the Moor

What Can a London Opera Star and an Escaped Dartmoor Prisoner Have in Common?

Opera star Maggie Lee escapes her opulent lifestyle when threatened by a powerful politician who aims to ruin her life. She runs off to the wilds of the moors to live in anonymity. All that changes the day she discovers a half-dead man near her house. Escaped convict Oliver Ward is on the run to prove his innocence, until he gets hurt and is taken in by Maggie. He discovers some jewels in her possession—the very same jewels that got him convicted. Together they hatch a plan to return the jewels, clearing Oliver's name and hopefully maintaining Maggie's anonymity.

Paperback / 978-1-64352-342-2 / $14.99